THE MEMORY KEY

CONOR FITZGERALD

BLOOMSBURY
LONDON · NEW DELHI · NEW YORK · SYDNEY

First published in Great Britain 2013

This paperback edition published 2014

Copyright © Conor Fitzgerald 2013

The moral right of the author has been asserted

No part of this book may be used or reproduced in any manner
whatsoever without written permission from the Publisher except in the
case of brief quotations embodied in critical articles or reviews

Bloomsbury Publishing Plc
50 Bedford Square London
WC1B 3DP

www.bloomsbury.com

Bloomsbury is a trademark of Bloomsbury Publishing Plc

Bloomsbury Publishing, London, New Delhi, New York and Sydney

A CIP catalogue record for this book is available from the British Library

ISBN 978 1 4088 4392 5

10 9 8 7 6 5 4 3 2 1

Typeset by Hewer Text UK Ltd, Edinburgh
Printed and bound in Great Britain by CPI Group (UK) Ltd, Croydon CR0 4YY

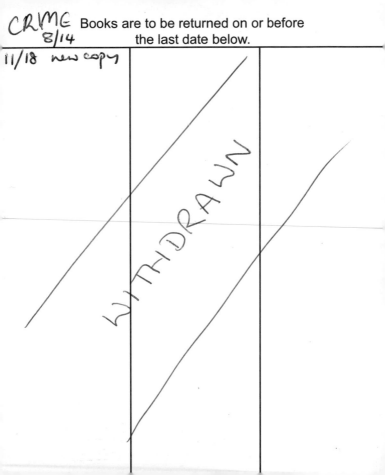

CRIME
8/14
Books are to be returned on or before the last date below.

11/18 new copy

WITHDRAWN

THE MEMORY KEY

A NOTE ON THE AUTHOR

CONOR FITZGERALD has lived in Ireland, the UK, the United States, and Italy. He has worked as an arts editor, produced a current affairs journal for foreign embassies and founded a successful translation company. He is married with two children and lives in Rome. *The Memory Key* is the fourth in his series of Italian crime novels.

BY THE SAME AUTHOR

The Dogs of Rome
The Fatal Touch
The Namesake
Bitter Remedy

To my brother, Cormac.
Thank you for everything you have done.

1

Central Italy, 1980

The unmarried woman in the thin blue dress turned to the old man on the broken bench and said, 'I think the clock has stopped.'

The old man sighed and glanced up at the wall. As he did so, the big hand dropped down a notch from one to two minutes past the hour, and the woman blushed and apologized.

A philosophy student with cutaway jeans, who had turned his oversized backpack into a divan and was reclining luxuriously on it, relit his self-rolled cigarette, more paper than tobacco, and laughed at the woman's embarrassment.

'They should have a second hand on it,' said the man in brown corduroys and orange shirt who was sitting opposite. She suspected him of trying first to look up her dress, then to look through it. Certainly, when she had crossed her legs a few minutes earlier, watching him from the corner of her eye, his head had swivelled in her direction and his eyes flickered over her thighs, which she didn't mind too much, because he had a nice and easily embarrassed face. He circled his finger to represent the sweep of a second hand moving across the clock face. 'That way you could at least tell if the clock was working, but time always slows down when . . . oops.'

He pulled in his legs as a boy went racing fiercely by, determined to win a race against his baby sister to whom he had given a two-step head start, one step for every year. The boy slapped the wall triumphantly as he arrived, which turned out to be the funniest thing his sister had ever seen. Her squeals then turned out to be the funniest thing he had ever heard. They were soon on the floor, egging each other on, until, finally, the mother stood up, took them by the hand and led them back to their seats against the wall.

'They should just rename the 10:05 the 10:20,' said an elderly woman pretending to address her very old husband but clearly aiming her comments at the entire waiting room. 'Then they could stop pretending to apologize. It's the same every Saturday.'

A girl with dark hair and a serious expression glanced up from her book and looked quickly around the crowded room. A woman with golden hair cascading in ringlets down her left shoulder, whose arrival had drawn the frank attention of the man in corduroys and furtive glances from almost everyone else, set a hefty suitcase down on the floor, then immediately picked it up again, as if testing its weight.

Two young women, one in jeans, the other in a multicoloured flared skirt, both unkempt and sporting Tolfa bags, bent their heads together and looked for a moment like they might actually kiss.

A robust man in a navy jacket and red shirt, with a neat beard, leaning against the wall crossed his arms and surveyed the people present with an appraising frown, as if they were unwanted guests in his living room, and shook his head in amazement at a private thought. A grandmother opened her large handbag and took out a cheap packet of biscuits and handed them to her grandson, who, mortified, grabbed them out of her hand and retreated to the corner of the waiting room before opening the crinkly plastic and beginning to nibble surreptitiously. A deeply tanned man in a beige safari suit with a powder-blue shirt kicked impatiently at his suitcase and puffed out his cheeks. A baby fell asleep, its face nestled into its father's neck, just below the bristle line. The father tried to pass the drooped bundle to his wife, who shook her head firmly, and warded him off with her hands. 'I have had enough,' she was saying.

An InterRailing English couple, who had been in Venice for three nights and had decided there that they would get married before finishing their studies, were now more anxious to get back to Bristol than to visit Rome. They came in, looked around, saw there were no free benches, and left, he saying something disparaging about the Italian way of life, she murmuring something more conciliatory. A minute later, the girl was sitting on the outside ledge of the window, her back against the glass. As she leaned down to say something to her grumpy fiancé, the lumbar curve of her spine was visible in bumpy relief beneath her blouse, part of which had ridden up her back a little, exposing a small section of smooth skin.

The moustachioed stationmaster walked by the open doorway, paused, slapped his thigh with a rolled-up copy of *Gazzetta dello Sport*, and started heading back the way he had come, but was waylaid by a Milanese businessman angered both by the delay and by three days in the company of the smug communists of this flat and red-stone city.

A mouse-grey suitcase, a plastic shopping bag, and a cheap tartan travel bag sat on a gunmetal table set in an alcove that might once have served as a ticket desk. The blonde woman lifted the tartan case, and looked around to see who claimed it. The girl with the book glanced up and gave a friendly nod of permission. The blonde woman pushed the tartan case back a bit, and heaved her own on to the counter, curtly refusing an offer of help from the bearded man. She pushed her suitcase towards the wall, and, in what seemed like a courteous gesture, pulled the few other pieces of luggage to the front of the counter, from where they could be more easily retrieved.

The clock ticked off another minute. The boy in the corner finished his biscuits, a non-stopping train on the far track hooted twice, then went hurtling by causing the glass panes to rattle. It clattered noisily over some points, then continued rhythmically on its way, its wheels beating out the sound of *tsk-tsk, ciao-ciao* on the jointed tracks, as if to mock the people it was leaving behind. As the train bid its last faint *ciao-ciao*, Adriano Celentano's voice could be heard singing 'Il Tempo Se Ne Va' from someone's transistor. A short, thick-lipped man stood up and in a grave Sardinian accent told the man holding the baby that he might take his seat, and then marched off quickly to avoid the embarrassment of being thanked. The running boy crashed into the blonde woman's elegant leg. Instead of looking bashful, he used her thigh as pivot, swung behind her, and reversed direction to run straight back to his mother, who threw over an apologetic glance but received nothing in return from the woman's grey-blue eyes.

The station speakers announced the imminent arrival of the train from Milan to Rome, and the people in the waiting room shifted, and raised the murmurs of conversation into a hubbub of preparations. The young woman closed her book, *Abba Abba* was its title; the mother gathered her unruly children. The student got off his backpack and set it upright, flexing his shoulder muscles in preparation for lifting it with a single manly jerk for the benefit of the two women on the far side of the room, who had yet to see him. The man with the corduroy trousers shook his head almost imperceptibly as the woman with the angelic hair, too young and way, way out of his league, walked out of the door. What must it be like to have a woman like that? What must it be like to *be* a woman like that?

The blonde woman's hurried departure registered on the minds of several people who assumed illogically that the train must have arrived already, without further announcement. Their preparations became more urgent and a sense of movement spread through the warm waiting room.

The woman in the thin dress stood up and smoothed the paisley-patterned acrylic above her knees. She glanced over at her admirer, who smiled at her. He was, like her, in his early thirties. 'May as well stay in here,' she ventured. 'There's hardly room to move on the platform. Saturday's always so busy.'

'Are you catching the Rome train?'

'Yes. You?'

'Yes, I live there.'

'Really?'

'You don't then?'

'No actually, I do, or I will . . . I have a new job.'

'Really? Great! What sort of . . .'

The old woman called her grandson over and ordered him not to leave yet and not to get lost. The grandson therefore returned to where he had been.

'We apologize for the delay . . . please stand back from the yellow line as the train approaches.'

'Never find a seat . . . unless they've added a carriage. Sometimes they do that.'

'I could have sworn it was in this pocket, I . . .'

'Careful, love.'

'Just like you.'

'I can't wait to see their faces.'

'Don't even think of eating that now.'

'Hold my hand.'

'. . . a great day.'

The blonde woman, whose name was Stefania Manfellotto, walked across the forecourt in front of the station towards a Fiat Ritmo driven by Adriano Pazienza, the man she would later marry in prison.

'All set?' he said as she ducked in and sat beside him in the front seat.

'Get me out of here.'

Adriano turned on the engine and drove away from the train station. As he reached the intersection, he glanced at his watch. 'Five minutes.'

'If it works,' said Stefania.

Adriano patted her knee, and ran his hand upwards towards the inside of her thigh, then took it away to change gear. 'It'll work.'

The suitcase that she had positioned beneath a supporting wall, contained 18 kilos of Compound B, an explosive usually found in land-mines, mixed with 5 kilos of nitroglycerine. The timed detonator activated at twenty-five minutes past the hour.

So powerful was the blast in the station that it pushed the late-arriving locomotive off the tracks.

No one who was still in the waiting room survived the blast and thermal wave; no one within 15 metres survived the fragmentation of metal, glass, plastic, wood, and brick. Collapsing masonry killed several more, and three people died beneath the wheels of the train that, though its engine and front three carriages were derailed, kept moving mercilessly forward.

2

Rome, Present Day

SOFIA FONTANA was on her way to meet Magistrate Filippo Principe for the fourth time. He promised her it would be the last, but she didn't believe it. She did not much like the investigating magistrate, and resented the fact that it was she who had to come to his office. It took her two long bus rides from Trullo to Prati. The first bus, the 871, arrived with the regularity of papal elections; the second, the 23, was overcrowded and full of aggression. Her cousin Olivia had told her there was an app for the iPhone that plotted out the route and told you when the bus was coming, which was great, if you had an iPhone. Typical of Olivia to give advice on public transport, which she had probably never taken in her life.

She felt bad about not liking Principe, because she knew he liked her. But to be liked without liking, a reversal of a lifetime of experience, was a sensation to be grabbed. She tried to use the meetings as she might a psychiatry session, though if anyone was in need of counselling it was the magistrate.

Six months ago, she had almost been shot dead in broad daylight. As Principe kept reminding her, if the shooter had been less of a marksman, she would not be here now. It had focused her mind and made her realize how much she loved life.

Her white shoes had collected some dirt, which was a pity, given what they had cost. But her pale blue jeans and silk blouse felt good on her, and she was especially happy with her plaid '60s-style red and green coat, a touch of London. Her new earrings were imitations of a pair worn in a painting of Princess Leonilla Sayn Wittgenstein. Sofia saw a portrait of the Russian princess once and decided that this woman was the idealized version of herself. If a few proteins had unfolded slightly differently and some genes, particularly those that were responsible for noses and backsides, had switched off earlier, and if others, such as those that grew legs and breasts, had worked a little harder, then she would look just like Princess Wittgenstein.

The weather was cooling now, which gave her a chance to try out the new jacket she had bought in the July sales. Leather, another new departure for her. Two months in London, the idea being to learn English, but she had spent all her conversation time with East Europeans and other Italians whose English was worse than hers. She saw that the English, who had no respect for their hair or shoes, and could be dreadful dressers, could also make odd combinations suddenly look very stylish and different, and their culture had more room for the plainer types, like herself. She felt that with a little more style, she might move beyond vulnerability.

She walked into the Palace of Justice and, having done this three times before, told the guard she had an appointment with Magistrate Filippo Principe. The guard's dead eyes made it clear that he would be unmoved if she had an appointment with the resurrected Christ, but she felt she had to say something.

The shooting had occurred in late March. It was on the day before the clocks went forward, and she had been visiting Olivia who, uncharacteristically enough, had stayed late at university to meet her boyfriend Marco (Sofia felt the usual mixture of desire and pity as Marco's face came to mind).

'And why were you at the university?'

She looked in disbelief at the magistrate. 'You have asked me that –'

'– over and over, I know.' The magistrate, who looked particularly ashen today, was continuously swallowing something invisible, keeping his pale lips tightly shut, as if to stop something noxious inside his body from seeping out.

'I was on my way from the Health Institute where I work. I was taking a short cut through the university grounds.' She pictured herself walking across the courtyard in front of the brutalist façade of the literature faculty, and, in spite of what was about to happen, envied her earlier self for the freedom of being out and about.

'Go on,' he prompted.

'There was what I thought was a girl with blonde hair, walking directly towards me. In my memory, we seem to be the only ones in the courtyard at that moment. The hair was bubbly, lots of ringlets, which is why I thought she was young, but as she approached, I saw she was far older. A mature woman, and the hair was peroxide bright.'

'Did you or she say anything?'

'No.'

But Sofia had raised her eyes with the intention of giving a friendly smile, which died at once when the blonde woman with stone-grey eyes looked straight through her. Even as she thought about it now, she felt smaller and uglier. The woman's eyes had conveyed something beyond disdain. Her eyes had registered a presence, but without a flicker of interest.

Urged on by the sad magistrate, she over-elaborated the moment to the point where she was not sure whether she was inventing things. The few seconds of the event now stretched out in her memory like a feature film.

'The woman passed me by, and I heard a slight cracking sound and an intake of breath.'

'You heard this?' The magistrate consulted his notes, which took some time. Eventually he said, 'This is the first time you have said anything about hearing something.'

'Then scratch that. Maybe I didn't. You keep asking me to tell the story, and the more I tell it, the more details come into it.'

'That's the idea.'

'But maybe by now I am just making it up. Not deliberately.'

'Don't worry, Sofia. If I make you relive the moment, sooner to later you'll invent your own soundtrack for it. I am not going to place too much faith in your actually having heard something, but maybe you did. You never know. Real details sometimes emerge.'

'OK, but something made me turn round, and there, ten metres away, lay the blonde woman on the ground.'

Other people were already running towards the spot, and someone was shouting something. Sofia remembered tiptoeing slowly back and craning her head forward to look at the woman, but not really wanting to see.

The eyes that had unnerved her a minute before unnerved her again, but in a different way. They were open and staring straight at her, but had lost their contemptuous expression. On the contrary, the woman now seemed to be looking at her with absent-minded fondness, as blood dripped from the side of her head and ran in rivulets down the concrete into the grass before it could form a pool.

Someone was shouting about a shot and someone, perhaps the same person, was saying they should take cover. But she had heard no shot, seen no flash, felt no ripples in the air.

'On second thoughts,' she told the magistrate, 'I didn't hear anything.'

'That's fine, Sofia.'

Watching some people run up the steps and into the building and others out of the building and into the courtyard, Sofia had felt like she was standing upstage and watching an audience panic. Behind her, centre stage, lay the woman with the bleeding head attended to by more and more people. Hours seemed to pass, though they must have only been minutes. Her legs, which had felt as strong and incapable of movement as two stone pillars, suddenly crumbled, as someone bore her weight and accompanied her to the ground.

She was still sitting there when the ambulance man in the huge orange jacket came over to her. Could the ambulance man not see that she was perfectly fine? He sent over his smaller female colleague, and Sofia became even angrier at the blatancy of the ploy. Carabinieri were on the scene as if teletransported there. A plastic tape had already been unwound and the chaotic milling crowd had been reconstituted into a neat circle of spectators. The blonde woman was being carted away on a stretcher. The paramedic insisted Sofia had to go, and Sofia shouted no. Screamed, as a matter of fact. She did not want to get into the same ambulance as that woman.

'We have another ambulance here just for you,' said the paramedic.

'I don't need it.'

'You have blood down on the back of your jacket and some in your hair. It's almost certainly not yours, but wouldn't you like us at least to check?'

It was then that she began to cry.

And now, praying that the magistrate would not try to comfort her by putting his arm around her or something, she began to cry again.

3

COMMISSIONER ALEC Blume was sitting with Chief Inspector Caterina Mattiola under a duvet on the sofa, as good as gold because Caterina's son Elia was in the room with them, watching TV. There had been an attack on a Catholic church in Baghdad, and the Italian reporter seemed to think that the atrocity was aggravated by the fact that today was All Souls' Day. Scores injured.

'I didn't know they had Catholic churches in Iraq,' said Caterina, drawing Elia towards her and snuggling her feet under Blume's legs.

'Well,' began Blume, who had not known either but was perfectly prepared to explain why her assumption had been so foolish.

'Oh look!' Caterina's voice rose to a squeal of delight as she pointed at an American army officer in fatigues fielding questions with a face that, though it wore a grave expression, had something of a George Bush smirk about it.

'What?' said Blume, annoyed at being interrupted. 'Oh . . . I see.' The caption below showed that the American army officer was called Lieutenant Colonel Eric Bloom. 'But it's a different spelling.'

'Still, Eric Bloom, Alec Blume, you've got to say . . .'

Blume shrugged. 'I suppose.'

'That's not a coincidence; it's not even close,' said Elia.

The kid had reached the age where he thought opinions were best delivered in scathing tones.

'Did you not see the name, love?' asked his mother.

Meanwhile, dead Iraqi Christians had been replaced on screen by a man floating and waving in the space station.

'When a game of football is played,' announced Elia, 'it is more likely than unlikely that two people on the pitch have the same birthday. That's mathematics, not coincidence. People get them confused all the time.'

His mother beamed at him, and nudged Blume's backside with her foot to get him to join in the admiration.

'You sure about that?' said Blume. 'We're talking about 22 people.'

'Twenty-three. You forgot the ref.'

'Yeah well, 25 if there are linesmen,' said Blume.

'They are not on the pitch,' said Elia in weary tones. 'They are behind the touch line. That's why they are called *lines*men. All you need is 23 people.'

'Really?' said Blume. 'That's really interesting. It's bullshit, but it's interesting you should believe it.'

'It's true!' Elia's voice was quite high-pitched for a boy. 'I'll show you.'

'You do that. Tell you what, if you prove it, I'll give you €50.'

'You're on,' said Elia, 'but you had better pay me this time.'

'No!' said Caterina. 'No gambling, and €50 is too much.'

'It's not as if he's going to get it.'

It was then that the phone rang to draw him out into the cold.

Half an hour later, he switched off the stereo and climbed reluctantly out of his warm car into the drizzle of the November night, and went in search of his old friend, investigating Magistrate Filippo Principe.

The magistrate, frailer and more stooped than Blume remembered him, was standing shivering on the perimeter of an area cordoned off by the forensic team, which was working quietly under arc lamps. They had set up a canopy above the slumped body of a young woman who lay with her back propped against the wall, in the attitude of an insolent pupil. The canopy, lights, the quiet team of forensic workers, the spectators outside, and the pillars clad in white marble at the university entrance gave the whole scene a theatrical effect.

The magistrate, who had not noticed his arrival, stood with bowed head in bleak silence. Blume reached out and tapped him on the shoulder blade.

'Ah, Alec.' Principe's smile was slow in arriving and did not last long. 'Thanks for coming.'

Principe's shivering was infectious. Near him, a young woman had her face buried in the shoulder of a man in his twenties, who held her in a tight embrace, trying to stop her shaking sobs and at the same time shield her with an umbrella. Her voice, muffled against the fabric of his fleece jacket, kept repeating the name 'Sofia'. Steam rose from the young man's shoulder every time the woman, a girl with fine features, lifted her face to say the name.

'Suit up and go in and have a look at her as soon as they let you,' said Principe. He nodded at the weeping girl. 'That's Sofia's cousin.'

'Sofia?'

'Sofia Fontana,' said Principe. 'That's the name of the deceased. A lovely girl.'

'You are shivering.'

'It's freezing, Alec. What do you expect? The one who is weeping is the cousin. Her name's Olivia. She had arranged to pick Sofia up here.'

'Right,' said Blume. He wanted Principe to go and sit somewhere warm.

'The victim's mother is on her way,' said Principe with stiff emphasis on the word 'victim'. 'She had no father.' He turned away and resumed his contemplation of the scene in front of him.

Blume was happy enough to get into a white suit, since he had forgotten to bring a coat and was getting wet. He fitted plastic covers over his shoes and crisscrossed a pair of elastic bands beneath, so any footprints he left would be recognizable. He pulled up his hood, and listened to the rain ticking noisily on the plastic, and waited to get the nod from the head of the Carabinieri SIS team, which was not a given, since Blume was from the wrong enforcement agency. If the Carabinieri decided not to cooperate, he could shrug and go back to Caterina, and tell Principe he had done his best.

But the magistrate must have primed them, because the SIS chief eventually gave a curt nod in his direction and Blume walked into the scene, at the centre of which lay the dead woman. She was young, but had crossed the fateful threshold that separated children, whose deaths no one ever got used to, from adults whose deaths people could even make jokes about.

The wound, a tiny hole, smaller even than the bullet thanks to the contraction of the skin, showed no signs of stippling, so the shooter had been some distance away. The abrasion ring was symmetrical and concentric. It could have been a long-distance shot. Blume turned round and looked at the two buildings opposite, flinching a little as he imagined himself to be still in the theoretical trajectory. As he did so, he saw two Carabinieri come out of the National Research building opposite followed by a technician in a white suit. Another technician was already preparing a set of bullet trajectory rods.

Blume looked at the girl, Sofia, slumped there, her coat shining with rain, her knee-high boots looking brand new, the cheap bead bracelet, pearl earrings, a small neck tattoo, small white teeth, perfect but now disturbing to see in the mouth which was open, in what was almost certainly a cry of pain. It looked as if a giant beast had picked her up and swung the back of her head against the wall, then dumped her on the ground like a pile of dirty laundry. Yet this was the work of a single bullet no bigger than half a thumb.

Blume did not really want to look at the devastation at the back of the skull. The explosive nature of exit wounds aggrieved him. He went over to the head of the crime scene team, who regarded him levelly. Blume was aware of his undefined status as an unaccompanied member of the Polizia di Stato in the middle of a crime scene being run by the Carabinieri.

'A high-velocity bullet?'

'Possibly. Fired from that building over there.'

Blume was gratified to find the SIS officer so helpful.

'One shot only?'

'Yes . . . Well, you can never be completely sure. Maybe they'll cut off her clothes for the autopsy and find a tiny entrance wound that we missed. But it looks like one shot.'

'Thanks,' said Blume.

'No problem,' said the man. 'Now that I've answered your questions, do you mind leaving the area again? You're standing where I'd like to set up my Leica.'

'Sure. In a minute.' Blume went back to have another look at Sofia. He had no information on her, nothing at all, but he felt confident that she was a student or recent graduate. Generally speaking, students are not victims of sniper fire. Not only was there a mismatch between the victim and the mode of her murder, but the very idea of a sniper was unlikely. The shooter, probably a jilted lover, could have been standing a few metres away. He could have called her name, pointed a pistol, then fired. Maybe it was another case of femicide: around 150 women a year, many of whom saw it coming and had asked for help. One thing about femicide, it made the case-resolved statistics look good.

A SIS agent came over and, glancing resentfully at Blume, inserted a trajectory rod into the chipped brick at the centre of the mess of blood and matter on the wall. After a few tweaks he had it attached and pointing upwards at an angle of around 30 degrees in the direction of the building opposite. Blume looked up and saw two men in white plastic overalls leaning out of the fifth-floor window.

He was just ducking under the crime scene tape on his way back to the magistrate when the girl's mother arrived. Unmistakable in her grief, she was calling her daughter's name, howling like an injured dog and, typically enough for this sort of situation, was pushing and shoving at two Carabinieri trying to keep her out of the crime scene. She had to see, or thought she did. They had to persuade her that her actions threatened to help the perpetrator. She would have time enough to see her daughter in the morgue, after which she would spend her life trying to erase from her mind the image that she now so badly wanted to impress upon it.

4

I T WAS past midnight and Blume and Principe were sitting in an Irish pub not far from the crime scene.

Principe drained his glass of Kilkenny ale and wiped his lips with the back of his hand. 'A few years ago, you wouldn't have been able to hear yourself think in here,' he said, 'but then they opened too many of these places all over the city, and it lost its cachet.'

Blume looked with disfavour at a sodden beer mat.

'I thought you'd like it here.'

'I don't drink,' said Blume.

'I am pretty sure we shared a drink in the past.'

'If we did I've stopped since then. It's not a big deal. I could probably have a beer.'

'Great. Want me to order you one?'

'No.'

Principe ordered himself a second drink, and Blume asked for a can of Chinotto. The barman told them he would be closing in half an hour.

'It's a role reversal: me the southern Italian enjoying beer in a pub, you the American giving me disapproving looks.'

'I am not disapproving.' He changed the subject. 'There is something familiar in the name, Sofia Fontana. Why is that?'

'She was a witness,' said Principe taking a long draught of beer. He put the glass down, his eyes watery, and suppressed some upsurge in this chest before continuing. 'She was a witness to a shooting. That's the direction your investigation should take.'

Blume clicked his fingers as the name slotted into place. 'She's the one who witnessed the assassination attempt on the terrorist Stefania Manfellotto.'

'Yes, that's her. I have been interviewing her off and on for months now. I found out almost nothing new about the Manfellotto case, but I got to know Sofia well. She was a beautiful, sweet, and generous girl.'

Blume deliberately ignored Principe's sentimental cue. 'It looks like someone was afraid you were making progress. That bitch Manfellotto isn't dead yet, is she?'

'Not yet.' Principe took another gulp of his drink. He looked terrible. 'We know where the shot was fired from inside the university – I am talking about Manfellotto now.'

'I get that, Filippo. I have just seen Sofia lying dead *outside* the university.'

'Yes, Alec. I am just sorting out my thoughts aloud.' Principe bent his head forward and massaged his forehead with finger and thumb. When he looked up again, there was less water in his eyes. 'Whoever shot Manfellotto almost certainly shot this poor girl. I called you in because I am afraid . . .'

Blume waited, but the magistrate seemed to have finished. Eventually he said, 'Afraid of what?'

The magistrate waved a hand at an annoying idea that seemed to be hovering in front of him. 'Nothing. It's just the absence of progress in the first case makes me fear an absence also in this one, which I would like to resolve. But we do have a lead, of a sort: Professor Pitagora.'

'Pitagora?' said Blume. 'Cool name. Like the actress . . .'

'Paola Pitagora? You're too young for her. She's more my generation.'

'I don't mean to intrude on the sexual fantasies of an old man.'

'Very funny. In both cases, it's a made-up name. A *nome d'arte*. I think the professor had it first.'

'Oh, that makes it a bit less interesting,' said Blume. 'So what's his real name?'

'Pinto. Pasquale Pinto.'

'Pasquale Pinto. Professor Pitagora. So he stuck with the letter P. Pitagora *is* better. Pasquale Pitagora?'

'Nope,' Principe shook his head. 'Just Pitagora. No first name unless you count Professor.'

'I have heard of him,' said Blume. 'He is one of those old-school Fascists. Monarchists, coup-plotters, mates with Cossiga, Gelli . . .'

'The Professor and Manfellotto were heard shouting at each other,' said the magistrate with another grimace. He stretched his hand out to his glass, then slumped back in an attitude of disappointment to find it empty. 'At the time Manfellotto was shot, he was giving a lecture on Ariosto to a class of over 50 students. The idea that he had taken a sniper's rifle and run up to the top floor and shot at her was never taken seriously. Cast-iron alibi and, above all, cast-iron friends. He put a lot of pressure on me for merely daring to question him.'

'But you didn't yield an inch.'

'Don't be stupid,' said Principe. 'Of course I did. I backed off at once. I know how it works. Except in this case, my conscience was clear.'

'Let me guess,' said Blume. 'Given who the first victim was, you didn't care all that much, but now you do because they have just murdered an innocent young woman.'

'Almost right, except I had already changed my mind.'

'About what?'

'Manfellotto. Not caring enough about her may have made me careless in my investigation. And maybe that is why Sofia was killed. My conscience no longer feels so clear.'

'Manfellotto deserved it,' said Blume. 'It was natural . . .'

'No, you're wrong,' interrupted Principe. 'You should meet her.'

'Why?'

'You'll see,' said Principe. 'So, back to that day. About two hours after Manfellotto was shot, a group calling itself the "Justice and Order" party called up the offices of *La Repubblica* and claimed responsibility with the words "Justice is done. Order restored." There were a few other calls of that sort, but this was the one we took seriously.'

'Sounds cranky to me.'

'The caller, a man, was using Pitagora's phone.'

'Ah.'

'Which he says was stolen from his office.'

'If he was behind it, using his own phone seems pretty dumb.'

'I agree,' said Principe. 'He has a good case. He was still giving his lecture when news of the shooting came through. The lecture was interrupted and Pitagora went back to his office with a few students. He said he did not notice his phone was missing until later. The call from his number was made about two hours later, from a point just outside the university walls on Viale Margherita. So our reading is that some student took it. It could just have been a prank in bad taste. Or someone trying to stir up trouble. I am assuming the phone was taken to embarrass him, but I am also convinced Pitagora knows which particular neo-Nazi splinter group is most likely to be behind the hoax, if that is what it was. And behind the shooting, too. He knows. That's his job, as you'll see when you

17

meet him. But I can't keep calling him in for questioning, not with the clout he has. I say professor. He's a professor emeritus now, well past retirement age, but somehow still sitting there in his office.'

'An old man in power refusing to give up his seat? I think I may have seen that happen before in this country,' said Blume. 'What did Sofia do for a living?'

'She was not a student. If she had been, it would be easier. Public outrage would give me a freer hand, including with Pitagora. But poor Sofia was just a lab assistant at the Health Institute on Viale Margherita. She explained to me once that she used the university as a short cut.' Principe shook his head. 'This case has sapped the last of my energy. I might get the office to assign it to a different magistrate.'

'I see,' said Blume, annoyed at the self-pitying tone. 'Remind me why you called me out on a freezing cold November night for a case you say you can't be bothered investigating?'

'Don't take it the wrong way. If I do give up, I want you to make sure things are done right. That's why I asked you to help. You might see things that I would miss.'

'That's what the Carabinieri are for. Don't you trust them?'

Principe sat forward, causing a dip in the signal strength to a radio playing in the background that Blume was only noticing now. 'I trust the Carabinieri more than you bastards in the police, if you must know.' He sat back and the radio fuzz stopped.

Blume stayed silent, absently wondering how much of the nasal singing voice in the radio he had been unconsciously enduring.

'Have I annoyed you?'

'Not as much as Eros Ramazzotti.'

'What?'

'On the radio,' said Blume.

'You do not have a stable mind, Alec.'

'Yet you want me.'

'Your thoughts hop around. It makes you hard to bear but good at working cases. Look, all I meant was that the Carabinieri will follow orders. So if another magistrate takes over from me, they'll follow his or her orders, no matter what. The Carabinieri are a very reliable force, up to a point. And I would like you to be there, watching from a distance up to that point where they stop being reliable.'

'And where will you be?'

'I'll be here. You'll report to me . . . differently from the Carabinieri. As a friend. This is a request, Alec. I really liked that girl Sofia.'

'I get that. You said you questioned Sofia over the past few months about the shooting of Stefania Manfellotto. So the obvious question is whether Sofia saw anyone or anything she shouldn't have.'

'She said she didn't. But it seems clear she did and never realized it. I think someone was taking no chances. If I had questioned her better, I'd have been able to work out what she saw, and maybe she would not be dead now.'

'Unless the two cases are not, in fact, related,' said Blume.

'That would be one hell of a coincidence,' said Principe.

'Maybe. You should talk to my nephew about that. He doesn't believe in coincidences.'

'Your nephew?'

'Elia.'

'Caterina's child? He's not your nephew, Alec.'

'What am I supposed to call him, my heir?'

'A normal person would say "adopted son".'

'I didn't adopt him. He was already there when I arrived. Part of the Caterina package. Besides, if anyone in that place is adopted, it's me.'

'Don't mess up that relationship, Alec. It's all you've got.'

'You said I should visit Manfellotto?'

'Avoiding the subject, Alec?'

'On the contrary, I am focusing on it. You are the one out of line. Isn't Manfellotto in a coma?'

'If you had been following anything, newspapers, the TV – Jesus, even the radio – you'd know she came out of her coma weeks ago. A month, by now. Everyone knows that.'

'Except me,' said Blume, finally sipping his Chinotto. 'I was out of the country.'

'I didn't know that.'

'We haven't seen each other in almost a year. And you're not my father. I was in Seattle, then down to Los Angeles, Nevada.'

'Las Vegas?'

'Yes.'

'Did you have fun?'

'I don't gamble,' said Blume. 'So Vegas was not much fun. I got to eat a lot of junk food, though. And drink root beer.'

'I thought . . .'

'Non-alcoholic. It's a bit like this stuff I'm drinking now, but with sassafras. Far better.'

'If you say so. But it sounds to me like you were looking for something other than root beer over there.'

'Do you want to investigate me, or do you want me to investigate the killing of Sofia?'

'*Tranquillo*. I was only asking as a friend. If you have people in the United States, good, because I remember your telling me you didn't. You're sort of the quintessential orphan. Not only no parents but no family anywhere. I am glad you went looking, and a little hurt you didn't tell me.'

'My mother's sister lives there. I thought you knew. But I never met her, or her kids, who aren't kids any more, I guess.'

'I hope it works out for you.'

'It won't. But thanks. Listen, Filippo, the last time I went off on a semi-official case without bringing my colleagues with me, I ended up buried in a hole in Calabria and a German Federal agent I was working with got killed. I blew my chances of upwards or sideways promotion, put myself in debt to Caterina, and gave the questore a large stick to beat me with.'

'Yes, and how is Caterina? Well, I trust?'

'She's good,' said Blume. 'Did you hear the rest of what I just told you?'

'Yes. But I am interested in you and Caterina.'

'It's all good. I need some ballast in my life.'

'Ballast,' said Principe. 'They don't use that word in love songs as much as they should.'

'Can we get back to what you're asking of me here? You need to appoint me officially, but even that will run into problems from the questore unless you can demonstrate that I have a particular skill the Carabinieri don't.'

'No. If I officially appoint you, the next magistrate can officially dismiss you.'

'So, don't let there be a next magistrate. What's all this talk about a next magistrate?'

They lapsed into silence. Principe took off his round spectacles and started polishing them with a soft cloth he had extracted from his breast pocket. He had managed to lose weight and gain flab. His eyes seemed to have lost colour in the dark light of the pub. Liver spots covered the back of his hands, and the same ugly hair that had sprouted from his ears coated the backs of his fingers. On their way from the car to the pub, Principe had walked with the stiff gait of an old man. He still had thin strands of hair on his head, but outside, when the wind had been blowing, he had seemed bald.

'I am not saying I will do this,' said Blume. 'But, if we assume the same person or persons who killed Sofia also shot Stefania Manfellotto, who would you say it was?'

'Neo-Fascist terrorists. Forza Nuova, or some such group. Definitely an internal feud.'

'Shouldn't they make sure Stefania Manfellotto is dead, too? In case she starts talking?'

'She is brain damaged. She's no danger to them.'

'Is she under guard?'

'She personally killed two young Carabinieri recruits in 1978, but was never brought to trial for it. We appointed the Carabinieri to guard her hospital room. They probably take long breaks.'

'Something doesn't fit. What sort of people kill a possible witness to an attempted murder, who seems to be no witness at all, but don't make a second attempt on the original target?'

'I told you, Manfellotto is harmless now. Total amnesia,' said Principe.

The barman came over and pointedly began to wipe down the table next to them. Blume pulled out his police badge, showed it to the barman, and said, 'If you need to lock up, go ahead. You can let us out later.'

'I'm closing the bar.'

'That's fine. We're not having any more are we, Filippo?'

'And I am taking a final reading on the cash register.'

Principe pulled out a €20 note and gave it to the barman. 'Keep the change.'

'Two beers and a Chinotto makes 22 euros.'

Principe added a fiver, and said, 'Bring me the change.'

When the barman had left, Blume said, 'Amnesia? Lots of ex-terrorists suffer from that prior to entering democratic politics.'

'You need to see her to understand. She's not acting.'

'So she can't remember, or says she can't remember the events leading up to her shooting?'

'She can't remember anything that's happened since 1979.'

'How convenient. The bomb she put in that train station was in 1980. An injury that turns out to be a moral cure.'

'Except she doesn't need to pretend, does she?' said Principe. 'She has served her term. Paid the price.'

'For all those lives?'

'She paid the tariff determined by the Italian state,' said Principe.

The barman came and stood by their table.

'All right,' said Blume. 'We're leaving.'

As they left the warmth, Principe buttoned up his overcoat against his skinny frame and seemed to shrink inside it. 'Sofia was so young.'

'A lot of victims are.'

They turned on to Via Merulana. The white marble façade of Santa Maria Maggiore, a church built in memory of a miraculous snowfall, stood out clearly above the large empty piazza in front. Principe buried his head deeper into his coat to protect himself against the corridor of cold air rushing up the street.

'I need to get back to the crime scene first thing in the morning,' said Principe. 'But it's best if you're not there. I'll send you all the details.'

'I still haven't agreed to this.'

'That's because you're disagreeable. But you'll do as I say.'

'Why's that?'

'Because I am one of the few people who's your friend.'

'You must think I am desperate, Filippo.'

'Yes, I do.' He gave a loud hoarse cough that sounded like it had ripped his throat. 'We'll catch our death out here.'

5

QUESTORE DE ROSSI was a tightly packed and compact man who carried within him vast reserves of destructive power. He wielded his small stature like a bully stick, and preferred to be standing up when he met people the better to display his shortness, for he enjoyed the tension this created, and enormously relished the challenge of cutting down those who gazed down on him from a height. Women whose eyes shone with pity, or whose impassive faces concealed their feelings of contempt, were brutally treated, and often left his office effectively demoted in function if not in rank. Tall men were his particular enemies, and Blume was a tall man.

'I hear you are moonlighting, Commissioner. Turning up without colleagues at crime scenes being adequately handled by the Carabinieri, not mentioning it to anyone.'

Blume was staring out the fifth-floor window of the Questura, across an empty space at the opposite wing of the building. He could see the dark figure of someone standing in a distant office staring blindly at Blume as Blume was staring blindly at him, like lonely travellers in passing cruise ships. Perhaps that man, too, was being upbraided by a small official with power. He half lifted his hand to give his doppelgänger a sympathetic wave.

'Commissioner, look at me when I am talking to you, and for God's sake sit down.'

Blume settled down in a chair, crossed his legs, and stretched his arms back to relieve a pressure in his chest.

The questore licked his finger and polished a lapel pin in the colours of the Italian flag. He watched Blume watching him.

'Not enough members of the force are proud to be Italian. Some members are not even Italian.'

'I got my citizenship papers a long time ago,' said Blume.

'Hah. You kept your American passport, though, didn't you?'

'Sure. If you give up your passport,' said Blume, 'they won't even give you a visa to visit the country. The US authorities can be very small-minded.'

'Really?' The questore was momentarily mollified by Blume's criticism of America, but, like a dog rediscovering a scent, he snapped his head up and said, 'I say they're right to take that attitude. People should be proud of their country.'

Blume inhaled deeply, expanding his chest, bulking himself out to three times the questore's size, and then exhaled slowly and wearily to give some idea of the fathomless boredom of his soul.

'You're not fish nor flesh nor fowl, Blume. You're not honest, and you're not corrupt; you're a commissioner but not a team player; your politics are undefined, as are your loyalties. I would be generous and say you're not a complete failure, but you're definitely not a success . . .'

'Sometimes it's just hard to measure up to your high expectations, sir. I frequently fall short,' said Blume, shaking his head in a mockery of penitence. 'Sometimes I feel pretty low about it.'

'Do you want a suspension right now?'

'Of course not.'

'Then shut up. I can't have my commissioners wasting valuable police time doing secret favours for their friends. Is he paying you?'

'Who?'

'Don't play stupid. Principe.'

'No! He's a magistrate.'

'That's all the more reason to be suspicious.'

'Why would he pay me?'

De Rossi shrugged. 'One out of three policemen in this country moonlights. At €1,300 a month, they have no choice. It's fucked up.'

'I agree. Too much money to the politicians – and to senior civil servants,' said Blume, looking levelly at De Rossi. In two years at most, this man would be recycled out of his life. Being short of stature and vile of personality was no impediment to prospering in Italian politics.

'I don't want your agreement, Blume. I want your obedience. Someone in your office informed me about your meeting with that magistrate last night.'

Now this was not necessarily true. The questore was probably trying to give the impression that he had eyes and ears in Blume's office, or perhaps that Blume had internal enemies. The obvious explanation was that the Carabinieri who had seen him at the crime scene had taken note and complained.

'My co-workers are all very conscientious,' said Blume. 'If they see an issue, no matter how small it seems, they will raise it. We are all slaves to the whims of magistrates, sir. I responded as I should, telling Magistrate Filippo Principe to go through the proper channels.'

The questore narrowed his eyes into what he probably thought were sly slits and struggled to keep a knowing smirk from his face. 'So you and he did not repair to the "Druid's Den" later on in the evening?'

'You said, "Repair to the . . ."? Can you repeat that?'

'*Druid's Den*,' said the questore, struggling with the strange vowel sounds.

'I beg your pardon?'

The questore now tried swapping the *i* and the *u* around in 'Druid' and lengthening the *e* in 'Den'. The 'r' travelled over to the end of the second word.

'A what Denner?'

'*E che cazzo!*' shouted the questore in broad Roman. 'Do you deny you went to an Irish pub with your friend the magistrate?'

'Oh, the *Druid's Den*,' said Blume. 'Awful dump. I hope you don't go there. A very low place.'

'Drinking and chatting, sharing information. Principe is an old fool, Blume. You and he were made for one another. *Dio li fa, e poi li accoppia.* In any event, I've been given assurances by the chief prosecutor that Principe will not be involving you or any of us in his damned case. He's made such a mess of it we're best out of it. He's completely mishandled the politics and now journalists are getting interested. I don't want to open *La Repubblica* and read that a senior police officer is now involved in the investigation into the attempted murder of that neo-Fascist woman.'

'You read *La Repubblica*?'

'I have others read it, and then bring me the interesting bits. I don't want to find you in any of them, if you value your job.'

'We hardly spoke about Stefania Manfellotto. We talked about the student who was killed, and not even much about her.'

'Do you think I'm stupid?'

Blume stayed silent, but noticed that he was nodding his head in unconscious assent.

'Obviously they are connected,' continued De Rossi. 'That girl must have seen something she shouldn't have. Not only was she killed by the same person, he even used the same weapon. That's the preliminary finding anyhow.'

'This is news to me,' said Blume, annoyed. Principe should have got that information to him first thing.

'Hah, well, it ought to be, but I don't trust you, Blume. I think you already knew that.'

'That you don't trust me or that the weapon used was the same? I knew nothing about the weapon, I assure you. I have not heard from Principe since. I told him I would not become involved without an official sanction, and he did not call me back. So I know of no new developments. You are better informed than me, Questore. You may choose not to believe me, but I turned Principe down. I said it would have to be an official appointment or nothing. Now you have called me in and explained very clearly that that is not going to happen.'

'Hah, well.' De Rossi seemed disappointed that the fight was coming to an end. 'I am glad we see eye-to-eye on this at last, Blume. I am sure you have plenty of work to do. Go now, and don't bother me again.'

Blume left the room, and walked absently down the corridor, half greeting one or two familiar faces as he went. Outside, the world was blustery, wet, and misbehaving. Leaves were held in a magical vortex over the roof of his car, and as he opened the door, plastic bags leapt off the ground and clung to it. One wrapped its way around his ankle, then whipped away, leaving a dirty stain on his trouser cuff.

He climbed into his car. The wind caused the dashboard vents to make a lonely and far-away howling noise that seemed better suited to a remoter and colder place than Via Torino in Rome.

6

'AN OLD weapon,' said Principe. 'The famous Carcano 91, maybe, a Mannlicher-Carcano-Parravicino. In any case, it was loaded with a 7.62×51mm NATO cartridge, and the shot came from around 60 metres away, from the building in front.'

'That's the National Research Council, right?'

'Yes. Easy to get into. Occasional security.'

'A Carcano 91, really?' Blume squeezed the phone against his head with his shoulder and mimicked holding a rifle. 'The weapon Lee Harvey Oswald used,' he said.

'The weapon every Italian soldier used for decades. The round was a 7.35 for Manfellotto, and a 6.5 for Sofia. The 6.5 bullet is back-heavy and unstable in flight. When it hits, it devastates like a dumdum.'

'Different bullets, but the same weapon was used in both incidents?' said Blume.

'Absolutely. The weapon fingerprint on the bullet is the same. In the first case, the distance was probably 400 metres, and the shot came from the side. That the shot was not fatal is nothing short of miraculous.'

'So a real marksman?'

'The techs were non-committal on this. If you have a good sights and a laser, then it's not all that hard, and both are easy to come by. Just ask a Russian in Ladispoli and he'll sell you both at a decent price. Then you'd need a bit of practice, or just be able to handle a rifle, calibrate the sights to the laser. Also, a professional would have a more modern weapon. This is the sort of ancient army surplus you would expect an outmoded Fascist gang to have stashed away somewhere.'

'Ignore the question of Sofia for a moment. Have you completely discounted the idea of a revenge attack on Manfellotto by one of the family members of her victims from the train station bombing?'

'Yes. Apart from anything else, it's a question of age. The angriest are those who lost children, but they are also the oldest, and much time has passed.'

Blume could not fault the logic. Even if someone who had lost a family member more than 30 or so years ago had suddenly snapped at seeing Manfellotto walking around a university campus and consorting with a Fascist fellow traveller, that same person was not the sort to go out and murder an innocent girl who might have seen something.

'By the way, what is it with the Russians up there? Why did they all decide to live by the sea near Ladispoli?' asked Blume.

'Caterina worked in immigration affairs,' said Principe, a trace of irritation in his tone. 'Ask her. Were you even listening to me?'

'Yes. So the unstable bullet took the back of the girl's head off, pretty much like what happened to Kennedy. Yet the same weapon was used for a cleaner shot that passed through the temporal lobe of Manfellotto, carving a neat and short canal through part of her brain and leaving the rest intact. God's never been much good at choosing who to save.'

'You have a funny idea of what "save" means. The bullet performed a lobotomy on Manfellotto. She can't remember anything, suffers from incontinence, loss of hearing, and incapacity to taste food, or remember what or if she has eaten,' said Principe.

'Not remembering what she has done, if that's actually the case, is another sign of God's special mercy for the worst type of human. As for the lobotomy and the incontinence, I never said He lacked a sense of humour.'

'Neither of them was lucky. If you do get shot in the head, pray it's point-blank up through the chin with a Magnum 44.'

'Lord, hear our prayer,' said Blume.

'Want to see for yourself what I mean?' said Principe. 'I'm going to the hospital to have a chat with Manfellotto in an hour. University Polyclinic, Ward 7, second floor, bed 33. Come along if you're interested.'

Blume put his phone down thoughtfully and left his office for the open-space area where Chief Inspector Caterina Mattiola, Chief Inspector Rosario Panebianco, and the new arrival in the office, transferred from Corviale, were crowded around the computer monitor on Panebianco's desk. They appeared to be watching something on YouTube.

'Busy, then, are we?' said Blume.

Caterina motioned him over and slipped her hand around his waist.

'Have you seen this?' asked Panebianco. 'Do you think they trained the dog to do that? I mean how would you even think of training a dog . . . wait, here's the best bit.'

Blume patiently watched a dog on waterskis. When the video was over, Panebianco leaned back in his chair and looked at Blume. 'I suppose you want to know if we've made any progress with the road rage case.'

'That would be nice.'

'You can ask Caterina. She's been hard on it.'

'I am asking you.'

Panebianco tapped his teeth with his pen, as if considering whether to answer or not, then relented, 'Well, it turns out the guy who got run over was not only a regular user of hash, coke, and alcohol, but he also used to sell them. All three. He had a pub, which was closed down five years ago when it turned out he was dealing from it. He blamed his staff, claimed he had nothing to do with it, and got a suspended sentence. He was also brought in twice on assault charges and was an active member of Casa-Pound, the Nazi group.'

'Illiterate nazis who claim inspiration from an American poet,' said Blume. 'Only in Italy.'

'They also like Tolkien, Irish hunger strikers, and World of Warcraft,' said Panebianco. 'And beating up schoolchildren, stabbing visiting fans from England, and starting riots in the stadium.'

'They tend to be Lazio supporters, don't they?' said Blume. 'That must increase their sense of alienation and loss.'

'I think you'll find they are mostly supporters of AS Roma, Commissioner. I would also point out that Lazio is second from the top of the league whereas Roma . . .'

'Fifteenth, yes, but the season's only begun. We always get off to a slow start.'

Caterina intervened. 'Let's not talk football, guys, OK? We're going off topic.'

'Fine,' said Panebianco. 'So the victim, Valerio, is on his motor scooter at a traffic light beside a silver-grey Citroen C4 Picasso driven by the accused, and, according to an eyewitness who came out of his furniture repair shop to watch the fun when he heard the shouting and horns blaring, was seen kicking at the door of the car, being in an excess of rage caused by a mixture of alcohol, cocaine, and the very disappointing performance of Roma against Siena, who are hardly giants of football, but that's what comes of trying to play like Barcelona without any of your players actually being any good at passing.'

'Seriously,' said Caterina.

'Yeah,' said Blume. 'Shut up, Rosario.'

'The argument continued at the next set of traffic lights, just after the Casaletto tram terminus, and we have a witness there, too. This time, Valerio got off his motorcycle the better to kick the Citroen.'

'Nobody saw the accused in the car?' asked Blume.

Caterina gave him a funny look. 'No, but we know who it was. The dents in the body work, the paint from the scooter, and of course, the blood.'

'But no one saw what happened?' he insisted.

'We have reconstructed the scene, and the investigating magistrate has ordered the detention of the accused on the basis of our reconstruction,' said Caterina. 'The driver of the car, Adelgardo . . .'

'Great name,' said Blume. 'He must be from Lombardy?'

'No,' said Caterina. 'Adelgardo Lambertini. He was born in Bologna, but has been resident in Rome for 60 years. Adelgardo seems to have accelerated on the downhill stretch at the beginning of Via Silvestri and struck the scooter from behind. The victim was hurled into the opposite lane but there was no oncoming traffic. At this point Adelgardo, according to the forensic expert from the Municipal Police who examined the marks on the road, seems to have executed a handbrake turn of around 130 degrees.'

'Not bad for a 72-year-old,' said Blume.

'He then realigned his vehicle, as witnessed by the barber in the shop who is the only one to have seen the whole thing from beginning to end. He accelerated back in the direction he had come, and drove over Valerio as he lay on the ground. The wheels crushed the victim's windpipe. He then stopped and once again turned the car round.'

'Another handbrake turn?' asked Blume.

'No, a slow and deliberate three-point turn, this time, clearly showing intentionality. He drove back over Valerio who was now thrashing about and trying to breathe. We should have dozens of witnesses for this, but none of the drivers on the road has responded to appeals to come forward, apart from one who arrived on the scene just after Adelgardo had passed over the body for a second time. Not that he deserves much praise, since he did not see fit to stop, but he did remember the first two and last two letters of the number plate, which may be because they are the same. EF and EF. When questioned, Adelgardo Lambertini denied having been in the car that day. He even denied owning a Citroen, even though it was registered in his name.'

'That was a bad move,' agreed Blume. 'He should have said it was stolen.'

'He parked it outside his daughter's house on the other side of Rome and got a taxi back. A patrol spotted the car a few hours later and we managed to track down the taxi driver, who has a clear memory of his fare. He remembers picking up an old man and being afraid that he might end up with a corpse in the back of his car, so white and feeble did he seem.'

'Also,' said Panebianco, 'the last number dialled on his mobile phone was 063570, which is the taxi company, and the call places him outside his daughter's house.'

'She removed the car, and the magistrate issued an arrest warrant against her for aiding and abetting,' added Caterina.

'An arrest warrant, no less,' said Blume.

'Arrest is obligatory on this charge,' said Caterina. 'The magistrate can't order custody only. Article 378 of the criminal code. He ordered the arrest to put pressure on Adelgardo. But either Adelgardo doesn't care about his daughter and grandchildren . . .'

'Or the magistrate's bullying tactics have angered him. We know he has a temper.'

'The magistrate's actions are perfectly legitimate,' said Caterina.

Blume looked at Caterina. He had been living with her for nine months now, and as each day went by, he felt he knew her less and less. He looked over at the new sovrintendente from Corviale, who had remained silent throughout. 'Am I the only one who thinks this Adelgardo is a fucking hero and we should be giving him a medal instead of arresting him and upsetting his grandchildren?'

The sovrintendente's look of serious concentration and deference was split in two by a smile of relief and agreement.

Panebianco's face showed no change, but he said, 'Of course he is. But we are agents of the law. Take it up with the investigating magistrate.'

'You know as well as I do the magistrate is not investigating anything. She's got all the evidence she needs and is just keeping the old man and his daughter in custody until they crack.'

'Commissioner,' said Caterina, all formal and hostile now that Blume had appealed directly to the young sovrintendente. 'This man has spent 72 of his God-given years on this earth. What do you think gives him the right to take the life of a man less than half his age? The right to drive over a helpless body lying in the middle of a road. Is that your idea of a hero?'

'Pretty much,' said Blume. 'Maybe not a top-tier hero. A lesser hero, let's say. The old guy has some anger management issues, but to do that after all those years without so much as a parking ticket is pretty impressive. Am I supposed to be sorry that an old man, instead of becoming a victim, pressed a drug-pushing thug into the asphalt?'

'He was only 30 years old.'

Panebianco intervened. 'His parents claim social benefits, yet he opened a pub when he was 25. So where would you say his income came from?'

Caterina's neck went blotchy in that unattractive way it had when she was angry. 'That's irrelevant.'

'From what I gather,' said Blume, unhappy to see her like this but needing to press home the advantage, 'his favourite pastime was beating up immigrants and spray painting walls with messages of hate.'

The new sovrintendente nodded in enthusiastic confirmation of this.

'His background is no longer relevant, since he is dead. And his killer was unaware of his past activities. He could have been a kid on his way home from school.' Caterina's lips had tightened to two thin lines. Her lips weren't all that great, Blume thought. Maybe that is why they didn't kiss so much any more.

'Twenty-one years in prison for a 72-year-old. And possibly four years for the daughter unless she starts cooperating. That's vindictive.'

'So is driving your car over someone's head,' said Caterina, and crossed her arms and bit her bottom lip. 'And you know he'll get house arrest at that age.'

She was right, but it was also a question of principle. The old man proved he was not a pushover for a thug. He had probably saved lives by taking out Valerio.

Blume disliked talking in this room. The fluorescent tubes in the ceiling were always on, adding to, rather than countering the greyness of the November day. Even when the light outside was bright and the air crisp, the fluorescent lights were constantly goading his patience, encouraging bad-tempered exchanges like this.

'OK, let's not argue the point. Caterina, you're still coordinating the evidence gathering.'

He went up to the sovrintendente, put his arm around his shoulder, and steered him away from the other two. When they had arrived at the window, Blume released him, and said, 'Claudio, how would you like to liaise with the magistrate in my place?'

'I don't think I could do that.'

'Are you not familiar with the facts and developments of the case? As far as I can see, you've been doing a great job of keeping up.'

The sovrintendente's face was taut and flushed in the effort of trying not to look delighted to be praised, even if he knew a request always followed flattery.

'I think you feel much the same as me about this case, and so I think you can represent me very well.'

'Magistrate Martone sent for you, not me.'

'Yes, so you'll need to get good at lying. You arrive, telling her I was called away urgently on other business. Tell her I have delegated to you, which is true. If she doesn't accept that, then she'll have to send for me all over again. But it's not likely. Like I said, there is not much more investigative work. And I don't think we need to bend over backwards to strengthen the case against the old man and his daughter, do we?'

Blume left the young policeman pleased and flustered in equal measure and went back to Panebianco and Caterina.

'Can you two come into my office?'

Blume had them sit down and dragged a chair across the room to join them. He told them about his visit to the crime scene at the university, his conversation with the questore, and his latest conversation with the investigating magistrate.

When he had finished, Panebianco asked him, 'What do you want us to say? It's pretty clear that you should not get involved.' He stood up. 'And that's all I have to say. If you choose to do otherwise, as you will, don't tell me about it.'

Caterina put her hand on his arm. 'Alec, don't even think of it. You don't need the hassle.'

Panebianco turned as he reached the door and added, 'Just one thing, Commissioner.' He paused till Blume was looking him in the eye. 'You give too much credit to Magistrate Filippo Principe. I realize he is a friend, but he has not always acted impeccably. There was a time when political types sent investigations to him to die.'

'I know that,' said Blume. 'But it's been a while.'

'Leopards don't change their spots,' said Panebianco. 'If he has turned completely honest, it's only because his political referents ceased to exist.'

'He never tried to block a murder investigation, Rosario. Not even all that time ago when all his friends were Craxi Socialists.'

'If you say so.'

First Caterina, now Panebianco. Everyone was being uptight and right-eous today. 'Hey, sorry if being consulted upsets you. I'll remember that next time.'

Panebianco opened the door. 'Good.'

Blume smiled complicity at Caterina and rolled his eyes as Panebianco closed the door, but got nothing back.

'He's right, Alec.'

So she was still on her high horse about Adelgardo and his road rage.

'Some support I get here,' said Blume bitterly.

She stood up. 'I think we're done here.'

'Yeah, go on, get out,' said Blume. 'The questore said someone in this office reported me to him, and I scoffed, thinking it was probably just the Carabinieri unhappy to see me in their case. But now I am wondering.'

Caterina looked at him in amazement. 'You're wondering if *I* reported you to the questore?'

He had gone too far, but the best he could manage was a shrug.

'You know who it most likely was?'

'Who?'

'Principe himself. He knows how pathetically predictable you are. If there is one thing bound to make you want to get involved in the case, it's a direct order from the questore to stay away.'

7

BLUME ARRIVED in the car park of the University Hospital, his head-lamps already on to penetrate the brownish gloom of the afternoon. He immediately spotted Principe, a forlorn figure who looked like a man who had forgotten where he had parked. Principe was still glancing about absent-mindedly when Blume sauntered up.

'Do you know what Caterina was saying about you, Filippo?'

'And how *is* Caterina?'

'Good. I told you that the other night. She wants me to rent out my apartment.'

'That makes sense. It would almost double your income. We public servants could do with a bit extra these days. Let me guess: you don't want strangers trampling all over your apartment, or that's what you're telling her. But she knows, you know, and even I know the real reason is you want to hold on to it to have a bolt-hole for when everything goes south.'

'Don't you want to hear what she says about you?'

'Well, what?'

'She says you know me almost better than she does and that you are the one who made sure the questore found out about my moonlighting, if that's the word.'

'That's obviously not true. It does not even make sense.' Principe started moving in short hurried steps across the crumbling asphalt of the car park. 'Come on, you've kept me waiting as it is. Let's go and see Manfellotto.'

Blume couldn't be bothered relaunching the accusation. Maybe Principe had second-guessed him. Why not? He had guessed right about this hospital visit.

'You knew I couldn't resist coming here, didn't you?'

'Yes, Alec. I was pretty certain. You need to see, touch, and verify for yourself. But, really, it's fascinating stuff. The bullet went right through a section of skull and came out the front, without expanding. It cut a clean tube through her frontal lobe. *Mannaggia*,' he said as a sudden swishing and drumming sound came racing towards them through the trees. 'Is it meant to rain this much in Rome?'

Principe opened a huge yellow golf umbrella, just as the rush of rain hit so hard that he had to raise his voice to be heard. 'Get under here. I knew you'd forget an umbrella, so I took the biggest I could find.'

'I didn't forget an umbrella,' said Blume, alarmed at the feebleness of the magistrate's arms. 'I always have one in the car.'

'Always there because you never take it out!' Principe had to raise his voice against the rain, which was coming down so hard now that the backsplash from the ground had already soaked the lower half of his trousers. Blume, as casually as he could, took the umbrella from Principe and lowered it to use as a shield against the wind and horizontal rain.

They climbed the flight of steps outside the hospital and pushed their way into a steaming mass of weather-watchers and smokers.

'Come on, there's a hot air dryer in the toilets,' said Principe who was beginning to shiver. He led Blume down a ramp and through a door marked 'Authorized Personnel Only'. Blume demurred, but Principe said, 'It's cleaner than the public ones, and the hot air dryer works. Besides, who more authorized than a magistrate?'

As they were drying themselves off, two doctors in white lab coats came in, gave them dirty looks, pissed, washed their hands, and left without drying them. Blume managed to get the front of his shirt around his stomach dry, but that was about it. Principe, too, gave up, and the quiet that followed the noise of the dryers was so pleasant that they stood in silence for a few moments savouring it.

'Just tell me,' said Blume. 'You made sure the questore found out that I had visited the crime scene, didn't you?'

Principe was looking at himself in the mirror and fingering the damp strands of hair on his head as if he was only now discovering how bald he had become. 'Why would I do such a thing?'

'Well, Caterina thinks because I am pathetically predictable, and that as soon as I was warned off the case by the questore I'd commit myself to it with zeal.'

'That's one cynical little woman you got yourself there,' said Principe. 'You don't seem surprised that the questore knows about it.'

'Oh, I am. I just used up all my shocked expressions after seeing my face in the mirror.' Principe turned round, his face grave. 'The Questura is a huge place, especially here in Rome. It's awash with rumour and backstabbing and spying. I used to know my way round it pretty well, and I am sure it hasn't improved over the years. Worse than ever, probably.'

It was not an explanation or an admission, but Blume did not really care. They left the toilets and turned into a corridor, at the end of which stood a ward sister who put her hands on her hips.

'I hope you're quick on the draw, Alec,' muttered Principe as they approached. Then, slipping off his round glasses and polishing them while looking at the nurse with his watery eyes, he said, 'Yes, Sister, I realize we are very wet, but this is official business.'

She merely tossed them a look of contempt and pointed to a waste bin that had been turned into a stand for wet umbrellas, then walked away. Blume was not sure whether she had been protecting the room or had happened to be standing there surveying her dominion, which reached all the way down the blue corridor.

'In here,' said Principe. He pointed to an empty plastic chair by the door. 'See, no Carabinieri on guard. Out for an endless cigarette break, if they even remembered to put someone on duty.'

'Does she get visitors?'

'That is what the guard is supposed to tell us. But it doesn't seem like it.'

'Will she be awake?'

'I don't know. We can wake her up if not. Awake or asleep, she lives in the past.'

The room had two beds in it, one empty. On the windowsill sat a spotted pink orchid plant, incongruous and defiant of the sheets of freezing water racing down the other side of the pane. Blume felt the claustrophobia of the room at once, and caught himself stooping as he approached the bed, as if his head might bump against the ceiling.

A woman was sitting propped up on pillows. The front part of her shaved head was bound in white bandages, and she was regarding them with frank interest and a pleasant smile. She looked far younger than she should, more late forties than early sixties. The folds of skin around her throat and the pronounced line of the tendons in her neck gave some indication of her real age, but the smile was splendid, and inviting.

'This is Stefania. Not bad for a 62-year-old figure of hate who has just been shot through the head, huh?' said Principe, without bothering to modulate his voice.

Blume was appalled at the comment. The woman was right in front of them, smiling, trying to be welcoming and dignified.

He tried to square his protective feelings with what he knew of this woman's history. When he lifted his eyes again, Stefania's blue-grey eyes regarded him levelly, a slight twitching preliminary to a smile was evident at the corner of her mouth, as if she knew him and was on the point of greeting him with a beam of happy recognition. She then turned her gaze to Principe, who had dragged over two chairs. Once again, she seemed poised on the cusp of recognition.

'You are wet, both of you. That is a terrible storm outside, isn't it? I can't remember it ever being quite this bad.'

Blume gazed questioningly at Principe. He had imagined flickering eyelids, tubes, a respirator, a waggling small finger that proved she was not brain dead. He had not expected small talk.

He noticed a book beside her on the bed, a biography of Garibaldi.

'This is Commissioner Blume,' said Principe, stretching out his arm. 'He'd like to ask you some questions, wouldn't you, Commissioner?'

Blume shook his head. He had not planned to ask her any questions at all.

'And I am . . . do you remember who I am?'

'Of course I do,' said Stefania Manfellotto with a smile. 'You are . . . I'm sorry, your name escapes me. But we have met, of that I am quite sure.'

She turned to Blume and gave him a conspiratorial wink. 'Don't be offended if I forget your name. I've recently been subject to fits of absent-mindedness.'

She touched her forehead with her fingers, and seemed surprised to feel the bandages there. For a moment, a look of panic swept across her face, then she relaxed.

'What day is it?' asked Principe.

'I'm afraid I've rather lost track of time.'

'Can you tell me what month it is?'

Blume saw her eyes wander over to the dark window. The rain had eased off a little.

'December?'

'Close. But it's November,' said Principe.

'Silly me,' she turned and Blume expected another wink, but this time he seemed to cause her to hesitate.

'Now, then, can you tell me your name?'

'Of course. I am Stefania Manfellotto.'

'And,' Principe glanced over at Blume, 'what have you done with your life?'

'My life's not over yet!' she said laughing. Blume realized her voice had a light timbre, more suited to a younger woman. Then she became serious and, for a moment, frightened, as she looked about the room. 'Unless I have some serious disease.' She cheered up. 'Which I don't, obviously, or I would remember!'

She looked over at Blume again, and he expected a wink, but, to his dismay, he realized she was looking at him with the same expression of contingent welcome of a few minutes ago, her eyes giving him cautious acknowledgement.

'What are you reading?' asked Principe.

Stefania glanced at the bedside chest, then at the book on her sheets. She picked it up and read the title. 'Giuseppe Garibaldi,' she said.

'Are you interested in history?'

'Evidently.'

'What about politics?'

'Oh yes, I am very political. I am afraid my beliefs are not shared by many.'

'Can you think of any recent political events? Here or abroad.'

Stefania nodded. 'A journalist got shot.'

'Who?'

'Mino Pecorelli.'

'Do you approve of his assassination?' asked Principe.

'He was hateful, wasn't he?'

'Who is the prime minister?'

'Giulio Andreotti, of course. It's always him. Foreigners always accuse Italy of having unstable governments, but it's always the same people moving around in a tight circle. We have fewer elections than most countries. Foreigners know nothing about Italy.' As she spoke, the confusion cleared from her face, and her eyes took on a more focused and intelligent look. She looked at Blume and said, 'Are you foreign?'

'No . . . I am, well . . .'

She cut him short. 'Good.'

Now it was Principe who winked at him as he said, 'Stefania, who's the president of the United States?'

'Jimmy Carter.'

'Who's the president of the Chamber of Deputies?'

'Nilde Iotti. She's a Communist.'

'Do you hate her?'

'I don't hate anyone . . .' She cast around for Principe's name but it was gone.

'Did you have anything to do with the kneecapping of the women journalists in Radio Città Futura?'

'Of course not. What a silly question.'

'Who is Emilio Alessandrini?'

'A judge, he got killed.'

'By a neo-Fascist group. Are you pleased at this?'

Stefania shook her head sadly, but her lips, still fleshy and inviting, tightened.

'Any recent news from abroad that concerns you?'

'The Communists have taken over Nicaragua. That is disturbing.'

'The Sandinistas, you mean?'

'Why, are you trying to tell me they're not communist?'

'No. I agree with you. Remind me when it was.'

'Last week.'

Blume had to stand up. He went over to the window, intending to open it, but the rain outside was still beating down, and the plant was in the way. Principe joined him.

'Where is she?' asked Blume, keeping his voice low. '1980?'

'No, 1979. I used an old almanac last time I was here. Cossiga was never prime minister, but she remembers the Sandinistas going into government. That puts her somewhere between July and August 1979. Close to 19 July, since she seems to remember the news from Nicaragua as being from the other day.'

Blume glanced back at the bed, where Stefania, smiling to herself, had picked up her book on Garibaldi. Principe followed his glance. 'Yes, she always goes back to page 1. A doctor told me that he found her reading page 64 the other day, which is apparently a record. But as soon as she's interrupted, it's back to the beginning.'

Stefania had glanced up from her book and smiled at them. Clearly, she did not recognize them any more.

'I take it you now accept that she is not malingering?' Principe said to Blume. 'Apart from the fact, it's kind of hard to fake being shot in the head. And she has no need to. She's not under arrest. She was released on condition that she signed in at a police station once a day, and that's now been waived pending her discharge from here. If she ever is discharged. No, she's not pretending. *Cui prodest?* That's the real question. If we can work out whose interests are served by her death, then we can make some progress.'

Blume was only half listening to the magistrate. His eyes were fixed on the woman who returned his stare much as a baby might do, without any embarrassment or looking away.

Principe followed his gaze. 'Yes, I know. It's hard to fathom. I don't even know whether to say she is trapped or living free in the past. There's a doctor, called Ferraro, who comes to visit her. He's loving every moment of this. He told me, without any embarrassment, that he's going to get at least one best-selling book out of her story. He's already organized a conference and invited leading neurosurgeons, psychologists, neurologists, and so on. A group came over last month. I think she's due to get a steady stream of visitors. But it will make no difference to her how many men in white coats peer and prod at her. She can't form any new memories. Her perceptions hang around for only a few minutes, then fade without trace. So she can hold a conversation together for a while, though it soon veers into the surreal, and then moves into the impossibly boring, but there is a fun game of political trivia you can play with her. Or *I* can because you're too young, and weren't even here.'

'You treat her like an animal in a zoo,' said Blume, hearing something of Caterina's moral tone in his words.

'Nah. I treat her like a sort of magic window into the late 1970s. Talking to her is like conversing with a time-traveller. Well, up to a point, because you can't really show her the future. She doesn't take it in. It's fascinating, but then it becomes hard to bear.'

'Why?'

'She makes me think too much about my younger self and how things used to be. I get pretty depressed after a while,' said Principe. 'That's why digital cameras, video, Facebook, and all that stuff is going to turn an entire generation into unhappy neurotics, trying to climb back into the perfectly preserved memories. Luckily, I won't be around to see it.'

Principe took off his glasses, which had fogged up again. Blume looked down and laughed. In the heat of the room, Principe's heavy knit trousers were steaming as the damp evaporated. 'You look like Lucifer standing there with smoke coming out of your ass,' said Blume.

'Excuse me?' It was Stefania. 'Are you planning to be here long?'

'No, I think we're going now,' said Blume.

'Why, are you expecting someone, Stefania?' asked Principe.

Her brow creased and then she laid down her book. 'My father is on his way.'

'Is he, now?' said Principe. 'From the print shop where he works?'

'So you know him!' She sounded delighted. 'Did he say when he was coming?'

'Soon enough. Maybe in the next half hour.'

Stefania nodded happily, as if Principe were confirming a certainty. She relaxed her rigid posture a little and leaned back against her pillows, closing her eyes.

'The father,' Principe said to Blume, 'was a monarchist. He fought on Mussolini's side at Salò.'

'Keep your voice down, damn it!' hissed Blume. He had never seen Principe this cruel.

'You still don't get it, Alec. It's in one ear, out the other with her.'

'Your words will still hurt going in,' said Blume, though he had no idea what he was taking about. 'Just lower your voice,' he motioned Principe to the far end of the room away from the bed.

'Have it your way,' said Principe. 'Her father's employers tried, and failed, to have him fired for using their presses after hours to print propaganda leaflets. He fought a hopeless campaign to hold a new referendum to bring back the monarchy. Essentially he was a nonentity, but it's where her politics came from.'

'What about her mother?'

'Touchy subject that. If you're having difficulty believing that woman over there is capable of so much violence, just mention her mother and watch her face. The transformation is remarkable.'

Blume looked over at the bald head resting against the pillows, eyes closed, and was reminded of a sleeping infant. 'No, I don't think I will.'

'Both her parents are dead, of course. Here's an interesting thing. Her father died in December 1979.'

'A few months ahead of where she is now,' said Blume.

'Yes,' said Principe. 'More to the point, she is living in a reality a few months before she went out and bombed that train station.'

'Are we absolutely and completely sure she is the person who did that? A lot of the evidence in court was contradictory, wasn't it?'

'Seeing her now makes you doubt it. I understand that. Look, it pains me as a magistrate to say this, but the trials were farcical for how much leeway she and her defence team were given. The evidence against her was overwhelming. The courts of the first and second instance found her guilty. The doubts, reversals, technicalities, and all that shit began with the Court of Cassation, when the political interference and back-room dealing really kicked in. She promised not to mention certain things, the Court went as easy on her as it could. I know how it works, especially in those days. She still served 27 years. It was her.'

'Back then I was an American kid living in Seattle.'

'So you were. But the trials went on for decades.'

Blume went quietly back to the bed, thinking he might leave the woman to sleep in expectation of a visit from her father, but as he approached, she opened her eyes and smiled. 'I'm sorry,' she said. 'I didn't realize we had been introduced. I'm afraid I can't quite remember your name.'

'Alec.'

'Pleased to meet you, Alec. You're quite tall, aren't you?'

Blume blushed, and she laughed. 'You're easily embarrassed, I see. I like tall men.'

'Thank you,' said Blume, feeling like a fool.

'You're welcome.' She winked at him. 'I hope you like blondes. Most men do.' She tossed her head, then frowned in puzzlement. He could hardly bear to watch as she raised her hand to discover her shaved and bandaged head.

8

THE RAIN had stopped by the time they left, but not before mixing the loose asphalt and crabgrass borders of the car park into an undifferentiated mass of water and mud that had soaked though their shoes. The wind seemed to have snuffed out the street lights, and a heap of black clouds in the sky blocked out the moonlight.

'I am assuming you looked into the families of the Carabinieri she killed before the bomb attack,' said Blume.

'Of course. The parents are dead in both cases. One of the Carabinieri was an only child. The other had two older brothers. One lives in Australia, the other in Canada. I even spoke to a woman who was the girlfriend of one of the young men at the time. She is married with three grown-up children, and lives in Livorno. All she could talk about was that she was about to become a grandmother. Not too many delayed-action killers there.'

'It's too cold to talk,' said Blume, who could feel his lower jaw beginning to tremble. 'I'm going back to my car.'

The rain had turned the piazza outside into a broad lake. While some motorists felt the best way of getting through was to pretend their cars were jet-skis, others became extremely cautious and stopped dead at the water's edge, unsure whether to proceed. It took him half an hour just to get down Via Regina Margherita, and then another half hour to drive upstream past a long line of motionless trams, past the commuters who had abandoned them and now walked like protesters down the middle of the road. But he didn't really mind. He had the hot air on full, and aimed at his feet. He had got used to the smell of wet leather and the musty stink of the floor mat, and was simply enjoying the sensation of the rubbery heat rising up his body. The radio was playing a long intricate piece of funk by Solomon Burke. Occasionally, he would turn the vent dial and direct the warm air over the windscreen to demist it. The rain was light enough to keep the wipers on intermittent. He felt so snug in the car with the music, that he almost welcomed the traffic jams. Passing by pedestrians trying to wrap themselves up like bears, then leaping like gazelles over the oily pools of water overlapping the kerbs and footpaths, he was almost tempted to offer someone a lift in his nice warm car.

His phone rang. It would be Caterina wondering where he was. She was probably stuck in traffic, too, though she had started out from a better location about half an hour earlier. He hoped she wouldn't ask him to pick up something in the supermarket. Reluctantly he turned down the music.

But it was Principe. 'Are you home with the wife or still stuck in traffic?'

'Stuck in traffic. She's not my wife, Filippo.'

'You should correct that. Don't end up alone like me.'

'You called me to say that?' said Blume.

'I called you up to talk about the traffic. About Manfellotto, too. I saw you in there. She fascinates you. I mean as a case. You know, I was thinking, maybe someone she knew in 1979, someone she remembers as a young man, is the person who just tried to kill her. We need to get her to mention the names of all her neo-Fascist *camerati*. Did you notice how cooperative she seems? Maybe you should go to interview her again, try and dig out all the names she has stored in there.'

'Are you afraid I am not involved enough?'

'Oh, OK, sorry. I just want you to keep monitoring the developments. You haven't met Captain Zezza. I'll need to arrange that.'

'I expect he's busy doing real police work.'

'What do you mean by that?'

'You know exactly what I mean. The Carabinieri will be following protocol and logic. This captain examining Sofia's murder will be checking out all her actions immediately before the event. He'll be questioning the people she met, spoke to, was seen by. But you know this, since he is reporting to you.'

'All that you say is true.' Principe sounded offended. 'But I don't understand your tone.'

'You phone me to remind me of what I am supposed to do, but aren't you the one losing focus? You should be prioritizing Sofia. Keep your focus on the most recent events. Otherwise, they will slip out of memory, evidence will be destroyed, alibis will be built, and other cases will distract your attention. You thought to draw me deeper in with this Stefania Manfellotto, but I had already given you my word.'

'I phoned for a chat about the terrible traffic . . . I am following the proper procedures, and the Carabinieri I am working with are good. Tomorrow I'll be talking with the last people to have seen Sofia, as well as with her parents and her cousin Olivia. You might have seen them arrive at the crime scene the other night.'

Blume recalled a young woman with straight hair weeping uncontrollably, her boyfriend's arms wrapped around her.

'The fun of disobeying Questore De Rossi wore off a while ago. This is starting to feel like unpaid work.'

'All your investigative work is unpaid. If you sat at your desk all day and did nothing, they'd pay you the same.'

'They'd probably promote me faster, too,' said Blume. 'I'm hanging up now, Filippo. I am almost home.'

'Speak soon.'

All the warmth was blown off him as he stepped out of his car, three blocks from Caterina's apartment (he doubted he could ever think of it as his), and thanks to passing traffic and wind, he was soaked again before he reached the building. No one answered the intercom. So he let himself in the front door and travelled up in the lift. Some bastard had been smoking in it and dropped the spent butt on to the wet floor. The damp air was laced with the nicotine and breath of the smoker, which almost made him gag.

The apartment was cold. He went straight into the bathroom, stripped, and stood under the hot shower until he had turned the room into a sauna. He then dried himself down slowly, relishing the luxury of it and deferring the moment he would have to open the door and let in the cold dark air. He dropped the towel on the floor, and swiped it around in a mixed effort to dry his feet and the floor. If he had been more organized in his mind, he would have turned on the heat and brought his clothes in here to change into. He decided he would make dinner, because the idea of bumbling about in the kitchen stirring something in a pot bubbling over a hot gas ring appealed to him. He heard a key scratch at the front door, then saw the shine of the light in the hallway under the bathroom door.

'Alec, you here?' called Caterina.

'Here I am, clean and, if I may say so, ready.' He flung open the bathroom door.

Caterina was standing there, three plastic shopping bags still in her arms. Standing next to her was her mother, who had already clasped one hand over Elia's eyes, the other over her own.

9

CATERINA SEEMED to be in two minds about whether it had been the funniest thing she had ever seen or a regrettable incident. When she thought about her mother, she found it funny; when she thought about Elia, she was less sure. Blume had no doubts in the matter. It had not been funny in the slightest, but it had helped them gloss over their showdown in the office earlier.

As they lay down in bed together, the boy already safely tucked away and not, it seemed, traumatized for life, the honest voice inside him, the small voice that saw him for what he was and had an ability to tighten his chest and curdle his stomach juices with a simple whisper, now told him that he was only pretending to be annoyed at what had happened. The advantages accrued from the incident had been considerable. Caterina's mother had declared she was never setting foot in the house again. After she left, Caterina had whispered something about him keeping the rash promise he had made. The incident had implicitly strengthened his case for keeping his own place, and now Caterina, sensing that he was still in a huff, seemed disinclined to ask him where he had been that afternoon. He might have told her, but he was glad for the opportunity not to, and he was also glad that she did not ask him what he was doing as he read the transcript of Professor Pitagora's interview with the Carabinieri. She would tell him to make his position official or get off the case, and then they would have another fight.

Depending on how he framed the question to himself, Blume reckoned he was either a dammed good lover or simply a good one, but he had to admit he had difficulties with the preliminaries. He found it hard to voice his requests fully clothed, though once the sex began, his tongue loosened, literally and figuratively. But before he could get to that stage, he needed to lie on his back, talk in matter-of-fact tones about some subject or other, and let his, or sometimes her, hands start exploring.

'I got a call from Magistrate Martone,' said Caterina, adding an 'oof!' as Blume lifted his hand from the sheet and plonked it heavily on her stomach. 'She's agitated.'

'Oh?' said Blume, shifting down the bed to align his hip with hers. He dearly wished she had not brought up the case again. Apart from everything else, it had no investigative merit. What happened happened: the rest was just administration.

'The old man . . . the road rage guy . . .'

'Mr Adelgardo Lambertini,' said Blume, keeping his voice neutral.

'Yes. He's got himself all lawyered-up. A real ball-breaker, too. He's retracted everything, and now says the whole thing was a ghastly accident.'

Blume slid a finger down. She was wearing cotton pants again, and yet he had definitely seen an entire drawer full of silk ones. He considered asking her about this.

'He is claiming his foot slipped on to the accelerator in an attempt to brake, and that the reversing back over Valerio's head was caused by senile dementia. He's lining up some doctors who will say this is possible.'

'Anything's possible,' murmured Blume, then, reverting to his normal voice, said, 'Anyhow, what the fuck do you care and why is this making you tense?'

'The magistrate thinks she's going to lose the case.'

'If she thinks that, then she will, and I hope she does.'

'I don't. If a crime like this goes unpunished, no matter who the victim was . . .'

'I don't want to discuss this,' said Blume. Had Caterina ever thought of shaving down there. Not all off. A landing strip. How could he ever broach the subject with her?

Was she really still talking about the magistrate and the murdered thug? She turned her body towards him, which was encouraging, but it meant his arm was suddenly too long for what he had been trying to do.

'I'm sort of in charge of the witness,' said Caterina. 'I was the first to interview him, and I accompanied him to the magistrate. And then this evening, Martone ordered me to go round to him again, and check that he was sticking with his story.'

If he responded she might finish the conversation quicker. 'What's he do, this witness?'

'He's a barber.'

'A barber. Well, people don't feel strongly about barbers. The court is not going to have any pro- or anti-barber prejudices.'

'You speak from experience?'

'No. Just, you know, people feel neutral about barbers. He'll make a good witness.'

'Your hand is hot.'

'If you want me to stop, just say the word.'

'No. It's just . . . This cold. I need to pee.'

A few minutes later, when she had stopped complaining about her feet being cold, he realigned himself and started again, with a little less hope and enthusiasm than before.

'It's nice and warm under the duvet,' she said encouragingly.

He grunted.

'Did you turn off the heat?'

'No. It turns itself off.'

'It turns off far too late, though,' said Caterina.

'So adjust the timer.'

'I don't know how.'

'Jesus.'

When he got back to bed, Caterina was almost asleep, and he wasn't having that.

'If you're so hot, let me take this duvet off and, turn round, that's it . . .'

Caterina lifted her arms and put them behind her head. 'You are such a romantic, Alec.'

10

For a man in his mid-sixties, Professor Pitagora had remarkably well-preserved pale skin. Close up it was a mass of tiny cracks like the surface of a white porcelain plate left in an oven rather than the melted latex look of an ageing rock star, though he did sport a disconcerting moptop Beatles' haircut that his silver hair made looked like a metal helmet.

The professor was well turned out. His suit was undertaker black but had an expensive cut, beneath which he wore a black shirt with a tiny priest-like collar. Around his neck, he wore a shimmering gold foulard, an unapologetically female piece of apparel. Rising from a broad red chair, he walked across the room towards Blume. The heavy, shiny brogues were masculine enough, as was the gait. If he lost the foulard and pushed his hair back, he would look like a normal person, Blume reckoned.

He seized Blume by his hand, and placed his other hand on the elbow, and shook it firmly, his face showing apparent delight, as if Blume were a favourite brother. On his wrist, he wore a dark gold bracelet.

'A police commissioner. A valorous and completely underpaid profession. I have always vigorously preferred the police to the Carabinieri, who are always ambiguous. The Carabinieri tend to treat themselves like a state within a state, don't they? Whereas you people, the *Polizia di Stato*, well, the name says it all. You are a reflection of all the imperfections of the Italian State. When the country is rotten, the police are rotten, but the Carabinieri hide their faces, collaborate in the corruption, then emerge as virtuous. Not so the police. So I'll try to be as helpful with you as I can, out of deference to your uniform.'

Blume glanced at his arm to check he had not inadvertently put on his dress uniform that morning.

'Are you political, Alec Blume? You don't mind me calling you by the name you were baptized with, presuming you were baptized at all.'

Blume wrinkled his nose to indicate he was not too happy with the use of his name, but the professor had crossed his arms and was tapping his foot, as if waiting for something else.

'Well, were you?'

'Was I what?'

'Baptized.'

'I don't think that's any of your business.'

'Do you consider it a taboo question?'

'An irrelevant one.'

'A millennial cultural tradition that defines your religious identity is not irrelevant. All your actions flow from what happened in infancy. Blume is a foreign name. Jewish?'

'Me?'

'There is no one else in the room, is there?'

Blume had never really considered the matter. His mother had been a non-practising Episcopalian who went through an evangelical phase, which swiftly transmogrified into aggressive atheism. He never remembered his father expressing a single religious idea in his life. He doubted they would have been able to tell him anything even if they were alive. He had an aunt in the United States whom he had failed to track down on his last visit, not that he had searched too hard. Maybe she could tell him something about his name. He was circumcised, but then again, that had more to do with being born in America. Or so he had always assumed.

'I am perfectly capable of decoding the meaning behind your long silence,' said Pitagora. 'It's what I do. You know of course your questore is Jewish? De Rossi. That is one of the oldest Jewish names possible.'

'De Rossi is Jewish?' Blume had never imagined it for a moment. He found himself unaccountably interested in the idea, then sceptical, and finally scornful. He would have heard about it. Overtly or covertly, Jews in power were always identified. 'No, he's not.'

'Thing is, De Rossi himself probably doesn't know. Do you have many dealings with the man?'

'As few as possible,' said Blume.

'Healthy attitude,' Pitagora tapped his nose, went back to his big red chair, and invited Blume to sit down.

'This fascination with Jews,' said Blume, crossing his legs, 'is it connected with your Nazi politics?'

'I could tell you were intelligent the moment you walked in. Intelligent, but very, very negative. You noticed my golden foulard and bracelet, and you thought they were affectations, but wearing gold on your person gives you the energy of the sun. I know, you don't believe me. You were trying to provoke me with the Nazi taunt, but of course the real problem with Nazism was the socialism. Without socialism, you don't get big assemblies gathering to serve a man-made ideology. Are you following me?'

'No.'

'You are, and you are evaluating me, too. Subtle Hebrew.'

'Drop the Jewish references, Professor.'

'I speak out of absolute admiration. Yours is a fascinating race. Do you know that the Jews of Rome pre-date the Christians? The Jews were here first. As a religion, that is. When the Emperor Titus, one of the greatest men this city ever produced, destroyed Jerusalem in 70 AD, many Jews fled here, to the centre of the empire. They settled in camps on one of the hills facing Rome, where the Etruscans used to be, what we now call Monteverde, and *they are still there*! Still in Monteverde and down the hill, too, in the Ghetto. That is some staying power, isn't it?'

Blume grunted what Pitagora took for acquiescence.

'The immigrants from Jerusalem were followed by St Peter and St Paul, both Jews themselves, who formed a breakaway sect called the Christians. And if the Romans didn't care much for the Jews, but could accept they had a case, they definitely didn't care at all for the flesh-eating, blood-drinking Christians. But the breakaway group got the upper hand, and then turned on their own people. So you see, the Jews are literally their own worst enemy . . . You seem tired. A bit flabby around the waist for a man of your age. I trust you have a woman? So what about your politics? As you can see, I love the light. I hate intrigue and I despise people who do not have the courage of their convictions. In what do you believe, Commissioner Alec Blume?'

'My opinions are my own business.'

'Nonsense. The only reason we have opinions is to present them to others. That's the definition of an opinion.'

'You neo-Fascists tend to have a lot of opinions, I've noticed.'

'I take it that, too, was intended as an insult? You notice our opinions because we have to speak them out. All the neo-liberal and capitalist propaganda is taken as a given, you see. It's not counted as an opinion if you talk about the importance of GDP growth and the bond markets. No, I object merely to the "neo" in "neo-Fascist". I advocate a return to the original ideology, to the idea that one stick is weak but a bundle of sticks bound together is strong. Finally, after many false starts and a period of hope in the 1970s, the time has come again. State corporatism, taxing the rich, strong governance and public spending, exit from the European Union, the jailing of Silvio Berlusconi and his lackeys. Don't tell me there are not some ideas in there you dislike?'

'I am here to talk about Stefania Manfellotto, and the recent murder of a young woman.'

'Ah, poor Stefania. Yes, we can talk about her. But you know I have an alibi?'

'Yes,' said Blume, adding 'unfortunately' in his own mind.

'Also, when the young girl was killed, I was in Lucca. Lucky for me, I suppose.'

'You were heard to fight with Stefania minutes before she left here and was shot.'

'I fought with her the week before, and she was not shot. And the week before that, and she was not shot then either. It was a dispute, not a fight.'

'Students heard voices raised.'

'Not so much that they could make out the words, though. You see, without words to report they may as well say they heard us moving furniture. Words are everything, as I know you know. When the Romans had destroyed the Second Temple in Jerusalem, Yochanan ben Zakkai fled to a place called Yavneh where he set up the first academy for the study of the Torah. Ever since then, Jews have been a people of the book, a literate and academic race. *Bildung* is everything. Your parents are intellectuals, am I right?'

Seeing he was getting no answer, he continued. 'Commissioner, you'll soon need to choose sides. The collapse is happening now. Late-phase capitalism turned out to be a perverted socialism, with the state paying bankers instead of workers. Your pay, let's talk about that. In a short time, you won't be earning enough to eat, but the pigs and the technocrats, the Germans, the IMF, the bankers, and the thieving politicians who never defended the interests of this country will expect you to be there, gun in hand, to defend them against righteous rage.'

'Let's get back to talking about your meeting with Stefania Manfellotto.'

'Why, what new skill do you bring to the questions that was not available to your Carabinieri peers? Read the reports they made. They contain precise accounts of my meeting with Stefania,' said Pitagora. 'I have deliberately crystallized my memory of the events. If I tell you, there will not be a single comma's difference between the statement I made to the Carabinieri and the one I will make to you. Also, you have no authority in this investigation.'

'So you checked my credentials before this meeting,' said Blume.

'Yes. My original plan was to throw you out of the office, but you brought in an aura with you that I simply have to understand and oppose. For your sake, too. I can make you feel better about yourself. Look at us here. Which of us is the happier man?'

'Ah, but which one of us is sane?' said Blume.

The professor got up from his desk and went to the large bookcase behind him and stared up at the long row of books as if they might speak to him. He walked around his desk. 'I think I may give you my book.'

'Thanks, but . . .'

Pitagora cut across him. 'I do not keep copies of it here, of course. It is too valuable.'

'All your copies are first editions?' enquired Blume.

'I understand what you are insinuating. My book was not written to sell in bulk. I have come up with an entire memory technique for policemen, did you know that?'

Blume indicated that he hadn't known. His manner suggested that he did not care very much either, but Pitagora was not deterred. 'You know the University for Forensic Investigators in L'Aquila? I was organizing a three-year course for the police there. It was all ready to go, when the earthquake struck. That was a setback, which has delayed the project by several years. But they tell me we can try again next September. I teach techniques for perfect recall, and I am prepared to put my knowledge at the disposal of law enforcers. In the meantime, in addition to my courses in literature, I give an interdisciplinary course in memory techniques. Hundreds of students from all faculties attend my seminars.'

'You were going to teach all your memory techniques to cops?'

'Technique is only technique. Memory is just the beginning of the ultimate knowledge.'

'I'll try to remember that,' said Blume.

Pitagora took a sheet of paper from the neat stack beside him and pulled a black fountain pen out of his pocket. He lifted a golden pince-nez from his desk, placed it on his nose, and started writing something, then handed it to Blume. 'Here, read this.'

Written in a thin spidery script was the following: *Zezza, Aaron Fisher, tin, string, Tiberius, Caligula, Claudius, Nero, Otho, wire, Vespasian, Titus.*

Blume glanced at the list. 'I would prefer not to get sidetracked, Professor. Can we get back to the matter in hand?'

'Have you read all the names on that list?'

'Yes.'

Pitagora took the sheet of paper back, ripped it into four pieces, and then walked over to an ebony box from which pieces of paper were already protruding, and dropped them in. Blume saw he limped slightly as he walked. He had an unexpected bald patch behind, around which his dead straight silver hair formed a sort of curtain. The effect was monkish.

'Do you recognize them all?' asked Pitagora, returning to his oversized chair.

'The first is the name of the Carabinieri captain in charge of the case, which I take as a reminder that I am not, which is fine. Then some random words and a few Roman emperors up to your favourite Titus, destroyer of Jerusalem. And there was another name. I have forgotten it already.'

'I am glad you have not heard of the second person in the list. He is a filthy plagiarist. A vulgar American who has stolen my ideas and is hawking them as his own. He has written a series of bestselling books using my memory techniques. I have sued him and his publishers in a Los Angeles court for plagiarism.'

'I'll ask you all about that another time,' said Blume, 'as soon as it becomes in the slightest bit relevant to anything at all. Meanwhile, how do you know Stefania Manfellotto?'

'We met here, in this very university, back in 1977. We shared a lot of beliefs. We were also sexual partners. I believe a man should have as many sexual partners as possible. Even this became a controversial position thanks to the AIDS conspiracy of the 1980s.'

'There are rumours about your relationships with students.'

'Some of them are grounded in fact, what of it?'

Blume shrugged. 'Oh, I don't care. They are all over the age of consent in here. Did you agree with Manfellotto's terrorist activities?'

'Who would ever respond yes to a question such as that?'

'You,' said Blume. 'You strike me as just the sort of person who might, Professor.'

Pitagora parted the curtain of his hair to find and fondle his ear. 'Thank you, Commissioner Alec Blume.'

'Let's get back to the evening you met her,' said Blume.

Pitagora was right about one thing: his version of events showed absolutely no change from what was in the Carabinieri report that Principe had shown him. Indeed, it was as if he had seen the report and learned it by heart. Manfellotto had been in his office between 5 and 5:45 in the evening. They had drunk some expensive peat-flavoured Scotch, reminisced about old times, and discussed the current political situation. The door to the office had been closed, and twice some student or other had knocked tentatively to see if he was there. He had not answered. At one point, around half past five, she had excused herself to go to the toilet down the corridor. He had opened the door for her, and waited on the threshold. Several students and staff had seen him there, and he could provide the names of some of them. Two students were outside his office, and he agreed to see them afterwards. When she came back, they talked some more, and then had that argument that everyone seemed to have heard.

'What was it about?'

'I'd prefer not to say.'

'Politics or money?'

'Well, since you were so succinct, you deserve a succinct answer. Both. Then we arranged to meet at a restaurant on Via Della Scrofa.' Pitagora wetted his finger with the tip of his tongue and consulted a black leather-bound desk diary. 'Look.'

He turned the diary around on the desk, and Blume saw the same spidery script with 'Ristorante Istria' written next to the line reading 8 p.m. It was the only entry on the page.

'Turn back a page, Professor, please,' said Blume. Pitagora obliged. There were no entries on either side of the diary. 'And another,' said Blume, motioning with his finger. The pages again were blank. 'You don't seem to have many appointments. Just the one that was supposed to be on that evening.'

'Stefania made me write it down. I use my memory techniques, but she likes to see things in writing.'

'All right. Stefania left here at 5:45. Then what?'

'I went to give a seminar in front of 50 or so students . . .'

'You went directly from here to the classroom?'

'Yes.'

'So you were on time for the seminar?'

Pitagora undid one silver cufflink and then the other, like a magician preparing for a show. He pulled up his sleeves.

'I have no watch, Commissioner. I may have been early, I may have been late. The fact is, my students are enthusiastic and come early, so they were waiting for me. I have not worn a watch for years, for the same reason you have not.'

Blume touched his wrist self-consciously.

'On some people, a timepiece cannot keep time. If it is mechanical, it loses or gains, if it is digital, it malfunctions from electromagnetic interference from the wearer. I am one of those people, Commissioner, and so are you.'

'Basically, you're saying you were late,' said Blume.

Pitagora redid his cufflinks with care. 'While I was there a student came in to say someone had been shot.'

'Who was this student?'

'I don't know. A friend of one of my students. I had never seen him before.'

'He came in and shouted it out, or . . .'

'More or less. "They are shooting people" he called out, or words to that effect. Then they all ran out. I have given the names of the students to the Carabinieri, and I believe they have been questioned. This means I am somehow a suspect, which is fantastical nonsense. And now, if you don't mind and even if you do, I have to ask you to leave.'

'Why?'

'I have students waiting for me.'

'Where?'

'Behind the door.'

Blume went over and opened the door. Sure enough, a group of about twelve students were standing about in the corridor.

He surveyed them, then said, 'One minute', and closed the door.

'Who are they?'

'Some of my best students. They are here for a lesson on Tasso. You know the epic poem *Jerusalem Delivered*?'

Blume ignored the question.

'The story of the Catholic knights who freed the erstwhile Jewish capital from the infidel Muslims? I know you know what I am talking about. I am transferring that poem to their memory. They must learn it by heart.'

'Literature students, then?'

'No. There is one, but the rest of them come from other faculties. But they understand that all knowledge is connected. The more you learn about anything, the more you know about everything.'

'Can I borrow one?'

Instead of asking why, Pitagora nodded and said, 'Take Miriam. She's the blonde one you noticed, almost to the exclusion of the others.'

'Who says . . .'

'You know who I mean?'

'There was a blonde girl there, yes, but . . .'

'Ask her her name. Go on.'

'I am not playing your games.'

'Blondes stick in the mind better. That's why women who want to be remembered should go for the blonde look no matter how poorly it suits them. It is also why so many saints and angels are fair-haired. What about that list from earlier, the one I wrote down. Do you remember it?'

Blume ignored the question. He opened the door and called to the students, who filed in sheepishly, as if they had done something wrong.

'Miriam,' said the professor. 'This is a police commissioner. He was looking particularly at you.'

The girl blushed, and arched her foot.

Blume opened his mouth to protest, then thought better of it.

'He says he wants to "borrow" you. Do let us know what he does with you, will you?'

'That is, if you don't mind,' said Blume.

The girl shook her head.

'Commissioner! I know you're going to want to talk to me again. Come to my home. I live on the Via Appia Antica, but you'll know that. I want to show you my memory theatre. It will expand your mind.'

Blume turned to the girl, whose scarlet blush was just fading.

'Just a quick favour,' said Blume, and ushered her out the door.

As he left the office, he let out a long sigh and shook his head and limbs as if coming out of the sea from a long swim.

'He's intense because he's a genius,' said the girl.

'Do you study literature?'

'No. Final year medicine. Where are we going?'

'I sorry, I didn't explain.' He had the girl give him her telephone number and they separated at the end of the corridor, him going up the stairs and her down. He climbed two more flights to the top floor, then walked down the empty corridor. The rooms he passed were stuffed full of smashed desks, and piles of books.

At the end of the corridor, he turned left, and entered a small corner room. The roof sloped down and he had to duck under a cross-beam piled high with dust so fine it billowed like icing sugar at his passing. He grabbed a broken brush handle from the floor. He made his way over to the window, familiar from the Carabinieri photos he had examined in Principe's office. It was small, circular, and iron-rimmed like a barrel. An iron bar ran along the middle dividing the window into two half-moon lights. The lower pane was intact and the upper one was missing, and he could imagine bats flying in and out. It was less dusty here because of the air coming in, or perhaps because the Carabinieri had swept it clean. It commanded an ample view of the concourse below. He took out his phone and called Miriam.

'Ready? OK, start walking now. Keep the phone to your ear.'

He stuck the broom handle out of the gap, and looked down it. Thirty seconds later Miriam's blonde hair appeared below. He took aim at the top of her head. Then he ordered her to stop. The figure below stopped.

'OK, I just needed to check that was you. Can you go back to the door and start walking again, this time all the way to where the paths meet in the centre of the yard?'

Twenty seconds this time. She was walking faster, impatient with his game. No problem. He kept the broom handle pointed at her beautiful head and fired imaginary bullet after imaginary bullet into it. When she reached the centre of the courtyard, he told her to keep walking. Ten seconds later, she was hidden by the protruding wing of the admin building.

He picked up his phone and thanked her, wishing her luck in her exams, and then he walked all the way down the stairs, and into the courtyard, counting one elephant two elephant three elephant as he did so, and ignoring the looks he was getting.

Well, he thought, as he exited the university campus, that doesn't really make sense.

11

GOD, THIS girl Olivia was bouncy. Her breasts bounced, her auburn hair bounced, her shoulders bounced as she shrugged off his questions with careless declarations of forgetfulness and a shake of the bangles on her wrists. Even her voice bounced up and down as she explored the dramatic potential of doing public double-takes, repeating what Blume said in incredulous tones to make sure he got the point that his questions were either cretinous or hard for her to fathom. She liked to make the most of her large brown eyes by opening them wide in exaggeration of surprise, or rolling them in melodramatic disbelief at the obtuseness of his questions. But he had a strong suspicion it was all a show for him, in which case she had misread what he liked. Her mood followed the general principle of bounciness, leaping from petulant bad temper to sudden flashes of sorrow for her lost cousin, then back to enthusiasm as she spoke about her boyfriend Marco and her plans for that evening.

They were standing on the road, just a few metres from where Sofia had been shot. The crime scene tape was still there, torn and fluttering. There were just four bouquets at the spot. Someone had washed down the wall to get rid of the bloodstain, and had inadvertently created the outline of a person standing against the wall, a bright shade.

In the hope of evoking a mood of reflection or sadness, Blume moved slightly to one side, so that the spot where Sofia had died was visible to Olivia, but the girl seemed not to see it.

'So the other night, you told Sofia to be here so that you could pick her up in your car?'

'I don't see why you couldn't have come into the magistrate's office with me this afternoon,' Olivia complained. 'You are asking me EXACTLY the same questions, and I am giving EXACTLY the same answers.'

'I had things to do on the campus. Besides, it's different here where it happened.'

'Yeah, it's colder,' she gave a cute little shiver that ran down from her shoulders to her backside. 'Can we maybe sit in a car or something?'

'This will only take a minute. We are standing more or less where you said you would meet her.'

'Yes. That is to say where I would be. She waited over there.'

'And you here.'

'It's practically the same point. What's the difference?'

'Why not exactly at the same point?'

Olivia shook her head in disbelief at having to explain it. 'Here, where we are is beside the road, right? So if I am picking her up outside the university, this is the place where I stop. I can't get any closer in the car. She liked to stay over there waiting.'

'Why?'

'Because it's out of the wind, it's sheltered, and she's got a wall to lean on while she waits.'

'Are you not always punctual?'

'With Roman traffic! And I'm the one doing the favour of picking her up.'

'How often did you meet here?'

'Lots of times. Twenty, thirty? Like I was her chauffeur.'

'And she always waited by that wall?'

'Yes.'

'I see. And who else knew about the appointment?'

'Anyone that she told.'

'Do you know her friends?'

'She didn't have any. At school, I used to lend her my friends, even though we were younger than her. Pathetic, huh? Can we go now? I'm cold.'

'Do you think when we listen to the recording of the call between you and her we'll hear her say she'll be at the wall?'

Olivia's eyes widened. 'You can do that?'

'Oh yes,' said Blume gravely.

'Well then, you'll hear her say "usual place" and then "thank you".'

'Are you sure?' he asked. 'You realize this is very important?'

'I *think* those were her words,' said Olivia. 'Why is it so important? I mean, obviously it's a murder and all, so everything is, like, really important, but why is where we decided to meet so important?'

'Because this is where she was killed,' said Blume.

'This is going to come across as bit heartless, and that's not at all how I mean it, but so what?'

'She was shot with a high-velocity bullet, probably from a rifle. The killer had to be waiting for her, so he had to choose his vantage point and had to know she would be here.'

'We just said the usual place. Except this time . . .' Her eyes welled up with tears, which she allowed to splash freely down her cheeks, smudging her mascara.

'I am sorry I had to bring you here,' said Blume mechanically. Tears irritated him no end. Was Olivia misjudging him again?

Olivia sniffed, and brought her face closer to his. The tears had gone already. 'Is my face a mess?'

'Your face is fine,' said Blume. 'You were very kind to give her lifts.'

'We were more like sisters than cousins. She was like a big sister.'

Blume accompanied her back to her car, parked fifty metres away. He patted the roof of the car, on which was painted a Union Jack. Two more Union Jacks were painted on the leading edges of its aerodynamic wing mirrors.

'Are you an Anglophile?'

'I don't understand.'

'These British flags all over your car.'

She laughed at him. 'They were there when I bought it. They were part of a set of optional extras, I suppose. I have a bag with that flag on it, too.' She paused, 'And a T-shirt and a pencil case and an iPhone cover. I just like the colours. And the shape's pretty cool. Better than the Italian flag, wouldn't you say? I mean the Italian flag on your car would just look silly.'

'And attract vandals if you drove it up north,' said Blume.

'But the British flag looks good. Besides, everyone loves Britain and all things British. Can I go now please, Inspector?'

'Commissioner. I am a commissioner.'

'Is that higher or lower?'

'Infinitely higher. You bought the car?'

'Sure.'

'You personally?'

'Well, my dad.'

'What does dad do?'

'Not much. Hangs out with friends, works in a hospital sometimes.' She shrugged.

'One more question. Sofia worked in the Health Institute on Viale Margherita. Why was this the usual meeting point for you?'

'Because this is where I study. This is my campus.'

'Yes, but isn't it a bit out of her way?'

Olivia shook her head, then recomposed her hair. 'I don't understand.'

'You're saying Sofia would come all the way over here to get a lift from you?'

'Because I am the one with the car. Besides, from where she worked, she could just cut through the campus.' She pointed a manicured finger at the entrance to the university.

'How long was the walk?'

This was the sort of question that provided an opportunity for Olivia to widen her pupils in surprise. '*I* don't know, Inspector. And I'm freezing.'

'Get into your car, roll down the window.' When she had done so, he leaned in. 'You often gave Sofia a lift because you both live in the same district, right?'

'We are almost neighbours. Our mothers are sisters, and they wanted to stay close after their mother died.' Olivia clapped her hand to her mouth. 'Ooh! Sorry! I called you Inspector again.'

'That's OK. What district is it?'

'We live in Trullo, unfortunately.'

'Why unfortunately?' asked Blume.

'Well, Commissioner, it's not exactly the nicest part of the city, is it?'

'I see. Thank you, Olivia. I'll let you go home now. But I want to talk to your boyfriend. Would that be all right?'

The question earned him an impatient toss of hair. 'You'll have to ask him, I suppose. What do you want to talk to him about?'

'It's how an investigation works. We talk to everyone the victim knew. Sofia knew Marco, didn't she?'

'Well, obviously, because there's me, isn't there?'

'Were you always around when they met?'

Olivia snapped her head round and looked straight at Blume whose face was just inches away.

'What a fucking stupid question,' she said, all the bubbles suddenly gone from her voice and movements.

Blume stood back from the car and did his best to look affronted. 'Sorry, but why is it such a dumb question?'

'Because if I am not around, by definition I wouldn't be there to see if they were meeting, would I?'

'Ah, I see. But they might have told you afterwards, or before.'

Olivia received this suggestion in silence, then she leaned back in the seat, fluffed her hair, and laughed. 'Sometimes I am so stupid! Everyone always said Sofia was the clever one. Of course, they could have met and then told me. I just didn't think of it.' She reached out her hand and gently touched him on the arm. 'I am sorry for my tone just now. I am very upset.'

'I understand,' said Blume. 'So maybe you'll ask your boyfriend to contact me, maybe drop by the Commissariato on Collegio Romano, phoning ahead to make sure I'm there?'

'Sure!'

'Great! Bye then.'

Olivia switched on the engine, revved it a little bit, turned, and gave him a lovely smile. He slapped the Union Jack on the roof of the car, and leaned down again.

'Did you ever drive around to Viale Margherita to wait for her outside her office?'

'No.' And with a final pitying shake of her head, she spun the steering wheel, and the mini nipped neatly out into the traffic flow.

12

BLUME SAT on a turquoise plastic bench that seemed to have been ripped out of the back of a bus from the 1970s. Until now, he had believed that the main problem with plastic was that it was non-biodegradable, but this seat was making him reconsider his science. Worn out by the shifting buttocks of people waiting for haircuts, it had fissured into millions of tiny scales like the surface of an old painting, and every time he moved, a tiny stream of blue plastic particles rose into the beam of sunlight coming through the window.

On the floor before him lay the curly grey locks of the customer before him, like the shavings of a sheep with scabies. Propped on the counter in front of the mirror and overhanging the washbasin was a small television set. On the other side was a portable DVD player. The cable linking them dipped into the washbasin. The DVD player was double wired with an electric shaver, and the TV was plugged into a socket behind Blume, who had been warned by the barber as he came in not to trip over it.

The barber and his customer, whose face Blume could not see from where he was sitting, were enjoying a film with Alberto Sordi, who was playing a marquis in a comic-historical romp. The barber would often pause his haircutting and point with his sharp scissors at the screen, to recommend an upcoming scene, whose screenplay both he and the customer seemed to have committed to memory. Then they would wait until the scene had played itself out, and the barber would prudently put down his scissors, so that he could safely wipe away his tears of laughter with the back of his hand. Then he would pick up the scissors again, sigh, and snip a few more hairs from the top of the customer's head, before pointing again at the screen in delighted anticipation of what was coming next. He seemed to manage about three grey curls per hour.

Fortunately, Blume had arrived when they were already far into the film. As the credits rolled up, the barber whipped out a folding razor and, with unexpected speed and dexterity, cleaned up the bristles along the customer's hairline.

Finally, he took the once-white apron off the customer, and with the theatricality of an onstage magician making a girl disappear, swiped it up and down in the air with a happy thwack. Millions of tiny black hairs and skin-toned particles joined the asbestos-like dust from the bench in the sunbeam. Blume thought fondly of the gas mask he used to have hanging on his belt while policing football stadiums as a young cop.

From a bent shelf made of slowly exploding plywood, the barber retrieved a bedside candlestick containing the stub of a candle surrounded by Gothic lacings of hardened wax.

'Candle treatment?'

'I need it?'

'Afraid so.'

'OK, not too much, you've got a customer there. Don't keep him waiting.'

The barber pulled out a soft pack of MS cigarettes from his pocket, opened it, extracted a disposable lighter, and lit the candle. Then, crouching down a little, he gently pushed the customer's head to one side and waved the flame about his right ear, and then proceeded to do the same with the other ear. A smell of burning hair filled the small space.

'Ow,' said the customer mildly.

'A few caught fire there. They won't be bothering you for a while.'

The customer, who turned out to be a large and angular man with the face of a mistreated horse, rubbed his ears as he stood up. He gave Blume a nod. 'Pity you can't get rid of nostril hairs in the same way,' he said with the cheerful complicity of a man spotting a peer. 'Tweezers. Don't talk to me about tweezers.'

The man paid €10 and left. The barber fetched a broom, swept the hair into a pile against the skirting board, and propped the broom against the wall. Then, with the solicitude of a maître d', invited Blume to take a seat.

Blume settled down into the damp warmth of the previous customer. The barber went over to the right-hand side of the sink, lifted out the video cable, rinsed the scissors, then dropped it back in. He popped out the DVD, a homemade affair with the title written in felt pen, blew on it carefully, and then wiped it against his apron, covering the disc in a million tiny hairs.

'Hold on a second.'

He disappeared around a skirting-board partition at the back of the shop, and Blume heard a door scrape close. After a minute or so a toilet flushed, the door scraped open again and the barber was back, DVD in hand.

'You look more like a man who enjoys Eduardo De Filippo. Am I right?'

Blume's knowledge was limited to snatches of old films glimpsed on Sunday afternoons. But he agreed that De Filippo was to his taste.

'What's your favourite film of his? One with his brother Peppino?'

Blume racked his brains for a title.

'Do you prefer the stuff from the forties or the fifties?'

'Oh, the fifties, definitely,' said Blume. A title popped into his head. '*Napoli milionaria.*'

The barber gave a knowing smile and nodded his head slowly, then displayed the disc he held in his hand. Inscribed in thick black felt pen was the very same title.

'That's uncanny,' said Blume.

'I am a good judge of character,' said the barber, inserting the disc and fast-forwarding through the opening credits.

'Short back and sides,' said Blume.

'Same style as you have now?'

'Style?'

'A wave cut down the back, flat edge above the ears instead of tapering,' said the barber.

'Right. Same style, then,' said Blume.

A few minutes in, it became apparent that the barber was waiting to see if Blume was one who appreciated the film as serious art or lowbrow comedy. Neither was the answer. The thing depressed the hell out of him. Seeing that his customer needed guidance, the barber would occasionally pause in his clipping, point at the screen, and allow an entire exchange to pass between Gennaro and his wife Amalia, then wait to see if Blume had enjoyed it.

'I suppose I'm in a grim mood,' said Blume after failing to laugh for the sixth time.

'I could turn it off,' said the barber in a tone of terrible self-sacrifice.

'No, no. It's me. My job. It gets me down.'

'What do you do?'

'I'm a policeman. But that's not the problem. It's the things we have to do.'

'I can imagine,' said the barber and snipped the air for emphasis. 'Just the other day . . .'

Blume interrupted him. 'You say you can imagine, but you're probably thinking it's hard to put up with the violence and senseless cruelty of criminals, the terrible acts of violence.'

'Ah, so you're *squadra mobile*. I was just saying, the other day . . .'

'Well, you're wrong,' said Blume.

'I didn't say anything,' said the barber, hurt.

'About criminals. You expect them to behave like that. You become immune to cruelty, you get used to violence, you regret seeing good people make terrible mistakes and throw their lives away. That's part of the job, the good part is when you can contribute a little to righting a wrong, or saving a person. But you know what the worst thing is?'

'Dead children, I imagine,' said the barber, clipping away at the back of Blume's head.

'Yeah, well, after dead children.'

The barber went to the DVD machine and stopped the film. 'I don't think light comedy is appropriate if we're talking about dead children.'

'But we're not. I was talking about something else. I was trying to say that what really gets you down is when the people who have been appointed to do justice do great injustice. What is a man supposed to do when he has to follow the instructions of a cruel magistrate? A bully?'

The barber listened in silence as Blume told him all about Adelgardo Lambertini, his imprisoned daughter, the mother of an infant son. The barber pushed up the short hairs at the back of his neck and quietly and methodically clipped away as Blume told him about Valerio and his drug-pushing, his Nazi beliefs, his history of violence, cowardice, and petty crime. When Blume had exhausted the full list of Valerio's crimes, some of which he invented since, from experience, he knew they were the sort of things people like Valerio did all the time, the barber, silent now, took out an electric razor. Blume stopped talking as the razor buzzed around his ears, around the back of his head. Then it stopped, and out came the folding razor. Blume was relieved to see the barber change the blade.

Five minutes passed in silence, then off came the apron and the barber said, 'Shampoo and rinse?'

Blume looked at the television balanced on the left edge of the basin, the DVD player on the other.

'Only €5 extra. Makes 15 in all.'

'In this basin?'

'Sure. I'll move the DVD player, first. Water would damage it.'

'And the TV, maybe?'

'I never splash in that direction.' He lifted down the DVD player, set it on the floor, and said, 'OK, head forward.'

He kneaded his fingers and knuckles hard into Blume's skull, then dried his head off with very vigorous and unpleasant towelling. He turned the hairdryer to full heat and blasted it into Blume's ears and heated his hair till he thought it might combust. He then swiped Blume's face with a soft brush caked in talcum powder, hit the release button on the chair, and as Blume sank down towards the floor, spun the chair around and said, 'That'll be €15.'

Blume gave him 20 and told him to keep the change.

'That's OK. It's my own shop. I don't need tips. Let me write you a tax receipt.'

'A tax receipt?'

'It's the law,' he tore off a receipt and thrust it at Blume. 'What about that policewoman, I spoke to? She was lovely. What am I supposed to tell her if she visits again?'

'Caterina,' said Blume.

'You know her?'

'I'm married to her.'

The barber stood back and looked at Blume as if seeing him for the first time. 'You. Married to her? You don't have a ring.'

'Modern marriage,' said Blume.

'Is this a joke?'

'No. Look, I haven't married her yet. But that's the plan. I do live with her, though. That's the truth.'

'She doesn't know you came here to see me?'

'No.'

'You want me to deny what I saw?'

'I did not say that.'

'You implied it,' said the barber. 'I'd hate to see her get in trouble.'

'I'm her boss. She can't get in trouble with me, and if any trouble comes down from higher than me, I'll be standing there to intercept it. For her, it's an administrative hassle. For that old man and his family, it's their entire lives.'

'And you sure about the woman inspector not getting into real trouble?'

'Absolutely.'

'Well, I'll think about it. Maybe what I saw that old man do wasn't as deliberate as it seemed.'

'You do whatever you see fit to do,' said Blume. 'I don't want you to do anything that goes against your conscience.'

'You already have,' said the barber.

13

Principe, dressed like the Italian idea of an English gentleman, raised his glass of gin and tonic and clinked it against Blume's coffee cup. 'You made a good impression, dear boy. Pitagora likes you. He sees in you a kindred spirit. He phoned me to tell me this.'

'I find that strange,' said Blume.

'That someone should like you? He invited you to his house, I hear. I hope you accepted.'

'Yes, I did. But only for you.'

'See, you are likeable.' Principe gulped down half his drink, set it on the table, swirled a few shards of ice with his little finger, then gulped down the rest. 'Did you get your hair cut?'

'Yes.'

'It makes you look older. The grey comes through.'

'Can I get you anything?' he asked Blume, signalling to the waiter.

They were sitting huddled against the cold in Piazza San Lorenzo in Lucina. Principe asked the waiter for another gin and tonic and for the outdoor heater to be moved closer to him and turned up. Blume suggested going indoors, but Principe shook his head.

'There is more life out here.'

A group of children in expensive fancy dress tumbled by. A small girl dressed as a pirate decided to take a short cut through the outdoor tables, and immediately got lost in the forest of human and chair legs. A young woman elegantly wove her way in and out of the tables without disturbing the patrons, swept the lost pirate up in her arms, and carried her back to the open piazza to run after her friends, who were milling about the steps in front of the church of San Lorenzo.

'Why are they dressed up like that?' said Principe. 'It's autumn, even if it feels like winter. Carnival is still three months away.'

'Halloween,' said Blume. 'It was a few days ago, but once you have the

72

costume, you may as well use it. There is a kid on the second floor of my building who goes round dressed as Batman from October to March. His sister is often a bee.'

'Another American import. No one paid any attention to Halloween a few years ago.'

'Time passes, times change. Here's your drink.'

Although he was wearing a heavy green woollen coat, red scarf, and a trilby, Principe shivered so much that his hand shook as he took his drink. He drank this one, too, in rapid gulps, then smacked his lips and hugged himself.

'Why don't we go in since it's so cold?' said Blume again.

'It's not so cold. You're sitting there in a jacket and open shirt, Alec.'

'I have a T-shirt beneath the shirt and the jacket is heavy. It's cold enough.'

'You are being polite. Back to the case. Pitagora has clout. I'm sure you picked that up. He knows where the bodies are. Maybe literally.'

'I hear that so often in this country,' said Blume. 'And yet no one ever finds the bodies. I am beginning to think no one knows anything.'

'Code of silence.'

'Except Pitagora never shuts up.'

'You noticed that, too?'

'He sits there and spouts forth an endless stream of bullshit,' said Blume.

'I sort of admire him,' said Principe. 'At least he believes what he says.'

'Unlike us, you mean?'

'Yes.'

Blume was going to argue the point, but Principe looked too haggard and vulnerable in his oversized coat, and by the time he had stayed his tongue, he was beginning to think maybe the magistrate was right.

Principe sipped at his drink, grimacing as if it were filled with bile. 'There is the sexual angle,' he said.

'I was wondering about that,' said Blume. 'What's the story there?'

'For years there have been hushed up scandals and rumours about him exploiting his students,' said Principe. 'Good marks for favours. Not only that, good marks, possible research posts, and influence over other members of staff, which means the good marks continue to arrive.'

'That's not much, though, is it? He's hardly the only professor who does that. Regular sex?'

Principe shrugged. 'These days who can say?'

'Just answer me, Filippo.'

'Yes. Taking into account rumour-mongering, envy, exaggeration. His house is swarming with young students. He teaches there.'

'You mean "teach" as in "fuck?" '

'I think he actually teaches, too.'

'Was Sofia one of his students?'

'No,' said Principe. 'She was a bit vague about the professor. I couldn't pin down what she wanted to hide. She seemed to know about his memory methods. Apparently her boss was a student of his. But she was not forthcoming on the point.' His voice turned throaty and he coughed at length. When he had recovered his composure, he waved his hand in feeble apology. 'I always hated old people who coughed like this and now here I am.'

'It was annoying,' agreed Blume, 'but you've stopped now.' He waited until he was sure the fit was over. 'I went up to the storage space from which the shot that hit Stefania Manfellotto was fired, and I did a little reconstruction using a student. She started walking from the building when I told her and . . .'

'How did you tell her if you were upstairs?'

Blume pointed at his mobile phone sitting on the table between them. The blush that covered Principe's face made him seem momentarily healthier.

'So, I ordered her to walk. After about 30 seconds, she came into sight from the window. At around 40 seconds, she cleared the shadow of the building, and that was by far the best moment for the shooter to pull the trigger. Every step she took thereafter simply increased the range. Worse, the point at which she was shot was at the very limit of the range. A few more steps and she was protected by the admin building. So why did the shooter wait till the shot was as difficult as possible? It would make sense if Manfellotto had been coming in the opposite direction, towards the window. Then we could say the shooter fired at the earliest opportunity.'

'I don't have an answer for that,' said Principe, still as embarrassed but whitening again.

'That makes me wonder,' said Blume. 'You have the diagrams, the reports, the ballistics, so why did it not occur to you?'

Principe took off his glasses and breathed on them, then tried to polish them on his woollen coat, with poor results. He placed the glasses on the table and peered with his watery eyes in Blume's direction.

'A little kindness, Alec. I am fallible, and I haven't been feeling great.'

'That's fine. You're fallible. I might not have thought about it either, but the Carabinieri? I know they will have reached the same conclusions, and I know they have a file on it. So, what worries me is this: either they did not point out an essential element of the investigation to you, in which case they are deliberately withholding evidence from you; or they did, in which case you are withholding evidence from me. Which is it?'

'There is a third possibility, Alec. Maybe they showed me, and I forgot. I am not withholding evidence from you. Why would I do that?'

'You forgot? I need to talk to the lead investigator of the Carabinieri. I am sure he won't appreciate my butting in. But it can't be helped.'

'Captain Giovanni Zezza,' said Principe. 'I have already asked him to meet you.'

'There's something else,' said Blume. 'Where there is more than one victim, you seek the point of convergence in their lives and concentrate there.'

'There is nothing in common between Manfellotto and Sofia. The girl must have seen something by accident.'

'What could she have seen? When the sniper dropped Manfellotto, they were in an open space. Even if she saw where the shot came from, and you tell me she didn't, she can't have identified anyone. No, the connection has to be the professor.'

'She wasn't a student of the professor's. She wasn't even a student.'

'What about the people in Pitagora's class. Did she know any of them?'

'She was just cutting through on her way to meet her cousin for a lift back home.'

'You didn't answer my question. Is that because you forgot to ask? Did she know who Pitagora was?'

'Everyone knows who Pitagora is,' said Principe.

'Yes, but did *she*?'

'Yes. I told you that. I asked her, of course I did.'

'Thank you,' said Blume. 'I just need to be clear. Unlike you. What about her place of work? Have you checked that out?'

'That's just standard procedure. Yes. Or no . . . I told her boss to present himself for questioning. I think I'm seeing him . . . I forget. I'll look into it. For the sake of procedural protocol. But like I said, there are interviews scheduled and the Carabinieri have asked a few questions.'

'So you have no objections if I go?'

'You have your own bastard way of doing things, and I'm not going to change that now.' Principe was slurring his words noticeably now. 'What's your lead?'

'No lead. I just want to learn something about Sofia. So far the focus has all been on who killed her. It's good to get an idea of the sort of background she came from. Including the workplace. As you said, it's standard procedure.'

He watched as the magistrate put away another drink. He had had one in front of him when Blume arrived. No wonder he was forgetting stuff.

'Stop giving me those disapproving looks, Alec.'

'Maybe it's envy.'

'Then have one.'

Blume shook his head.

'Too bad,' said Principe, with a hint of aggression in his voice. 'Pitagora and Manfellotto are on opposite sides of a power struggle going on within the parties of the extreme right. Both of them are figureheads more than anything, but their opinions count. Manfellotto, believe it or not, was playing the role of the moderate. She was in favour of an alliance with Berlusconi or whatever creature comes after him. Pitagora, on the other, hand, is following the line of Forza Nuova: no abortion, reinstatement of the Lateran pacts giving the Catholic Church complete control over education, public morals, and so on, expulsion of all non-Italians and a few other points I can't be bothered remembering. Basically, she is anti-Catholic but pro-establishment, he is pro-Catholic and anti-establishment, if those things can go together.'

'All this fighting over 2 per cent of the vote.'

'They'll soon get a hell of a lot more, mark my words. Pitagora is also a leading light in Our Own Nation, if you have heard of them. Anyhow, their big platform is that the banks and high finance are running and ruining the world. And since that is indisputably true, I think they are going to start picking up a lot of support, and I'm not the only one who thinks this. A lot of powerful people are taking long positions on the rise of these parties, and Pitagora is a natural interlocutor. This is one of the reasons he is hard to touch – Excuse me,' Principe stopped the waiter and ordered yet another gin and tonic for himself and, without asking, a cappuccino for Blume.

'They're not still killing each other, though, are they? Last time I looked, internecine strife on the far right consisted of Alessandra Mussolini doing her angry fishwife act on television.'

'It might be starting again. As I say, the far right is on its way to power.'

'We have had 20 years of the Northern League, so what's the difference?' said Blume.

Principe propped his elbow on the table and fumbled around a bit with his glasses before getting them back on his face. 'The Northern League is a spent force. Italians need something just as nasty, maybe a little less comical than fat men with green handkerchiefs, to take its place. But you're right. It's all happened already and will happen all over again. I'm just explaining why people take Pitagora seriously.'

'No one so much as Pitagora himself. You can't be Fascist and have a sense of humour,' said Blume.

'But to get from that to shooting his old girlfriend and *camerata* is a hell of a stretch,' said Principe. 'How would that work? They met, they argued. He took an old high-powered rifle . . . Ah-ha.' He took his glass from the waiter's proffered silver tray, and drank one-third of it before Blume had finished watching the sugar sink beneath the foam on his cappuccino.

As the waiter walked away, Principe said, 'Did you see the look he gave me? Like I had asked for a personal favour.'

'You asked for the bill, but he's been putting the receipts under the drinks as he brings them out. Maybe that was it, or maybe it's the fact that you've gone through half a bottle of gin in about half an hour and it's not midday yet. What's going on, Filippo? I don't remember you drinking like this.'

'It's the loss of my wife.'

'I'm sorry, but that was two years ago, and drinking won't help.'

'That's not what I meant. Now she's finally gone, I can drink as much as I like,' said Principe with a forced laugh that turned into a cough and then an attack of spluttering. The waiter came over and, without saying anything, placed a glass of water beside him. Principe downed it, and thanked the waiter.

Three minutes later, Principe stood up and said, 'I need an old-man piss', just too loud, drawing looks from the tables around. He swayed slightly as he made his way into the bar.

He was a long time coming back. The sun had already left the piazza, and Blume was beginning to feel cold and impatient. When Principe finally emerged, he announced that he had paid the bill. He threw a thin arm around Blume's shoulder and with his free hand, rolled his fist playfully against Blume's chest before releasing him. 'Loosen up, Alec. Have a drink now and again. Smile a bit more, learn to like people and appreciate all this,' he swept out an arm and turned in a full circle, staggering from left to right foot as he completed his twirl.

'Is this because you're upset about Sofia?'

'Is what about her?' said Principe, his words coming out with a flanging effect caused by the mucus in his throat.

'Your drinking, messing about like this.'

'Told you, my wife . . .' He grabbed at Blume's arm

'I'm not listening to this,' said Blume, pulling away so suddenly that Principe stumbled and might have fallen had he not caught him. 'Damn it, Filippo.'

Principe straightened his trilby. 'I think I may stop the drinking. It's not as much fun as I expected it to be. It just makes me so very tired.'

'And maybe less effective as a magistrate,' suggested Blume.

'That would be bad. I have to solve this case. It is my last one you know.'

'You're retiring?' Principe certainly looked like he was at retirement age, but Blume knew he had just turned 63. 'Is it ill health?'

'More than that, Alec,' said Principe. 'I'm dying.'

Blume stood back and looked at Principe from head to toe, and saw it was true.

'Dead man walking,' said Principe, then put a histrionic finger to his lips, drawing the attention of the tables around them. 'Shh. Don't mention it to anyone.'

'I won't. Sit down before you fall down.'

Principe sat down heavily. Allowing his head to loll backwards before he manoeuvred himself into a more assertive posture, he continued, 'I don't know why I told you. I haven't even told my daughter. And you made me sit down but stayed standing, which is just psychological bullying. I like you, Alec, but I would not choose you for a confessor.'

'You just did.'

Principe stared at him, eyes glassy from drink, then stood up again, rocking back and forth on his feet. 'Have you ever thought of becoming a grief counsellor, Alec?' He swayed dangerously, and Blume caught hold of him again.

'Come on, I'll get you home.'

'We can walk from here, it's quicker,' said Principe.

'I know. We'll walk. It'll do you good.'

'I'm afraid I might crash into all the people walking in the opposite direction.'

'I'll guide you.'

14

Blume knocked again on the double doors, but they were designed to be pushed through, not knocked on, and the sound he made was no more than an ineffectual rap. He raised his voice again and called out, 'Professor Ideo!'

A voice, raised but sounding distant, shouted something back that Blume failed to understand.

A woman in a white coat clacked quickly across the corridor behind him.

'Excuse me?' She ignored him. 'Excuse me!'

Reluctantly she turned round, pushing ringlets away from her forehead to clear her field of vision. She was young, but her face was severe and filled with snappish authority. She seemed very unimpressed by what she saw and allowed her hair to fall forward again. It was the white lab coat, Blume decided. Put an ordinary person in a white coat, or a police uniform, come to that, and watch them grow in contempt for the uninitiated.

He pointed to the double doors which had a circular wire-mesh window through which he could see another identical set of double doors three metres further on.

'I'm looking for Professor Ideo. Can you go in there and fetch him for me?' asked Blume.

'I hardly think so,' said the woman.

'Well, do you think *I* can?'

'Do as you wish.'

Blume turned back to the door, hesitant. A large yellow triangle announced 'BIOHAZARD!' and below that, in bright red letters, was written: 'Strictly no admittance for unauthorized personnel'. Below that was written: 'Suits MUST be worn at all times'; and finally: 'Keep this door closed'.

He turned round to ask for more advice, but the woman was gone.

Gingerly, he pushed his way through, and took a few steps to find himself standing before another set of identical doors with exactly the same message. It was like being in one of those dreams that pretended to be about frustrated progress, but kept you thinking about death for the rest of the day.

He knocked again. Nothing.

He thumped with his fist and called out. 'Professor Idco!'

One door opened with a small gust of air that carried with it the tang of antiseptic, followed by a more complex funk of something familiar yet alien that nagged at his memory. A small head with wispy hair poked out and looked around. The wide mouth, which sat like a gash below a small nose Blume immediately suspected of plastic surgery, emitted a laugh that sounded more like a bark.

'Don't just stand there knocking, come in.'

The reptile cage at the zoo. That was it.

Seeing Blume hesitate, the man, who was sporting an ill-advised stretch-fit black shirt that strained against its buttons, came out of the room and stood with Blume in the no-man's-land between the sets of double doors. He waved a short dismissive arm at the wall, flashing a glimpse of a fat Rolex and releasing a smell of onion peel. 'Oh, never mind those signs. They're just for civilians.'

'I am a civilian,' said Blume, taking a step back from the door, wondering what sort of deadly bacterial strains had just covered him.

Ideo frowned, then had a bright idea that split his round face into a smile. 'I know, let's go to my office! I'll get my lab coat first!'

He pushed the inner doors open, giving Blume a brief glimpse of dozens of cages, and seconds later re-emerged with his lab coat which he started putting on, even though he was now leaving the lab, and all the signs were he was too warm already.

'Lab mice, rats, and, above all, shrews. I am very interested in shrews. Care to look?'

'Another time?' suggested Blume.

They walked back into the main corridor.

'And you are?'

'Commissioner Blume.'

Ideo stuck out his hand but as Blume reached for it, he pulled it away and burst out laughing.

'Sorry! I really need to wash that hand before giving it to you.' He walked over to a stainless steel sink set into an alcove and rubbed an alcoholic gel all over his hands. He dried off with a paper towel, concentrating most of the wiping effort on his watch. He crumpled and threw the paper towel towards an overflowing bin, and missed by a mile.

'So, you want the tour? My office is down there . . . Oh, here!' He stuck out his hand to be shaken. He allowed Blume to touch the top half of his fingers, which were still damp, then slipped them out of his grasp. 'Is this about me not getting round to making my statement?'

Blume put his hands behind his back and rubbed his fingers clean against his trousers. 'No, what statement?'

'The magistrate invited me, or should I say, instructed me, to go to make a statement to the Carabinieri. About Sofia, of course,' he added.

'It's about her, yes,' said Blume. 'But this isn't about the statement.'

'I haven't had the time, you know?'

'I understand. Have you been interviewed at all?'

'By phone, yes. Magistrate Principe. A very courteous gentleman.'

'No one came to see you?'

'Not until now.' Ideo made a comb of his fingers and pushed some hair from behind his ears upwards and over the bald middle part of his head and patted it down gently.

A door to the left was flung open, and the movement of air undid his hair dressing in a single blow.

'Oh, sorry, Professor!' A youngish man backed into the room when he saw Ideo and Blume standing there. Inside were two women and two men, all of them between 30 and 40, peering at a large empty cage. Ideo put his hands on his hips and seemed to be counting.

'Where's Chatterjee?'

'Lunch,' said one of the lab assistants.

'What?' Ideo consulted his watch. 'OK. That's reasonable. Any luck?'

There was a collective shaking of heads. Ideo turned on his heel and waddled down the corridor, calling over his shoulder to Blume, 'That is where Sofia worked when she was not with me in the labs.' He dropped his voice to a stage whisper. 'She had twice the personality of any of them.'

They entered his office. 'Damn!'

'What?'

'No chairs. They took my chair again. I understand they need a chair and the state gives us no money, but it shows a lack of respect, don't you think? Just because I am in the lab all day. There's no chair for you, either. We'll have to stand.'

It was more a storeroom than an office. Blume found the spot where he was least likely to knock over lab equipment, books, or papers, and stood there. Where the piles of equipment and paper moved higher was the desk. On the wall was a calendar from 1982 and a poster showing Darwin's face circled and crossed in red, like a no-entry sign.

'That's just a bit of fun,' said Ideo. 'I am not anti-Darwin. I just think I have moved beyond him. Just like you can believe both in string theory and in Newtonian physics. Do you smoke?'

He pulled out a pack of Camels and shook it at Blume. 'Totally forbidden in a public building. Institute of Health, no less. But no one ever uses this room.' He pulled out a chrome lighter and lit up. 'Ah. That's good. I love a good smoke. They are not as bad for you as they say, you know.'

'No?'

'Not if you prime your mind first. Power of thought. You can put a little distance between yourself and the holon if you try.' He blew smoke at Blume. 'Do you know what a holon is?'

'No. I don't need to know that now.'

Ideo inserted the cigarette into the corner of his mouth, and made an unsuccessful attempt to insert his hands into the tight front pockets of his black jeans. They were small hands, but the jeans were tight, and he did not seem to be able to squeeze his thumbs in. He aimed a kick at a ball of grey dust with his short legs, and Blume saw the triple stripe design of Adidas runners.

'We are all going to miss her. She was a wonderful girl. She had a way with animals that was . . . exceptional.' His eyes took on a shrewd look as he squinted against the rising smoke. 'I don't know much about investigations, but is it normal to be questioned by one force and then another?'

'It happens,' said Blume.

Ideo pulled the cigarette out, touched it with his tongue, flicked ash at the wall, then put it back on the opposite side of his mouth. 'Don't you usually interview in twos, or is that just the films?'

'Films,' said Blume.

'The Carabinieri must watch more films than the police, then. There were two of them.'

'I thought you said they didn't interview you.'

'They didn't. They came here – two of them – to tell us the terrible news, asked a few questions of several people, told me the magistrate would be in touch, and went on their way.'

'Do I call you doctor or professor or just … ?'

'. . . Either is fine,' said Ideo.

Blume had mentally filed away Ideo's first name, which was Matteo. Matteo Ideo – why do parents do that to their kids? 'And what do you do here, *dottore*?'

'Do you know what an ethologist is?'

'I know what an etiologist is,' said Blume. 'Is it similar?'

Ideo waved his hands as if trying to stop Blume from uttering some terrible obscenity.

'No! That's like me saying I know what a travel agent is and asking if it is similar to a policeman!'

'Is it? I wouldn't be all that upset.'

'Or a travelling salesman.'

'Just tell me what you do.'

'My official title is Professor of Behavioural Neuroscience. I study animal behaviour.'

'That's what an etiologist does?' He couldn't help himself.

'An ETHOlogist. Not an ETIOLogist.'

'I beg your pardon. Can we use animal behaviourist?'

Ideo shook his head in disbelief and exasperation. 'No, because an ethologist does it in the wild, a behaviourist works in the lab.'

'But you work in the lab,' Blume pointed out.

'I do *now*. But I am an ethologist. I spent an entire year on the island of Lampedusa. You know, we think of Lampedusa as ours, but if you go there, you'll see it's really part of Africa.'

'All the illegal immigrants?'

'No! Are you being deliberately stupid? The flora and fauna.' He grabbed a sheet of paper covered with equations and dropped his cigarette butt into it. He crumpled it into a tight ball, which he dropped on the floor.

They watched the paper ball unfold itself a little, and then waited a little longer to see if it would burst into flames.

'It's so sad,' said Ideo. 'Poor Sofia. But, you know, in a way she lives on.'

Blume suspected a religious gambit in these last words. He parried by pulling out his notebook and flicking it open as if to check something. 'My notes tell me you studied in La Sapienza?'

'Just across the road. Graduated, travelled the world, wrote some pretty groundbreaking studies and three books, the last of which I wrote directly in English. It was published by Duckworth, and they didn't even come back to me with any corrections: it was that precise. And then I ended up working more or less where I studied. Story of my life.'

'What do you mean?'

'Nothing. Just an expression. It's as if I were born into a circle that I have to stay inside, even if I have travelled widely. I get up in the same house as I did 30 years ago, go to almost the same place as 30 years ago.'

'You live in the same house?'

'I travelled the world for years. I didn't save for a home, and I, too, served my time as a poorly paid research assistant.'

'The address I have here is the family home, then?'

'Exactly.'

'And does anyone else live there?'

'No. Apart from my mother, of course.'

'So, you're not married?'

'Don't your notes tell you that?'

Blume nodded. 'They do, they do . . . So, now Sofia has gone, what happens her job?'

Ideo rubbed his small hands together. 'It's open. That lot in there will start fighting each other for it. That's why I set them on a project together. Also, I made sure it's a particularly pointless project. They have to modify the feeding system in the cages, then design a fish maze. Fish, by the way, have terrific memories. I think if we could hear them scream we wouldn't be so blasé about angling and trawling. There's definitely more going on in their heads than we know. But, yes, before you say it, I am doing a little bit of experimental psychology with my researchers. Don't tell them, though, if you are going to talk to them, will you?'

Blume promised he would not. 'Can you confirm that you are 48 years of age?'

'Almost 49,' said Ideo.

'Yes, you're right.'

'Of course I'm right. It's my birthday next week!'

'Have you been following the murder investigation?'

'Absolutely!' Ideo could not find his cigarettes and whipped off his lab coat in the hunt for them.

'There,' said Blume. 'You left the packet next to that . . . that . . .'

Ideo snatched up the packet as if rescuing it from a thief. 'Thanks. It's a centrifuge. Broken, of course.' He lit another cigarette, smacking his lips.

'We move through life at the speed of light,' he announced. 'Death is just a sudden deceleration and a movement into a different and slower dimension.'

'Uh-huh.' Blume was keen to avoid this sort of talk. He stayed quiet to let the philosophy blow over, and watched Ideo's nervous movements as he sucked and tapped at his cigarette. 'So who will replace her?'

Ideo shrugged. 'I'm not sure, but she'll never be as good as Sofia.'

'She?'

'Well, you saw in that room. They are all women.'

Blume pictured the room. There had been as many men as women. Plus one on his lunch break.

Ideo seemed to read his mind. 'The suitable candidates for the post are women.'

'You prefer to work with women?'

Ideo opened his wide mouth showing yellow teeth. 'Don't you?'

'It depends,' said Blume.

This time Ideo chose to stub the butt out on the floor. He watched the ashes and sparks scatter, and when he raised his face it had a serious expression. 'What do you think women want?'

Blume shrugged. 'I wish I knew.'

'You, too, huh?'

Blume did not like the assumption of complicity. 'No, I'm fine with women.'

Ideo's eyes lit up 'Successful, you mean? Is it your rank? Maybe the weapon you carry? They like power.'

Blume felt increasingly disinclined to agree with the man in front of him. 'They like strength.'

'They don't like a man to have any weaknesses, do they?'

'Not true,' said Blume 'They love men with weaknesses. They just don't like weak men.'

Ideo went for another cigarette, then thought better of it.

'Well . . . I am working, and this is my time you are wasting. Tell me what you need.'

'Nothing, really,' said Blume. 'I just like to meet the people connected to a case, no matter how peripherally. I wanted to make your acquaintance, and now I have.'

It was a relief to get away from Ideo and his smoke, and from the Institute and its smell of antiseptic and rodents.

Blume returned to the station and spent most of the early afternoon doing paperwork. The only person in the front office when he arrived was Rospo, a man so disliked by all that he had become as essential as electricity to the smooth running of the department. Whenever two colleagues were bickering over something, whenever a betrayal of trust had taken place, or someone had made a joke that did not go down well, whenever someone was not pulling his or her weight, or was slacking off, Rospo was there to remind them all that human beings could turn out worse in looks, conduct, and intelligence. Even better, some of the higher-ups in the police and judiciary thought he was a useful spy. Thanks to Rospo, sending disinformation up the chain of command was a cinch. Of course, the more intelligent senior officers knew that Rospo was an unwitting conduit of false information, but the more intelligent senior officers were also the ones who did not rely on spies.

'Rospo! Working hard, I see,' said Blume as he passed by. Rospo had tried to shut down the gambling site he was visiting, but the screen was covered in multiple pop-ups advertising sex sites, free music, poker apps, and video games.

Towards five, Caterina came in without knocking, leaving the door open behind her, as if they had nothing to hide, which they didn't, but that did not alter the fact that doors were for closing.

She collapsed into a chair. 'Where were you today, Alec?'

If she had not looked so haggard and exhausted, he might even have reminded her to shut the damned door. They had a deal. He would take his shoes off as soon as he came in and never lie on the bed with his 'outside clothes' on. He had adapted, but she couldn't be bothered.

He walked over, shut the door to his office, and decided the bad news about Principe could wait.

'Left it open, sorry,' she said in a totally unsorry voice.

Blume looked at her face, and realized she, too, was ageing: where her lips ended at what had once been the merest shadow that threw her bright cheeks into relief had become a fold, so that the cheeks were now divided. It was not that they were sagging, it was just that it was now possible to make out where the sag line would be. Her hair was lank and had an unwashed look, and she seemed to have gained weight around the throat so that the tendons were no longer visible. If this was the result of her dieting and jogging three times a week, she might be better off giving it a rest, but he did not want to get into that conversation again. She was wearing no make-up. He appreciated this in her, or had always appreciated it, but now, as he looked at her, he thought she might look a bit better with lipstick and whatever that stuff was women used to give their face colour. Rouge – or was that a word from a different century?

'Meeting Principe.' Blume waited for her to ask why, but she sat there like a fattening, ageing doll, and asked him nothing, too involved with her own tiredness.

'I just spent the afternoon with a family of fucking troglodytes,' said Caterina. 'One's worse than the other.'

'Valerio's family?' asked Blume.

She nodded. 'Me and Panebianco. I wish I were more like him. He really detaches, you know? Floats away in a cloud of indifference. I can't do that. These people. We should have been comforting them, instead we were threatening them that if they took any action against Adelgardo or his family, they'd end up in jail. Not that our threats made any difference.'

'You still think a man like that should end up in the same prison as a hardened criminal?'

'I think it is the natural result of what he did. What do you want, a special prison for the middle class, because that's basically your problem here, Alec.'

'He's an old man.'

'Sorry, a special prison for the *elderly* bourgeoisie,' said Caterina. 'And we both know he's not going to prison, so why argue?'

'No, he's not,' agreed Blume. He remembered something. 'How's your father?'

She shrugged. 'Not good. He's entering the aggressive stage. Apparently it commonly comes at the end of stage three, before he enters a total vegetative state.'

'Maybe it won't come to that,' said Blume.

'Meaning let's hope he dies before then.'

A while ago, she had told him that the fact her father had Alzheimer's greatly increased her chances of the same. 'I need to you plan what to do if that happens,' she had told him. Blume had not thought much about her eventual Alzheimer's; instead, he had obsessed about her assumption that they would reach such an advanced age together. Now as he looked at her slumped in the chair, and thought about Principe, about Stefania Manfellotto propped up on her pillows, he tried to imagine her in hospital, an older version of himself standing there, wisely deciding on throwing the switch, or stopping the feeding, or using his service pistol, fighting with Elia, now a man calling him a murderer.

'You've had your hair cut,' said Caterina.

'No . . . Well, yes, just a trim.'

'It wasn't long. You had it cut two weeks ago.'

'I just caught sight of myself in the mirror this morning, and I decided I needed a haircut.'

'How vain. Where did you go?'

Blume waved at the wall. 'Down there . . . just off the Via del Corso. There's a place.'

'I'm surprised a barber can afford the rent,' said Caterina. 'Was it expensive?'

'No, no. Ordinary price. Fifteen, no twenty . . . -two. I had a shampoo, too. I guess the shop must be his own. He bought it years ago when prices were lower.'

'He told you this?'

'No, of course not. I'm just imagining that's how it must be.'

'So he was old.'

'Yes, an old barber,' said Blume. He switched subjects. 'You know, you don't look all that great. Are you coming down with a cold? It's chilly out.'

'You sound like my mother. By the way, she's got over her shock at your penis, and is prepared to visit the house again to help with Elia.'

'Help him with what? I mean how old is the kid?' said Blume walking into his own rhetorical trap. Maybe she wouldn't notice.

No such luck. 'Are you asking me that because you can't remember?'

'Sure I can,' he lied. 'My point is, isn't he old enough to look after himself after school?'

'He gives structure to my mother's life, Alec. Who is she supposed to cook and wash and clean for now that Papà's in hospital and is never coming out? Would you deprive her of that?'

Blume figured he would, at least for a while; just long enough for Caterina's mother to work out she was there on his forbearance and was not really needed.

'So how old is he?'

'Thirteen,' Blume spoke confidently.

'Wrong.'

'Fourteen.' Maybe the kid was only twelve.

'I'm going home now, Alec. Will you want dinner when you get in?'

'Actually, I'm going to be a bit late. I've got something I need to do.'

'OK.'

He was relieved she had not asked for details, and furious at her incuriosity.

15

BLUME TOOK out his notebook, and wrote out all that he knew about the case so far. It took him an hour to get everything down as he wanted it. He looked at what he had, and picked up his desk phone and called Principe's mobile phone, but it went straight to voicemail. He had to go to the old steel cabinet next to the window, slide open the sticky drawer, and retrieve an old Rolodex he had thought he had done with to get Principe's landline number.

He dialled it and finally got a reply.

'Yes?' Principe sounded weary. Everyone seemed so tired and irritable. It had to be the weather.

'It's me,' said Blume. 'Your mobile is switched off.'

'I forgot to charge it,' said Principe, a hint of reproach in his tone, as if to say he had other things on his mind. His voice was muffled as if he had put his hand over the receiver.

'Can you tell the Carabinieri Captain . . .'

'Giovanni Zezza.'

'Tell him I want to talk to him.'

'Sure . . .' Principe sounded vague. 'I tried to set up a meeting. He didn't call you?'

'No.'

Principe sighed. 'Get out of the office and go home to Caterina.'

'How do you know I am in the office?'

'Well, are you?'

'Yes, but that's just a lucky guess.'

'Is Caterina in the office?'

'No, she's gone home,' admitted Blume.

'Go to her.'

'If we're handing out free advice, why don't you phone your daughter and tell her you're sick?'

'If you go home to Caterina now, maybe I will. Deal?'

'Deal,' said Blume.

Muffled up in a Crombie greatcoat that he hardly ever got a chance to use because it made Caterina laugh, Blume pulled the door to his office closed, greeted the two *agenti* coming in for the night, and went down to the garage for his car.

Before turning on the engine, he called a number he had just looked up in the office. He identified himself to Sofia's mother and asked if he could come round and ask a few questions.

Sofia's mother mumbled, her voice clouded and indistinct. Blume recognized the tone. It was the indifference of grief, the indifference to the weather, the passage of time, sleep, food, night and day, the things people said and did, the niceties of communication, the need to separate words when speaking, the expectations of people who didn't know that you were still supposed to shop, pay bills, wash, acknowledge the check-out person, reply to questions, stop at traffic lights.

Half an hour later, he was walking down the centre of the concrete and grass piazza that ran the length of Via Ventimiglia, looking for the address of Sofia's mother. Deep in his warm pocket his phone vibrated. He pulled it out, and saw the name 'Valentino' on the display.

Valentino was the nickname he had given to the man with the fat tie and huge collar from the estate agency, whose name had gone straight out of Blume's head as soon as they had met, and whose calling card he had binned.

'Alec!'

Like they were old friends or something.

When Blume first met him, the man had been wearing a chocolate-coloured Valentino suit. After 'Valentino' had called a few times about the apartment, Blume felt obliged to list him in his phone book. The only thing he knew was that Valentino's name was not Valentino, though he would not have reciprocated the cheery first-name greeting even if he had been able.

'You still there?'

Blume allowed a reluctant grunt of confirmation.

'Sorry about the hour, but you know, I never stop working for my customers. You especially. So, are you sitting down?'

Blume continued on his way towards the ground-floor apartment that gave on to a patch of communal grass in the middle of which sat a lethal-looking children's swing and slide, all sharp metal edges and heavy iron, a rusted relic from the carefree 1970s.

'Well, are you?'

'Yes,' said Blume. He had to go around the garden to get to the door. But now he had to hold back until the clown he was talking to had got to the point.

'Do you know what IFAD is?'

'The Something Food and Something Development Something, part of the UN,' said Blume.

'Exactly. They pay 90 per cent of the rent for staff on transfer, so people working for IFAD don't mind paying a bit above the odds.'

'Are you telling me someone from IFAD is going to rent my apartment?'

'I am. And wait till you get this . . .'

Blume waited.

'When I heard the foreign accent, I thought I would throw out a few casual questions before we got down to the question of price. The woman . . .'

'A woman?'

'A whole family, Alec,' he said as if the additional people were a bonus extra. 'I was able to get her to reveal that she worked for IFAD, and I decided there and then to up the price, try our luck.'

'It was advertised at €1,200 a month,' said Blume.

'I always said you put it too low. I simply told her that the price had been misprinted and was supposed to be €1,800. She hesitated, so I dropped it to €1,750. That hooked her and she made an appointment and I've just been through the place with her – maybe you could have cleaned up that study a bit more? I am in the car heading back and, guess what, Alec?'

'She took it?'

'Two years!'

'That's great,' said Blume.

'Two years at €1,750 instead of €1,200. That's €13,200 extra I just negotiated for you! You could buy a car with the difference. A small car. A Citroen C3, say. You don't need a new Citroen, do you?'

'No.'

'Not necessarily a Citroen, of course . . .'

'No.'

'OK. No problem. Hey, €13,200!'

'Yeah, you said.'

'I'm doing the paperwork tomorrow. She's coming in with a three-month deposit. Usually, we keep an extra one-month deposit to cover damages, so that makes a total of €15,000 basically I just got you.'

'Like I said, great.'

'You don't sound so pleased. I do you this favour and you react like your dog died or something. *Oddio*, your dog hasn't died or anything? Sometimes I say things and then, you know . . .'

'I don't have a dog,' Blume reassured him.

'Thank God for that. Listen, one thing . . . No two things . . . Three things. The family, two teenage boys and a husband are moving in immediately. Like the day after tomorrow. That's fine?'

'Sure.'

It looked like he would have to move in with Caterina after all.

'And another thing. They asked for the study to be cleared out. Can you deal with that?'

'I wasn't expecting that. I have nowhere to put the stuff.'

'Look, it's no problem. I can organize everything: removal, a warehouse. I can get you a really good deal. We can talk about it.'

'Fine.'

'And another thing?'

'How many more things do you have lined up to tell me?'

'Just this one. The woman's name is Prisca Mutungi.'

'Is it?'

'So that's OK?'

'Is the name supposed to mean something to me? Has she been in the news recently charged with arson?'

'Mutungi. She's from,' Valentino paused delicately, 'Tanzania.'

'Are you trying to tell me she's black?'

'She seemed very educated nonetheless. Very respectable. But she is very visibly black. You can't help but notice that about her. Shiny black, you know that look? Then, damnedest thing, her husband is totally white.'

'Totally?' said Blume. 'That really is something.'

★

Her phone beeped to tell her the line to Blume was now clear, but it was too late. They had started dinner. It was up to him to call anyhow.

Caterina smiled at Elia, and cut a piece of breaded pork with a steak knife. The meat in the middle was pink, slightly undercooked, and she was about to tell Elia not to eat his and let her fry it a little more, but he had already covered it in ketchup.

'I wish you wouldn't put ketchup on everything,' she told him, getting a scowl in return.

She hated that he was like this. It was normal, she knew. Children became adolescents. But Elia had done it almost overnight. According to Alec, that was what had happened to him, and, he assured her, it was a tough moment in life. A teenager can have 700 times more testosterone than an adult. One minute, he said, you are a child full of trust and innocence, the next you are a twirling mass of testosterone unable to stop thinking about violence and rape and death, and you think you are the worst person in the world. Which you are, Blume continued in that unremitting way of his. If you want to kill a village, baton-charge peaceful protesters, machine-gun intellectuals, shoot dead an honest magistrate or politician, send in a young man to do the job.

Caterina suspected there was some truth in his jaundiced vision, but she resented the implication that Elia was beset by evil. Alec was just using it as an excuse to continue not . . . what was it he did not do for Elia? He was really fond of him. But there was something missing. In the end, blood is thicker than water. Elia, when in a bad mood or when egged on by his grandmother, sometimes regarded Blume as an interloper, and the worst part of it was that Blume himself agreed, and therefore refused even to rent out his own apartment, let alone sell it. She used to argue that they needed the money, but that made no impression on him. She would make that a precondition now. He had better rent his apartment or else.

It was Elia's favourite dish, which is why she had made it, but the smell of the meat and cooking oil in her nostrils was making her feel nauseous. She cut the piece of meat on her plate, and her hastily prepared breadcrumb-and-egg batter slipped off like a scab revealing a pink piece of undercooked pork beneath. She pushed the batter back on, and dropped it all into her mouth, and as it slipped down her throat, she was overcome with an overwhelming desire not to swallow anything so revolting. She retched, then retched again. She held up a hand, warning Elia away, but also trying to tell him it was OK, and ran to the bathroom, vomiting just before she reached the toilet bowl. Then, seeing what she had vomited, vomited again.

'Mamma?' Elia's voice had gone back to childhood. 'Mamma! Where are you?'

'In the bathroom. Don't come in! I'm all right, but don't come in.'

'Who should I call?' he said, becoming a little more grown-up now that she had reassured him.

'No one. I'm OK. Sometimes I really hate meat' – the very word made her feel ill again.

'I can call him, if you want.' Elia found it hard to choose what to call him, 'Zio' Blume was stupid, but they had used it, 'Alec' was odd, and Alec himself didn't like it. Recently Elia had taken to calling him Blume, and Alec seemed to like that.

'No. Don't. I just have an upset stomach. Go back into the kitchen, throw out your meat. I didn't cook it properly.'

'I've finished half of it already!' Panic filled his voice. 'Will I be all right?'

'Perhaps it was something else. If you feel sick later, we'll know. But you'll be all right. I made a mistake not eating all day . . . Diet.' It was exhausting having to explain through a closed door to a frightened child trying to be an adult. But at least he had offered to call 'him', which was something of a breakthrough. She could do with someone to make her a cup of tea and warm her up. Where the hell was he?

16

B LUME PRESSED the intercom button marked 'Fontana'. No other
surname of course. No father. The buzzer sounded without any
voice enquiring who he was. He glanced at his watch. Half past nine.
Who else would it be at this time?

The door to the apartment, a few steps from the main entrance, was
opened by two women in their early fifties. One was considerably fatter
and more buxom than the other and less elegantly dressed, but they were
unmistakably, almost comically alike. Blume identified the larger woman
at once as Sofia's mother. In part, he remembered her outline from the
night he had seen Sofia's body slumped against the university wall, but the
look in her eyes was unequivocal. The other woman also wore a look of
sorrow, but not the hollow look of a parent who has lost a child.

Blume offered his hand first to Sofia's mother. Mirella Fontana. 'I am
Commissioner Blume, and I am investigating the murder of your daughter. I am very sorry for your loss, and would like to ask you some questions.'

It didn't matter that he sounded mechanical and stilted. Everything
sounded so to the recently bereaved.

The more elegant woman stood forward. 'I am the sister.'

'Silvia, Olivia's mother?' asked Blume.

'Yes.'

They stood back to allow him in, and he followed them through a dark
corridor, so short it was almost square, past a red lamp burning under a
Sacred Heart and into a room of peeling paint. The room smelled of
mould overlaid with a chemically fresh scent of some sort, either floor
cleaner or one of those cancerous air fresheners people like to plug into
their walls. The horizontals of the room were dominated by a large table
topped with imitation wood, the verticals by a black flat-screen television
taking up most of the wall on the right. A plastic and glass chandelier with
six candle-shaped bulbs was failing to give much light to the room, though

one corner, with three mismatching chairs, was better lit by a tasselled lamp. There were two windows looking back into the garden. A roll-down shutter obscured one.

Blume sat on a lumpy armchair and the two women sat down opposite. All of a sudden, he was unsure of his right to be there, intruding. The Carabinieri were dealing with this. They would be doing a good job. He should be at home with Caterina, not probing at the pain of a woman who had lost her only daughter.

His eye wandered around the squalid little room in search of inspiration, and came to rest eventually on the aluminium frame window, which was protected outside by a heavy metal grille. Sofia's mother seemed to have been following his gaze, for she said, 'The bars haven't always been enough. We've been robbed three times now.'

Blume nodded. How long would she continue saying 'we'?

'Do you work, Signora Fontana?'

'Call me Mirella.'

He smiled. The name sounded nice. It suited her. 'What do you do, Mirella?'

'I clean other people's homes.' Her choice of words expressed her sense of humiliation, and sensing that she had perhaps overstepped some boundary, she moderated her tone a little. 'I am lucky to have the job, and the people I work for are decent. I will only work for decent people.'

'Did Sofia ever help?' A grieving parent thinks of nothing other than the lost child. Nothing was to be gained by avoiding the subject, so you may as well be direct. It was Principe who had told him that.

'Clean houses? Absolutely not.' Her voice was hoarse, and she probably had no more tears left for the day. He imagined they would flow freely when she woke up in the morning, the loss dawning on her all over again.

'Did she ever babysit for any of them?'

'No. She studied. That was the deal we had.'

It had been a long shot, but one worth taking. Any connection was relevant. 'Excuse me, Mirella, I realize you have been questioned by the Carabinieri already and it is painful.'

'Yes. It is. But I need to know why, so keep asking questions.'

Grieving mothers will always want to know why; fathers want to know who – Principe again. In this case, there was no father.

Blume asked some more questions, unsure whether he welcomed or was distracted by the presence of the sister, who had sat there making small noises of approval and grief as appropriate. After a while, he turned his attention to her.

'I see you live on the same street.'

'I live three doors down,' she said. 'How did you know that?'

'It's on the files. Getting together a full list of names, addresses, and phone numbers of the family is one of the first things we do in a case like this. So your apartment is pretty much the same as this one?'

The sister reddened. 'Well, they all have the same floor plan. They are based on the one model. Mussolini built them.'

'Mussolini had other people build them,' corrected Mirella suddenly, with more life – and venom – than she had shown when he asked his routine questions. 'She always puts it like that: as if Mussolini was down here in person breaking ground with a pickaxe, hero of the working class.'

Her sister gave a tight little smile of indulgence, and looked meaningfully at Blume, as if to say that unreasonable outbursts like this were to be expected from a grieving mother.

'And what do you do?' Blume asked her.

'I am an artist.'

'Really?' said Blume. 'An artist. You paint?'

'Yes, I paint. I also write.'

'Poetry or prose?' asked Blume.

'It's hard to tell,' interrupted Mirella, whose seething anger at the attribution of building prowess to Mussolini seemed to have momentarily seared through her cloud of grief.

'You've always hated my artistic side,' said her sister, her veneer of compassion cracking. 'The artistic genes were passed on to me, not to you, and you've always resented it.'

'I don't resent it, Silvia,' said Sofia's mother in what seemed like a gentle tone, but she followed it up with the less than tender observation: 'It's just you're no good. No one wants your paintings, no one will publish your poetry.'

'No one that you know, but you don't anyone worth knowing, do you?'

'So have you been making millions selling your paintings to cultured folk? People who understand. People who don't think your paintings look like dogshit from a distance, and dogshit from close-up, too.'

Blume had been forgotten, but that suited him fine. Family dynamics were always interesting, even amusing, unless you were inside them.

'We at least tried to do something meaningful.'

'We?'

'Olivia and I.'

The breath came out of Sofia's mother as if she had been punched in the stomach. Her head fell forward and, for a moment, she reminded him forcefully of the image of her daughter slumped against the wall. A similar sound now broke from Silvia, who went over and hugged her sister. Blume was caught off balance by the sudden shift in emotions. He expected a fight to last longer than that.

'I loved her, too. I love you,' Silvia was now saying. 'I don't know why I say these things.'

Mirella stroked her sister's face. 'It's all right. I know you loved her, and I love your Olivia. That's what will keep us going.'

When they had composed themselves, Blume said, 'The main reason I am here is for you to tell me anything that you think might be relevant.'

'What sort of things?' asked Mirella, gently pushing her weeping sister away.

'Anything.'

'Well . . . no. You'll just think I am being stupid.'

'No, tell me. I will think nothing of the sort.'

'It's almost as if she knew, you know what I mean?'

Blume nodded and made a sound that could be interpreted as assent, but he had no idea what the mother meant. He hoped she would continue.

'I thought it was London, but she was down a lot of the time. She was even short with me. Then she would make up for it. But it's like she saw something was going to go wrong.'

'This is after she witnessed the shooting of Stefania Manfellotto?'

'No! Before. That's what I mean. It's as if she knew.'

'But she said nothing,' prompted Blume. 'Did she mention any problems at work, anything along those lines?'

'No.'

'Was she involved with some group, some cult, a former boyfriend perhaps? Someone else?'

'Like a married man, you mean?'

'Anything,' said Blume, aiming for a tone halfway between reassuring and pleading. 'Nothing can harm her now. But any knowledge you have might help us get whoever killed her.'

Silvia now took it upon herself to praise her niece to make up for the fight a minute before. 'Sofia did not have much time for boyfriends . . .'

'She had some boyfriends,' interjected Mirella.

'All I meant to tell the policeman was that Sofia was a serious-minded, lovely girl. She was always ready to help my daughter Olivia with homework when they were in school. If it hadn't been for Sofia, I don't think Olivia would even have done her *maturità* and gone to university. Olivia, you see, has an artistic temperament like me, which means she is not so good with certain subjects like Maths and Science.'

'Or History, Geography, Languages, Music, Philosophy,' added Mirella.

The emotional swings in the small room were making him dizzy, and he blurted out his next question more to stop a resumption of hostilities and weeping between the two sisters than because he had any clear intention. 'Where is Olivia now?'

'Olivia?' said Silvia, flashing her sister a dirty look. 'She's at home.'

'Just wondering. Anyone there with her. Your husband, perhaps?'

'No, he went out. Olivia is there with her boyfriend Marco, as it happens.'

'Ah, now that's very handy,' said Blume getting out of his chair. 'Because I was hoping to talk to him. I thought we would meet tomorrow, but if I can talk now, that would be great.'

Silvia looked doubtful. 'These are young people. They need their privacy.'

'I am sure you can ring the bell rather than use the front door keys. Or phone ahead,' said Blume.

'Yes, but we promised them privacy.'

'I see,' said Blume. 'Is that why you're here and your husband is out?'

Silvia glared at him. 'I would have been here anyhow to help my sister.'

'I can imagine,' said Blume. 'And your husband, where does he go when Olivia needs a free house?'

She looked at him trying to see if there was a trick to his question, then, seeing none, said, 'He has a regular place, a bar across the street. It's closed now, so he'll go to the multi-screen at Parco de' Medici. Sometimes he drives down to Ostia afterwards.'

'What's your husband's job, Mrs Visco?'

'He's a manager.'

'Really. Our records must be out of date, then, because when I looked him up his occupation was given as hospital porter on sick leave for the past eight years, poor man.'

'Why do you ask questions if you know the answers?'

'Because I didn't have the correct information, as you see. That's why it's always a good idea to double-check. So where is he a manager?'

'In the hospital. He manages the shifts. You'll have to ask him.'

'Tell you what,' said Blume clapping his hands loudly. 'Let's give the kids a surprise.'

It took a bit of persuasion, with an undertone of threat but, with the encouragement of Mirella who did not seem sorry at the prospect of her sister's departure, Blume managed to get her out of the house. From an investigative point of view, Silvia, Olivia, and Marco seemed more interesting than poor Mirella, to whom he had taken a liking. As he was on his way out, she clasped his hands in hers.

'Catch the right person, please.' Her hands were warm and dry and, despite her job, soft. 'Commissioner, your hands are freezing. Your fingers!'

'It's cold,' said Blume.

'You must wear gloves.'

'I don't have any gloves,' he said.

'You must learn to look after yourself.' She released his hands, and he was sorry to lose the warmth.

17

CATERINA ATE eggs resentfully at breakfast, battling down the nausea. Scrambled, boiled, boiled, and scrambled, sometimes mixed with spinach and always with a dose of what Blume referred to as 'Dukan dust', she sighed and chewed and looked weepy and angry morning after morning. She had even started snarling at Elia. It was a deep and lasting nausea that went beyond eggs.

When she had mentioned that the diet recommended meat, he had had visions of sirloin steak fried in butter and onions every night. Instead, it was boiled chicken, strips of Bresaola so thin they wouldn't offend a vegan, and, a recent and ghastly addition, tofu. He had started finding reasons to stay out for dinner. Once, he had even sneaked back into his old apartment and made himself a big beautiful lasagna.

A week earlier, Blume had made the mistake of speaking his mind.

'I think you should give up this diet. A million eggs a month can't be good for you and you hate them anyway, almost as much as you hate the fish you have to eat. It's only making you miserable. Besides . . .'

'Besides what?' she snapped.

Shocked at the sudden aggression in her voice, Blume lowered his chocolate muffin and spread his hands in a what-the-hell? sort of gesture.

'No, you started this conversation,' she said. 'Say what you were going to say.'

Blume played for time by thickly buttering a piece of toast with exaggerated care. 'I don't trust that French guru you're following. I mean, have you seen the smug little face he has? Reminds me of a three-toed sloth.'

'Of course I've seen his face. It's on the front of the book.'

'That's another thing. What sort of person puts his own face on his book?'

'Maybe a successful person who has done something in his life? I don't see your face on too many best-sellers.'

'I was trying to say something that I find hard to say,' said Blume. 'But now . . .' he shook his head sadly.

'Tell me what, Alec?' She relented, and softened her reproach. 'I appreciate you are making an effort here. If you have something that you think needs saying, say it.'

He swallowed the rest of the muffin and pointed his finger at her plate. 'I think all those eggs are making you fat.'

Since that conversation, Blume had been inventing appointments to get him out of the house earlier in the morning so as not to meet her at breakfast. She knew what he was doing, of course. By the time they met in the office or in the field, she seemed to be in a better mood, at least until dinner time.

Over the past few months, Caterina had taken charge of his scheduling, and he was coming to depend a little too much on her. He was also beginning to resent the way she double-checked that he had understood, as if he were an idiot. At her suggestion, he had also taken to using a computer bag to carry his stuff around in. It was padded, had compartments that kept papers separate and uncreased, sat nicely on his shoulder, and could accommodate anything from a pistol, though he had never used it for that, to a packed lunch and a few paperbacks. He still pretended he resented having to give up on his old leather briefcase just to please her, but the truth was he would never go back to it.

She had warned him several days ago that a mid-morning conference in the Giulio Cesare Hall of the Campidoglio, originally scheduled for 10:30, had been put forward an hour.

The coming conference was on the theme of racism and the police. It promised to be a pleasant affair. The right-wing government of Rome was not convinced that the police had much to answer for in respect of racism, and, by happy coincidence, all the delegates from the Police and Carabinieri were of like opinion. The only irritant was that they all had to turn up at the conference and pretend to be concerned about a problem that they didn't believe to exist.

There was one point of contention. The City had recently announced that the police would no longer travel free on the metro and buses. The questore was proud of his smooth delivery of hard political truths, and he thoroughly enjoyed having a captive audience. He would have a few telling words to say about bus privileges.

Blume got up quietly, but Caterina was a light sleeper, especially recently, and immediately mumbled, 'Don't forget the conference', before rolling over.

He was tiptoeing out when she sat bolt upright. 'Where were you last night?'

'Hmm?'

'OK, don't answer then,' she lay down again.

Blume put his socks on in the hallway, away from Caterina. Did she suspect him of an affair? Where would he find the time? And who? He thought about the meeting last night with Olivia, who was wearing a short kimono robe and a scowl when she opened the door to him and her mother.

Stupidly, he had followed Olivia into her bedroom, a place so full of clothes – piled on chairs, on the bed, hanging over the closet door, strewn on the floor – that sounds were muffled. The remaining surfaces were filled with bijoux jewels and white electronic items. The walls were covered in photos of Olivia at every age from birth and in every pose imaginable. A 6-year-old version of her a fairy had been blown up to poster size and stood innocently next to a stylized monochrome photo of her face in half shadow.

In the middle of this Bower of Bliss had been a young man with full lips, smooth bronzed skin, and long legs. He had black silky hair, a thin nose, and long delicate hands. He was wearing socks and jeans, but was bare chested. If he had not looked so trapped and uncomfortable sitting in the squalid, overcrowded room, he could have stepped out of a Cinzano or Armani advertisement.

'Marco,' Blume had said. Marco nodded, which seemed to be all he had in his repertoire. To any question Blume asked, he received a slow nod in reply. It was either gross insolence or gross stupidity.

Olivia had intervened and steered the conversation wherever she wanted. In the end, Blume had ordered the young man out, telling him it was a ten-minute walk now or a full day in the police station tomorrow. He expected Olivia to make a scene, but she merely crossed her smooth legs and smiled her gracious permission at them.

Marco was as handsome as possible, and well-built, but not someone you would want to rely on in a fight. The first few paces as they left the house suggested he wanted to infuse a dash of unconcerned swagger into his walk, but as they turned the corner and the icy *tramontana* wind hit them, he had to stop, zip up, and huddle down defensively. Even his physique was unreliable. By the time they had walked around the block, Marco was stooped over in the attitude of a prayerful penitent, silent, with his chin buried deep in his chest.

In hard facts, he learned nothing new from Marco that he did not already know.

'My father is a retired Carabinieri captain,' he told Blume. 'Parachute regiment. I've got an elder brother who's in the force.'

'Have they met Olivia?'

'Sure. First thing my brother did was make a move on her.'

'At least it wasn't your father.'

'No, that came after. But Olivia is a match for them.'

'Sounds like she earned you a bit of respect, then. Are you sure she doesn't play you?' asked Blume.

'Are you saying she sleeps around or something? She's free to do what she wants.'

'And you? Does she give you the same freedom?'

Marco laughed. It was a real laugh, as if Blume had just said something funny. 'No, she doesn't. No way. You get a girl like Olivia, though, you do as she says. I'm lucky to have her.'

For one so lucky, he didn't seem all that happy.

'What about Sofia?'

'I knew her, that's all.'

'Anything between you?'

Marco hunched down deeper into himself, and it was not the cold wind's fault.

'Tell me, Marco.'

'No, nothing. But I think . . .'

'Come on.' Blume was getting impatient with this weak young man.

'Nothing . . . I didn't. I think she was worried about something.'

'Sofia. When?'

'Nothing. That's just the impression I got.'

Blume got nothing more out of him, despite walking him round the block once more, listening to him complain about the cold. When they finally came round to Olivia's again, Blume left him. As he reached his car, he turned round to see Marco still standing there, shivering, and he thought Olivia might have refused to let him back in, but as he watched, Marco raised his hand and pressed the buzzer. Seconds later, the door buzzed and he was in.

Blume left the house at seven when Caterina was still in the shower. He climbed into the car and dropped the bag beside him, and steeled his nerves for the traffic through town. The morning sky was flat and white, as if the sun had been replaced with a fluorescent tube, and everything around him seemed dirty and broken. Dirtiest of all was his own windscreen. He flicked the lever to squirt water on it, and the rubber blades moaned their way with the window three times, evenly distributing a thin patina of sperm-coloured ice that completely blocked his view. This was Rome, not Seattle. Global weirding, they called it. He switched on the demisters.

From his bag, he extracted his new Kindle. He had bought it for himself several months ago, charged it, turned it on, and been very disappointed to find himself looking at what seemed to be a glorified Etch A Sketch pad. But he did not want to start filling Caterina's apartment with real books. He still did not know what to do with all the books he had left behind in his own place.

He switched it on. It was simple, and he keyed in Pitagora's name. Amazon had never heard of him. He conjured up Pitagora's memory test from the other day: OK, there had been Zezza, a group of Roman emperors, Tiberius and Titus the Jew killer, and some others, details he had wiped away, since he didn't need them. A whole string of names, 'string' was one of the words, or 'wire'? Both? A string of emperors, string, wire, a can of worms, a tin of worms, used as bait on the end of the string . . . someone fishing . . . a Fisherman – Aaron Fisher.

He keyed in the name into his Kindle. There it was: *The Memory Key* by Aaron Fisher, with the inevitable self-help subtitle: *Expand your mental capacity by 2^7*. He hesitated a second, then pressed 'buy', then went back to the main menu, and, sure enough, there, sitting above a line of dots, was the title on his home menu.

Amazing. And he had not even noticed the price. He clicked through the first few pages, then noticed the windscreen had demisted. He checked his wing mirror and, after making it clear to the uninterrupted line of angry drivers on Viale delle Province that he was pulling out no matter what, he edged his way into the traffic flow that would bring him in fits and starts into the centre of town, multiplying twos in his head. Two times 2 is 4, which is 2 squared, cubed is 8, 16, 32 . . . Aaron Fisher promised to improve his mental capacity 128 times over.

While stuck in traffic outside a school, he pressed his Kindle again and, after the irritating business of pressing the side button several times just to get to the start of the book, discovered that it did not handle illustrations well. To make a start on expanding his mind 128 times, Aaron Fisher was suggesting he remembered the number 1 as resembling a magic wand, and had included a Harry Potter lookalike to help him. The 2 was a swan – notice it is black! emphasized Fisher, as if this should excite him. On the Kindle, the black swan was grey. Things improved with the number 3, which he was instructed to remember as a pair of breasts nestling beneath a lacy bra. Here the ink-line drawing seemed to work just fine, with all the laciness in evidence. The 4 was the sails of a sailing boat, or a sailing boat drawn by a 4-year-old. The 5 was a fish hook and the author, with a lot of exclamation marks, drew attention to this and his own name, Fisher. The 6 was a hangman's noose. He edged forward 10 metres in the line. The car moved when he released the clutch and before he touched the accelerator: something he needed to get seen to . . . Here was a pistol, shaped like a Walther PPQ, in representation of the number 7. Eight was a snowman. The number 9 was a tadpole. Very unsatisfactory, thought Blume. Tadpoles were tiny, and sailing boats were large, and 9 was greater than 4. So far, Aaron Fisher was making his brain feel smaller.

Someone beeped at him and he felt his hand shoot up in the air in an automatic gesture of defiance before he noticed the road ahead was clear and he was holding everyone up. He turned his gesture into an unconvincingly apologetic wave at the last second, and got another blast on the horn for his trouble, so he turned the wave back into a *cornuto* gesture. Cars were now pulling out and roaring pointedly past him through the junction. The light turned red again, and looking in his mirror, he watched with interest as the man in the car behind him jerked about in a seated dance of spasmodic rage. Why hadn't he just pulled out and gone around like the others? Probably so much up his ass he didn't have space to pull out. Fat bastard, he was, car registration DF 145 LE. Domodossola-Firenze-145-Livorno-Empoli or Delta-Foxtrot-145-Lima-Echo. No need for mnemonics for number plates. He wondered what the book had to say about memorizing letters. The 145 would be a magic wand, a sailing boat, and a fish hook. Wand, boat, fish hook. It would be 128 times easier just to remember 145, he figured. There used to be an Alfa Romeo 145, Article 145 of the Highway Code. That was the one about stopping at stop signs. Speaking of which . . .

DF 145 LE behind him was ready with the horn within nanoseconds of the light changing colour. Blume proceeded at a snail's pace through the junction. DF 145 LE overtook, shaking his fist as he sped by, then came to a halt 30 metres further on at the next traffic lights. A Skoda saloon behind him allowed two cars to steal into the lane. The Skoda had also sat still at the traffic lights. A patient driver driving a wise car, basically a Volkswagen with a different label, which meant it cost a few thousand less. It, or another Skoda, had been on Viale delle Province when he pulled out.

To the right was the road leading down to the university and the site of the shooting. He was going to be early, far earlier than any of his colleagues, to the Campidoglio. Without quite coming to a decision, he found himself turning down Via del Policlinico. Within a few minutes, he had returned to the site of the shooting, and he pulled up on to the kerb beside a group at a bus stop and got out. Casually glancing back, he saw the Skoda saloon arrive, pass him, the driver, a man with curly black hair, almost an Afro, staring straight ahead.

The wall was pockmarked by pollution and rain, but Blume had little difficulty in individuating the small clean chip mark left by the bullet. He placed his thumb in the hollow and stared up at the research institute opposite.

He glanced at his phone, and decided he had time. When he got to the other side of the street in front of the institute, he was more amused than intimidated to see, 50 or so metres distant, the back end of the Skoda sticking out where the driver had unsuccessfully tried to insert it into a small parking place. He pushed open the doors to the CNR building, gave the faintest of nods to a porter who was busy sucking a pencil and studying the *Settimana Enigmistica*, and walked down the hall.

Undisturbed, Blume wandered around the corridors of the building, peering into wards, a lab, several utility cupboards. The only challenge he got was when he tried to enter the radiology department. He showed his badge, received a shrug, and was warned the dangers were mainly to himself.

At the far end of the hall, through a door that gave every appearance of being locked but was not, he found a stairwell that smelled of lift grease and dust. He climbed up to the top floor, pausing at each level as he did so. Every communicating door was open, and the corridors were mostly empty. Finally, as he rounded the last flight of stairs, he was surprised to see a group of six people in white coats, smoking and holding small plastic cups. One of them, a young man with sideburns, stepped forward as if to say something, but Blume stared pointedly at the cigarette in the man's hand, and shook his head like one disgusted to see smoking in a public building. The man half hid the cigarette by cupping his hand, and stepped back. The little crowd then parted to let him through and he saw they were all standing in front of a coffee machine.

'This is the top floor?' he asked.

'The stairs stop here, so what do you think?' The speaker was a woman, and she had no cigarette in her hand. 'Who are you looking for?'

'No one. A place rather than a person.'

'Which office?'

'You're very nosy,' said Blume.

'No, that's you. You're the one walking about the premises. I work here.'

He imagined asking her out to dinner, and felt the stirrings of being turned on by the contempt that would drip from her voice.

She was still looking at him, with an expression that, if he didn't have Caterina . . .

'I suppose you want the room with the police tape stretched across it, and the lonely Carabiniere standing outside it?'

'That sounds like it might be the place,' said Blume.

'So you're a policeman?'

Blume showed her his badge, then, for good measure, flashed it at the rest of them. The young man with sideburns dropped his cigarette into his plastic cup and crumpled it up.

'That way, then,' said the woman pointing at the door into the corridor. 'The lift works, you know.'

'Yes. Just . . .' Blume patted his stomach. 'I thought I'd lose some weight.'

He did not expect her to say something like 'What would you want to lose weight for?', though that would have been nice, but he was hoping she would at least lower her glance and take in his presence. Instead, still gazing straight through him and speaking to him as if he were on the end of a phone line, she simply said, 'Second door on the left.'

The Carabiniere started smiling nervously when Blume was still a few metres away. The red flash of his police badge had been enough to convince the poor kid, who already thought he had done something wrong.

'Did you let someone in there?'

'No!'

'Captain Zezza is convinced you did. He's in a fucking rage downstairs. They're holding a reporter who says he went in, took some pictures, and is claiming you let him in. Zezza wants you down there.'

'I never . . .'

'You'd better go. I'll stand guard here till you're back. Hey . . .' He gave the kid a light punch on the shoulder. 'Good luck.'

The kid broke into a run before he reached the end of the corridor.

The seal on the door was intact, and Blume was not happy at breaking it. He pulled out his phone and called Principe, who did not pick up until about the tenth ring. He sounded exhausted.

'Did I wake you or something?'

'Yes.'

'Sorry. I thought you'd be in the office by now.' Blume took the phone from his ear to glance at the clock display. 'Well, maybe in half an hour.'

'I'm taking the day off,' said Principe.

'I am sorry to hear that.'

'Don't be. Also because I'd prefer not to talk about it on the phone. So . . .' The magistrate tried unsuccessfully to inject lightness into his tone, 'What are you breaking my balls about at this early hour?'

'Two things. There is a Carabinieri seal on a door here . . .'

'You're in the CNR building in front of the crime scene?'

'Exactly. I wanted to break the seal, have a look around inside. Can you OK that?'

Blume pulled back the tape, broke the seal, and pushed his way into the room, which was full of grey filing cabinets and stacks of red and blue hardcover books. The air was filled with the smell of must and rotting bookbinder glue. The window the shooter must have used was covered in dust, but thick flakes of cream paint lay on the sill and on the ground where it had been opened. The area directly in front of it had been disturbed, no doubt by the forensic team, but also by the shooter himself.

'You're in there already, aren't you?'

'Yes,' said Blume softly, unable to raise his voice to a normal pitch in a room that smelled so strongly of books.

'Just don't . . . don't trample all over it. Zezza will tell you all you need to know,' said Principe, the tiredness taking over his voice again.

'Can't you tell me now? Anything particularly interesting?'

'That's definitely the room the shots came from. Or shot. The shooter was very careful to leave no traces, and may even have been wearing a plastic suit from one of the labs. No DNA, no prints but the shooter made one very bad mistake.' Despite his evident exhaustion, Principe could not resist playing the magistrate game, hiding his hand, making Blume wait.

'Go on, then,' said Blume. He pushed up the window and leaned out. The sill was thin and the shot angled. Whoever fired was not doing it for the first time.

'If you go to the window – I am assuming you're there already, you can see that it's not a perfectly clear line to where Sofia was shot. So the shooter had to balance the rifle on the outside sill. It looks like he took more than one shot at Sofia, but we found no trace of the second bullet. Anyhow, the shooter lost a cartridge. It fell on to the street below. It was recovered and is still under examination.'

'You're still holding back.'

'I was hoping Captain Zezza would tell you all this, so he could build up a rapport with you.'

'I am sure we'll get on just fine no matter what,' said Blume. 'What about the cartridge?'

'It's a 7.35 × 51 mm calibre. Issued to the Italian army in 1938.'

'You mean a 7.62 × 51 mm,' said Blume.

'Nope. A 7.35 × 51 mm, apparently. Except it wasn't.'

'Because they don't exist,' said Blume.

'Not any more. But they did, once. They were used for the Carcano M38, which no one in the world used except for the Italian army. And

Lee Harvey Oswald, of course. So the cartridge alone identifies the rifle, which is quite a break. I wanted Zezza to tell you all this.'

'So you said. The shooter used a round from the end of the War? He's lucky it didn't blow up in his face. Presuming it's a he.'

'Lucky for him, unlucky for poor Sofia. Or he adapted his own ammunition. They need to examine the bullet that came out of the girl, but I'm told the wound was consistent with the type of bullet.'

'Meaning?'

'Horrible. A vile thing. The Carcano bullet was designed to be reasonably steady in flight, but the low velocity gave it some yaw as it travelled so that it became unstable as it hit flesh.'

'There is no such thing as a nice bullet,' said Blume. He looked out the window again. 'We're talking about 45 to 60 metres from here.'

'Fifty-two metres.'

'So it would take a good shot, but not have to be a marksman. As for the Carcano, doesn't every family in Italy have one in its attic?'

'I am sure there are plenty about, but not in working order. We're talking about someone who knows how to adapt ammunition.'

'Conclusion?' asked Blume.

'A collector. Ex-military, military, police. Or maybe someone with access to tooling equipment.'

'I see.'

'You said you wanted to ask me two things, Alec. What was the other?'

Blume held on to the window frame and turned away from the crime scene to look in the opposite direction. 'Yes, there was something. Are you having me followed?'

'What would I do that for?'

'That's a no?'

'Of course it is. Who's following you?'

'Someone who's not very good at it. No handover, no backup, no safety space, just a lone guy following me. He did manage to do a half-decent drive-by furiously ignoring me, but then ruined it all by picking a bad parking spot 50 metres farther on.'

'What street?'

'I don't know its name. Just off Piazza Aldo Moro.'

'You mean where you are now? You can see him?'

'The vehicle, not the occupant,' said Blume.

'Do you want me to send someone over?'

'No. I'd have done that myself,' said Blume. 'I think the best thing is to go down and talk to him.'

'That doesn't sound like a great idea.'

'Have you got a better one, Filippo?'

By way of reply, Principe made a sort of gurgling noise, followed by a long exhalation of breath.

'Are you all right?'

'No. No, I am not. Christ! I need to go, Alec.'

'What did I say?'

'Nothing. The pain comes in waves.'

'You could have told me. I wouldn't have bothered you.'

Blume left the room and followed the corridor to the far end, crossed another stairwell, went through an emergency door, and continued until he had reached the opposite end of the building to that he had entered.

Taking the lift down, he took a hard left and walked throughout a side door. As the door swung open in front of him into the rain, he caught sight of the shimmering outline of the man with the curly hair standing under an umbrella on the opposite side of the road. Blume would just walk behind him and –

'Hey!' The young Carabiniere was running towards him, his face no longer quite so innocent as it had been. 'Hey, you!' he repeated, all traces of deference gone from his voice.

Blume stepped outside into the rain and quickened his pace. The Carabiniere ran after him shouting, then caught up with him, and started to place his hand on his shoulder. Blume swung round. 'Don't even think of it.'

The commotion had attracted attention and as he watched, the umbrella closed and the man seemed to vanish with it.

'*Porco giuda! Deficiente!*' Blume cursed at the Carabiniere who stood back, suddenly uncertain again. Blume stepped into the road, almost under a bus. He jumped back and the bus passed him. He tried again, standing in a channel of water that soaked him up to the knee. The Skoda was nowhere to be seen. He spotted a high-backed vehicle moving faster than the others. One of the few not to have switched on its lights. Pushing at the skin on the side of his temple, he tried to bring the area around the number plate briefly back into focus. He might have seen a B as the first letter, and that was it, but then he realized that could not be right. The B registrations were from years ago, and the car was newer than that. Maybe an E, then.

The Carabiniere was standing beside him. The two of them were soaked through.

'You just lost me a lead.'

'You just lost me my job.'

'No, they won't fire you.'

They two of them walked back in silence to the building, passing empty conference rooms, labs with wooden tables, and orange hosepipes. Everything belonged to the 1940s and 1950s, when Italy was youthful and growing and even provided training for its scientists. No one stopped him, no one looked at him. He opened a door to where a meeting was going on, and they all turned to look at him, then continued talking.

'Now what are you doing?' said the Carabinieri. 'And how do you know Captain Zezza?'

'Maybe you should get back to your post?'

'I will in a minute. I need your name.'

'Commissioner Alec Blume,' he said opening another door, this one leading into a utility room. Two wheeled laundry carts were gathering dust. A pile of wrinkled plastic lab suits were piled like used condoms, on a black shelf containing detergents and plastic basins. Blume took one, and held it up. It was pretty much the same sort of CSI suit the police wore.

He balled it up and stuck it in his pocket. It bulged a little, but not very noticeably. He pulled it out again and unfolded it. The killer could have taken one beforehand, or improvised as he came in. A suit like this was perfect. It made you look like a lab technician who belonged in the building, it disguised you, and it made sure you left almost no DNA traces at the scene. He was convinced the killer had been wearing one of these suits. Almost certainly, he would have got rid of it thereafter, and these discarded suits should have been taken away by the Carabinieri for tests. He liked to think the Polizia would not have committed such an egregious oversight.

'What are you doing?'

'If I told you that Zezza may have missed something important here, what would you think?'

'You need to explain yourself better.'

Blume did. The young man nodded, taking it in. He seemed intelligent after all. He had been closely following the case in which they had assigned him such an unimportant role.

'Word of advice on how to cover your ass. Make your report about me,' said Blume. 'But don't file it. Have it ready if you find I destroyed evidence or something. Otherwise, who needs to know?'

'I am reporting the event and this conversation.'

'Good for you. You're right. How about we say you found these used jumpsuits, one of which might have been used by the shooter. Would that help?'

'I am still writing a truthful report.'

'I didn't say not to. I am just suggesting that if we agree that you rather than I found these jumpsuits, it might help neutralize the mistake you made. I'm not asking for anything in return.'

'It will mean you have a lie you can hold over me, Commissioner.'

Blume nodded. 'You'd better get back to your post, *appuntato*. You have too much integrity to go far,' he said.

As he drove down Via Cavour, the rain eased off and he opted for a detour by the Circo Massimo and a leisurely, luxury breakfast at Cristalli di Zucchero. Parking outside the rose garden and the American residence, he strolled down towards the United Nations building and, for old times' sake, bought himself a copy of the *International Herald Tribune*, being mildly surprised to find that it still existed. It had been his father's paper, or, better, it and the *Guardian Weekly* had been the newspapers for all the ex-pats in the days before the internet and globalization, in the days before graffiti and economic decline, in the days before the damned euro, 'in the days before Rock and Roll,' he said out loud in his best Van Morrison voice, drawing a sideways glance from an African woman hurrying to her UN job.

That reminded him, he needed to check out his new tenants – or did he? What was the etiquette? One thing he needed to do was tell Caterina he had finally rented out his apartment. She would appreciate that.

He spent a pleasant hour and a half in his own company, getting warm and dry again and even venturing into the crossword at the back of the newspaper, and reading the comic strips which, like the newspaper and the act of leisurely reading in the morning, seemed to belong to another, better age, when most people kept their thoughts to themselves, and opinionists were rare creatures that lived in newspapers, and nobody blogged.

Full of cappuccinos and pastries, and marvelling still at how much they had just made him pay, he drove up the winding hill behind the Vittoriano and parked his car next to an overexcited couple, him in a morning suit, her in a cream dress that cost more than the car they had come in, on their way to get married in the registry office. It was now about 11:40. Ten minutes late for a conference was like being half an hour early.

As he reached the portico of the Palazzo dei Conservatori, he noticed the groom was carefully following one of the lines of the white marble pattern set into the cobblestones, while his bride swept forwards across the ground, past Marcus Aurelius on his horse, holding up the hem of her wedding dress above her ankles but letting its trail sweep the wet ground behind. The young man was now looking up at the sky in wonderment at what he was getting himself into.

Blume climbed Michelangelo's elegant staircase, prepared to be bored and irritated in equal measure for the next two hours. He pushed the doors of the debating chamber open, then found himself staring straight down the aisle at the questore who was standing in front of a stature of Julius Caesar saying something about the burdens of responsibility. The questore stopped in mid phrase to stare at Blume, then continued, but not before everyone else had also looked at him. All the front row seats were taken. Blume slid into a seat next to a commissioner from Tor Vergata with pointed sideburns and a moustache who looked up from his game of Angry Birds on his mobile.

'Good entrance.'

'Thanks,' said Blume. 'How come everyone's early?'

'It's the cold, makes us all feel northern and efficient.'

'Still it's only ten minutes . . .'

'You know it was rescheduled to start at 9:30?'

'No! She told me 11:30.'

'Who?'

'She said it was put forward an hour. The meeting was moved forward an hour from 10:30: that makes 11:30.'

The commissioner destroyed a complex pig stronghold and rubbed his hands in satisfaction. 'Yes! They moved it forward by an hour. There was a circular. It's not as if you missed anything'. The commissioner's finger hovered over a slingshot containing a fat white bird, and he glanced at the object on Blume's lap. 'What's that?'

'It's called a Kindle. It's a sort of unfriendly book.'

'Let me see.'

Blume let him see, and waited patiently as the commissioner lost the place in the book, explored the submenus, and looked critically at an image of Mark Twain.

'It's all in English,' he said, handing it back.

18

Say you want to remember the contents of a business report, a book you just read, a film, or maybe a name, a face, or a childhood memory, a moment from the distant past. What do you do? You focus and focus and think and think and then in a flash it comes to you. Right?

The hell it does.

The more you obsess about what you can't remember, the less you remember what you can.

The trick, then, is to look away. Some people swear this is the best way to find actual objects not just thoughts. If you have lost your car keys, pretend for a bit that you're not looking for them and, hey presto, there they are!

My daughter tells me that this works because you lull the keys into a false sense of security, and they come out of their hiding place, which I think is a fantastic metaphor for what happens when we try to catch a thought. Remember, if it went into your head once, it is in there still.

So how can you practice this looking away? Well, one way would be for you to wait till the next time you forget something, which isn't very practical. The other way, which is the way we are going to do it, is for you to capture your dreams. Not all of them, because that is what crazy people do. Just some of them.

Capturing your dreams is beneficial in all sorts of other ways, too, especially if you are a creative person.

But wait, I can already hear the impatient ones among you, those less interested in creativity and more interested in exams and success, looking for short cuts to effective memory. OK, how about this: Marilyn Monroe: picture her. Now picture her nude. She was born in 1926 but died in 1962. The 'but' is there because her life was too short, but it also serves to draw attention to the reversal of numbers. Is this useful information? Perhaps not, but it sticks in the head, as does the image of her in the nude. Those dates and that image will still be in *your mind, bugging you at the end of this book, like a pesky pop song, which is just what you want when trying to memorize something.*

There seems to be a puritanical belief that learning should be abstracted, and involve no tricks. Personally, I think this comes from the fact the Puritans didn't like images. This was not a problem for medieval monks. Some of the holiest books have dirty pictures in them. And check out some of the scenes you get in the frescos and bas-relief of cathedrals in Europe. X-rated stuff, and totally memorable.

What about the idea that there is something lazy in using tricks to expand your memory? Well, our brains are busy things. They <u>have</u> to be lazy and a bit careless when dealing with stuff – including stuff such as seeing. We 'see' about 10 per cent of our surroundings. The rest we fill in. If you want to call that lazy, fine. In fancy talk, it is 'heuristic', which means making the most of a bad job (the bad job is done by the eyes, the brain does magnificent work with what it gets).

So we have the number reversal method, which George Orwell used in 1948 to name his book <u>1984</u>. There are other more useful tricks coming right up, don't worry.

I am going to go straight to the method that people find hardest to accept, the one they say is over-elaborate, and requires more work than is worth the effort. It is also the method used by those 'magicians' who can remember thousands of random numbers. These magicians are not cheats – and I am not just saying this because some of them are my best friends. But when people find out about how they learn all those numbers, they tend to say – 'Oh, but that's just a trick!' That, my friends, is where the puritanical impulse is hiding itself. Because a method is effective and maps the way we think, it is cheating to use it? If that is what you believe, close the book now.

Can't really do that with an e-book, thought Blume.

I am not just going to give you the trick here. Instead, I have chosen to include the 'Major System' or Memory Key as an appendix to the book. Why? Because those who already believe that you can learn 5 decks of cards, all your telephone numbers, history dates, and so on will go straight to the back of the book and learn it now. Those who don't will read on as sceptics. I welcome sceptics. I was once one myself. But as you continue, the contents of this book will start seeming more and more surreal as we start applying the system. Memorization using this

method draws on the same parts of your mind as dreaming, Dreams are surreal,
they can even be disturbing, but they are pretty easy. Easier than studying.
  So go to Appendix I at the end of my book. Or just read on.

Blume made a few fruitless attempts to get the e-book to go to the appendix, then gave up.

If you read the Appendix, you now command the means to remember any
number up to ten thousand. Learn those letters and the numbers associated with
them now – it's the hardest task in this entire book. If you didn't, I hope to
make you want to.
  How can you learn the system and, generally, what is a good method for
remembering? One method that I and many others have found very useful, as
well as extremely enjoyable, is called 'lucid dreaming'. As you lie in bed tonight
and the first odd thought comes into your head, the first thought that seems
slightly out of kilter, slightly illogical, let it float about for a moment, and then
accept that it was the first thought of a dream. Don't look at it too closely, or
you'll wake yourself up. And if you have problems in relaxing, let your mind
free-associate, float . . .

The commissioner from Tor Vergata gave him a sharp nudge and the
Kindle fell out of his hands and hit the floor with a clatter.
  'What?' roared Blume, furious at the assault and ready for battle.
  The questore paused in his speech. A roomful of inattentive and bored
people became momentarily alert and hopeful of amusement.
  'What … ?' repeated Blume more quietly.
  'You were snoring.'

19

THE *CORDONATA* leading down into Piazza Ara Coeli was glistening wet and treacherous in the midday sun, but Blume was still strongly tempted to walk down it, cut down past Piazza del Gesù, and get some air that, if not fresh, was at least cold and invigorating after the interminable conference and the breathy heat of dozens of public officials.

But the Municipal Police, who had their headquarters nearby, got quite defensive about parking rights on the Campidoglio. Odds were they'd leave his car alone, but even if they did, he'd still have to come back for it at the end of the day. His present desire for a wake-up walk was unlikely to recur in the evening, when it would be dark and probably raining again. So, reluctantly, he made his way to his car, and drove the short distance to the station, waving to the cop standing on the corner of Via della Gatta protecting the side of Palazzo Grazioli where, probably at this moment, Berlusconi and his followers were cavorting with a gaggle of girls. He liked them young and leggy. A baron with traditionalist tastes, essentially.

He was pretty sure by now that Caterina had deliberately failed to tell him about the conference being brought forward by an hour. Maybe to avoid an argument like they had last time, when she told him an interdepartmental meeting scheduled for a Wednesday had been moved forward by two days. For Blume, that meant it was now on the Friday; for Caterina, it meant Monday. The upshot was that he missed it.

He was going to have to disabuse her of the idea that their personal problems could be brought into the workplace. He might even discipline her, put a demerit in a report. It would shock her, but maybe that's what she needed.

He took the stairs rather than the lift, as he always had. Caterina had told him a while back that her French guru recommended always using the stairs. Blume, who had avoided lifts all his life, started using the one in the office for a week after that, just to make a point, but soon grew tired of it. All that helpless waiting, and standing still, door closing, and button pushing stressed him out. He liked to take stairs three at a time and feel the muscles on the back of his thighs contract and stretch as he did so.

No one noticed as he entered the operations room. He could see Caterina sitting at her desk, looking, he had to admit, pretty good this morning. Her diet might not be working as she had hoped, but he liked the flushed smoothness to her face and, for once, she seemed happy and relaxed. Beside her, on the same side of the desk, whispering to Caterina like an old friend, sat a figure capable of putting any woman in the shade, Olivia.

As Blume watched, he could see Agente Rospo bobbing up and down on the far side of the room, trying to steal glances at the two women. Meanwhile, the new sovrintendente from Corviale had found a reason to sit at the wrong side of his desk, which gave him a direct line of sight to Caterina's desk. Inspector Viviano, who rarely passed this way, had a file folder in his hand, and had stopped to lean against the cubicle partition and was still chatting to the two women about a funny bureaucratic moment in his life.

Olivia was drawing all gazes towards her and no one had seen him enter. The inspector continued trying to be entertaining. The look on Olivia's face, as she listened to him turning a non-event in his dull life into an anecdote with a punch line, was that of a vivisectionist watching the spasms of a dying animal on the table. As she turned away from the inspector and back towards Caterina, the detached and contemptuous expression lingered for a moment, before dissolving into a smile of complicity and sisterhood. Blume called out Caterina's name across the room and moved towards the group. The inspector was already pleading busyness and taking his leave, dislike for Blume stamped all over his big, lop-sided face.

Blume realized he had momentarily forgotten how young Olivia was. She could have been their daughter sitting there. No trace of contempt or malice remained on her face; on the contrary, she had the unclouded look of happiness that he had seen only on the faces of young people and children. He felt a sudden protective urge towards her, and guilty at the way he had projected his own negativity on to her.

'Commissioner!' said Olivia with a laugh. 'It's good to see you!'

'Why is it good to see me?'

'Because we have been talking about you all morning, haven't we?'

She turned to Caterina, who nodded and smiled both at her new friend and at Blume.

The waiter from the bar across the road arrived wearing an impeccable white uniform with gold braid. He bore a tray full of steaming cappuccinos, coffees, and pastries, which he set down on Caterina's desk. Everyone gathered around to help themselves.

'Is it someone's birthday?' he asked.

'No, no,' said Caterina. 'We just all felt like some decent coffee. We're going Dutch.'

Sure enough, everyone was settling up in pairs or separately with the barista, a young kid with a good head for figures. Panebianco came over, nodded at Blume, and paid for his cappuccino and pastries. 'How was the conference on racism?'

'Long.'

Even Rospo was invited to the party, though he paid for his coffee alone and took it straight back to his desk.

'We didn't order you anything,' said Caterina apologetically as the waiter left. 'We didn't know when, or if, you were coming.'

Olivia, who was sipping her cappuccino, which someone had paid for, waved her hand generously at the two pastries left on the tray. 'You can share mine. It's the one with the chocolate.'

'I'm fine,' said Blume.

Caterina picked up the other pastry, a hooked cornetto with a bright yellow *crema pasticcera* filling and bit into it, her eyes smiling at him before she had to tilt her chin upwards to catch the falling flakes and powdered sugar.

'Your diet!'

'I've given it up.'

Blume looked at Olivia, who winked at him. 'It'll be better for both of you. Trust me.'

'Look, I need to talk to you alone,' said Blume.

'Sorry, which one of us did you mean?' said Caterina, gently brushing the front of her blouse to remove sugar and pastry off the curve of her breast. She tore open a sachet of sugar and stirred it into her cappuccino, then lifted the phone on her desk. 'I'm going to call the bar, get them to bring you something. I can't bear to see you sitting there so miserable.'

'I'm fine,' said Blume. 'I have had my coffee and pastries today.'

Caterina used her bottom lip and tongue to clean foamed milk from her upper lip, and pointed at the remainder of her pastry. 'These are delicious. Try a bite.'

By way of reply, Blume turned to Olivia. 'Can I ask what you are doing here?'

He was alarmed and a bit frightened to see the girl's eyes suddenly seem to be brimming with tears.

'Thank you for asking, Commissioner. I am fine. I just suddenly had an image of Sofia.'

Blume looked at Caterina, then back at Olivia. 'Have you been talking about that?'

'Of course we have,' said Olivia. 'Chief Inspector Mattiola has been absolutely fantastic and so kind to me, and she has not stopped praising you either.' She quickly flicked a tear sideways from her eye. 'Sorry.'

'No, that's . . . not exactly, but you weren't to know . . . what made you come here?'

She tilted her head slightly as if appraising him, then reached out and touched him briefly on the arm, before drawing back, as if slightly confused by her own actions. 'I came to see you. I came to apologize for the unfriendly reception I gave you last night and my poor behaviour the other day. I have discovered that I react to grief with aggression. It sounds strange, but maybe you can understand it?'

'Understand it? He invented it,' said Caterina.

'Well, I guess you two have things to talk about,' said Olivia, standing up.

'What things? Where are you going now?'

'I came by to apologize. I have done that now,' said Olivia.

'She waited here all morning for you,' said Caterina. 'Now I know where you were last night, by the way.'

Olivia nodded with the air of a sage marriage counsellor. 'People often refuse to offer the simplest, most innocent explanations. I never understood that. The truth is always best, isn't it?'

'Lies have short legs,' said Caterina.

Blume looked at Olivia's long legs and nodded.

'How did Marco behave himself last night?' Olivia asked Blume. 'He's a nervous type, you know. Making him feel better about himself is my project.'

'Your project?'

'Yes. He's my project,' said Olivia. 'Nothing wrong with that I hope?'

'I thought he was your boyfriend.'

'He's that, too.'

'Olivia, can you step into my office?'

She glanced at the white gold watch on her wrist, as if time was suddenly of the essence, then said, 'Sure!'

His intention had been to demand to know how much she had told Caterina, but as he closed the door, he realized it would make him look weak. He had a feeling that Olivia had already worked out for herself that he was running a sort of one-man show.

She disconcerted him. She was transformed, like she had drunk some magic potion. Sexy, provocative, pouty – and therefore essentially irritating as well as attractive – yesterday evening; now she was beautiful, relaxed, and poised. Her hair, which had been sprayed and lacquered flat yesterday, now unruly and thick and carelessly pushed back, her eyes deep and dark and searching as she waited for him to say something.

'Is Marco really your boyfriend?' It was the best he could come up with.

'Of course! Poor Marco is one of those guys who just can't manage by themselves.'

'He'd be lost without you?'

She touched her chest with her hands in a flutter of self-deprecation. 'It's not me. I am nothing special. Marco is just one of those men, boys, who can't manage by himself. It would be so cruel to leave him. He's not strong like you. Can I leave now?'

He agreed, and watched her as she graciously bade farewell to all the other cops, some of whom had seen all the tricks. Even Panebianco seemed charmed.

He tried contacting Principe again, to no avail. The magistrate had failed to put him in contact with Captain Zezza.

He came out of his office a few minutes later with the intention of asking Caterina about Olivia and perhaps repairing a few broken bridges, but found she was not there.

He called over to Panebianco, who told him Caterina had been asked to pay a visit to Magistrate Martone. 'Something about that hit-and-run case.'

'Adelgardo Lambertini? Any progress there?'

'The opposite of progress, to judge from her face. I think a witness she thought she had secured has withdrawn his testimony. A barber. The magistrate will blame Caterina instead of herself. Good news for old Lambertini, though.'

20

Wither the aid of Google images, Blume identified the car that had followed him that morning as probably a Skoda Octavia saloon. He leaned back in his chair and closed his eyes, trying to bring back the details. He imagined himself coming down the stairs of the research institute, noticing the rain, the man with the curly hair standing in the rain. Why would he do that? Presumably because he was looking to see where Blume had got to. Had he been standing there for long, for all the time he had been inside?

A thought was pushing itself to the front of his mind and frustrating his attempts at relaxed recall: why he had failed to call backup? All it would have taken was a phone call, a patrol car would have been there within minutes, they could have pulled up beside the Skoda, asked the driver to step out, and then he would know who was following him. So why had he not done it? Pride. He thought he could handle it easily himself, outmanoeuvre his follower by coming out of another door. It was a reasonable assumption, seeing as the person was no professional. But he had blown it.

The best way to remember was to think of things around the object, such as that bus that almost knocked him down. Bastard. The car was silver-grey, same as all the other cars, same colour as the rain.

He was going to fall asleep. He could feel it. That was no good. Maybe Aaron Fisher had some advice on recall. Not that recall had much to do with memory.

He pulled the Kindle out of his bag. Part of him was disappointed to discover the search feature. He was hoping the product would be more useless.

Simonides: The man who knew where the bodies are buried

Recalling faces is a funny business. You may not be able to conjure up the face properly, but when you see the person again, you have no problem in recognizing them. You may forget the name, but probably not the face. Even if you cannot call up the features of a face, you often 'feel' the identity in your head. For instance, think of the last time you were at a meeting, or sitting in a classroom. Now try to recall the person to your left. Or just try to recall one or two people. Not only will at least one come to mind, you will also remember where they were sitting. And this, folks, is the second big secret of all those memory masters, of those people who can recall lists of emperors, presidents, pi, mathematical formulae, all the bones of the human skeleton, and, a popular one these days, all the cards played in a game of poker or bridge. I am about to tell you this great secret, which, in fact, is not so much a secret as something that was forgotten for many years and is now being recalled. But it is great, and it will help you ace your exams and acquire considerable knowledge with far less effort than you thought possible. Ready? Yes, well, first, I want you to go back, and check you have really learned the Memory Key. Done that? Really? OK, then we have time for a little story.

It concerns a Greek poet called Simonides of Ceos (I like to think of him as Simon), who lived around 550 years before Christ. He was, they say, a bit of a miser, but very good at writing victory poems – boastful ditties for kings and warlords. If he were alive today, he'd be composing songs for Mexican drug lords, or, maybe he'd go it alone as a rapper singing his own praises.

One day, Simonides was at a banquet in the palace of a rich guy called Scopas, who had asked him to write some poems in which the hero was . . . you guessed it: Scopas. But the poet put in too many references to the twin gods Castor and Pollux, sort of squeezing Scopas out of the picture, and, to make matters worse, there was a whole room full of guests to witness this insult. And so Scopas decided that he would not pay Simonides for his poems after all.

At this point, a messenger came in to say there were two young fellows outside who were seeking Simonides. So the poet, suspending his row with Scopas, went out to see who they might be and what they wanted him for. It turns out the two fellows waiting for him looked pretty darned alike. Like two twins. Like the twin gods, Castor and Pollux, whose praises he had just been singing, in fact.

As Simonides stepped out of the doorway, an earthquake struck the city. Down came the palace behind him, crushing Scopas and all the guests. The twins, being magical, vanished, and there was Simonides standing beside a pile of rubble and feeling lucky and – well, we'd have to know him a bit better, but there might have been a part of him that was pretty pleased at what happened to

Scopas. Not to the guests, though. In fact, soon the mothers, wives, children came running and there was great lamentation. Not only had all the poor guests been killed, but the collapsing rubble had disfigured them horribly. No one could identify the bodies of their loved ones. Maybe we'd call in the FBI and use dental records nowadays, but this was ancient Greece.

Simonides snapped his fingers and said, 'Wait a minute! I remember where they were all sitting and who was who.' And he walked around, pointing to one corpse after another, pronouncing the name of each one.

It was not a great feat, but it got him to thinking. It is easy to remember the position of real things. Just try it now. In your mind's eye, think of the furniture in your sitting room. Now the furniture in your best friend's sitting room. Pretty easy, isn't it?

Simonides developed a system for remembering that has become known by several names. The Memory Theatre, the memory room method, the memory palace, and the 'loci' method. Loci is just Latin for location, and the Latin is used because Roman orators, and later medieval monks, used and refined Simonides method.[1]

Anyhow, in the method I want to show you, theatres don't come into it. We'll just call it the 'mental walk'. And instead of saying 'locus', we'll say 'stop point'.

Now there are two schools of thought about where we should go next with this. One school says that the best mental walk is one that takes you around your own house, school, or neighbourhood. After all these are places you know very well. There is no remembering to be done. The other says that it is better to invent a place in your head, and 'walk' your way through it. The effort is a little greater to begin with, but the results are better. Why would this be so? Well, one reason is that a mental walk that brings you into, say, your son's room, might bring up the image of your son and the smell of his trainers, and much as you love him (that's why he comes so readily to mind), he might be 'in the way' of something you are trying to remember. Sad to say, but the best memory palace is a lonely place.

RULE: Whether you use your own house or the place I am about to describe, you must be absolutely consistent in your route. Make sure you know which room leads to which. Do not change direction. Never change the route.

---

[1] Some writers, including some contemporary ones, have tried to copyright the ideas of Simonides, a guy who lived 2,500 years ago. I'd say that qualifies for public domain by now. I even know of an Italian professor who seems to think that no one else should have the right to use the title 'The Memory Key' for a book. Good luck with that one, Professor!

The other reason I want to create an imaginary place is that I am here and you are there. I don't know what your house is like! And the people reading this book will have all sorts of houses, so we need a common virtual ground.

This place may sound lonely, but remember, there are thousands of us who are familiar with it, or with a version of it, since each will be very slightly different from the next, like parallel universes.

But, you've guessed it, I have relegated the palace to the back of the book. Appendix II . . .

For fuck's sake. Blume went online and ordered a proper version of the book. There.

21

Dinner with Caterina that evening was conducted in the sort of stilted silence that used to make him hate his parents when they did it. He could see Elia stealing furtive glances at them both. Poor kid was dying to say something, find out what was going on and stop it, or just break the evil mood. The looks he was directing at Blume were no more hostile than those at his mother, which made Blume feel grateful and suddenly tender.

It only took him three minutes to wolf down his pasta. Caterina took her fourth or fifth forkful and eyed him levelly. He had complained in the past about her pushing food around her plate, but he was not going to bring that subject up tonight. She seemed to be considering making one of her remarks about him eating like a savage, but whoever made the first criticism would become the guilty party in Elia's eyes, so they both held their peace.

Elia, closer to Blume than his mother in eating speed, fidgeted.

'I was followed today,' said Blume suddenly, addressing himself more to Elia than to Caterina.

Elia's eyes widened. 'Who by?'

'Some amateur,' he said. 'Nothing to worry about.'

'This is the first I am hearing about it,' said Caterina.

'I didn't give it much thought.'

'Is it in connection with the university thing?'

'Possibly.'

'Did you get a look at the person, the vehicle?'

Blume relented. He had not wanted to discuss the case with Caterina, but he couldn't think of anything else to talk about. Besides, Elia seemed to be enjoying the break in the tension.

When he had finished telling an abbreviated version of his morning, Caterina said, 'So did you look up the reports of stolen vehicles afterwards?'

'No,' said Blume.

'How do you know the car was stolen?' Elia asked his mother.

'She doesn't,' said Blume, 'but it is an intelligent suggestion. It shows she is cleverer than me.'

'I don't get it,' said Elia.

'If what Alec has been telling us is the truth, love, and the person following him was really an amateur, and he is not just saying that to put my mind at ease, then we have three options: the person was driving his own car, he was driving a friend's, or he was driving a stolen one.'

'That applies to anyone in a car,' said Elia.

'You're right, of course. But let us suppose that this person now fears that Alec has the details, then he may well be tempted to report the car stolen. That's what some people do in a hit-and-run. They report their own car stolen. It never works, but they do it. It makes our task easier, because they give a full description of the car, make, model, registration, none of which was known before. Then we find the car and we find the owner, and usually the owner is the guilty party, or his best friend is. It's depressingly easy.'

'Sometimes,' said Blume, 'they report the car stolen *before* using it for a criminal act.'

'So they are driving around with intent in a car that is on a watch list?' asked Elia. 'Nobody can be that dumb.'

The two of them turned and spoke almost in unison.

'Oh, yes they can,' said his mother.

'Dumber than that, even,' said Blume. He surreptitiously swiped his thumb across his empty plate and sucked it. 'That was delicious pasta, Caterina.'

'Thank you.'

'All that effort, you could have made a little more?'

The following morning, they drove in to work together. The sun had made a glorious comeback and every surface was glistening. Even his car looked bright and new.

'I can look for reports of a stolen Skoda Octavia when I get in, keep my eye open during the day,' said Caterina.

Blume patted her knee, 'I appreciate that.'

She swung her legs towards the door. 'Don't do that. It's patronizing, and the fact you mean it humorously makes it worse. And you never really explained who you think might be following you.'

Blume put both hands on the steering wheel and looked straight ahead.

'There is something important I need to tell you,' she said.

'Go on.'

'I think . . .' A rippling roar and a figure flashed in front of them, but Blume continued driving without interruption, as if nothing had happened. If anything, he had accelerated a little. '*Dio mio!* Alec, did you not see that motorcyclist?'

'I saw him,' said Blume. 'And he saw me, the fucker. If he wants to drive like that, it's his funeral.'

'You can't just . . .'

'I didn't do anything. I kept going straight at the same speed. If he wants to cut in at speed inches from a vehicle on a wet road, that's his problem. Sooner or later he'll slide under someone's car.'

'Let's try not to make it ours, OK?'

'You're talking as if I aimed at him.'

'You didn't try to avoid him.'

'Not the same thing.'

'Sometimes I don't understand you,' said Caterina.

'I am easy to understand. I'll tell you what's hard to understand is motorcyclists who think they're immortal. They try to bully you on the road as if they were in a Sherman tank or something, but it's the other way round. Just the tiniest tap with your car and they go skittering across the road like rag dolls.'

Caterina stared out the side window. Her husband, Elia's father, had been killed while on a motorcycle. Maybe by a driver like Blume. No doubt Blume had forgotten this detail of her husband's death, which in some respects made it worse. He had been a better man than the one beside her now.

It was not until they were heading across Piazza Venezia that Blume said, 'You were going to say something?'

'Was I?' said Caterina. 'Maybe I was going to say I'll drive myself in tomorrow.'

★

Blume spent the entire morning writing up a report for a magistrate on his minor role in what turned out to be an interesting enough case of a jeweller's wife organizing to have herself robbed by a gang that was supposed to return some of the proceeds, but then did not. The police had still been chasing up the identity of the gang members and examining some video evidence when the wife walked in and named them all.

He made a special effort to be succinct. He rather prided himself on it, even though he knew it was regarded as a failing by certain magistrates, whose love of formal language and meandering, inconclusive sentences knew no bounds. Once, paraphrasing someone, he had added a note, 'I am sorry this report is so long, I did not have time enough to write a shorter one', and the magistrate called him in and reprimanded him for facetiousness.

At mid morning, he phoned Principe, who turned out to be at home.

'Not feeling well?' asked Blume.

'No.'

'I could call round.'

'No.'

'I am coming around anyhow.'

22

BLUME WAS shocked into a sudden sympathy when Principe opened the door. The magistrate's fine suits had hidden a lot. Now that he was dressed in a round-necked sweatshirt and loose-fitting tracksuit bottoms, he seemed three times thinner and 30 years older.

'I seemed thin, but not emaciated, right? I know. I didn't quite realize it myself until I looked in the mirror this morning. I almost never look in the mirror.'

'Me neither,' said Blume irrelevantly.

'The Gemcitabine they were giving me made me vomit, the cancer kills my appetite. Weight Watchers have got a lot to learn from me. I think I'll write a book. Any ideas for a title?'

'*Yes, we cancer,*' suggested Blume.

'I was thinking more along the lines of "Fast, pray, and die".'

'That's good, too.' It seemed inconceivable that three minutes ago he had still been intending to attack Principe for the way he was conducting, or not conducting, his inquiries. Now he had a different criticism. 'Why the hell did you stay at work?'

'What else could I do with my life?'

Blume felt aggrieved. Principe had just given him an emotional sucker punch. 'You could have given me fair warning.'

Principe pressed his hand to the small of his back and grimaced. 'Alec, I am so sorry. I didn't know it was going to suddenly be this bad.'

But Blume's anger was not satisfied yet. 'Why the hell were you drinking when I met you?'

'I was trying to hurry things along,' said Principe.

'That's just . . . irresponsible.'

'Maybe, but it worked. Since then I have been hardly able to move.'

'What about hospital?'

'What about it? I want to die here, in my own house.'

'Yes, but there is no one here to help. You can't. Actually, I think it's illegal for me to walk out of here now without calling an ambulance.'

'Failure to provide emergency aid, pursuant to Article 593 . . .'

'I am being serious.'

'I know.'

'We all die alone anyhow.'

'Where is your daughter?'

'United States. Where you came from once.'

'Call her.'

'I can't. I don't have her number. I don't know where she lives.'

'How did that happen, Filippo?'

'You suspect me now, don't you? I must have done something terrible to lose her like that. I didn't. It's not always the parents who are at fault. Evil can be spontaneous, and emerge in a child for no reason.'

'You can't call your daughter evil,' said Blume.

'Evil is a stupid word.' Principe fell silent as he breathed heavily through his nose. Sweat slid off his forehead. 'Selfish. She simply never cared for us. We were never good enough. It broke her mother's heart.'

'I definitely remember your mentioning a grandson, once. You went to the beach. That was with her, I assume. It wasn't so long ago.'

'Six years. There was some idea the grandchild might bring us all together again. I didn't even like the boy all that much.'

'It sounds like you might have something to do with the rift. I'll call her.'

A sudden burst of energy passed through Principe's body. 'No! That would be gross interference.' Even the yellow pallor around his eyes whitened for a moment as he stared at Blume. 'She did not come to her mother's funeral, I don't want her by my deathbed.'

'I'm not a psychiatrist −' began Blume.

'No, you're not.'

'But . . . look, you told me you were sort of in love with that young girl, Sofia. That's why you called me in.'

'I'm sorry. I think that was a side effect of the drugs. In fact, it seems I got you into this mess as a result of a pharmacological side effect. All life is chemicals reacting and running into each other anyhow. Still, I'm sorry.'

'Stop apologizing. Did Sofia remind you of your daughter?'

'It's logical you should think that.'

'Well, did she?'

'No. She reminded me of my wife. We married when we were very young.'

'Why didn't your daughter come to the funeral?'

'I don't know. Ask her. That is to say, don't. Don't contact her.'

'She's your child. If I had a child . . .'

'You might end up very disappointed. Look, I was going to call you anyhow, apologize, and tell you to forget about the case, if you can. It doesn't matter. I don't need to know what happened. I thought I did, but I've done with it all now. Sorry.'

'*Porco Dio*, Filippo. Stop apologizing. Did you put me on the case to see you die?'

'Maybe. For the company.'

'You could have chosen someone better.'

'Not true. I am not as good a person as you think I am, Alec. You can tell just by looking at my address. If I was completely clean, I wouldn't live here on Via della Pigna. Have you any idea what this place is worth?'

'Your annual income is pretty high, and you've been living here for some time. I am sure it was cheaper when you bought it.'

'Not that much cheaper, and my annual income is €66,000. My pay grade does not account for 300 square metres on the top floor of this building, and it never did. You think I'm exaggerating? Sure, this house is small enough, but here's something I bet you didn't know: my neighbours pay me rent. That doubles my income, and I declare only one of the rents. I also have considerable savings. Several million. How do you think that happened? And what was the point of it anyhow?'

'I don't need to know this.'

'You might find it is of interest to you. Will you visit again?'

Blume realized he was being dismissed and stood up and walked across the oak floor and past the polished mahogany and the dull shine of the solid gold mantel clock and the tarnished silver plates, the scrolls and coin display case, and reached the triple reinforced door.

'I could drop in anytime. It's a 45-second walk from the station.'

'No need.'

'I will anyhow. I want to clear up a few things with this Captain Zezza.'

'Sure. Or I'll leave a message.'

'And your daughter?'

'I'll think about it.'

23

As he left Principe's apartment, Blume called Pitagora, and announced that he wanted to see him.

'I am at home, and my invitation to you still stands, Commissioner. I hope you won't bore me with too many questions. I am interested in you personally. You are a melancholic, with a strong impulse towards self-destruction. Sometimes you mix fact with fiction, and you sometimes find that you can't quite distinguish between what you dreamed and what really happened. Am I right?'

As if he was going to answer that.

Pitagora continued: 'This may seem a drawback for an investigator, but it is not. It gives you depth of vision, you see. You get the details wrong, but you can see into the heart of matters. Sometimes you know you are right without knowing why.'

'Enough of the horoscopes, Professor.'

'That was no horoscope. Still, if I had to guess I'd say you must be an Aquarius. It fits you to a T. Honest and loyal, independent and intellectual but also intractable and contrary, perverse and unpredictable, unemotional and detached.'

Blume felt a slight thrill of shock and then pleasure. Then, as his intellect reasserted itself, he suddenly felt foolish.

Pitagora giggled. A girlish sound. 'That got you for a moment, didn't it? I looked up your date of birth. Astrology is a false science. But the interesting thing is I managed to get through your defences just by recognizing some of your qualities. That's what I'd like to talk you about.'

'And I'd like to talk to you about the shooting of Stefania Manfellotto and now the murder of an innocent girl.'

'I am not sure I want to talk about that any more, and you can't make me. On whose authority are you acting?'

'My own for now. Principe's, too, if I ask.'

'This is not in your best interests, commissioner. You risk reprimands, suspension, your career, all for what, a whim?'

'It's what I do.'

'Your will to power, Commissioner. *Wille zur Macht*. Come round later, then: after three? *See you later, alligator.*'

Blume had to block an almost Pavlovian urge to reply, '*after a while a crocodile*'. How the hell had Pitagora picked up on that phrase?

Blume had turned away from the station with a vague idea of walking off the bad feeling he had got from Principe. As he marched purposefully with no destination in mind down Via del Gesù, dodging the puddles and scooters, he found he was now hitting the pavement rhythmically as the song expanded in his head. '*Well, I saw my baby walkin' with another man today . . .*'

The phone in his hand rang, and he looked down at the name. About time, he thought to himself as he answered.

'Commissioner Blume?'

'Captain Zezza?'

'Correct. I think we should meet.'

'How about now?' said Blume.

'I agree. Will you lift your left hand a moment?'

'I beg your pardon?' said Blume. He had reached the end of the street and was looking across the Piazza del Gesù.

'Please just do as I say.'

Blume was reluctant to obey, but he understood the request. He lifted up his arm and waved. A tall man with a square chin like a comic book superhero, standing on the steps of the Jesuit church, raised a furled umbrella and waved back. They put their phones away at the same moment; Blume crossed the road and joined the captain in the middle of the square.

Captain Zezza was as tall as Blume, which was rare. Dressed in a charcoal suit and looking as much like a Carabiniere as was possible without actually wearing a uniform, he held out his hand. Blume took it, and Zezza crushed his fingers, while staring at him with intense blue eyes. His hair was so closely cropped it had no colour, but the overwhelming impression was of whiteness and hardness. His whole head seemed like a large molar.

'How did you know I was coming here?' asked Blume.

Zezza rubbed his broad chin. 'Ah, a coincidence. I don't much like coincidences. I was going to ask you the same question.'

'I didn't know you were here,' said Blume.

'Good, good. That answers that then,' said Zezza, his brow unfurrowing. 'You are here by chance. I called by to speak personally, and I found out you were at the magistrate's. I thought I would let you and him talk for some time, and I came here to pray for him. As I came out of the church, I called you, and I saw a man answering your description bring a phone up to his ear. I am taking this to be a good omen.'

'Pray for him?'

'Yes, I pray. I don't think it is very effective, but it is a healthy mental discipline. Have you had lunch?'

Zezza led the way to a place in the Jewish Ghetto. The food was not good, and the service was terrible. The owner was sulky and the decor was depressing, but none of this seemed to matter to Zezza who ordered a salad and a sports drink.

Blume decided a toasted sandwich would be fine. Well toasted, he specified. Almost burnt.

Zezza smiled and placed a square-shaped thumb into the dimple that appeared on his cheek and stroked his eyebrow with his index finger and stared intently at Blume.

'Magistrate Filippo Principe is most unwell.'

'I know.'

'Anyone who meets him can tell he is ailing, poor man. Resolving the killing of this girl is very important to him. It's his last case.'

'Let's not be too hasty.'

'He says he has seen you grow up over the years. He's proud of you, I think. He sees you as very worthy but very . . . well, it's not for me to say.' The captain turned the side of his smooth face towards Blume and looked away for a moment. 'Principe is handing over the case to a colleague. It is all for the best.'

'So I expect you want me to pass on everything I know to you?' said Blume, with more than a hint of challenge in is voice.

'Oh, I don't expect you know anything, really,' said Zezza. 'Nothing that we don't know already.'

A burnt cheese sandwich arrived. Blume ignored it. Zezza ate a lettuce leaf.

Blume tentatively suggested the attempted murder and murder were unconnected with the victims of the 1980 bomb, just to see if he drew any response from the captain. Nothing. He hinted the attack on Manfellotto might have something to do with the hidden politics, which, in fact, was something he had now stopped believing. To all that he said, the captain nodded in a matter-of-fact way, occasionally picking out pieces of carrot from his salad and inserting them between his square teeth. The reuse of the weapon, Blume observed, was unprofessional, as was the choice of weapon itself. The captain nodded slowly and chewed, but said nothing. He drank some of his bright orange drink.

'And what about the convergence between Manfellotto and Sofia? Have you checked what she was doing in London, her colleagues at the Health Institute?'

'Yes, we have.'

'And?'

'I do not think it is your concern. This is your handing back to me what you should never have touched to begin with.'

'Speaking of things not being touched . . .' Blume mentioned the plastic jumpsuits in the CNR offices, and was pleased to see a crack in the captain's vexatious self-composure.

Zezza finished his salad and placed his fists on either side of the bowl. Blume could see the shape of his muscles through his jacket. 'We made a mistake there,' he admitted. 'But the chances are slim that he wore one of the suits you found there. Which you should not have touched, of course.'

'Little mistake by me. Big mistake by you guys.'

'Oh no, not so big, really,' said the captain. 'Not compared to sending away a Carabinieri guard under false pretenses and breaking a seal.'

Blume pushed away his cheese sandwich. 'This is a horrible place, by the way.'

Unexpectedly, Zezza grinned. 'Yes. It is an awful place, and the owner's a crook. But it is quiet. No customers, see. And the owner likes to stay as far away from me as possible. Now, I am sorry you got dragged into this without a proper briefing. I realize you are a friend of the magistrate, and you were doing him a favour.'

Blume nodded.

'At the risk of angering you on behalf of your friend, it was apparent from the outset that magistrate was not up to the task. At the start, we presented him with our findings as we made them, but it was soon clear that he did not quite understand them, or was ignoring them. His orders were vague and contradictory, and if we had really followed them, we would have wasted a lot of time. So we did what you do when the magistrate theoretically in command is an incompetent . . .'

'He has cancer,' said Blume outraged. 'Terminal.'

'In my prayer earlier, I hypothesized cancer.'

'If you get the prognosis wrong, does Jesus ignore you?' asked Blume.

The captain leaned his bulk back into the chair, which squeaked in protest. 'I see you are a non-believer. Where is the poor man's cancer?'

'Oesophagus, but the thing with cancer is it goes everywhere in the end.'

'Drinking,' said the Captain, shaking his large head in sad reflection. 'I notice he drinks. Lead paint in old buildings, the dust from file folders, living in the centre of Rome as he does. These are all aggravating factors. I live in Casal Palocco. The air is better there.'

'What about the long drive in every morning? All those cars and fumes in front of you?'

'I get up early, miss the traffic. Does the magistrate smoke?'

'Toscano cigars,' said Blume.

'Well, there you go, then,' said the captain, completely satisfied.

'So you started withholding evidence from him?'

'Not withholding, Commissioner. You are deliberately taking the wrong attitude. And I am sure you have done the same thing yourself in the past when faced with incompetent or not entirely honest magistrates. We made sure the evidence was unequivocal and complete, then we presented it. I have sought to make the magistrate's life simpler. The sniper on the top floor, we discussed that with him. He seems not to have grasped its significance.'

'Which is?'

'I don't think you need to know.'

'I think I do.'

'No, I am afraid not, Commissioner. And now the case passes under the command of a new magistrate. Alice Saraceno. A very able woman. Please, do not interfere in this case any further. I can see you are a wise and cautious man from the fact you did not eat that cheese sandwich.' The captain stood up and retrieved his furled umbrella.

'Wait!' said Blume. 'The target was moving towards the shooter.'

The captain propped his umbrella against the wall again, and tilted his head inquisitively. 'Explain.'

'You know exactly what I mean,' said Blume.

'I re-enacted the shooting from that room. There is no reason for the shooter to have delayed until the last moment as Manfellotto crossed the courtyard below. The shot was fired just as she was about to leave the line of sight. At the very last moment, in other words. The hardest shot possible. I can't think of a good reason for that, can you?'

'Maybe the shooter was nervous, and had doubts.'

'I thought about that, too,' said Blume. 'But that does not fit in with the idea that this was a political assassination of some sort. All right, it might be that. I am sure political assassins get nervous sometimes, and some assassins may have last-minute second thoughts, but it is simpler to assume that whoever pulled the trigger had made up his or her mind, and fired at the earliest opportunity, knowing that even if the first shot missed, it was unlikely the target would even notice, and would keep coming closer. Are you following me?'

'The person moving towards the shooter was Sofia Fontana,' said Zezza.

'Precisely,' said Blume.

'You believe Sofia was the intended target?'

'And you don't?' Blume didn't hide his surprise. He had fully expected Zezza to be following the same line or logic. Now he was not sure.

'Not Manfellotto?' asked Zezza.

'No! Manfellotto was the unintended victim. In a delicious twist of fate, she was the innocent bystander.'

Zezza wiped his mouth with the back of his hand. He looked worried, which was gratifying.

'Before the station bombing,' continued Blume, 'she murdered two young Carabinieri. So it's easy for you people to imagine she is the victim in her turn of an assassination attempt. But I did not think this consideration would be blinding you. The person walking into the line of fire was the person the shooter was aiming at. Sofia. But surely you knew this? You were disappointed that Principe had not worked it out, which is why you were not cooperating fully with him.'

'No, Blume. We were worried by the magistrate because his health is failing. He is slow to issue orders and has difficulty in following details. Your theory about Sofia is interesting.'

Zezza had put all his effort into controlling the tenor of his voice and trying to come across as sceptical and a little bored, but Blume had seen the look in his eyes as he took in the explanation. He was sorry now he had played his winning hand so badly. He had given the Carabinieri captain the key and got nothing in return. At this point, he may as well do his best to push the captain in the right direction. Maybe he could count on gratitude later.

'What about the fact that no further moves were made against Manfellotto?' said Blume. 'If having her dead was so important, wouldn't they try again?'

'She's practically brain dead, from what I hear, why risk it?' said Zezza.

'She's alive, she could remember and become a risk.'

'I am going to let you in on a little secret here, Blume,' said the captain, his moment of doubt beginning to dissipate. 'We only apparently left that room unguarded. It has been under observation just in case. Or it was. After a few weeks, we ended the surveillance. Too much manpower. No one turned up.'

'Which is my point!' said Blume in exasperation. 'She was not the target. No one is out to get her. If someone had made a second attempt on her, then, yes, I would clearly be wrong, but no one has. Sofia was the target. One miss, one hit.'

Zezza's eyes darted sideways as if to check that no one was listening. 'I may look into your theory, Blume.' He was still modulating his voice to sound bored, Blume could see he had at least managed to plant a seed of doubt. Zezza's movements were a little hurried now, and though he made a show of favouring Blume with an indulgent smile, he spoiled the effect by striding out too quickly.

Blume looked at the retreating figure and at the umbrella he had left propped against the wall. He did not call out. It was a nice umbrella with a real wood handle.

24

With his new umbrella held up against the rain, only a light drizzle now, Blume walked towards the University Hospital, which adjoined the Umberto I Polyclinic. He would make one more round of the people in the case, starting with Stefania Manfellotto, then the professor, just in case the Carabinieri were right and he was wrong. If nothing interesting came from them, then he would finally let it go.

This time he had to use his police badge several times over before he was finally allowed through to the neurology department and into the ward where Stefania lay alone, asleep. It was as if the other day, in the rain, the hospital had decided to suspend its vigilance and suspicion of visitors, perhaps because of some instinctive feeling that a public building in the rain, like a church in war, was a legitimate place of refuge.

The shutters in the room were drawn halfway down, and the dullness of the day meant very little light was filtering in. The room was surprisingly cold, too, which he welcomed, rather than the stifling heat that made hospitals doubly unbearable. He approached the sleeping woman quietly. Although he had come to speak to her, he did not dare to wake her up. It might harm her, and she might scream. He walked over and looked down at her face, which, since he had seen her last, seemed to have grown smoother and younger. The bandaging around her head had been changed, and her hair had already grown back to the length of that mad Irish singer he remembered had ripped up a picture of the pope. What was her name? It had something to do with quietness or shade.

He needed to call someone into the room. A helpless woman in a room like this, a man standing over her. A woman who was the object of great hate, and who was the victim of a murder attempt. This sleeping, ageing, damaged, and vulnerable woman had killed two Carabinieri and 80 civilians.

'Are you a relative?'

The voice, deep and full of authority, came out of the darkest corner of the room.

'Jesus Christ,' said Blume, spinning round. 'Don't do that! Were you there all the time?'

The man stepped out of the shadows. He was elderly but robust, with a broad chest. He was wearing a white doctor's coat and had a white beard and wore shining round spectacles. If anything, he should have been particularly visible in the shade, but Blume, who fancied himself as observant, had missed him.

'I repeat, are you a relative?'

'No,' said Blume. 'I'm not.'

'If you were, you'd be the first to visit her. But since you're not, what are you doing here?'

'I am a policeman.'

'Oh.'

'You sound disappointed.'

'Yes, I am. I don't like the police. Are you here to make sure she doesn't say anything awkward, because I can assure you there is no danger of that. You can tell your bosses she may as well be dead for all the danger she poses.'

'What are you talking about?'

'You know exactly what I am talking about.'

'The train station bombing?'

'What else?' The doctor came over and stood disconcertingly close to Blume, then lifted up his glasses and peered into his face. 'You're very tall. Generally, tall people are wealthier and stronger and live longer, more profitable lives. They dominate others and get ahead in their careers, all because people don't realize how primitive instincts guide our decisions. Have you found that?'

'Have I found that I'm wealthy and at the top of my career? No,' said Blume. 'That we are primates, yes.'

The doctor nodded approvingly. 'Self-irony. That may explain your lack of career success. But it is a good quality: very rare to find in policemen and politicians.'

'And completely absent in doctors,' said Blume.

'Hmm. Would you say?'

'What was the message you wanted me to report to my superiors?'

'That she,' the doctor jerked his thumb at the sleeping head in the bed beside them, 'is *non compos mentis*, or *non compos memoriae*. She poses no threat. She won't be able to tell anyone about which senior policemen facilitated her and her Fascist fellow-travellers.'

'I'll be sure to pass that message on,' said Blume.

'I see your irony extends outwards, too, Mr Policeman. You know, in the 1980s I used to have fantasies about having a murderous Fascist like this at my mercy, and my wish has come true.'

'And is it as good as you hoped?'

'It's different. I'm older now, and in my fantasies, the bombers were never women. They were particularly not bewildered old women whose minds have been wiped clean of all guilt. But, even so, I am still pleased that this has happened to her. I am happy that I have been able to use her as opposed to a decent ordinary person, as a case history for my students. We spent all morning exhausting her with tests. That's why she is sleeping. But when she awakes, she won't remember the tests, or that she slept, or that we subjected her to almost cruel stress all morning long. She has both anterograde and retrograde amnesia.'

'So she is literally incapable of holding a grudge,' said Blume.

'That is one way of looking at it, I suppose.'

'Which in the here and now makes her a decent person. More decent than either of us.'

'I can vouch to the anterograde, but I am still suspicious of the retrograde, since it wipes her conscience so marvellously clean. I am trying to think up a way of forcing recall.'

'You think she's faking?'

The doctor went over and placed a finger on the side of Stefania's temple. 'The bullet entered here. I don't know much about ballistics or even head trauma, which is not my field, but it must have been a strange sort of bullet. The impact with the skull changed its trajectory from horizontal to almost vertical. So it came out the top of her forehead.' He tapped her on the head with his thumb, and she stirred and made a sound as if in pain. 'Even the exit wound was small, which is why she is still here among the living. All these bandages,' he gave the top of her head a small slap, again causing her to cry out softly in her dissipating sleep, 'are the result of an operation to remove half her skull: basically to allow her bruised brain the space to swell up. This,' he knocked her head with his knuckle, 'is acrylic, not bone.

Amazing advance in medical technology. We are so far ahead compared with, say, 30 years ago. Maybe we'd now be able to save some of those who died in her bomb blast. So the bullet took out a section of the temporal lobe, which is probably the cause of the amnesia, then spun upwards into the frontal lobe.' He tapped her forehead.

Blume reached out and lifted the doctor's hand away. 'That will do,' he looked at the name badge above the doctor's breast pocket, 'Professor Marcelli. What are you a professor of?'

'Experimental Psychology.'

'I am not sure what that means,' said Blume.

'It means my students and I come in here to experiment on her, not to cure her. Which is fine by me, Mr . . . Inspector . . . ?'

'Commissioner Blume. What sort of experiments?'

'Nothing evil. Tests. Mental tests. Like quizzes or puzzles. Checking her orthographic, phonological, and semantic processing. A lot of subjects find them fun. Looking at pictures, learning to draw diagrams, lists of words. That sort of thing.'

'I don't suppose you know a professor of animals. Guy called Ideo?'

'The ethologist?'

'That's what it's called,' said Blume. 'Yes, him. So you do know him?'

'Professionally. I have read his stuff. I can't really say I know him personally. You know he is utterly insane?'

'No more than the other academics I have met,' said Blume. 'Why insane?'

'He believes in Lamarckian evolution based on memory,' said Marcelli, shaking his head in humorous despair at the folly of it all.

'And that's a bad thing?'

'Well, of course it is! The heritability of acquired characteristics?'
Blume shook his head.

'Soft inheritance, Jean Baptiste de Lamarck?'

'I am afraid not,' said Blume sadly. 'You may as well be speaking Arabic.'

'The idea that if you learn something, a skill, say, or if you adapt your body to deal with something in your environment, you can pass on this ability to your children.'

'And you can't?' said Blume. 'Seems a pity.'

'Lamarck thought giraffes stretched their necks to get to softer leaves in trees, then passed this characteristic on to their offspring, who stretched their necks even further, and so on.'

'And this theory is insane?' asked Blume. 'It sounds pretty good to me.'

'Forgive me, Inspector.'

'Commissioner.'

'Commissioner. That's simply your ignorance. Not your fault.'

'I accept that,' said Blume, doing his best to sound humble. 'But as mad professor theories go, it doesn't sound totally insane. That was the word you used.'

Marcelli laughed a big exaggerated Father Christmas laugh. It was the sort of laugh he probably used to put down a student who dared challenge him in public. 'That is just the beginning of it. Ideo thinks that plants talk to each other. He has this idea of "morphic zones". So a rose grows into a rose not because of its genes or because of evolution, but because other roses around it teach it.'

'Flowers teach other flowers to grow?'

'Not just flowers. Everything. People, plants, animals, stones, whatever becomes what they are because they partake in a sort of massive collective memory. Ideo says this solves a mystery of foetal development – how some cells know to become skin, others to become legs, feet, hands, head.'

'I have sometimes wondered about that,' said Blume.

' "Immanent morphism", he calls it. Demented stuff. He links it to how dogs know about their owners' whereabouts and health. You know, the way a dog seems to know its master is on his way home long before he arrives.'

'Smell?' said Blume.

'Exactly. That's what a normal person would say. Not Ideo. He has done experiments to show that the dog "knows" before smell is possible. Like when the owner is leaving the office in the city and about to take the train. He says it is because the dog has started sharing the morphic space of its owner, the same zone that controls development. They form a "holon". Lunatic.'

'Cats never do that, do they?' said Blume.

'Of course not. But neither do dogs. Ideo is raving.'

'Does Ideo have many followers?'

'Oh no. No one pays any attention to him.'

'What about students, impressionable young minds? They can be persuaded.'

'I don't think so,' said Marcelli. 'In fact, from what I hear, Ideo has difficulties in hanging on to staff. They quit him and his madness as soon as they get a chance. And while we've been talking, someone has woken up.'

Blume glanced uneasily at the woman beside them. Her eyes were moving back and forth, as though she were following every word of the conversation with perfect understanding, though she had not said a word. Her eyes met his and she smiled. Blume smiled back.

'Hello. I don't think we've met,' she said. She lifted an unsteady finger and pointed it at Professor Marcelli. 'I don't know this gentleman either. Perhaps you might introduce me?' Then she dropped her voice almost to a whisper, 'Or maybe don't bother, eh?' She smiled and gave Blume a wink.

Marcelli, who had missed Stefania's aside and wink, grabbed his arm and propelled him across the room hard enough to make Blume consider retaliating with his fist. 'There is no point in engaging in any conversation with her. I mean, none that will lead you anywhere. Are you trying to find out who shot her?'

'Are you trying to stop me?' asked Blume.

'It was probably a family member of one of the victims, wasn't it?'

'No,' said Blume. 'It almost certainly was not.'

'If it wasn't a revenge attack, then it is likely she was shot by a former *camerata*,' said the doctor. 'Or some neo-Fascist organization. Perhaps it was some organ of the secret state, someone connected with the police or the secret services, am I right?'

The doctor stood back looking pleased with himself, as if he had just proved that for someone like him, investigation was child's play.

Blume knew he should just ignore it, but the moral contradiction in the doctor's reasoning annoyed him too much. 'Let's admit the possibility that a former right-wing terrorist – no, scratch that – a still active right-wing terrorist, or a person with such sympathies, got wind that Stefania was planning to confess and took action to stop her. But what if Stefania has repented? Perhaps she was finally persuaded by the plight of the families and wanted to tell what she knew. You need to allow for these possibilities, too.'

'Unlikely though they are.'

'Unlikely though they are,' Blume conceded.

'Look, Commissioner, first of all, remember what she did. Secondly, I am not treating her harshly. At least she serves as a lesson for my students. A lab rat, basically, which is a fitting end for her.'

'*Ammazza*, you have got a lot of hate, Professor.'

'No, she's the one who hates. Or hated.'

'What sort of tricks do you get her to perform for your students?'

'We show her a complicated diagram and ask her to draw it. Every time the diagram seems new to her, and yet her ability to copy it is improving. Her semantic memory is blown, but her procedural memory works just fine.'

'There is absolutely no point in my trying to jog her memory to find out who shot her?'

'No.'

'Will she live?'

'Hospital will kill you pretty quickly, and seeing as no one even visits her, it's hard to imagine someone being prepared to take her home. And now, I think I have been helpful enough. I try to avoid talking to policemen.'

As the doctor reached the door, Blume said, 'You must be frightened?'

Marcelli paused. 'Of what?'

'Of ending up like that,' said Blume, pointing to Stefania, who wore a mildly puzzled but friendly expression as she watched them from her bed, 'and then of meeting someone like you.'

25

'Not a very nice man,' observed Stefania, as Blume approached her bed.

'You know him?'

'Oh no, we've never met, but you can tell, even from a distance. And you are?'

'Commissioner Blume.'

'Pleased to meet you. I am Stefania Manfellotto.' The name gave her pause as she said it, but then, having consulted with some functioning part of her mind, she nodded confidently to find herself confirmed in herself.

The hand she proffered seemed whiter, thinner, and softer than only a few days ago. Blume took it and shook it as formally and firmly as he could, then, asking permission first, sat down on the chair at her bedside. The door was open and people passed in the corridor, but no one looked in.

'I am not a doctor.'

'Oh, I know that!'

'How?'

'You can tell, even from a distance.'

'Can you guess what I am?' asked Blume, suddenly interested.

'You are not a family man. That is obvious. Also, you have no ring. You are taller than most Italians of your age, so I think your parents may have been from northern Europe or America. You have pale skin and eyes that change from blue to green, depending on the sky. Not many professional foreigners settle in Italy, so they may have been artists or scholars, and you may have followed in their footsteps. You dress slightly differently, too. I notice you don't care for your shoes, which is a sign of a non-Italian, and you speak with a very precise manner, though without an accent, so if you were not born here, you have been here for a long time. I think you have problems in your family. Maybe your mother has died recently? You close your eyelids slowly, which means you are sad, but I don't know if that is always or just now. When you sat down you were angry with someone, but you are not now. But when you were sitting down I saw a holster, but I don't think you enjoy . . . you need to . . . What *you* need to do, before it is too late.'

Blume leaned in to the bed. 'What do I need to do before it is too late?'

Stefania pushed her head back into the pillow, and he pulled back again, apologizing. She blinked, and smiled at him.

'You were saying, what I needed to do?' prompted Blume.

'What do you need to do?'

'I wanted you to tell me that,' he said. He looked at her face, which was gazing at him with patient indulgence.

'You have the look of a man who has forgotten what he was going to say,' said Stefania. 'That happens to me sometimes.'

'Not all the time?'

'Oh, no. Not all the time. I'm Stefania, by the way.'

Blume sat back in his chair, and pushed his feet out and realized the room had grown dark.

'What's the matter?' asked Stefania. 'You seem a bit down.'

'I'm fine,' said Blume. 'Look, you know we are in a hospital?'

She looked around her, a slight look of disapproval clouding her face. 'Yes. I suppose I knew that.'

Blume decided to give one more shot at an idea he no longer believed in. 'Someone put you here. Someone tried to hurt you. They tried to kill you.'

As soon as he said it, he regretted it. Stefania's face was contorted in fear and she jerked her arm out of the bed, seeking to grab hold of him. Even as he took her hand and reassured her she was safe now, he could feel the fear beginning to subside.

'It's OK. That's not really what happened. It was an accident, probably.'

Stefania looked relieved. But he had to continue, just to make sure Zezza was not right. It would be hard to take that, Zezza being right and him wrong.

When he reckoned she was calm enough again, he said, 'If I ask you the name of a friend or enemy, who comes immediately to mind?'

A sly expression stole fleetingly across her face. 'I have friends and enemies in abundance.'

'All right, how about Professor Pitagora?'

'Who is Pitagora? Apart from the triangle guy and music philosopher.'

'You have always known him. You knew him in 1978.'

'No.'

Blume realized his mistake. 'He was not known as Pitagora then, was he?'

'Who?'

Blume recalled the name Principe had told him. 'Pinto.'

'Pasquale Pinto?'

'Yes. That's him.'

Stefania frowned as if trying to conjure up something, but all she came out with was, 'Pasquale is a sort of friend. Pasqualino. We called him that even though he was older than us. He has quite a high-pitched voice.' Her voice took on a confiding tone, and she winked at him again. 'He has a lot of money, you know. All from his father.'

'Pasqualino's my friend, too,' said Blume. 'But can we trust him?'

Stefania narrowed her eyes as she looked at Blume, then, apparently finding him to her liking, said, 'Pasqualino is an envoy.'

'An envoy?'

'He passes from one side to the other. He is guaranteed safe passage. It's how we keep in contact with the authorities. Of course, no one likes him!' She added this last remark as if Blume had just suggested the preposterous opposite.

'Can we trust him?' asked Blume

'He believes only in himself.'

'Is he dangerous?'

'Who are we talking about here?'

'Why, Pasqualino, of course,' said Blume.

Stefania thought about this for a while, then said, 'When I talk about him, I want to be scrupulously fair.'

'Absolutely,' agreed Blume, wondering if what he was doing had any practical value whatsoever.

He waited.

And waited.

'You were saying about Pasqualino Pinto?'

'Ah, Pasqualino! You know his father left him a lot of money?'

When the woman before him murdered a waiting room full of people, her accomplice was Adriano Pazienza. Like her, he was tried three times before receiving a conviction that was surrounded by controversy and obfuscation. Reporters, especially on the left, liked their conspiracy theories. They were less interested in the facts, which were set out quite plainly in the trial papers. Like most investigative work, court proceedings were dull. It was more fun to invent theories.

'What do we think of Adriano?'

'Adriano?'

'Pazienza.'

'I know who you mean, but I don't understand why you're asking.'

'You think it's pretty clear-cut?' suggested Blume.

Stefania looked at him so sharply that he was convinced for a moment that she was faking everything. Then she said, 'I'm afraid I can't quite place you.'

'My name is Alec Blume.'

'Pleased to meet you. My name is Stefania.' She offered him her soft hand, this time looking in dismay at her own frail wrist. She looked around in confusion as an electronic trill spiked the air between them. 'What's that noise?'

'It's for me,' said Blume, and to Stefania's utter astonishment, he pulled something out of his pocket, opened it, and spoke into it as if this were a perfectly normal thing to do.

But he was having difficulties with the machine in his hand, or he could not hear properly, because he was asking the person on the other end of the line to repeat what he was saying, and still he seemed to have difficulty following. He folded away the phone and turned his face briefly towards her. The roll-down shutters at the window shuddered in the wind, and suddenly it was raining loudly. The room was too dark to see his features clearly but she could feel the aura of fear and anger around him. She knew it was not directed at her, and she felt sorry for the man who was now turning away from her and rushing out of her presence, his face a mask of anxiety.

26

B LUME HEADED across town from one hospital to another, and when he reached his destination, he found he had no memory of the trip he had just made. Panebianco was waiting for him in the main lobby. Blume appreciated the gesture. It saved him the necessity of seeking out someone to ask where to go, and someone else to tell him what was happening. In fact, from the second he saw Panebianco's face, Blume knew he could relax a little. Panebianco looked grave, but not stricken.

'This way.' He led Blume upstairs and down corridors. The walk had a surreal quality to it. The air in the hospital, passed through the mouths of patients and their visitors, lost most of its oxygen content and grew heavier and warmer as they went deeper into the building. The panic in his soul was becoming swamped with a sense of lethargy.

After what seemed like an hour, Panebianco stopped and said, 'There.'

The door in front of him was definitely closed to casual visitors. It even looked as if it might be locked.

Blume made to push it open, then stopped. 'How … ?'

'She is going to be OK. Don't worry. You can't talk to her, though. They have administered a general anesthetic, but she'll wake up soon. Those are the doctor's words.'

'How do you know all this?'

'I got here about twenty minutes after she was admitted.'

'I mean how do you know she is going to be all right?'

'The doctors told me.'

'And you believe them?'

Panebianco nodded firmly. 'Absolutely. I trust doctors when they are being optimistic. Pessimism is the default mode, you see. If they say things could go wrong and they do, then they were right all along. If they are wrong and everything goes fine, you are so thankful you forgive their miscalculation.'

Panebianco was still talking and Blume tried to tune in, but found a single large thought sat sideways across the front of his brain blocking his ability to take in information. He had to dislodge it first before he could hope to be of any use.

'Where was she?'

Panebianco said something unconnected with the question, so Blume repeated it. Finally, Panebianco stopped talking and peered at Blume as if only now realizing that he had not been listening. But suddenly the words were devastatingly clear.

'She was talking to a witness who had decided to retract his testimony in the road rage case,' said Panebianco. 'The witness who said he saw Adelgardo Lambertini run over the scumbag.'

Blume gave a tight nod. The back of his neck hurt and his brain felt as if it had shrivelled and hardened inside his skull.

'Magistrate Martone instructed Caterina to go and talk to him. Apply some pressure. I don't like the magistrate, to be honest, but you can't really pin this on her.'

'A barber, wasn't it?' asked Blume.

'That's right. The witness was a barber.'

'Then what happened?'

'Kids on a motor scooter. They hit her from behind, but it wasn't entirely their fault. Apparently, she staggered into their path. One of the kids is in hospital, too. The passenger hit the side of his head against a car.'

Blume shook his head, shaking off this extraneous information. 'Rosario, talk to me about Caterina. What happened?'

'I just said. She sort of fell into their path. The kids weren't even going so fast according to the witness.'

'There was a witness?'

'Sure,' said Panebianco. 'The barber again. He was standing at his door and saw it all. He is saying Caterina had already fainted before she got hit. In fact, he says it was almost as if being hit by the scooter woke her up, and it looked like she was going to land quite softly, all things considered, but the kerb is high there and she landed badly. First on her stomach and groin, then her face, and she fell back into the road for a second time. I can't say exactly, since I wasn't there. She fell once, then again, is how he put it.'

'You've spoken to him?'

'No. I got this from the two *vigili* who arrived on the scene. So this is his word filtered through them, which puts us at a distance from the events themselves, I realize that.'

'No one from our force?'

'It wasn't a serious incident, Alec. That's good news. When she lost consciousness in the ambulance . . .'

'Did you tell me before that she had lost consciousness in the ambulance?'

'I can't remember. I don't think so. But if it hadn't been for that maybe she would have been a code yellow.'

'The doctors told you that? A code yellow for a person knocked down? That's an automatic code red, Rosario. What sort of fucking doctors are these? Code yellow . . .'

'Calm down, Alec. That was just me saying that. I was just trying to minimize, make you feel better.'

'Yeah, well, where are the doctors? I want to go in there, but I'm afraid I'll do more harm than good, bringing in germs and the outside cold.'

As if on cue, the door in front of him opened, and a slow-moving man in white emerged, head down consulting a piece of paper in his hand. Incredibly, he seemed prepared to walk right between them, ignoring their presence. Blume stuck out a restraining arm, though the man was almost small enough to walk right under it. He stopped and, without looking up properly, said, 'Family only.'

Blume glanced at Panebianco. 'Does her family even know?'

'No. I thought . . . We thought maybe you would want to . . . seeing as you're her . . .'

'Get them in here. Her son Elia. Her mother.'

Panebianco drew his phone out of his pocket and moved away. The doctor, who had kept his head bent, looked up and revealed himself to have a bent nose, like a witch from a fairy tale.

'You're family, then? Partner or husband. That's fine. Do you want to sit down?'

'No,' said Blume.

'Fine. No need I suppose. Your wife . . .'

'Partner. Why is she like that? Is she paralyzed?'

'Paralyzed? Good God, no.'

'But she can't wake up?'

'Of course she can. She's in a pharmacological coma.'

'What's that?'

'We put her to sleep. She's having a long nap. It will help make her better.'

'Don't talk to me like I'm a child.'

'You are the one who didn't know what a pharmacological coma was. We are monitoring her for internal bleeding, closed head injury, concussion. She also suffered a cracked rib, and a hairline fracture in her wrist. We have scheduled a CAT scan. But she gets 12 on the Glasgow scale.'

'What does that mean?'

'The top mark is 15. So 12 is pretty good. Better than some people walking about in the streets right now would probably get.'

Was this doctor trying to be facetious?

'Some of her speech was incomprehensible and then – excuse me, you are standing too close.'

Blume stepped back a little.

'As I was saying, her speech was incomprehensible, then inappropriate.'

'What's the difference?'

'Incomprehensible is, well, incomprehensible. Not connected with reality. Inappropriate, which is an improvement, of course, means she was saying certain things. Does she usually use a lot of bad language?'

'Not really,' said Blume.

The doctor made a quick note on the piece of paper. 'It's probably nothing. You'd be surprised at the foul language that comes out of some very demure women when giving birth. That's because there is nothing demure about giving birth. Were you present at the birth of your children?'

'What's this got to do with her head?'

'It's our main worry now.'

Blume tried to take a deep breath, but his lungs rebelled against the hospital air, and he felt his nostrils flare and his cheeks puff out as he attempted to control his frustration. Doctors did this to him. They talk normally for a bit, then suddenly go all first person plural on you, and you weren't sure if they were talking about a consultation with other doctors, patronizing you, or using the royal we of themselves.

'Whose main worry? I mean what main worry?'

'Abruption. That's what we fear. She could lose it, but I'd say it is sixty–forty in favour right now. That's good. Seventy-thirty,' he corrected in reaction to Blume's expression. 'I am sorry to have to tell you this. It depends on the way she fell. Even a minor knock, if it happens in the right place – that is to say, the *wrong* place, ha ha! – can cause the placenta to abrupt, and once that happens, the foetus can't survive but there is grave danger to the mother, too. Even if the abruption turns out to be harmless, and I assure you it often is, the danger comes from the passage of blood from the baby to the mother. If the baby – foetus, I should be saying – if the foetus has a different blood type and some of its blood gets into the mother's system, this causes the mother's body to manufacture antibodies, which then start attacking the blood in the foetus, leading to Rh disease. Of course, that only happens if the foetus has a different blood group, which is common enough.' The doctor scratched the end of his nose and glanced up at Blume. 'Do you happen to have a different blood group from your partner?'

'What?'

'Well, the baby – sorry, the foetus – does. So we know that father has type O positive blood.'

'Like me. I mean, that is me.'

'Are you sure you don't need to sit down?'

Blume allowed the little man to guide him into an armchair, incongruously soft and cushiony, set into a small alcove a few metres away. Vague notions of the diseases lurking in the threads of the material and the dangers these posed for Caterina floated through his mind.

'What sex is the child?'

The doctor, who was finally a little taller than the seated Blume, looked at him and shook his head in pity at the ignorance of laymen. 'Indeterminate. The foetus hasn't decided yet, so to speak. Or won't tell us. Are you sure you're the father?'

Blume stood back up again.

'I am merely explaining why it was decided to give . . .' he checked his notes, 'Caterina an intramuscular injection of Rho(D) immune globulin.'

'Is it possible that she did not know she was pregnant?'

The doctor pursed his lips, producing an effect that, combined with the nose and his receding hair, made him one of the ugliest people Blume had ever seen. But even as he thought this, he was overwhelmed with a wave of immense gratitude for the little medical troll as he set about explaining how he was trying to save his child, and secure Blume's place in the world.

'It is possible, yes. But it usually takes a particularly ignorant, young, or underweight sort of woman not to realize what missed periods mean – along with all the other signs, from mood to tenderness.'

'Nausea? I thought morning sickness was after . . .' Blume stopped. He had no idea what morning sickness was. He had merely heard the term and somehow associated it with babies and therefore with the aftermath rather than the process of pregnancy.

He hadn't a clue.

'Oh, yes. Nausea is common.'

'And what about contraceptives?'

'Someone was not using them,' said the troll with what could have been a leer.

'She was dieting.'

'Dieting while pregnant is very foolish and, if I might add, morally reprehensible. But it would explain a lot, and, from an aetiological perspective, I am very glad you mentioned it. If she was dieting, that would explain her fainting, and we can concentrate on the effects of the accident rather than searching for its cause. Good.'

The doctor started shuffling away.

'Wait! Can I go in there?'

The doctor made a victory sign. 'Two minutes. No more. She is unconscious. You'd do better to go in, say hello, then come back tonight. Except on second thoughts you can't, because no visitors after seven, so come back tomorrow.'

Half an hour later Caterina's mother arrived. She stood behind the glass and gazed in at Caterina with far more calm that Blume was expecting. Still looking at her daughter, she said, 'I have already spoken with the doctors. They assure me her injuries are not serious, and I believe them.'

'So does Rosario.'

'Is that one of your colleagues?'

Blume nodded, feeling foolish. Had the doctors also mentioned the pregnancy to Mrs Mattiola? If so, she was giving no sign.

'We cannot stay the night. That is also a good sign. If a loved one is likely to die, they allow you to stay.'

Blume nodded as if all this had occurred to him.

'I have taken Elia off your hands. I am sure you'll be glad of that.'

'No. I like Elia. We get on great.'

Finally she turned round and regarded him levelly. 'I am delighted to hear that. Thing is, you like him, but he *needs* me.'

'And you *need* him,' said Blume before he could stop himself.

Caterina's mother did not seem offended. 'This is my family. This is what it has all been about. My entire life. Will I see you here in the morning?'

'Of course,' said Blume.

'Well, good night.'

'Good night, Mrs Mattiola.'

While Blume was driving back to Caterina's, Pitagora phoned to tell him he had missed his appointment. Blume listened to him without a word, then hung up.

27

Blume went back to the hospital at eight the following morning. Caterina's mother was already there, but not Caterina, who, he was frostily informed, was out of the coma and now undergoing a 'battery' of tests, which was an excellent sign. Only she didn't say Caterina, she said 'my daughter'.

Blume said he would stay, though he did not relish hanging around in the hospital with Mrs Mattiola.

'You don't have to stay. I am sure you have work to do.'

'It can wait.'

'No, do it now, because you will be needed later. Do I need to remind you that my husband is in a nursing home?'

Blume said he did not need reminding.

'Good, because I need to see him, too. And someone needs to be ready for Elia when he comes home from school. That someone has always been me. Unless you want to pick him up, give him lunch. He has karate in the afternoon.'

Blume started to speak.

'I understand,' said Mrs Mattiola, shaking her head in automatic disagreement with whatever it was he was planning on saying. 'It's hard to predict your schedule, isn't it?'

Blume had said nothing about schedules.

'That is why it is better for you to come here this afternoon,' concluded Mrs Mattiola. 'Whenever you get a chance. I shall cover the morning shift. Go and get your work done so you can be free later on. Agreed?'

Blume agreed.

Fifteen minutes later, he turned off the Via Appia into the recess in front of Professor Pitagora's villa. The gate before him was shut. The back of

Blume's car jutted out on to the narrow road behind, at risk of being hit and possibly killing anyone travelling too fast, which was everyone, across the slippery cobbles.

He pressed the intercom button on the gatepost.

The gate swung open, revealing a lawn that might have once been tended but was now knee-high with soaking crabgrass and wild oats. A swimming pool surrounded by ferns and covered with a sagging tarpaulin gave the appearance of long disuse. Goosefoot, dandelion, and shepherd's purse had pulled up the tarmac on the drive. He got back in his car and drove up to the house, a sprawling three-storey villa, to which a modern excrescence of cheap concrete and gold-coloured aluminium windows had been added sometime in the 1970s, like an illegal extension to a low-quality pizzeria. The fine old villa had been repainted a delicate rose, but the new part had been left to sag and rot.

Pitagora, dressed in a pink jacket that matched the outside of the house, with a deep blue shirt and a gold tie, was waiting for him in front of the front door.

Blume stepped back and made a point of surveying the villa.

'I see what you are doing, Commissioner. You are making me aware that you see how large this villa is. Far too large for a man who earns public sector wages as a university professor, but this is my family pile.'

'I was just stretching my back against the dampness of the day. I am not from the Finance Police, so what do I care? And,' he waved a hand at the garden, 'the state of the garden is testament to your integrity. A man with undeclared earnings would hire a gardener. Berlusconi used to have a Mafia boss as his gardener, or was it a stable hand?'

'I prefer the garden like this,' said Pitagora. 'Those are my weeds of forgetting. When I use my house and gardens as a memory palace, I never place anything here. And there will be wild flowers in the spring.'

The professor led the way into the house, and Blume was impressed. It wasn't just the fine furnishings, the view of the entrance to the Christian catacombs, the overlaid Persian carpets, the long palatial corridor stretching out in front of him with a *trompe d'œil* wall painting at the end, nor was it just the beeswax and flowery scent that assailed his mouth and nose and made the inside of the villa smell like summer, while outside the sky remained dark and wintry; what really impressed him were the frescos that covered the walls and ceilings.

After a few steps, he simply stopped and gazed up at them in frank wonderment.

'What you're looking at there is a Pollaiuolo,' said Pitagora. 'Those three figures represent the Goddess Isis, or the Virgin Mary if you prefer, Hermes Trismegistus, and Moses. It's an original work . . .'

'No, it's not,' said Blume. 'Unless you had the fresco ripped from its original place and brought here. This villa is, what, 200 years old at most?'

'The foundations and the cellars merge with the catacombs, but you're right, it's not original in that sense.'

Blume was still staring at the fresco above him. 'Obviously, you didn't have it ripped from its original site. The colours are too bright and the more I look at it, the less impressed I am. But it does have a wow factor on first impact, I'll give you that. Where is the original work?'

'I thought you'd know that. I hear you're something of an art expert, Commissioner.'

'You heard wrong.'

'I don't know if I believe you. The original is in the Vatican, so you can see why it is unlikely I had it ripped from there.'

'I haven't been to the Vatican in a long time,' said Blume.

'It's in the Borgia apartment.'

'And who did this?'

'Me,' said Pitagora, clasping his hands in front of him in what seemed to be a practised gesture of modesty. 'With help.'

Blume squinted at the ceiling again. 'It's not a proper fresco, is it? It's just painted on to dry plaster.'

'Correct. Also, we used modern acrylic paints.'

'You managed to get that soft touch to it, though,' said Blume. 'From here it still has that chalk and milk effect. How did you do that?'

'You are the first person in *years* to notice that. I applied a thick coat of plaster after it was finished, then sanded it down till the painting below was visible again. I deliberately left a few pieces covered, so it looks as if the work has faded with age. There was no need to do that, but I liked the idea.'

'Congratulations,' said Blume. 'The effect is persuasive.'

'You still haven't seen the centrepiece,' said Pitagora. 'Come on!' And breaking into a trot, he hurried down the corridor and threw open double doors at the end.

'Isn't this something, Commissioner? I mean, just look at it.' Pitagora swept his hand in an arc, turning on his heel as he did. They stood in a circular room topped by a dome in the centre of which was a cupola forming a roof lantern, though not much light was coming in from the bleak sky outside. 'Wait, wait till you see.' Pitagora flicked up a row of light switches and bathed the room in the bright light from a series of spotlights revealing the work in all its glory.

'It's the same size as Bramante's Tempietto di San Pietro on the Janiculum,' said Pitagora. 'Exactly the same size. To the millimetre. The floor plan, the height, everything in perfect Fibonacci harmony. You know what that is?'

'Remind me.'

'The golden section: A plus B is to A, as A is to B.'

'Oh, that.'

'The golden mean, the basis of all life and harmony, from seashells to the distance from your chin to your navel, the spirals of the galaxy, Florentine architecture. The magic number, 1.6180339887 . . .'

'I think that's precise enough for me, Professor.'

'I know it to 2,800 places. It unfolds as a story before my eyes. It's an infinite number, like pi.'

'Shouldn't it be a bit more precise if it's really so golden?' asked Blume. 'A number that just keeps on going – I don't see that as golden. Pretty annoying, if anything. A beginning without a middle or an end.'

The professor looked delighted. 'What a way of thinking you have! I think that you and I, Alec, we have got to . . . We can't be enemies. We just can't. There is so much natural sympathy here.'

'Who says we're enemies?'

'Stop. You're spoiling it with your tone. You scoff too much, but I can see you are impressed and, yes, envious, at what I have. We can get back to business in a minute. But for now, please.'

Blume relented, and gave himself over to contemplation of the dome above, which was decorated with the twelve signs of the zodiac in blue, white, and gold. Although the first impact had been considerable, he found his eye skipping over the mannerist depictions of the symbols, and a feeling of rebellious boredom was stealing up on him, as when his parents dragged him round museums.

'Here I have divided the images and set them into the twelve sections, starting with Aries, then Taurus, Gemini, and so on all around. What I want you to look at though are the images at the top of the wall, along the drum of the dome. These are the thirty-six decans. Some of them are a bit clumsy, I admit. I copied from woodcuts, paintings, prints, and one or two I simply made up on the basis of descriptions I found in Marsilio Ficino's translation of the Pimander. I want you to look and see if you can find yourself. Because you are there, believe me.'

Blume turned his attention to the figures arranged around the top of the circular wall, where the twelve triangular sections into which Pitagora had divided his zodiac paintings were widest. He kept his eyes on the symbols also because he knew his face was far too readable for a policeman, and that the sudden realization that the professor was insane was now written all over it.

Under each symbol were three panels containing figures drawn by a clumsier hand than had decorated the rest of the house, or perhaps it was simply a question of being able to see the work up close. The boards, he saw, were treated wood, and the paint was modern, as were the faces of the figures. One showed a black man, an African, with flaming red eyes, another showed a woman in a red dress apparently vaulting a goat. Next in the sequence came a pale man holding a hoop of some sort. The next figure was a fleshy naked man holding a golden key sitting on a bull. Overlapping this was a scene in which a guy wrapped in a bathrobe was holding a snake and a fish while leaning against a white horse. In the following quadrant, a woman saying something to a child with fat thighs. Farther on, someone was playing a clarinet, someone else was praying, people were digging. Next came a massive lobster such as might be seen on a restaurant billboard in New England. Someone strangling an eagle or a dragon, it was hard to say which. A man with a crow's face (or a crow with a man's body) sat on a throne grasping a spear in one hand, a sickle in the other, a dragon under his left foot. A woman playing cards sat next to a man playing a trumpet and reading a book at the same time. Someone had speared a fish and someone else was watching a dogfight. A woman was stabbing her husband or lover, and a pigeon fancier was releasing a bird. A young couple, naked, seemed on the point of fucking in what, to Blume's increasingly jaundiced eye, looked like manga porn. Two young men on a different panel seemed to have similar intentions.

'I am supposed to be one of those?'

'Never mind. It was a stretch to ask you to self-identify, but take my word for it, you are there.' The professor seemed suddenly deflated. 'Remind me to show you my theatre afterwards.'

'You have a theatre in the villa?'

'A model. It is a model for the memorizing mind. You need to learn it, Blume. You have a figurative bent. You think in images. Perhaps you are not so Jewish after all. Certainly the Mishnah Torah means nothing to you.'

'You're right about that bit,' said Blume.

'You wouldn't even need to see my memory theatre. It's really to help people who can't build one in their own mind. They need the physical analogue.'

'Like the one that guy talks about in his book? You have a scale model version?'

'No!'

'What, you don't?'

'I mean no, don't tell me you bought the book by that charlatan and plagiarist from America?'

'You told me you were suing him in an American court.'

'I am.'

'So I was interested in finding out.'

'You bought his vile plagiarist book!'

'No, not really. I bought it on my Kindle. It's not really the same thing.'

'What is a Kindle?' asked Pitagora.

'An e-book.'

Pitagora nodded, but Blume could see that the exchange had left him as lost as Blume had been looking at the 'decans' in the round room.

'He still gets royalties when he sells an e-book containing my material?'

'I suppose,' said Blume. 'Not my area. Maybe he gets less. Maybe he pays for me to download it. I have no idea. It cost me next to nothing.'

'That is because it is worth next to nothing.'

'Is that how publishing works?'

'Of course it is,' said Pitagora.

The professor brought him into a smaller room, dark and lined with books. He indicated a bulging horsehair chair for Blume.

The professor went over to a shelf and took down a large brown book, which he placed in Blume's lap. 'That is for you.'

Blume read the title, instantly forgot it, read it again: *Damnatio Memoriae imaginis. La fuga della mente moderna dalle Verità dell'Imagine.* He opened the volume, then slammed it shut with a thump to squash the silverfish he had seen scuttling about on the page. A cloud of paper pulp and bookbinding glue rose up into his face and made him sneeze.

'*Salute!*'

'*Tah-huu!* Thanks.' He opened the book. It was so long the publisher had used thin onion-skin paper, such as he had not seen since last looking through the *Encyclopaedia Treccani.* He slid in his thumb towards the end of the book and glanced inside. Page 875, and there were still more to go.

'It's got an introduction by Federico Zeri and Mario Praz,' said Pitagora, the look on his face like that of a father gazing at a child. 'Mario Praz was a good friend of mine.'

The guy who wrote *The Godfather*? Surely not, thought Blume to himself. Surprise seemed to be the reaction called for here, and it came naturally enough.

'And Pietro Boitani has promised to write a foreword to the new revised edition, which I am still working on.'

'A revised edition?' said Blume. Wait, Puzo was the name of the guy who wrote *The Godfather.* He had no idea what the professor was talking about.

'Yes, I'm expanding it,' said Pitagora.

Blume opened the first page and politely began reading a sentence. He had to bring the book up towards his face to read the small print. After a while, he found his eye was scanning ahead looking for a full stop, but page 1 had only commas and semicolons to offer; he flicked over and saw a lonely dot towards the end of the second page.

'You're a fast reader, Commissioner.'

'Yes, well. Later. I definitely look forward to it.'

'So maybe you'll read the original work instead of that populist junk by the thieving half-caste Aaron Fisher who stole my work.'

'Half-caste?'

'Jamaican mother,' said Pitagora with disgust.

'That's bad?'

'Miscegenation. I am not completely opposed to it, not within a European context, but it is a filthy habit.'

'Why did you meet Stefania Manfellotto on the evening she was shot?'

'Is that really what you want to talk about? There are so many more interesting things I can show you.'

'Maybe later, Professor?'

'All right. Stefania and I met once every three or four months. Once per academic trimester, basically. She always came to me, I never visited her. That was the deal.'

'What deal, Professor?'

'Reciprocal control. A code of self-conduct, mutual betrayal, catching up with old times, the emergence of new tendencies, political developments. Recently we were talking about the emergence of left-wing extremists, the Black Block groups, the anti-TAV protests, the Askatasuna movement. Turkish activists throwing metal objects at Italian police. Surely you can't accept that. And then what is happening in Greece with the collapse of the euro-project. It's coming here soon.'

'OK. How about we stop and we go through what you said step by step and you explain in simple terms what you are talking about,' said Blume.

'I know you are intelligent, Commissioner. You are the embodiment of Saturn, you realize that. There is almost nothing solar or jovial in you at all. Saturn is good, if you want a long life, but an unhappy one, full of pessimism and loneliness and doubt. Your wisdom is dark, you see.'

'And you're Mr Sunshine?'

'My aim is to incorporate everything, to find the divine in the human, and to forge a unity by the application of the *mens* to the earthly. I have to embrace and subsume the darker elements, like you and Manfellotto. God is darkness and nameless as well as light and all things.'

'What are you into, some sort of Masonic cult?'

'This is far greater than Freemasonry. The purpose of Freemasonry is to promote Freemasonry: there is nothing there. Just a bunch of English bricklayers with a dim understanding of the art of the mind – I deal with them in Chapters 6 and 7 of the book you are holding. Do you believe in God, Commissioner?'

'No.'

'And yet you do. I can tell. The problem is the name. Either we shall not name him, or we must name him with all the things, visible and invisible, of the universe. But they are infinite, and cannot be named. As you believe in the universe, Commissioner, so you believe in God.'

'Well, that's that settled, then,' said Blume. 'Let's get back to Stefania Manfellotto. You say she and you met regularly. Why?'

'I just said. Reciprocal control. Her job was to report to me on new currents, moods, shifts, and ideologies among the hidden right to which she belonged. Then, without betraying any specific confidences, I would convey the information to some old friends whose job is to monitor these things and make sure the sham of democracy continues to convince.'

'What people?'

'Do you want names?'

'Yes.'

'I thought you were less lazy than that. Find out for yourself.'

'Should I be looking into the secret services, branches of government, magistrates? The shadow state?'

'They are not all that hidden, Commissioner. Everyone knows they are there and many know who they are. Maybe you'll miss a few, and I am sure there are younger operatives I don't know about. But I am referring to my generation – that's the group that people associate with Cossiga, Andreotti, Gladio, the Americans from the OSS, the monarchists, Almirante, Pope Pacelli . . .'

'Do you still believe in all that – the excommunication of Commies, the recruitment of the Mafia to the cause of Fascism, Fascism itself, and the restoration of the monarchy?'

'I still think it would have been better than what we have now, an invasion of scum from East Europe, the gypsies, abortion, graffiti, and degradation, Italian kids bastardizing their natural expressiveness with New York nigger gestures, the rise of the EU.'

'Anything good happen in the last 65 years or so or has it all been downhill?'

'Israel. The cleansing of the misplaced hatred between Zionism and Fascism. They are natural allies. As are environmentalism and spiritualism. We need to create a synthesis, and some young people understand this. But you Jews have really shown the way.'

'I am not rising to that bait,' said Blume.

'You should be proud to be a Jew. If we accept that the word of God created the heavens and the earth, then we must remember that word was spoken in Hebrew. Keter, Hokhmah, Binah – that's you – Hesed, Gevurah, Rahaimin . . .'

Pitagora's eyes were shining as he spoke.

'And what does Manfellotto get from you?'

'Freedom. Yesod, Malkuth . . . aren't you interested in these names?'

'How can you give her freedom?'

'Not me. The people I report to, or the people they report to. It's all part of the peace deal that ended the political violence of the '70s and '80s. But when we met, it wasn't like a spy reporting to her handler or anything like that. We reminisced about the past and worried about the future. I'd ask her if there was any news to pass on, she'd mention something, or tell me there wasn't. That's all there was to it, though it's fair to say she was particularly good at what she did.'

'In what way?'

'No one was better at reading people than Stefania. Occasionally a spy would turn up in among the activists – someone sent there by the Ministry, the Internal Security Agency, you people, or the Carabinieri – and she always, *always*, identified them immediately. She noticed things. She was very quick.'

'And she'd tell you she had spotted them, even though you were reporting what she was telling you back to more or less the same authorities who were sending in the spies?'

'She would not tell me until after she had rooted them out. She never worked against the interests of the various groups to which she was affiliated. She was extremely faithful. Whenever an internal feud broke out, she could play the role of arbitrator.'

'I thought that was your role, and that she was the woman of action.'

'She spent a long time in prison. People change. We were both mediators in the end.'

'She was faithful, yet she betrayed some people. How does that work?'

'No, Commissioner. She betrayed nothing and no one. That is perhaps the essence of her being. Always faithful to her own ideals. Everyone knew she met me and everyone knows I have connections in politics. She was like a statutory auditor in a company.'

'They say you run a cult, you think you're some sort of messiah.'

'Of course they do. I am not the messiah and I am not mad.'

'And that you exploit young people.'

'I exploit no one and no one has made a complaint against me.'

'Of both sexes.'

Pitagora made an expansive gesture with his arms. 'I embrace all experience. All forms of *eros*. The work of magic is to draw things together. The parts of this divided world are united and made whole again by what Saint Dionysius calls Eros, which is like a perpetual circle, from good through evil back to good.'

'This perpetual circle allows you to fuck your students?'

'If you're interested in joining, and you seem to be, bear in mind that most of the intercourse takes place among themselves. My physical participation has been decreasing with my growing age and wisdom.'

'There is a kid called Marco Aquilone. Do you know him?'

'Yes, he's one of my students. Not much hope for him. *Bello ma non balla*, if you know what I mean. Fine body, but dull of mind.'

'Is he part of your fuck-circle?'

'Are you trying to shock me with crudity? That's hardly going to work. All it does is reveal your own prurience.'

'Please answer my question.' Blume was beginning to doubt his own theory. The professor made such a good suspect.

'No.'

'What about, back in the day – or hell, even now – Stefania Manfellotto?'

'Definitely not. Stefania was not into any of that. She was very highly sexualized as a young woman, but then she changed, and became almost monastic.'

'Did she lose her sex drive before or after she killed 80 innocent people?'

'More shock tactics?'

'Why would someone try to kill her, do you think?'

'I really don't know. The thought has been torturing me ever since. She hinted at nothing that would make her suddenly a target. I can't think why.'

'Thank you for the book, Professor Pitagora. Or Pasqualino Pinto as Stefania remembers you.'

Pitagora loosened his golden tie and leaned forward so that his face was half in shadow, and he lowered his voice either to convey a confessional tone or a subtle threat. 'If I were you, Commissioner, I would consider the possibility that whoever shot Stefania and murdered that young woman is the same person or persons who have just put your wife in hospital as a warning.'

Blume interpreted his words as a threat, and his reaction was not good.

28

O   N THE shimmering horizon, just beyond the range of her understanding was a crowd of thousands of places and people. If she
could reach out and touch them, then things would be clearer, which
would mean better. With clarity restored, she would know whether the
man now coming towards her was a friend or not.

He did not feel like a friend. The grin on his face was cocky and full of
malice. She shrank back for a moment. She could feel his controlled cruelty,
the absence behind his eyes. He was looking without seeing. Not all that bad-
looking. Was that lust she saw around his throat? No, but it was anticipation
of some sort. She raised her hands to pull back her cascading hair and was
shocked to find it all gone. Part of her head felt like the nap of a billiard table,
and the man in front of her was looking at her now. She had just seen him
come in, damn this all to hell, it was frustrating. And now her head filled with
that music again. *Sail away, away, ripples never come back* . . . She could even hear
the scratch in the LP. *Gone to the . . . click, click. Other side* . . . Pinto gave it to
her as a present. Little Pinto, getting his little prick and his hopes up!

There was a book beside her about Garibaldi. She couldn't remember
reading it, but she knew all about Garibaldi. She glanced out the window.
Winter, no sound of anything. Withered brown leaves were clinging to
the tree as it danced in a silent wind. What did that mean? Oak leaves did
not fall until the spring, until the new generation took over. Out of a dark
of which she had not been fully conscious, this man in the silky suit was
suddenly there, a smooth political face, a Christian Democrat fixer down
to the tips of his pointed bright shoes, a negotiator without qualms. She
knew the type and braced herself to resist his blandishments and threats.

'. . . as long as you agree to be bound by the terms of the agreement
and not engage in any hostile actions again.'

She apologized, but she had not been listening properly.

'It means you are free.'

'Free.'

'You can leave this place. I'd say the sooner the better. You can get dressed right now. Shall I leave you to prepare your things?'

She did not trust his smooth face and told him so. Escaping prisoners are often shot, or are sent out as agents of confusion to sow tares among the wheat, erect barriers between those who still trusted and those who feared betrayal. Some *camerati* had been turned by the authorities. And then someone came and you were given the chance to prove your absolute mettle. A conviction beyond all appeal, so that she would never be doubted. The lonely intro of 'Down to the Waterline' was playing as he came up to her, and his reasoning spilled out as eloquently and melodically as Knopfler's guitar work, music that was acceptable to the Right, but not to the Left. Like Massimo Morsello's ballads, except she really liked Dire Straits, and no one really liked Morsello, not even his mother. And then, when he had persuaded her, what had she done? She could not quite remember. Little Pinto, the treacherous envoy, his grandfather probably a Jew from the Castelli Romani, was all for it, then all against it.

Shoot the women first. Always shoot the women first. Men hesitated, and men seeing dead women gave up easily. Nothing killed a man like a woman being killed. Didn't she agree? The woman – where had she been? – smiled conspiratorially. We are of the same cut, she said. Put something on your feet before we go, the floor is cold. There had been a man there a moment ago, surely?

She wasn't authorized to say, and she might not even be attending the interview. You know how these things go. The woman by her side was dressed up like a Sunday visitor, and wore make-up, which she had put on inexpertly. Her bag was too practical and her shoes were flat and made for running. The shining black slacks she was wearing did not suit her, and were too wide at the hips, and the glasses were not to be trusted. Clear glass, possibly. The woman never wrinkled her nose or peered or pushed her head forwards like the short-sighted person she was meant to be. She touched them too often, because she was not used to them. Finally she found the words she was looking for to describe her.

'You are undercover.'

The woman smiled and complimented her, then lowering her voice, said, 'Only you and I know this. We can't just walk down the corridor, you understand that? You can see why that is not an option?'

She looked around. Everything was unfamiliar, and she did not trust the woman beside her, but now she had no choice. The stairwell was cold enough, but when the woman pushed open the door the wind cut right through her. She looked down.

'I am not even dressed!' She laughed to hide her embarrassment at finding herself in a nightdress, belonging to someone else, it seemed, standing outside in the cold in front of everyone, but the woman who had been at her side was gone. A smooth-faced man in a shining suit stepped forth from behind the door. It was strange he should be there, and she felt dizzy, and moved quickly back towards the door, but he had his back against it.

'Remember me?' he said. The music was in a loop in her head now. It was impeding her thinking.

She looked at him. He was not police. He was the type that chose bodyguards and organized security details, calmly set aside political and moral scruples, and engaged in straightforward and brutal negotiations. She knew the family and genus, but not this particular species.

'I don't think we've ever met,' she said.

'You know something, if you're faking this, you're doing one hell of a good job. Except it's just too weird. You really don't remember me?'

The music stopped dead, and her mind went silent. She felt cold and frightened, and was sorry she couldn't remember. She shook her head and smiled apologetically.

'Allow me to present myself.' He stretched out his hand, and she took it, mistrusting but shy. His hand was so warm she felt like putting her other hand into it.

'You didn't give me your name,' he said.

'Stefania Manfellotto,' she said, looking into his calm grey eyes.

'Thank you for the confirmation, Stefania, I'd hate to go to all this trouble just for some random mad old bitch.'

He grabbed her other hand and pulled her towards him, allowing her to feel his warmth, then, with an almost casual nod he smashed her nasal septum with the side of his forehead and as she gasped and fell deeper into his embrace, he spun her around, placed his hand on the back of her neck while effortlessly locking her arms behind her back with his other free hand. With two steps he brought her to the edge and flung her into cold space.

29

B Y ROUGH-HANDLING Pitagora and pushing him down his own painted corridor, Blume released a lot of the anger that had welled up in him, which enabled him to think a little more clearly. The problem with the clear thinking, however, was that he realized he was making a career-ending mistake, so as his rage subsided, his tension rose. An unexpected movement at the end of the hall caused him to push Pitagora against a wall showing a grinning winged lion standing on its hind legs with a sewing needle piercing its knee, and Blume found himself pointing his pistol towards the startled face of a young woman, and he realized the vastness of his error. He put away his weapon as quickly as he could, but even this sudden movement caused her to whiten and he saw her knees beginning to give way. She steadied herself, and he tried to make as many reassuring gestures as he could. He was afraid she might lose control of her bladder, and the last thing he wanted was for her to lose her dignity simply because he had lost his temper. Finally, without a word, she ran silently down the corridor and disappeared.

He turned to the professor, who was leaning against the wall in an attitude of studied indifference that was belied by the whiteness of his face.

'This is assault, you realize that? I am still prepared to forgive you for this,' said Pitagora. 'I heard about your wife through perfectly legitimate channels, and no threat was intended. All I was saying is that some equilibrium has been upset. No one ever knows what's going on, but I used to know a bit more than most. Now I realize I am out of the loop. I have no idea who wanted to harm Manfellotto. No, that's not right. I had no idea that they would do this. Now that they have, I think I know who it is.'

Pitagora brushed himself down, and waited for Blume to show some more interest.

'Lousy wall painting,' said Blume. 'Looks like it was done by a 5-year-old.'

'It's an allegory. It doesn't have to be well done,' said Pitagora. 'Gospel of St Mark, in case you're interested.' He nodded at the phone in Blume's hand, 'Good, you're holding a phone instead of your service pistol, but it won't work in here.'

Blume looked at the display and saw flashing empty bars.

'I have a mobile phone jammer operating here. It's in the hallway and covers the entire house. Silence is golden, Commissioner.'

'That's illegal,' said Blume.

'Well, you can add that to my charge sheet. Remind me again what the other charges are.'

'Shut up,' said Blume. 'Let me think.'

'I did not threaten your wife.'

'We're not married.'

'That's what we philosophers call an *ignoratio elenchi*. The point is I did not threaten her, and I am not responsible for what happened her. I was simply suggesting that it might not have been an accident, and so you need to be careful. It was meant as a goodwill gesture. A friendly warning.'

Blume had had threats couched in careful language in the past. It was all a question of the tone in which they were delivered. He realized, too late, that Pitagora was not threatening him. He was already over the hurtling sensation of fear that the mention of Caterina by the professor had caused, though he could not quite shake the sensation that something awful had happened. He needed to talk to Caterina now.

'How did you know about Caterina's accident?'

'Zezza told me. Apparently, someone in your office told him when he phoned looking for you.'

Blume felt a soft thud on the inside of his forehead, followed by a fuzzy sensation that was not entirely unpleasant, but was the harbinger of a migraine. He reckoned he had about half an hour before he would be almost incapable of thought or speech.

'Are you all right, Commissioner?' Pitagora's voice seemed to come from too far away for him to be able to tell if the tone was solicitous or mocking.

'I am fine. If my phone doesn't work in the front garden, I'm going to shoot you in the head,' said Blume.

'You are in a state of rage, Commissioner. You are about to do yourself enormous harm.'

But he was not in a rage now. He felt strangely at ease in his pre-migraine world.

'It's raining,' said Pitagora as they emerged from the villa.

'So?'

'I can't go out in the rain just like that.'

'What are you, a sugar cube?' Blume gave him a push, but kept it gentle.

Like that damned memory book and Pitagora himself had said, images are very powerful in the mind. He had had an image of Caterina lying completely motionless on the bed come to him, and then an image of her as she was the other day, her breasts rounder, her forehead glowing, he should have noticed that, too, and now pale . . . his child inside. Rage had boiled up. If she didn't answer, it meant she was dead.

He pulled out his phone and called the hospital. He was halfway through explaining who he wanted to talk to when he had a better idea and hung up. He called her mobile and she answered immediately.

'Caterina? Are you all right?'

'Alec! You called. That's something, at least.'

She sounded all right to him. The feeling that something had gone wrong was ebbing. No one had died after all.

'Are you coming in, then? We need to talk,' she said.

'Of course, I am coming.' His sense of relief was so strong that his earlier anxiety about her well-being seemed exaggerated. Now that she was fine, there would be time. 'I'll just finish up here and be on my way,' he told her.

'I am scheduled for a scan . . . you had better hurry.'

'The main thing is you are OK.'

'That's relative. I was better before being hit by a scooter.'

He could feel the conversation beginning to curve back upon itself. Soon it would form a circle, with the same things being said over and over again. He promised he would call back.

'Not call. Come,' she said.

He promised that, too.

The professor had recovered his equanimity and was regarding him with a teacher's indulgent smile for the gifted but unruly pupil.

The rain was solid, and the fat drops sounded like a series of slaps as they bounced off the professor's strangely flat hair. Pitagora was quite an old man, he realized. The brightly coloured jacket and shirt seemed out of place in the overgrown and wet garden.

'Commissioner, let's go back inside and dry off.'

Blume held his phone stupidly in his hand.

'You, Commissioner, are a centrifugal force, spinning on your own energy and flinging people away from you. Manhandling me is supposed to represent your affection for the policewoman, but you are here. If you cared in the way women expect you to care, you would not be here. You would be by her bedside. Women expect that, which is one of the many reasons I am not married.'

'I don't know what you are talking about, Prof. I am on my way to her right now. Just one thing. Ideo. Professor Ideo. He was a pupil of yours?'

'First you ask me about Marco, one of the dullest students I ever had, and now about Matteo, one of the best ever. That's going back a fair while, isn't it? He became an animal behaviourist, and developed his own theories. Actually, they aren't really his, they belong to Bruno.'

'Who's Bruno?'

'Giordano Bruno, the philosopher.'

Blume pictured the statue with the cowl on Campo de Fiori. 'Oh, him. I thought you meant a real person.'

'Bruno was more real than anyone.'

'A live person. The dead don't count.'

'That's a bad attitude for someone who works in homicide. Maybe you should think of a career change.'

'I have other people working on just that, thanks,' said Blume. 'Skip the bit about Bruno and his philosophy and tell me what sort Ideo was.'

'Intense. A bit tragic. You see, like Bruno and followers of Hermes Trismegistus . . .'

Blume held up a restraining hand. 'Please, Professor.'

'All I was going to say is Matteo was very persuaded of the idea that all things are connected, and that they are connected through memory.'

'Fine, but what was he *like*? Popular, gregarious, funny, lazy, politicized . . .'

'He was not very popular, no. That was sort of his tragedy. He loved the idea of all things being connected, except he himself was not. He was disconnected. A loner.'

'Did you like him?'

Pitagora looked pleased. 'It's very pleasant to hear you actually ask my opinion, Blume, I wouldn't have expected it.'

'Just answer yes or no.'

'Not as much as I should have, given his deep understanding of the mysteries of Hermeticism.'

'When is the last time you met him?'

'Oh, years ago. But he did call recently. Just after Stefania was shot, as a matter of fact.'

Blume felt an unfocused sense of anticipation, like when he knew something good was in store but had momentarily forgotten. His stomach turned quietly over.

'What did he phone about?'

'He wanted me to write a review of his book.'

'Will you?'

'I am not sure. I haven't read it yet.'

'Did he mention anything about the shooting?'

'No, no. He gave me the impression he had not even heard of it. I hear he spends almost all his time in the company of captive animals. It's perfectly possible he knew nothing about it. He mentioned something about dropping by, but I never saw him,' said Pitagora, turning around as the orange light on the gatepost began flashing and the gate started swinging open. 'I must have visitors.'

'Did someone in the house open the gate?' asked Blume, thinking of the girl he had alarmed.

'A few people have keys. No, well, look who it is.'

A dark blue car with a red stripe and two flashers came rushing through and stopped bumper to bumper with Blume's car. Another identical car followed, and behind that an unmarked silver car with a magnetic flasher on its roof. Two uniformed Carabinieri jumped out of the second car.

Zezza, wearing a suede jacket, came strolling towards them. He had huge white trainers on his huge feet. He walked with a slight fillip to his step, as if considering breaking into a sprint, came up to them, and nodded. If he was surprised to see Blume, he did not let it show.

'Professor. Commissioner.'

'Captain,' said Blume and Pitagora in unison.

'Everything all right here?'

'Oh, I think so,' said Pitagora. 'We may need to sort a few things out.'

'Anything to do with the student who phoned?'

'Ah, she phoned,' said Pitagora. 'Good for her. I thought she had just run away.'

'We were on our way anyhow. There has been a development. The girl said something about someone kidnapping the professor. That was you, Commissioner? Or have you just rescued him from a kidnapping?'

The point of the captain's nose was flat and almost cube-shaped. It was a small nose. Blume felt the headache descend from his forehead into his eyes, and he squeezed them shut.

'What are we doing in the wet?' said the captain. 'Let's go inside.'

Blume found himself back in the same study, this time in the company of Pitagora and Captain Zezza. One of the Carabinieri cars and its occupants had returned to barracks, but there were still two other Carabinieri wandering about the house somewhere.

The captain looked at ease in his surroundings. He was a young man. At first glance, he might be dismissed as all university and gym, and no street action. But this was likely to be to his advantage. Captain now, he was clearly marked to keep rising. This much was visible from his body language, the relaxed way he had about him. He leaned back from the desk and folded his arms. 'Stefania Manfellotto fell to her death 90 minutes ago from a fire escape at the hospital. It may have been an accident. It may have been suicide, and it may have been something else.'

Professor Pitagora crossed himself. 'God rest her wretched soul.'

The captain bowed his head. 'Amen,' he said, and stole a triumphant glance at Blume.

30

B LUME, PITAGORA, and Zezza sat in silence, nodding their heads slightly like three wise men contemplating the transience of life. Blume felt his headache rising and beginning to cloud thoughts that had seemed clear only moments before. The murder of Manfellotto, if that's what it was, caused him fresh doubt.

Pitagora asked the question for him. 'Is foul play suspected?'

'It is too early to say,' said Zezza, still unable to stop smirking at Blume. 'I saw the scene. A sheet, blood, a half-naked old woman lying in a cold courtyard. Then I went up and looked at where she fell from, and it gave me the shivers, because I do not like heights. I can't imagine anyone willingly going out there, especially in this slippery miserable weather. But then again, she was no longer sane. So, once the magistrate came along, I came here, leaving her and the technicians to look at the circumstantial evidence.'

'You left the crime scene just like that?' asked Blume. He was angered in equal measure by Zezza's attitude towards him and by his disrespect for Manfellotto. He was angry at being made to look wrong. He probably had been wrong, and Manfellotto had always been the target. The whole thing was about her. It certainly looked that way now.

'I was there for forty minutes, and I'm going back. No, Commissioner, you can't come.'

'I don't want to, I trust in your expertise. But I am not sure I believe you when you say you have not formed any opinions. Not even a preliminary idea, Captain?' said Blume.

'Her face was a terrible mess,' said the captain leaning back and looking at Blume. 'Like a huge overripe plum.'

'And her arms?'

The professor was looking back and forth between them like a tennis spectator. 'What are you trying to say, Commissioner?'

'I see that when the professor has a question, he asks you,' said Zezza. 'Have you been briefing him, maybe explaining your theory to him?'

Blume did not reply, but the professor, sounding like a plaintive child, said, 'Can someone answer me?'

Blume turned to him and snapped, 'If you were going to throw some poor fucker off a balcony —'

'A fire escape,' corrected Zezza.

'A fire escape,' continued Blume without missing a beat, 'there is a very good chance that they would drag you over, too. Or at least cause a hell of a fuss, a bit like you're doing now. Even if they were small and weak. So rather than grapple on the ledge, the best way to do it would be to knock them out first, or stun them, then throw.'

'Good God,' said Pitagora. 'Poor Stefania.'

'Actually it's a mercy, because she was almost certainly unconscious as she fell. She will have suffered less,' said Blume, pinching his eyes shut.

'Let us pray that it was so,' said the professor who looked thoroughly aghast at what he was hearing. Through the thickening fog of his headache, Blume noticed the tremor and fear in the professor's voice, and saw Zezza was noticing it, too.

'I think that's probably how it went, Professor,' said Blume more gently. 'If she was unconscious she would not have instinctively tried to shield her face with her arms. That's why particularly devastating facial injuries and intact arms suggest unconsciousness during the fall, and therefore point to murder.'

'None of this is certain,' said Zezza. 'They'll have to examine her arms, see how they are fractured. Maybe she did try to protect her face at the end.'

'This confirms what I have been saying. She was assassinated for sure,' said Pitagora. 'And I am afraid I wil be next.'

'Well, it's interesting, though, isn't it?' said the captain, addressing himself to Blume. 'I never really thought that Stefania Manfellotto had been attacked by a surviving relative of one of the victims of the train station bombing, but obviously that was the first line of investigation I was obliged to follow. For political reasons, too, you understand. I could not be seen to assume this was an internal settling of accounts among Fascists. They made me investigate civil rights movements campaigning for truth about this and the various other terrorist outrages. Now at last we can all stop pretending and focus on the Fascists, can't we, Professor?'

Pitagora was biting a knuckle and seemed not to be following.

'An internal settling of accounts,' said Blume. 'Neo-Fascists killing the whatever the opposite of neo is.'

'*Vetero*,' said the professor absently, and resumed his knuckle chewing.

'Neo-Fascists killing *vetero*-Fascists, then,' said Blume. 'Or, more likely, *vetero*-Fascists killing each other.' He spoke the words out loud. They made perfect sense. After all, that is what had just happened to Manfellotto, unless it actually was an accident. He had thought everyone else was looking in the wrong direction, but it was him. Was that possible?

'I tend to agree with that second hypothesis,' said Zezza. 'Professor? Anything to contribute?' When Pitagora shook his head, Zezza continued, 'One line of inquiry regards Manfellotto's past activities and the possibility that she was planning to betray an old confidence, reveal some secret pact. It is the most delicate because a lot of her former *camerati* reformed and acquired respectability and power, including within the hierarchy of my own force: yours too, Blume.'

'Some didn't reform, yet they still rose to positions of power,' said Blume. 'And the professor here is a fine example of just such a person. Molotov cocktails and baseball bats in the 1960s, beating up students, cooperating with organized crime, shooting people in bank raids.'

'Alec! I reject these accusations.' The professor sounded genuinely hurt. 'I did know people who did these things, but I was and am and always have been a mediator.'

Zezza looked askance at Blume as the professor blurted out his first name. 'We can look at Manfellotto's past activities and connections, or we can look at her new connections with the neo-Fascist groups. In other words, we can look at the old, or we can look at the young. Even before the Manfellotto case the Ministries of Defence issued a circular to warn about an upswing in terrorism.'

'I got the memo, too,' said Blume. 'They send one out every other year, just to make sure their budgets aren't cut.'

'You may not take it seriously,' said Zezza. 'But I do. The new groups are growing in number and strength, and it is only a matter of time before they reactivate. Terrorism is back in fashion. Already there have been several shootings of Africans by right-wing extremists. We are waiting for some atrocity, another train station, a shopping mall, a school, something like that.'

'We?'

'We law enforcers, Blume. Apart from the memo, the people I talk to have been saying that Italy is about to explode.'

'Italy is always about to explode.'

'Fortunately there are some serious men in law enforcement. If the new extremists are renewing themselves, militarily speaking, they'll want to get rid of the old guard. I think the professor is right to be afraid,' Zezza filled his tone with threat, 'which makes me wonder why he is not cooperating with me more.'

By way of reply, Pitagora simply left the room. Zezza seemed about to stop him, but then relaxed.

'He's not going anywhere,' he told Blume.

'You hope not.'

'I have reported you, you know. For interference. I did not have much choice. I hope it does not cause you too much trouble.'

Fuck you, and your big white head, Zezza, thought Blume. He massaged the webbing of his hand, a trick Caterina had taught him to keep his headache at bay . . . Caterina. *Fuck*, he had forgotten.

The professor came back with a box of Moment tablets. 'Always keep these handy – I forgot the water!' He paused. 'There is a lot of tension in this room.'

'Thanks,' said Blume popping five pills into his hand and then his mouth – pills, he realized, he had not asked for. 'Never mind the water, I'll just chew.'

'The commissioner is leaving. He has a sick wife to visit,' announced Zezza.

'She's not his wife,' said Pitagora. He turned to Blume. 'You were going to forget this. Don't.' He handed him the book. 'There is stuff in there that cures headaches, too.'

31

'Fool me once, shame on you; fool me twice, shame on me.' When he was lucid, her father liked to quote that phrase at least once a week, as if it were an ineffable truth. But Caterina could hardly think of a less appropriate motto for a man whose forgiving nature everyone, from the neighbours to her mother and herself, took advantage of. Eventually she guessed he intended it for her, so that she might turn out tougher and less forgiving that he had been. But when the dementia began to take over and swallow up the man whose character directly rebutted his favourite phrase, many of the people whom she thought he should have forgiven less became kinder. Even the neighbour who had exploited her father's good nature to rob, there was no other word for it, a plot of garden attached to the apartment that had once been theirs, even he turned out to have hidden reserves of generosity, going out of his way to call in favours to find the best doctors he could for them, giving her father lifts to the clinic and then the hospital, getting her father to join a bowling club and then making sure he went there and spoke to people and remembered who he was and why he had come – human contact being the only cure for the incurable.

As for the unforgiving and self-righteous phrase itself, she had assumed it was some local saying from the town of Pescara where he came from, like 'the daintiness of the boor', a phrase he always rolled out when someone helped himself to almost all the food on a platter, leaving a small amount for appearances. But in the days just before his mental decline became undeniable, she had asked him about his motto. It turned out it was not a local saying. He had heard it from an American pilot from the 376th Bombardment Group, who had returned after the war and set up a motorbike repair shop – in a town he had helped to wipe off the map – and given her father his first proper paying job. That shop beneath the railway embankment on Via Rieti was one of the last fragments in his blasted memory.

And Alec? How many times had she let him fool her? She thought she could give him one more chance. She was not asking for much. She did not even want to marry him, though it would be nice to be asked, and it might give Elia some more stability. But for now, she would be content if he simply lifted up his head, focused his eyes, and *saw* her. It was not an unreasonable hope. It was not even to ask something of which he was incapable. On the contrary, he was very observant of people, as long as they were not her. Or himself. About himself he had absolutely no idea.

All people, he had once told her, are neurotic or psychopathic; it was just a question of degree. Half of humanity was stuck in its own childhood, the other half in its adolescence. The people who were stuck in adolescence could be reasoned with. Not so the people stuck in childhood, which, he solemnly informed her, included all the psychopaths.

And him.

The chewing gum incident. Now that was scary. In one of his increasingly frequent raids into the kitchen, he had come across a tube of Air Fresh Vigorsol chewing gum. Hers. He didn't even like chewing gum. He had often told her so, which she took as a criticism of the fact that she did. But he chewed his way through the entire contents. She had complained about it the morning after, and he had been very dismissive. She had perhaps upped the ante a bit too much, turning the gum into a *casus belli*.

That evening, she had opened the cupboard to take out some pasta, and there, occupying the entire top shelf were five industrial-sized sealed plastic packs of chewing gum. Hundreds of packets. Thousands of pieces, enough for a lifetime.

She knew he had his answers all prepared. 'I thought, seeing as chewing gum means so much to you . . .' She could almost hear him saying it. So she said nothing. She never touched or mentioned them, and two weeks later threw them all out.

Whereas she should have thrown him out instead.

Three weeks later, he apologized for his stunt.

Fool me a hundred times, shame on me. When she thought of him now, she saw him standing in the kitchen gulping down water, slightly stooped to de-emphasize his height, his big face wracked with despair and the pain of migraine as he tried to pretend he was just fine. Except he wasn't there, was he? That's why she had to imagine him standing by her bedside. Nor could she relax in the knowledge that he would be there for

Elia, protecting him if something terrible happened her, as it almost had. He was not to be trusted.

He was no father to Elia, but he might learn to be a father yet. She knew he wanted to become one. Once, after they had made love all afternoon, she had found a used condom under the bed. He was usually so fastidious about getting rid of them. He hated them. He made jokes about it being like 'washing your feet with socks on' and all the usual masculine objections, but they revolted and frightened him. She could see that from the way he had to leave the bed immediately and remove them, wrap them up, throw them away, and wash. Except this once, when they had spent almost an entire day in bed, and he had begun to relax, and she found one, used, curled up like an onion peel under the bed, and she had picked it up with considerable less fastidiousness than he did, only to find it was split. Split and therefore relatively clean of semen.

She did not confront him with it, gave him no opportunity to disappoint her with a lie, and went on the pill. One evening, when he was muttering and struggling with a condom, she told him.

Thereafter, he told her, sex had been far better for him. No comparison, he said. But it had become immeasurably worse for her. He was rough and demanding, pushy, careless, and arrogant that time and the next and the next, until she had cried out, and then cursed him. She issued him with a warning, and began to train him, always amused at his debilitating embarrassment as she put into plain words acts that he had absolutely no compunction about putting into deed. She coached him into becoming gentler, slower, and more considerate.

But she did not forget those three of four times in which she had been assaulted by a man who was angry she was denying him the fatherhood for which he was evidently unprepared.

Then she skipped the pill for two weeks. No reason. Motivation follows action, as Blume liked to say, preferring to illustrate the truth of his point with cheerfully explicit references to gruesome acts of violence.

She had the beginnings of an explanation for her foolishness. It started when her gynaecologist observed that she was now 36 years of age, which was a time when a lot of women considered coming off the pill. Her blood pressure was a little high, and a blood test suggested she was building up levels of visceral fat. So she had come off it, and concentrated on diet, and said nothing to the Alec the first few times, as if some magic aura protected her. Then she told him, and he sulked and refused to go back to condoms.

Her following actions had been even more mystifying for her. The first missed period she put down to getting the timing wrong. The second she attributed to the considerable weight loss she had achieved thanks to the Dukan diet, and she even interpreted it as a good sign. And then the morning sickness had started and she attributed this to all the eggs she was eating.

And then she knew. She woke up after a nightmare involving spiral staircases and Elia, and lay in the bed, looking through the top of the window at the cold sky and listened to Alec breathing steadily and quietly, for once, and she knew with absolute certainty, and marvelled at how she had ever thought otherwise.

She had felt happy, relaxed, and ready, despite everything. Her thoughts were crystal clear all morning long, and she was able to look evenly and calmly at the idea of quitting her job. Almost miraculously money was not going to be a problem. The rent Alec would get on his house covered her lost earnings, and she was about to receive a large lump sum from a young woman called Emma, whose inheritance she and Blume had once helped save. She had always known that as soon as she accepted that money, her career in the police would almost certainly have to end, which is why Blume had completely refused to countenance it. He had to pretend to need his job so he could say he hated it.

New motherhood. Still getting up at all hours, but to feed and cuddle rather than step out of a bed into nightmarish scenes of human decrepitude and brutality. All those reminders of how futile, fragile, and ugly human life could be superseded by evidence of the opposite. Except for the fragility. That was a constant.

Everything had seemed so clear that morning, and then the sky darkened and the rain had started, and then Blume had had one of his homicidal moments in the car, and she postponed telling him. The sky continued to darken, and a few hours later, as she stepped out of the barber's shop, once again ready to invite Alec to the next level, a motor scooter slipped on the greasy road just as she lost her balance. It had been painful, too.

Now nothing was clear any more, not even if she shared the doctors' anxiety to save the child inside her. She had told the doctors to say nothing to her mother, though Caterina had caught her that morning looking at her differently.

A series of tests mid morning, then she would, probably, be free to go home and stay in bed for three days, ordered to rest for three weeks. Those were the recommendations. And she still had not talked to him about it. She did not even know if he knew. Almost certainly not, for even he could hardly be so –

Someone knocked softly on the door of her room and the knot of anger in her stomach immediately began to unravel and she sat up expectant, ready to forgive and be fooled again.

But it was Chief Inspector Rosario Panebianco who walked in.

The disappointment must have been written all over her face, because he immediately apologized for being who he was, and for intruding.

Panebianco sat down at the head of the bed, in the seat she already considered her mother's.

'Are you all right, Caterina?'

That was nice of him. Panebianco had difficulty in using first names.

'Fine, thanks. But I won't be back at work for a while. Three weeks at least. And then a few months until – look, can you prop up the pillow behind me?'

Panebianco did so, then sat down again, and, as she feared he might, took up the conversation from where she had trailed off.

'Until when? Have you applied for a transfer or something?'

'Now there's an idea. So, how are you all managing without me?'

'Fine. Operation Full House has been cancelled – or suspended.'

'Really? What happened?'

'The gang seems to have gone quiet. It now seems evident that they have abandoned the planned Ostia heist. It's as if they knew we would be waiting.'

'Someone tipped them off?'

'Or they have logistical problems. We'll see.'

'Too bad,' said Caterina. 'We were working well with the commissariato in Ostia.'

'Yes, I'm sure we'll get another chance. And the cooperation with our colleagues in Ostia . . .'

'Very useful,' said Caterina.

'Fruitful and valuable,' said Panebianco. They had reached the end of subjects in common.

'You know you don't have to stay here for my sake, Rosario.'

Panebianco bounced out of his chair like a man released. She thought and hoped he was on his way out, but instead he marched back and forth across the narrow space a few times, banging his open palm with his fist, then spun round and addressed her from the end of her bed.

'There is something I need to tell you.'

'OK.' If she didn't know he was gay, she might have expected a declaration of anguished love.

Panebianco glanced around to check they were alone. 'It has to do with your accident.'

He paused again.

'Go on,' she prompted.

'First thing, the *Vigili Urbani* have just caught the kid who ran you over and fled the scene leaving you and his friend on the ground.'

'He's only a kid. How's his friend?'

'Fine. Actually, I don't know. I haven't heard anything, or tried to find out. But seeing as it was you they hurt, I didn't want to leave the investigation entirely to the *vigili*, and so I detailed two men to ask a few questions, and I went to talk to the barber myself.'

'That idiot barber is too stupid to know if he's a witness or not,' said Caterina. 'I wouldn't depend on him.'

'As a matter of fact, he was able to supply the number plate, make of the scooter, a description of the kids, and an almost perfect estimate of their ages. When he saw them getting up after the crash and preparing to ride away, he even went after them. A good citizen and an excellent witness.'

'Which is the exact opposite . . .'

'I know,' interrupted Panebianco. 'I know.' He drew a long breath, and she shut up. She could see he was trying to tell her something. 'The barber withdrew his testimony and Magistrate Martone ordered you to go to him and apply a bit of moral pressure. I know all about that.'

Panebianco paused again. 'When I was talking to him, he said, "Oh, so now you want me to be the perfect witness because a cop got hurt." That pissed me off, and I told him we treated all cases equally.'

'Even if you just told me you went all the way out there because I am police,' said Caterina.

Panebianco glanced sharply at her, and she realized that she had just made it easier for him to tell her something she was not going to like.

'I pressed him on his attitude, and started asking him about the other case, too, and why he had withdrawn the statement he gave you about Lambertini. And he told me he had been pressured into it. I asked him by who, and he claimed it was a policeman. So I asked him if the policeman had identified himself and he said no, but that the policeman had claimed to be your boyfriend.'

Caterina felt a wave of nausea pass over her. Her hands and feet felt cold and clammy underneath the bedclothes, which minutes ago had seemed too warm.

'So,' continued Panebianco, 'I asked him to describe the policeman, and the description he gave fits Blume. It was him. I checked the day and time, and Blume was out of the office then.'

'It's not as if there is any doubt.'

'No, I'm sorry, Caterina. Blume asked the barber to withdraw his testimony.'

'Have you confronted him?' she asked.

'No.'

'Who else knows?'

'No one. Just you and me and him. And the barber, of course. I need to know what you are going to do, Caterina.'

'Do you think I am going to report him?'

'Forgive me if I'm getting this wrong, but from the look on your face a moment ago, I think you might.'

32

IT WAS past three when he arrived at the hospital only to find Caterina's room empty, as he knew he would. Casually, he asked at the nurses' station if they had any idea when she might be back. They didn't. They were able to tell him, however, in bright tones, that he had just missed her and that she had had a visit just before him.

'Who?'

'I don't know. Fairish hair, neatly dressed. Clean, he looked very clean.'

Panebianco. Blume felt grateful.

'I can't say how long I she'll be. You can wait. Not as long as that book's going to take you – at least I hope not!'

Blume had Pitagora's book under his arm. Twice on his way up he had considered just leaving it on a counter somewhere. Maybe someone else would like it.

He sat down on a bucket seat in the corridor and considered that he was the one responsible for sending Caterina to where she was injured. The worst of it was that he did not even know if he was going to tell her. It was not only his cowardice that was bothering him; it was that he did not know how he himself was going to behave.

He resolved that if Caterina lost the child, then he would tell her. He would admit what he had done when his admission would be hardest. That way, he could be sure he was no coward. If everything worked out for the best, he would maybe tell her some other time. When the baby was out. When he would have a son. A male heir. A mate for Elia. He did the maths. It would be a long, long time before they would be mates. But the arrival would mature Elia, bring them all very close, and all this would be true even if it turned out to be a girl, which he doubted.

Pitagora's magnum opus sat on the seat next to him. He bent down and pulled the Kindle out of his bag.

In the year 1596, an Italian Jesuit called Matteo Ricci set out to teach the method of the memory palace to three Chinese students, sons of a wealthy provincial governor, who needed to pass a difficult examination to enter the upper echelons of the bureaucracy of the Ming dynasty. To do this, he had to write in Chinese, which he had learned using the very same memory palace.

It is possible to learn a language using the techniques given in these pages. The reason people do not, I think, is that they are as unfamiliar to people today as Matteo Ricci's memory palace was to his Chinese hosts, and as their ideograms were to his Italian mind. People shy away from what seems strange. One helluva pity, in my opinion. Sometimes strangers and strange things can simplify our lives.

Look at this Chinese ideogram signifying war.

Blume did, and decided that this just went to show that e-books were useless. The spatial aliasing was distracting, the image was in the wrong part of the page, and too small to see properly. The painkillers had eased his headache for half an hour, but now it was on its way back.

How did he remember that symbol? Well, I can give you a sneak preview by saying that the right part of the image looked to him like a curved sword and the two upright lines on the left side were the hands of a man grabbing hold of the wrists of another man wielding the sword in an attempt to stop himself being killed. If you have seen <u>Saving Private Ryan</u>, you might remember the hand-to-hand combat scene between the American and the German soldiers in the closed room. Personally, I can never forget it, the American kid saying, 'Wait, wait' as the German leans down with the knife inches from his chest before plunging it in. I digress? That's the point. I want you to digress like that. Let the images take over and the words fade.

Words are overrated, by the way. Next time you're looking for a really good book, one that you can really get into, consider this: there are many very good writers out there, but there are very few good storytellers. In fact, you might find that your favourite storyteller isn't much of a writer at all – and will be despised by the critics and the clever people. But he – or she – shouldn't be. A good storyteller is far harder to find than a good writer. And what do storytellers do? They put images straight into your head. The images take over, and the words fade. That's why I'm not so worried if some people dislike my conversational and folksy style here. I could be more academic, but I want you to learn!

A word of warning, folks. We don't like bad memories and nasty images, and our brains will play all sorts of tricks to suppress them. So save the traumatic images for traumatic words like war, OK? Right, back to how to learn a language.

The peg system, which we looked at in Chapter 4 and will look at again in Chapter 9, is the first step. What is the peg system again? What, you forgot?! No problem. A peg is something you hang a memory on, but you know what? I don't like the term. I would have liked to call it the 'cloud' system, but nowadays everyone thinks of the cloud as a place where you store your files remotely. But think of how a cloud forms. A droplet of moisture attaches itself to a piece of dust, which attaches itself to another droplet, and a piece of dust, to another piece of dust, and so on. Eventually you have a big dark cloud ready to burst and rain down information. The point is everything we know now we learned by associating it with something else. At some stage, you say, like when we were really small babies, there must have been a moment when we just learned something without associating it. That's actually a pretty deep question of the type that gets Greek philosophers and Noam Chomsky worked up, so let's not go there. Let's just say that the basic rule is this: anything you learn you learn by associating it with what you already know.

One of these Greeks was a man called Protagoras, who is supposed to have said that man is the measure of all things, a point of view I agree with. He is also credited with inventing the genders masculine, feminine, and neuter for nouns in those languages that make such distinctions. Jacob Grimm (fairy-tale guy) did the same for German. My point is they might as well have called them air, rain, and sand nouns as masculine, feminine, and neuter. Like plant classifications, it is a system made up by humans, and essentially arbitrary. The word 'table' is feminine in Spanish, masculine in German, both in Italian, nothing in particular in English. It is arbitrary – though, obviously, words like mother and woman are going to be assigned to the 'feminine' gender.

No technique for remembering this demented system, invented by academics, not nature, can be considered 'cheating'. The original arrangements of plants, dates, nouns, words – everything – is arbitrary and made up by brains just like yours. There is nothing intrinsically male about, say, a cup or the floor or a tree, but if we are learning German we find that they are masculine, and so we are supposed to think of them as having some of the qualities of a 'male'. It's like the old joke about whether a computer is male or female. It's female because it stores all your mistakes in permanent memory for later retrieval and it uses a *language all of its own to communicate. On the other hand, it's male because you have to turn it on before it will work for you and it holds a lot of information but is still very stupid.*

In short, there is no 'cheating'. If instead of trying to associate a word with an arbitrary gender, you decide instead to 'put' it in an arbitrary place of your own deciding, that will help you remember.

Personally, I put all masculine nouns from all languages in a huge big field with a copper beech tree that I remember from my childhood, I leave female ones floating on the open ocean, which is not very chivalrous of me, and I throw neutral nouns into the darkness of space. You need big places if you want to learn a lot of words. Smaller places will do if you want to learn a shorter list.

All pretty weird, right? It seems like too much effort, but the brain reorganizes things pretty quickly. If you can type, play an instrument, ride a bicycle, knit, or drive a car, you'll know the truth of this. For a while it was a HUGE effort, slow, complicated, impossible to learn, frustrating, and, above all, so mechanical and laborious – not to say dangerous in the case of the bike and the car. Then it became natural, so natural that you can sing while playing guitar, chat while knitting, compose while typing, and text while driving (that's a joke, by the way).

Let's go back to the Chinese character for war: 戰爭 . . .

Blume's phone rang. It was Panebianco.

'Commissioner?'

'Hi, Rosario. Listen, thanks for coming in to see Caterina today. I am at the hospital now. What's up?'

Panebianco did not answer.

'What is this about, Rosario?'

'I think you need to come in now.'

'But I haven't seen Caterina yet.'

'You'll have plenty of time later, I promise.'

33

WHAT DID Panebianco mean by telling him he would have plenty of time later? As he walked up the steps into the Collegio Romano station, a policeman, whose tight uniform bore the sheen of age and many overheated ironings, made some comment. Blume missed the content, but the tone had been friendly enough.

'Thanks, Roberto,' he called without turning round, delighted with himself at remembering the name in time.

He walked quickly through the staff room on his way to his office, throwing greetings left and right, but they were not returned.

'What, did you all come in to stare at me today?' Blume made his way over to Panebianco, who obviously had something to say.

'This is scandalous!' said Panebianco with some venom. 'Come on, into your office. This is fucking unbelievable!'

Panebianco closed the door behind them, and leaned against it. 'Alec, you have been suspended from service.'

'What?'

'You heard me.'

'They can't do that. I got no notice.'

'They can. You have been served with an interlocutory order for immediate suspension, pending the commencement of disciplinary hearings within 40 days.'

'But I haven't been informed.' Blume squared his voice against hitting a plaintive note. 'My phone has been on. Apart from you, no one called.'

'This is totally unacceptable. You need to talk to your SIULP representative about this,' said Panebianco. He shook his head in disgust. 'I am sorry. I don't know why they are doing this. For all I know they have every reason to suspend you. I can think of a few reasons myself, but that is not the point. It's the way they have done it. They let everyone know before you. That is deliberate humiliation. It is an offence to the dignity of your office. You can get the union on your side on this. I am willing to be a witness.'

Blume felt like a spectator in a theatre watching himself and Panebianco act out a scene on a stage far below. He recited another line: 'Witness to what?'

'The fact that news of your suspension was leaked to your colleagues before it was officially communicated to you as the directly interested party. What else have you done, if you don't mind my asking?'

'What *else*? I'm not sure I like the way you framed the question.'

Panebianco gave him a look that stopped him dead. There was genuine contempt in his eyes.

'I annoyed a Carabiniere,' said Blume with a touch of humility. 'I came in late to the questore's speech. With the questore, I think it's sort of cumulative hatred.'

'I just want you to know that I am opposed to the way they did this, not necessarily the fact of the suspension.'

'Well fuck you, too.'

'And if the image of the *squadra mobile* has been deliberately insulted by the questore, I think people need to remember that you gave him and his office plenty of opportunity.'

'Spoken like a real friend.'

'Like a colleague whose dignity of office is threatened by the antics of his commanding officer.'

'Did I say "fuck you" a second ago? Because just in case I didn't –'

His desk phone rang.

'That thing never rings any more.'

'That will be them now,' said Rosario. He glanced at his watch. 'It is now 16:03 p.m. Make sure you don't delete the incoming call on your phone. Date, time, details. Log everything. Record them if you can.'

'I don't know how to.'

'But you had better answer the phone, Commissioner.'

Blume looked at the display. It was a short number, the Rome prefix plus 46861, the switchboard of a public office. He glanced at Panebianco, who flashed him a heartless smile and left the room. Blume went over and lifted the receiver.

★

200

The appointment with the questore was set for an hour later at the offices off Via San Vitale. If he went to the hospital, he might not make it back in time, even if he used his siren and the public service lanes. And even if it were possible, how long would he have with Caterina? Five minutes? Ten? Fifteen tops, but then the anxiety of the appointment would distract his attention. He descended the steep flight of steps leading straight out to the piazza outside and walked away from the station. He did not want to be within the earshot or even the line of sight of his colleagues until he had this all worked out. He called Caterina on the off chance, and was shocked into silence when she actually answered.

'Alec?'

'Hi. I didn't expect you to answer . . . so quickly.'

'Well, here I am.'

'You're fine, then?' This was met with silence, so he added, 'I was in earlier and you were having tests, so how did they go?'

'You're talking like they were multiple choice or something. It was a CT scan. Presumably they'll tell me.'

'Your mother is coming in soon.'

One beat, two beats, three, four, five. It was time enough for her to remove all inflections of outrage from her voice. 'I see. You're not coming.'

'Something important has come up. I wasn't cancelling.'

He waited for her to ask him what had come up, but it seemed she wasn't interested, and he was damned if he was going to volunteer information. The silence stretched a few more seconds, then he said, 'OK, like you said, I'll call later. You sound fine. I hope you are.'

'Wait.'

Here it comes, he thought. She had to realize he must have a compelling reason not to visit. She had to know something serious was happening. But her next question was too female for him to have anticipated.

'When's the last time you saw Elia?'

'Elia?'

'Yeah, you know, that kid who lives with us. My son, the child you refer to as your nephew. How I ever let you get away with that.'

Blume felt his temples throb, a reminder his headache was just biding its time.

'Your mother started that uncle thing.'

'Where did he spend the night? No, don't answer that. It was at his grandmother's.'

Thoughts too deep in him to get out caused him to sound prim and defensive. 'I would have been perfectly happy for him to stay with me.'

'With you. In my house? That's very kind of you.'

'Caterina, you said we had to talk. I think I know what about. Can we save all this until later?'

'Sure. It's not as if I am going anywhere.'

She was refusing to tell him she was pregnant. As long as she withheld that from him, what was the point in trying to do the best by her?

The conversation had filled his muscles with immanent ticklish energy. He had to walk. Cutting through Piazza Collegio Romano and past the Trinity pub, he emerged on to Via del Corso, which had become less busy over the past few years as the tourists vanished and the shops moved to out-of-town malls. It was easier to walk down, but there was little to look at. Moving quickly to keep his blood warm against the wind, he headed straight up Via dell'Umiltà as far as the Foreign Press Centre, then stopped, realizing that at this rate he would arrive too early at the Questura with a raging and ungovernable headache.

He doubled back, and stood for a moment underneath the entrance to the Forza Italia headquarters. Far less movement around here in recent years as the party sank back into the murky oblivion from which it had emerged. Just two policemen stood guard outside, whereas half a division was still posted around Berlusconi's pleasure palace down the road.

One of the guards came out, took a look at him, and nodded. Blume nodded back, unable to place the man, who had either recognized him in person or, as often happened, simply recognized him as a colleague. A squad car was parked where the road opened to become a small piazzetta. A uniformed officer leaned casually against it, watching the world go by, but straightened up defensively as Blume approached. His colleague was nowhere to be seen, which gave Blume an idea.

'Where's a good place near here to get something to eat?' He was five minutes from his station, but Via del Corso acted as a sort of line of jurisdiction for him and his colleagues, including for the bars and cafés. Anywhere around the Pantheon and Campo Marzio was home territory, but this was foreign ground as far as eating was concerned.

The policeman relaxed again, as he realized the unwarranted absence of his colleague was not going to be an issue.

'Sitting or standing?'

Blume checked the time on his phone. 'Sitting, I suppose. But a panino or something. Not a hot meal.'

The policeman crooked his finger and pointed down the lane to Blume's left. 'There on Via di San Marcello. The old Peroni brewery. Nice and warm, and not so many tourists now. It's a bit pricey, but if you just want a roll or something. There's no police discount.'

Blume thanked him, and walked a few paces down the narrow street, which was slick from the rain that had stopped falling an hour earlier but continued to drip from the dark buildings on either side of him. The lights of the Antica Birreria Peroni cast a golden glow on to the cobbles in front of him, whether from the ochre of the building itself or from the brass fittings inside he could not tell. He stopped just short of the entrance door, and considered. The door opened sending a gust of warm air laden with the scent of fried food and hops towards him, and a uniformed policeman came out, paused, nodded to Blume, and went on his way.

Blume rubbed his hands, which were perfectly warm but he wanted to remind himself of the cold, stamped his feet for the same reason, and walked quickly into the bar. When he had been a student, this place had been too expensive to frequent, but he had spent some evenings here, before the city filled up with its horrible Irish pubs. He remembered they used to serve fat-fried potatoes and German sausages, and wondered if they still did.

Half an hour later, walking quickly now, his stomach feeling very pleasantly bloated, his head still light but no longer threatening migraine, Blume was considering, with detached wonderment, at the mechanism by which he had ended up drinking a half litre of beer without having had the slightest intention of doing so. To cure his headache, he supposed, and it had worked. He felt pretty good, all things considered. Pretty damned good.

There was no reason for him not to drink; it was simply that he chose not to, or had chosen not to, after an attractive American woman was scathing to his face about his 'dependence' as she called it. He could smell the fried food coming off his own coat now.

He took the flight of steps that led up to Via 24 Maggio. To clear the hoppy smell from his breath, he took the steps three at a time, as fast as possible. He reached the top and tried to maintain his speed, but had to bend down and place his hands on his knees. He felt like he might faint. A doorman in livery watched him impassively from the Hotel Bolivar. He sucked in deep breaths, to get rid of the expanding pain in his chest. It was not a heart attack. A friend of his had had a heart attack, and said it was unmistakable. 'If you feel like there is an elephant sitting on your chest, it's a heart attack. Anything else is just wasted panic.'

Blume straightened up. More a heavy dog than an elephant. He recomposed himself, and walked with aplomb across the road.

34

BLUME HANDED over his badge, pistol, and handcuffs to a young man in a well-ironed uniform, who gave him three separate receipts and made him sign several papers, then asked him to take a seat, as if this were a job interview rather than its opposite.

They did not keep him waiting long. He was expected to sit and listen, which he did, as Questore De Rossi, his voice aching with regret, told him that there was simply no choice but to issue an interlocutory order. The vice-questore sitting beside his boss, nodded his head in rhythm to the beat of his boss's careful emphasis on certain words such as 'honourable' and 'shock' and 'unfortunate' and 'service' and 'embarrassment' and 'standards'.

Blume stayed silent as he was upbraided for unauthorized interference in an ongoing investigation, with actions verging on perversion of the course of justice. Failure to obey a direct order, failure to file a report, prejudicing interforce harmony, breaking a seal to gain unlawful access to the scene of a crime, neglect of duty, interference with and possible destruction of evidence, interference with witnesses, unlawful interrogation of suspect, unwarranted interviews with a terrorist, who then died in mysterious circumstances.

He kept his face set to impassive, but flinched a little when the questore moved on to an exaggerated version of the attempted arrest of the professor. He had not been expecting that. Zezza had not just filed a complaint, he had filled in all the details giving a running commentary.

Modulating his regret into a convincing imitation of concern, the questore wondered whether Blume had really been 'brandishing a pistol'.

'*Balle,*' said Blume dismissively.

The questore smiled as said he was pleased to hear it was bullshit. He had not believed it for a moment. A note of concern crept into his voice, and he wondered if Blume had considered the possibility of counselling.

Blume said the only counselling he intended to take was with the union and solicitors, whereupon the questore dropped the pretense of concern, which was a relief for all of them. Questore De Rossi told Blume to consider the prospect of life outside the police force; Blume counter-attacked, accusing the questore of caving in to political pressure. At this point, the vice-questore, a hunched creature with freckles way past the age in which it was normal to have them, intervened to say, 'Do I smell alcohol on your breath, Commissioner?'

'Absolutely not. I don't even drink.'

'I must be mistaken.'

'Maybe you should have that checked out,' said Blume.

'What do you mean?'

'Olfactory hallucinations can be the sign of a temporal lobe stroke.'

A bit of to-and-fro came quickly to an end when Blume, whose mind was now focused exclusively on his bladder, stood up.

'Are you walking out of this hearing?' asked the vice-questore in a high-pitched voice that he might have intended to sound indignant but came out as a squeal of undisguised delight at Blume's self-destruction.

It wasn't a hearing, but Blume hadn't time to insist on the point. 'I need to go to the toilet. I'll be back in a second.'

As he reached the door, the questore called to him. 'Commissioner?'

He turned round impatiently. 'What?'

'Turn right, second to last door on your right, just before the stairs. And, Commissioner?'

Blume waited, knowing what was coming.

'Don't bother coming back. We've finished here.'

Standing in the toilet, leaning with folded arm against the wall, Blume marvelled at a fun fact about beer that he had forgotten. As much as you drank was as much as you pissed. This rule did not seem to apply so inflexibly to other drinks.

Unlike in his station, the taps here gave forth a steady stream of warm water, and both the soap and towel dispensers were full. The mirror was remarkably clean and well illuminated by the overhead lights, and there-fore unforgiving of his face. Blume tried out some grins and smiles, then some sneers as he dried his hands, and then suddenly thought of the two-way mirrors in interrogation rooms and stopped. Soberly, he straightened his hair, his collar and breathed on to the palm of his hand and brought it to his nose. It smelled of pink bubble-gum from the soap he had just been using.

He stepped out the door, ready to turn directly on to the stairs and leave the building, but the neat cop who had deprived him of his badge and Beretta was standing there waiting for him.

'They want you back in, sir.'

'That's not what they just told me.'

'I don't know what they told you, I only know what they told me.'

When he entered the room again, the two men were sitting in the same places as before and attempting to wear the same expression, but something had changed. They were slightly more anxious, whereas he felt more relaxed now. Lighter without his badge and pistol, his bladder empty, his future a wide open range, he could not see what other harm they could do to him today. Perhaps at the disciplinary hearing itself, but that was at least six weeks away. He was suspended on full pay, and they suddenly needed him back to tell them something. His sense of ease increased when Questore De Rossi nodded to his freckled deputy, dismissing him.

'Look, Blume, seeing as you have got yourself involved in this, can you at least answer a few questions?'

Blume shrugged.

'Did the professor kill Stefania Manfellotto?'

'*Macché!*'

'I don't mean in person in the hospital. Did he order her killed, do you think?'

'No.'

'Is he involved in her murder?'

Blume was less sure about this. 'Probably not,' he ventured after a while.

'You don't sound too sure.'

'I can't be. Someone called while I was in the toilet,' said Blume with a grin. 'Right?'

The questore ignored his question. He picked up a pen, clicked it, clicked it a second time, put it down again, and then began moving a piece of paper in front of him. 'I am in two minds here. We have got a lot of pressure from the Carabinieri and the new investigating magistrate, who are all very anxious to see the back of you, and who wouldn't be? But Pitagora has friends, too, and they are even higher up, and the pressure from them, when it comes, will be even greater. For now, the professor seems to believe in you. He sent me a message – not directly – asking for your arguments to be listened to.'

'It *would* look good it you helped him in his hour of need, resisting the pressures of the Carabinieri.'

'You realize that I cannot lift a suspension even if I wanted to?'

'Of course,' said Blume.

'But if you have something that might help the professor recover his peace of mind, that would be welcome.'

'The professor is innocent,' said Blume, becoming more convinced of the idea as he spoke it.

'Give me your evidence.'

Blume shook his head. 'For now, it's only negative. I have no proof, and now thanks to you, I have no badge, so getting proof is going to be hard.'

'Just tell me your theory.'

'Not until it's fact.' Blume expected the questore to explode, but his expression was almost meek.

'What about this Manfellotto business?'

'Probably a political assassination.'

'You think someone dragged her out of bed, took her to the fire escape, and threw her over on to a group of doctors smoking in the courtyard. Who would have killed her, Blume? You spoke to her – improper conduct and all that aside.'

'The professor probably knows more or less who ordered it, but he's not behind it. It could be an accident, or suicide.'

'She was brain damaged?'

'Yes, but also perfectly sane, and perfectly harmless,' said Blume.

'Tell that to the people she shot and the 80 people she blew to pieces,' De Rossi said.

'Sure, if you think talking to the dead makes sense,' said Blume.

The questore eyed him levelly. 'My inclination is to back the professor. And that means you.'

'Good old Pitagora. He's scared, you see. They killed Manfellotto.'

'He should have been scared after the first assassination attempt, too, then.'

'Maybe he was,' said Blume. 'But I can see how this second one is more frightening for him.'

'How?'

'Well, apart from the fact they succeeded, they decided to get rid of someone who was only marginally dangerous. The professor is no doubt marginally dangerous to some people, probably the same people. Anyhow, sir, seeing as you cannot un-suspend me, can you get me clearance into the computer forensic labs at Tuscolana?'

'What do you want there?'

'I want to look at Facebook messages, emails, that sort of thing.'

The questore folded his arms. 'This *is* to do with the case?'

'Of course. It's the only thing I can do without getting under the feet of the Carabinieri. Without them knowing.'

'And this will help clear the professor?'

'Maybe. In any case, he will see that you have been trying to help.'

De Rossi picked up the phone on his desk. 'When were you planning on going?'

'I don't know, the next few days. I sort of lost my sense of urgency with the suspension.'

'How about right now? If you ever want back on the force.'

'Now's also good.'

After the questore had finished on the phone, he ordered Blume to wait at the front entrance on Via Genova. 'Someone will come to collect you.' He pointed a pudgy finger at Blume, 'If you're wrong . . .'

'Then you will suffer political embarrassment,' said Blume, 'but you will make damned sure my career goes down in flames.'

'Your life, Blume. Your whole life. You had better be right.'

35

O N H I S way through the courtyard of the Questura, Blume pulled out his phone and called Caterina. He let it ring, his satisfaction that he was fulfilling his duty without paying the price of conversation tinged with anxiety that she was not answering. It was a pity her phone would limit itself to telling her he had called, but fail to report that he had conscientiously let it ring and ring.

As he turned right into Via Genova, the air filled with a rushing sound as if a sharp breeze had come spinning through invisible trees, and then the rain came smashing down, bouncing off the four squad cars parked in front.

Blume leapt back under the loggia of the building, where the police-man standing guard was shaking his head in disgust.

Within five minutes, the loggia had filled up with functionaries, cops, steam, and cigarette smoke. Some of the braver souls, jeered and ironically applauded by their colleagues, pushed up umbrellas and ventured out. The ones with suits made calls, and unmarked dark cars flashing blue lights occasionally pulled up, opened their doors, and whipped them away. Someone offered Blume a cigarette, which he declined with regret. He remembered how there was something very satisfying about lighting up in the rain and standing in a fug of soft wet smoke, especially in company. He called Caterina again. Still no reply.

A few seconds later, a blue Alfa Romeo Giulietta pulled up in front of the building, causing a tiny interruption in the conversations around him as everyone noted, then ignored, its arrival. The back door opened and the vice-questore called Blume's name.

Blume ducked, ran, and swung into the car, bouncing down beside the freckly bastard, who moved over to the far side of the seat, and pouted out at the rain. The car was warm and smelled strongly of the air-freshener tree hanging from the rear-view mirror. The driver hooked his arm over the back of his seat and stared at Blume without seeming to see him, reversed blindly towards the fire station on the corner of Via Genova, then stopped to await instructions.

'This is where our appointment was,' said the vice-questore.

'It was raining,' said Blume. 'Use your head.' He tapped the driver on the shoulder. 'Via Tuscolana.'

The driver hesitated, awaiting confirmation from the vice-questore, who nodded irritably.

Even with the vice-questore acting like a personal pass key, it still took over an hour before Blume finally found himself where he wanted, which was inside a room that looked like a graveyard for old PCs, and for the careers of the two men inside. But they were remarkably cheerful. The first thing they did was offer Blume a ham sandwich. It was wrapped in cellophane and seemed innocuous, and he was hungry, but the fact it had been pulled out of a desk drawer full of computer components made him uneasy. The vice-questore sat at the door, fingering his freckles.

The one who had offered him the sandwich presented himself as Enrico. He pointed to his companion who was peering into a big red bag of Saiwa potato crisps. 'That's Sandro.'

Sandro looked up and nodded. He had the greasy-skin small-eyed look that Blume associated with all-night stake-outs.

In the middle of Blume's explanation of what he wanted, Sandro suddenly got up and left, muttering something unintelligible as he passed the vice-questore at the door.

'Never mind him, he'll be back,' said his partner. 'So you want to check the Facebook page of the victim? You had to come all the way here for that?'

'Yes, he did,' said the vice-questore. 'Let him ask the questions, so we can save time.'

'Sure,' said Enrico, rolling his eyes conspiratorially at Blume.

After a few moments of silence had passed, the vice-questore snapped. 'You're allowed to talk, you know. Commissioner, ask him whatever it is you need to know.'

'I am not sure what I am looking for,' said Blume. 'Probably nothing.'

Some more silence ensued. There was no sign of Sandro. Eventually, Enrico said, 'So you're American, Seattle. What's that like?'

'How do you know that?'

Enrico looked confused, then pointed at the vice-questore. 'He told me?'

The vice-questore wore a very convincing look of confusion and outrage. 'I did no such thing. I didn't even know he was American.'

'No, not directly, sir. You told us who was coming to visit. The rest –' Enrico waved his hand at the five lit computer screens, 'came from there. You have a small internet footprint, Commissioner. A Mafia boss would be proud to be so invisible.'

'Thanks for the comparison,' said Blume.

'Ndrangheta to be precise. The Camorra, on the other hand – all over the internet. Those guys *love* Facebook.'

Sandro re-entered with a fresh bag of crisps. He ripped open the bag and offered them around.

The vice-questore looked revolted.

'No, thanks,' said Blume.

Sandro sat down on a swivel chair beside his colleague and Blume, as Facebook pages appeared on three screens. He dug into the crisps, pushed them into his mouth.

'So, why do they call it Facebook?' said Enrico. 'It's not a book.'

Sandro swallowed his snack. 'But it does have faces.'

'Yeah, but it's not a book.' Enrico seemed quite exercised by the question.

'It's got pages,' said Sandro soothingly. 'Therefore, book.'

'Not even close.' Enrico had turned away from Sandro. 'I get the face bit, but it's not a book.'

Sandro used the opportunity to fill up with more crisps, and Blume realized the question, or accusation, was being directed at him.

'It's an American thing,' said Blume.

'I *know* it's American,' said Enrico. 'Everyone knows that.'

'In high school in America, they have what they call yearbooks. It's a photo album with all the faces of the people in the school divided by class. It's a book. You can find your classmates in it. That's where the idea came from.'

Enrico regarded him sceptically.

'I have two of them myself. Yearbooks, that is.'

They lay disintegrating under his parents' books in the study . . . speaking of which, he needed to clear the room out for his tenants.

'Is this from your days in Roosevelt High School?' asked Enrico with a grin that faded as he saw the look on Blume's face. He waved at the computers. 'Hey, it's all there. I was just checking.'

Sandro licked the salt and grease from his fingers and tapped on a keyboard to bring up an old-fashioned-looking data list, all text and no graphics. 'So, this Sofia. She didn't have so many friends. But she wasn't that active either. The photos are pretty sober, not your usual pouty teen-age-girl face.'

Blume peered over his shoulder and the vice-questore came over to take a look, too.

'Like you're a real expert on teenage girls,' said Enrico

'Like any of us here is,' said Blume. 'Except Sofia wasn't a teenager any more.'

'Lots of dogs,' continued Sandro. 'Rodents in cages, which is a bit weird. And this guy.'

'That's her boss.'

'Ideo – yeah his face is tagged,' said Sandro. 'He also sent her some emails.'

'What about?' asked Blume.

'Work. Nothing interesting. Except one, I guess. He's annoyed with her for making some stupid mistakes. She sends him one back, apologizing, then there is nothing more for a month, and suddenly, she sends him an email saying she is quitting.'

'Quitting? Show me,' said Blume.

Sandro tapped on the keyboard.

Dear Professor Ideo, I think you know what I am going to say to you. I cannot work in these circumstances. I will not. Unless the situation has resolved itself by Friday, I shall have no option but to resign my post. I do not want to do this. Frankly, I value my post above our friendship. If I find I have to quit, I will make sure people know why.

Yours sincerely,

Sofia.

'That was the end of it,' explained Sandro. 'The professor never replied. And she didn't resign. They must have worked it out, because there is another work-related one weeks later.' He called it up. It was a long message to do with a press release he wanted her to write. Ideo was planning to launch a campaign against the sterilization of pigeons on the grounds that immigrants ate pigeons and would end up ingesting the sterilization treatment. Ideo suggested this might be a deliberate campaign to stop immigrants from having children.

The three men read it in silence. The vice-questore remained in the corner, tapping on his iPhone.

'Leftists are weird people,' said Sandro at length.

'Do immigrants eat pigeons?' Enrico wanted to know. 'It's the first I've heard about it.'

'Go back to Sofia's threatened resignation,' said Blume. 'What does it sound like to you?'

'Sexual harassment, for sure,' said Enrico. Sandro crinkled his crisps bag in agreement. 'But it looks like it could have been resolved.'

'When was all this?' asked Blume

'Last January. Ten months ago. But there's no more. This one email is all we got.'

'That's her wall,' said Enrico. 'Links to serious sorts of stuff. Museums, medical stuff, biology, science sites. Poetry.'

'Her poetry?' asked Blume.

'No, some guy called Emilio Dickinson or something. All about death and stopping.'

Sandro pressed the buttons flicking between code and ordinary Facebook pages as Enrico continued the commentary. 'We've checked all this. There is nothing there. No threats, no hints of trouble, nothing. She had a boyfriend in London. Looks to us like that's where he still is. This is the condolence page. So you can see for yourself: 42 friends but 381 expressions of condolence. Nothing suspicious there. Young people *love* posting on a death page. It's the same mentality that makes people slow down at car accidents. No trolls, no hate. Traffic has collapsed to zero now.'

'Let me see the messages from Olivia and Marco,' said Blume.

'On the condolences page?'

'No. All of them. Can you extract them?'

'Sure. But they've been checked. I thought she was killed because she was a witness. If so, her killer is hardly likely to have friended her on Facebook.'

'I suppose not,' said Blume. 'Still, can you pull up the conversations for me?'

'You know there's hardly any need. She hardly ever used Facebook, and she was only on it for a year. You could read through everything in a few hours,' said Sandro.

'OK, I'll do that then,' said Blume. 'But I thought all young people were on Facebook.'

'They are now. But Sofia was just old enough to have found out about other sites and services. She used email, which a lot of young people don't really do.'

'Email is for old people?' asked Blume.

'Yeah,' said Enrico.

The news disturbed Blume. He was just getting used to the idea that CDs were not cutting edge. 'Did she have anything before Facebook?'

'MySpace. But she never did anything with it. And a Hotmail account that she used to chat on,' said Enrico.

'Can you recover her chat history?'

'With file carving, if we knew what we're looking for. But the best way would be to go to the ISP.'

'What about her email?'

'Well, for a while she was using Outlook, so it's all here. Again, we've looked at that. But there's not much to see. Mostly college stuff, funny video links. Harmless. The girl was a studious and serious person.'

'Did she have an address book?'

'Sure. About 300 names in there. Excluding sign-up addresses, companies, institutional addresses, and so forth, about 30 real people . . . Here. See for yourself.'

A bar chart overlaid with a jagged line and a red curve line popped up onscreen.

'What am I looking at?'

'We cross-referenced email addresses with Facebook contacts and generated a composite chart based on frequency and message or chat length. The long bars are the names of the people she was most in contact with over the past three years. They are identified by email addresses . . .'

He clicked on another button and a wall of numbers with dots leapt out at Blume, 'by IP addresses and . . . So let's see . . . Olivia_v@hotmail.com, and then Marco_08@hotmail.com, and Brian_93@yahoo.com are the three main contacts. There is also a Pitagora@sapienza.uni. That was one of the names you asked us to look for.'

'It was,' said Blume. 'She was in contact with the professor?' He felt a nervous knot in his stomach at the idea he had missed something.

'No,' said Enrico. 'That was Marco_08 forwarding something from the professor about a lesson. There is no direct traffic between her and the professor.'

'Who's Marco_08?' asked Enrico.

His partner answered. 'That's the victim's cousin's boyfriend. He's attached to Olivia, right, Commissioner?'

'Right,' said Blume.

'And this Brian?' asked Enrico. 'The guy whose IPs are in London. He comes in late.'

'Boyfriend of the victim,' said Sandro. 'Or friend. Still in the UK by all appearances.'

'And why is Sofia's name in red?' asked Blume.

'No reason,' said Sandro. He hit his keyboard and her name reverted to black. 'I highlighted her name in red so you could see it better in the cc field sent by this Pitagora person.'

'Sofia_347. That's her?' asked Blume.

'Yes.'

'Why 347?'

Enrico shrugged. 'A name like Sofia is going to be used already, even if you add the surname. So often the site will suggest you tack a number on at the end. A lot of people choose their year of birth, but if your name's really common, or you just don't care, you may accept whatever random number you get given. She didn't seem that interested in social media and computers; my guess is she just clicked OK OK OK agree agree agree, like any sane person should because even if you don't agree they are still going to steal your data and sell it to companies.'

'I always used my full name, and that's never happened to me.'

'You probably got there first. If you try and sign up a main account now with, like Google, Facebook, Hotmail, or LinkedIn, you'll find you have less choice.'

'I have never even heard of LinkedIn,' said Blume. 'So why would you think I would have got there first?'

'All I meant was you're pretty old,' said Enrico.

'He means in internet years,' said Sandro. 'They're like dog years.'

The vice-questore was grinning like a skull in the corner.

'I think I have seen enough here,' said Blume.

36

IN THE meantime, Caterina had gone offline. A frustrating back-and-forth with the hospital finally revealed the news that she had been discharged, and, no, they were not able to say if this had been her own decision.

Blume considered, then dismissed calling Caterina's mother to find out what was happening. A few months ago, Caterina and he had agreed to let the Telecom Italia landline lapse.

'Nowadays, we phone the person, not the building we think the person might be in,' said Caterina. 'I don't see why you object to that.'

Something about a phone ringing in an empty house appealed to him, as did the idea of sitting by a ringing phone in a room and not answering it. It was something to do with the possibility of not being there, but he had never properly explained it to himself, let alone her.

Now, standing at the front door of her building, Blume finally admitted to himself that he was ashamed and afraid to meet Caterina. He had keys, of course. He always had keys. But something about slipping into the apartment like a thief made him pocket them and press the buzzer. He needed to announce himself this evening.

When Caterina's mother answered, he told himself he had been expecting this. After all, Caterina had been in hospital until only a few hours ago, and she was now an expectant mother. Tired and injured, calling on the help of her mother as well as her partner.

When Mrs Mattiola said Caterina was not at home, Blume told himself he had been expecting this, too, since it made sense for Caterina to go to her mother's where she could help and be helped, and maybe pick up Elia, who ate most of his meals there. The flaw in this logic was that Mrs Mattiola ought to be in her own home with her daughter.

A neighbour from downstairs was coming out now, and kindly held the door open for Blume.

'The weather's cleared up at last. I couldn't take another day of rain,' said the neighbour with apparent friendliness.

'Still chilly, though,' said Blume.

'Yes, well, it's November, what do you expect?' said the neighbour, walking out. Blume let go of the door, which closed with a snap. What was it with people? A conversation about the weather had ended up with the implication he was an idiot for not knowing that it got cold in November.

As always, he shunned the lift, more trouble than it was worth with its flappy little swing doors. Depressing, too, with its Bakelite fixtures and peat-dark mirror, wet floor, and constant smell of mechanical grease.

Mrs Mattiola, who had been very fond of him once, had not even buzzed him in. She had been so encouraging in the early days but then something happened. It might have been the deteriorating condition of her husband, or the absence of any marriage proposals, or perhaps the realization that a commissioner, despite the elegant title, was just an under-paid pleb with no real power, but she had grown colder towards him month by month so that, without any direct exchange of fire between them, they were now enemies. Blume felt if he had arrived a few years earlier, he might have enlisted Caterina's father to his cause, but that chance was gone now.

He reached the front door and knocked softly with his hand. Mrs Mattiola was waiting behind it. She opened it very slightly, keeping the chain on. It seemed thin enough to cut with his fingers.

'This is very hard for me to say, Commissioner . . .'

'Don't call me that.'

'It's a bit late to start using first names.'

'Where is she?'

'At my place, of course. Please don't go round there.'

'Fine.'

'Thank you. She promised you would be reasonable. She also asked me to tell you not to come here either. As of tomorrow, when she comes back.'

'I have things in there that belong to me.'

'Most of what I see in here belongs to my daughter.'

'That's because from where you're standing you can't see my pants drawer.'

'Are you trying to make light of this?'

'I need some clothes. That's all I'll take.'

'You can work that out with Cate'. I am not letting you in.'

'I do have a key,' said Blume.

'She said you were to put the flat and building keys into the door on your side and leave them there. And to walk away.'

Blume felt the energy drain from him. 'OK. I'm going to leave them in the lock. Did she say why?'

'She said you would know why. She said if you thought about it honestly, you would be able to come up with at least ten reasons.'

'I just wish she had had the courage to do this herself.'

She slammed the door in his face, then, to his surprise, threw it open, and stared at him, her face chalk white. Her eyes, which usually peered absently at him from behind owlish glasses, were steady as two laser beams etching her contempt all over his face as he stood there, keys still in hand. 'Courage! My daughter came out of hospital today, her body black with bruising, her beautiful face swollen, her legs, stomach, and back gashed open and painted brown with antiseptic. She spent four hours with the doctors this morning, and then fought and cried until finally, against all their better judgements they let her out of hospital for the night, but only because they needed the bed and she threatened to call in her colleagues if they didn't let her go. She came home, comforted her son, who was worried sick and completely abandoned to his own devices, while I tried to look after my damaged daughter and helpless husband, while you . . . you . . . worm!'

He heard a tiny metallic click from down the hall as a neighbour cracked open a door to see what was going on, and he could picture himself from the neighbour's perspective, head down, neck burning in bright humiliation as he stood there.

He held out the keys. Mrs Mattiola, perhaps thinking he was offering to shake hands or reach out in some way, shrank back from him in alarm.

'The keys. I'm giving you the keys.'

She slammed the door in his face again. It was a fearful insult but the disappearance of her face and the muffling of her voice were very welcome. 'You are supposed to put them in the door and walk away!'

Blume fumbled for a while slipping his own key ring off, then inserted the flat key into the door in front of him. 'The keys are in the door. Tell Caterina I . . . tell her I did what she asked. I am walking away now.'

There was no reply.

Part of him was enraged at what was happening, but another part of him felt relieved to have it confirmed that he was the sort of person who deserved to be alone. Besides, he felt like having a drink.

Downstairs on the street, he called 6645, gave the taxi dispatcher his name and Caterina's address. They asked for a phone number, and when he started with the 333 prefix, told him they would prefer a landline number to a mobile. Eventually, his voice heavy with suspicion, the dispatcher told him there would be a car along in ten minutes.

He moved away from the front entrance to avoid meeting Mrs Mattiola if she came out. He did not want her to think he was standing there like a stalker. The air pressure was high enough to give a cold night sky, with the stars visible in spite of the glow of the city lights. He walked up and down trying to keep warm. If he had known the number of another cab company, he would have called it. No doubt the other companies had warm cars right now cruising softly past, one street away.

His phone trembled in his pocket and he pulled it out and cupped it against his cold ear. 'Taxi. Lima Roma 147. Two minutes,' said a voice in broad Roman. 'Confirm?'

'Yeah,' said Blume, turning and walking back quickly. Without quite realizing it, he had walked all the way down the street. He had also failed to notice that the street sloped down, so that the front door was out of sight, and the taxi driver would not see him. He had also failed to calculate how hard it was to walk fast up even a gentle incline.

As the front door of the apartment block came back into sight, he could see the taxi sitting there. Then the door to the building opened and someone walked out, and even from this distance, he recognized the careful gait of Caterina's mother. The taxi driver tapped his horn and now she was going over to him. Blume slowed down his pace, and watched as she drew back and looked warily about her, like someone who had just been informed of a spy. Then she caught sight of him. He could not see her face from where he was, but he saw the way she stood stock-still and looked all the way down the street, past the few other people still out and about, to where he stood. The only other person on the pavement at that time. She raised her arm and pointed at him. The taxi flashed its lights and came down towards him.

Blume hopped directly in the back seat and hunkered down.

'You weren't there,' said the driver grumpily. 'I almost drove off.'

'San Giovanni area. Via Orvieto,' said Blume.

The driver pressed the address into his satnav and started pressing buttons.

'It's just off Via La Spezia, I can tell you where to turn.'

The driver continued working at his machine. There was €5.50 on the meter already.

'You don't need that to tell you where Via La Spezia is, do you? How long have you been driving a taxi?'

'Look, you do your job, whatever it is, I'll do mine.'

'Yeah, but your job is to drive, not play video games. Via La Spezia. Go down to the bottom of this road, go straight, go straight again, and after that go straight. I'll give you plenty of advance warning of anything so radical as a turn.'

'If I don't like your attitude, I don't have to take you anywhere. There!' He pointed triumphantly at the satnav, which showed a big green arrow pointing straight ahead.

Blume got off at the corner of Via Orvieto, then spent a fair while collecting the exact fare from his pocket in as many coins as possible and putting them one by one into the driver's dirty hand.

He walked across the courtyard, surprised to notice that it had a familiar smell all of its own. The voices, the crooked venetian blinds of the building opposite, the missing shutters from the third floor, the chrome pipes stuck to the outside of the buildings in the mid 1990s, bringing, for the first time, proper drinking water to the complex, just in time for the whole world to start drinking bottled water anyhow, were all powerfully familiar. He realized how much he had missed them. In the summer, he could hear too much of his neighbours, but now it was cold and shutters were closed to keep in the heat, and the complex was uncharacteristically quiet. It might almost have been Germany. He opened the front door to his building, and breathed in the heavy smell of the oil-fired furnace in the basement.

A brown package had been jammed halfway through the narrow slot of his letterbox at the bottom of the stairs. He pulled it out and ripped it open and found himself looking at Fisher's book. He pulled out a few bills and flyers and stuffed them in his pocket as he made his way up.

Outside his own door, he paused, took breath, and prepared himself. This was going to be a little embarrassing, but it was necessary. He checked his phone. It was almost midnight. Definitely too late. He would need to explain himself clearly, and be very apologetic. He pressed the doorbell.

'*Keee ay*?' A man's voice, sounding slightly frightened, perhaps, or was it the faltering Italian pronunciation.

Speaking English, Blume introduced himself from the outside of his own front door, explaining that he was the landlord, and that something unexpected had happened, and that he was hoping he might perhaps be allowed in for no more than thirty seconds to collect something. He knew his speaking English should act as a guarantee, but the man still did not open.

'It's almost midnight!'

'I realize that. I am terribly sorry.' He fingered the key in his pocket. You only ever hear of tenants' rights, he thought. But Mr Almost Midnight was standing in his house on his carpet, farting into his sofa and eating off his kitchen table. It hardly bore thinking about.

Now a woman's voice, deep and sonorous, could be heard remonstrating and Blume distinctly heard the words, 'Let the poor man in!'

The soft clunking sound of the key being turned in the lock told him that his tenants were cautious people, locking themselves in at night. The door swung open to reveal a man, with wispy fair hair and a thin blond beard. Blume made to step across the threshold and the man came forwards as if to block him.

Blume stood back and regarded his adversary. 'You're not called Mutungi,' he accused.

'No. I'm Walker. Peter Walker. Mutungi's my wife's name,' said Walker in an annoying accent of some sort.

Blume stared at the insubstantial pale-skinned Englishman in front of him. 'You're the husband?' He felt aggrieved. 'I was told you were a Tanzanian couple.'

'I am Tanzanian,' said the Englishman.

A broad-hipped, broad-shouldered black African woman wearing a silk bathrobe bustled into the room, relegating Walker to the periphery of Blume's mind.

'Hello Mr BLUME!' she said, emphasizing his surname in way that made him feel important, welcome, and appreciative of the beauty of his own name. She gave him a dazzling smile, 'And what can we DO for you so late in the day?'

Blume was lost in admiration for a few moments and failed to speak.

'We really like this APARTMENT. You have such good *taste*.' The inflection she gave the word suggested that his good taste had come as a completely unexpected and delightful surprise to her. Seeing that Blume was evidently a slow-witted man, she asked him if he had come to welcome them.

He apologized for the intrusion. 'I wouldn't do this if it wasn't an emergency. Of course, now that I *am* here, I am happy to welcome you and if there is anything you want, don't hesitate to ask. If the kitchen radiator is cold, by the way, just bleed it by loosening the valve. Count to forty, then tighten it again.'

'And you are most welcome here, Mr Blume.'

A weak sniff from behind his back reminded him of the thin Englishman. Apologizing again, he explained he needed to pick up a few things, and would take only two minutes.

'Of COURSE! Where are these things that you wish to pick up?'

'In here,' said Blume walking towards the study. 'May I?' He opened the door and switched on the light just as Mrs Mutungi came bustling up quickly behind him. 'Mr Blume, that is where –'

It was like walking into a dream in which a familiar place suddenly turns into something else. The overcrowded study, full of posters and paintings, papers, and books, carpets, boxes, old clothes, and coats, which were what he had come for, was empty of everything except two new pine beds in which slept two children with perfect brown skin. He snapped off the light as one of them, a girl aged perhaps 6 or 7, began to stir in her sleep. The after-image of the empty shelves remained impressed on his retina and then floated upwards.

'The removal men you sent arrived this morning. They took everything away to the warehouse. We very much appreciate how quick you were to send them. The children are VERY happy with the room. It is such a NICE room. Big. They can play there, too.'

'They took everything? I had all my clothes in here.'

'Has it not all come to you, Mr Blume? Is something missing? That is it! Something is missing.'

'No, no, nothing is missing. At least I don't think so. It went into storage. I don't even know where.'

Prisca Mutungi, who was almost as tall as him, put a comforting hand on his elbow and steered him back into the living room, where the Englishman was slouched on the couch watching rugby highlights on Sky Sports. 'You can call me tomorrow, yes? You can tell me if anything is missing and I will look for it for you.'

'Thank you very much for your hospitality,' said Blume, stepping out the door.

'You are most welcome, Mr Blume,' she said. 'I am MOST happy to have met you.'

Blume walked back downstairs. Now he needed a place to spend the night. Tomorrow, the first thing he would do upon waking would be to cancel his subscription to Sky.

37

ANOTHER TAXI got him to the station at Piazza Collegio Romano. After midnight, hours were always longer and journey times through the emptying streets compressed, so that he always felt he was ahead of himself at night, getting to where he needed to be slightly before he was ready for it.

As he walked up the steep marble staircase to the main hall, a four-strong *Celere* patrol preparing to go on to the graveyard shift was coming down. They saluted him with exaggerated cheer, and Blume had to remind himself not to wish them good luck. It was one thing being suspended, but wishing good luck to a patrolman who then got stabbed or shot would really end his career. Even if they got a flat tyre or someone scalded his tongue on hot coffee, Blume's ill-advised good luck would be remembered in perpetuity.

'Go kick someone's head in,' he recommended, to general laughter and profanity. They assured him they would do their best.

The duty officer dropped his eyes in embarrassment at seeing Blume, and mumbled a good evening, which Blume scorned. He would have preferred a direct challenge of his right to be there.

He went up to his office, and took a clean shirt and a round-necked sweater from a narrow locker in the corner of the room. He also took a disposable razor and washed himself in the toilet.

Sleeping in the office was out of the question. Or rather, it was an absolute last option, which he really did not want to take. The suspension was damaging enough in its way, but some colleagues might even give him kudos points. Sleeping in the office because homeless and without anyone who liked him enough to put him up for the night was guaranteed to undermine his remaining authority.

At half past midnight, carrying no gun, badge or bag, he left the station without a clear idea of where he was going. He passed the great silent hulk of the Pantheon and reached Piazza Rotonda, where some people were still out, huddled around gas heaters, having cocktails. With his new tourist's eye, he saw the Albergo del Sole on the east side of the piazza. He shrugged. It was off season, and maybe he'd get a discount since he'd only be staying a few hours.

The concierge glanced up as he walked in, then down at a large guestbook on the counter. Blume wondered if he spent the entire night in a monastic vigil, standing and reading the names in the book.

Blume asked if they had a room. The man pursed his lips and shook his head in awe as the great Book revealed to him that there was, in fact, a room available. It was a double room. Would sir be interested?

Blume shrugged. He might as well be extravagant this once. He took out his wallet and was pleased to see he had brought his credit card, which he hardly ever used. He pulled it out, and asked how much.

Blume made the concierge repeat the amount twice, not because he hadn't heard, but because he was hoping to see the man collapse in shame at the price he had just quoted. But if anything, the man's spine stiffened and the tone became haughtier.

'I did say a night, not a week. You understand?'

'I'm afraid it's evidently you who doesn't understand, sir. That is the rate per night.'

Blume gave his best basilisk stare at the jumped-up night porter who, finally, flinched and then relented enough to offer help. 'If sir wants, I can try to see if there are other places with more modest rates.'

'Never mind. I'll sleep in the doorway of the Pantheon with the drunks,' said Blume.

He left the hotel and headed towards the Gelateria Giolitti, which stayed open until two. As a young man he used to consider this place expensive, but he calculated he could buy himself 400 ice-cream cones for the price of a night in that hotel.

He had a Torta al Caffè and, what the hell, an Amaro Marcono, and then another. He thought he might simply walk around the city all night, but he wanted a bed. He could only postpone sleep when working a fast case with a team of people.

He walked quickly past government buildings, nodding at the two listless cops standing by their Iveco van waiting for the night to pass. At the taxi rank at Largo Chigi, there was just one car. He climbed in.

'Where?'

'I need a hotel. Cheap.'

'You didn't book?'

'No.'

The taxi driver nodded slowly, taking in the information. 'Everyone books nowadays. You book from your smartphone, see? If you're a walk-in, they'll charge you more. Does it have to be central?'

'I suppose not.'

'Clean, good food?'

'I don't care. I just need to lie down.'

'There's a place just outside the city on Via Aurelia, next to the station. It's a massive hotel, and usually empty. It used to be luxury, back in the 1970s. It's run by the priests, and they sometimes use it for conferences, Catholic scout jamborees, that sort of thing. But even then, I've never seen it even nearly full.'

'Any idea how much it costs?'

'A tourist mentioned it the other day. I think he said €55 a night.'

'Then that,' said Blume, 'is where we're going.'

38

CATERINA LAY in her childhood bed listening to the rain. Her child, like a visiting adult guest, slept in the living room on the sofa bed. Her mother was next door, happy to have her hands and home full again.

It seemed Alec had behaved exactly as instructed, as she knew he would. Walking away came naturally to him. She would miss him, but she would manage better without. He never expected meals, his shirts ironed, or her to clean up after him, and if anything, he was fussier than her about tidiness and hygiene; but she found herself looking out for him, which had become indistinguishable from looking after him. He needed mothering, and she was not sure that is what she had in mind when she entered the relationship. The idea of looking after him and his child, as well as Elia, her failing mother, and her failed father was overwhelming.

Her phone buzzed silently. It was three o'clock in the morning, so she knew it would be him. Ever since her mother had come home with the news that he had left without even collecting his clothes, she had been waiting for this call. It was typical of him to put it off so long.

It was easier to speak to him at night. Blume listened in the dark. When he felt invisible, he dropped many of his defences. She dropped the phone on to the pillow, and laid her ear against it, closing her eyes and whispering as she spoke to him.

When he had got through his apologies, he said, 'But, the thing is, I haven't been able to think of anything else. We're going to have a child!'

She felt the anger stir in her stomach again, and lifted her head for a moment while his voice, tiny from the middle of the pillow, continued speaking.

'So you knew,' she said. 'And though you knew, you still managed not to visit.'

'I did visit, Caterina. While you were asleep, and when you were away for tests. I discussed the situation with a doctor, he told me about the danger of an abruption, but that it would probably be OK. It *is* OK, right, Caterina?'

She said nothing.

'When did you find out, Caterina? Were you planning to tell me soon? I wish we had had a better moment together. Caterina? Are you still there?'

'I'm here, Alec.'

'The baby. It's OK, isn't it? Do you have to go back for more tests?'

'Alec, you know a habit of yours when you have a bad conscience?'

'What?'

'You ask multiple questions. You don't give people time to reply between one and the next because you don't really want to hear the answers.'

'Sorry. I'll ask just one question at a time. First of all, how are you feeling?'

'Physically I'm fine.'

'Good. The physical part. Sadness is something we can work at resolving.'

'I said nothing about being sad.'

'You didn't need to. And the baby?'

'Gone.' Suddenly this seemed the easiest thing to say.

He made a swallowing sound, and then fell silent. Twice he cleared his throat to speak, and twice he said nothing. The silence stretched on. Then in a voice not quite his own, a voice streaked with mucus and tuned to the wrong pitch, he said, 'Oh God, I am so sorry.'

She knew he was. She also knew he was not speaking to her only; he really was invoking the God he avowed not to believe in, and he was saying sorry to Him, too. He was accepting his culpability, but it would not survive the daylight. Tomorrow, he would be atheist again, and careless of her and others. Tomorrow he would be distracted when it suited him, and focused only on what interested him, which was not even police work, but rather, showing other people that he was good at police work.

The wind whipped the rain against the window, making a sudden rattling noise that drowned out his voice.

'What? I missed that, Alec.'

'I was saying that that accident . . . Look, can I do anything?'

'No,' she said.

'This is all my fault.'

It probably was, but the statement still sounded self-aggrandizing. He still saw everything as related to what he did or did not do.

'It's weird,' said Blume. 'Everything is going along just fine then . . .'

'The Skoda.' She needed to change the direction of the conversation.

'What?'

'You asked me to look out for a stolen Skoda Octavia. Before I left to see that barber.' She stopped. Every conversational turn was an exercise in excruciating tact and half-truths. She could not live like this. 'No Octavia Skoda was reported stolen.'

'It doesn't matter,' said Blume. 'I had forgotten about it.'

'Shut up, and listen. When I drew a blank, I did what I often end up doing, which is trying to second-guess you. I ran a cross-check of Skoda ownership on the various people involved in your case. But that, too, produced no results. In my research, I did find that the father of a certain Olivia Fontana, cousin of the girl who was killed, has a criminal record. His last arrest dates back to 15 years ago, but he was involved with some bad people back then. Did you know that about him?'

'No,' admitted Blume.

'Well, once I discovered that, I cross-checked Skoda ownership with the names of some of Visco's brothers-in-arms, so to speak. Nothing. So I branched out even further, and drew blanks all round. Finally I got a sort of near-hit. A Skoda Octavia is registered to a Paolo Aquilone, brother of Olivia's boyfriend, Marco. But this Paolo lives in Naples. And he's a Carabiniere.'

'That's interesting,' said Blume, his voice suddenly stronger and less contrite as he forgot about lost fetuses and her. 'Very.'

'Could this Paolo be involved?' asked Caterina, getting drawn in despite herself. 'I don't see how he fits.'

'Have you been following the case, Caterina?'

'Yes. The cases, as I prefer to think of them. I would separate Sofia Fontana from Stefania Manfellotto.'

'Really? I think you're right.'

'I think if a woman was investigating you might have got further. There is too much emphasis on men.'

'I don't follow,' said Blume.

'Of course you don't,' she said.

'No, I really don't get your meaning. It's all to do with women. The two victims are women. Are you saying the perpetrator is a woman, too?'

'That's not what I meant. You suspect Olivia, don't you?'

This was met with silence. He hated to be second-guessed. Eventually he said, 'She has a financial motive.'

'It's your case.'

'I still don't get what you said about men.'

'I meant nothing by it. Try to see things from a woman's perspective every now and then.'

'Which woman?'

'Women in general, Jesus, Alec. Sofia. The poor girl has been interpreted by a bunch of men since the start of all this, then probably killed by one, too.'

More silence.

'Alec, are you going to say something?'

'Can I see you?'

'No. I don't think so. Not for a while at least. I need to rest.'

'Goodnight, then. I really am so very sorry.'

'I know you are.'

'Goodnight.'

'Goodnight.'

She closed the phone cover slowly, and slipped it under her pillow. He would not call back, but if he did, if he became desperate, she would answer. Up to a point, she would be there for him.

39

B LUME DROPPED his phone on to the floor, and peeled the top sheet off his legs, then detached the back of his legs from the lower sheet and contemplated the quilted bedcover. It was the colour of dark jam and the seams were lined with thin strings that looked like they might have dropped off the ceiling where black pieces of cobweb floated. Some previous occupant appeared to have been playing in the bed with a fingerprint kit to judge from the smudges and marks around the headboard and wall behind. Convinced he would never sleep, he got up, turned off the light, and lay down. He knew he was not going to get much rest in this filthy, hot bed, whose presence in a room so small was a mystery in itself, unless they had taken the door off, or hauled it in the window, or maybe it came in pieces. That must be it.

No one could possibly sleep in a room like this.

He was therefore very surprised to wake up to the sound of birds and rain against his window. He took his phone off the floor and it confirmed that he had not just dozed off but slept seven hours.

He decided to forgo breakfast, not that he saw any sign of it anywhere in the hotel, which, in the morning light, turned out to be far larger than it had seemed late at night. He traversed the vast empty lobby to the reception desk, where an incongruously cheerful receptionist stood waiting for him with a smile. He asked her to call a taxi. She did so, and as he sat waiting she looked at him appraisingly. Blume considered the curve of her breasts and imagined her without her frumpy uniform on. He wished he cleaned himself up a bit better. She gave him another smile – nice fleshy lips, too – and said, 'Somascan, am I right?'

'I beg your pardon?'

'Somascan father, I can tell.'

'What the hell is a Somascan?'

'Oh. I'm sorry, you're not a priest?'

'No.'

The young woman blushed, then disappeared into the back room and emerged with leaflets, which she pressed into his hand. 'I am so sorry. I didn't realize you were an ordinary person. A tourist, I mean.'

Blume shuffled through the pamphlets on the Colosseum, the Trevi Fountain, Piazza Navona, the Bocca della Verità, and the Vatican.

She pointed to a blue brochure. 'That one has a good map of the city centre in it.' She smiled at him, seeking secular forgiveness.

'Thanks,' he said. Trying to squeeze them into his pocket, but finding they were too bulky.

'Don't mention it. Do you need any bus tickets?'

Why not, he thought. Four seemed a good number to buy, but he made it five when she could not find change.

'What about sightseeing coaches? There is a double-decker bus with an open top. The ticket costs €12 if you get it at the stop, but just €8 if you get it here.'

'I think I'll give that a miss,' said Blume. 'It's a bit wet to sit on the open top of a bus.'

'You can sit inside downstairs.'

'I may as well get an ordinary ATAC bus then.' Still free for policemen thanks to the efforts of the questore.

She glanced at him with the beginnings of suspicion. 'You sound Roman.'

'No, no.' He had to stop her from looking too foolish.

'Where are you from, then?'

He thought about it. 'All over the place, really. Nowhere and everywhere.' He saw her eyes narrow again, and he grabbed a random town from his mind. 'Chieti. That's where I'm from originally.'

She seemed to accept this, but was now determined to be disappointed. 'So you'll have seen Rome already?'

'Not as a tourist,' he assured her. There, thank Christ, was his taxi pulling into the turning circle in front of the hotel.

He had the taxi let him out on the Via del Corso, and headed up Via dell'Arancio where he slipped inside a café frequented by shopkeepers rather than policemen. There he had two cornettos and three cappuccinos until his feet felt grounded in reality. Dropping the pamphlets into an overflowing white dumpster, he began his walk back towards Piazza Collegio Romano.

Panebianco was in the office, and made no secret of his displeasure at seeing Blume walk in.

'You shouldn't be here. It's bad for you, bad for us.'

'It's a courtesy visit,' said Blume. 'Nothing wrong with a courtesy visit, is there? I need to check the database.'

'I'll do it. What do you need to know?'

'There is a kid called Marco Aquilone. His father was in the army. His brother's in the Carabinieri, too. Look them up.'

'Anything else?'

'Check out what the inheritance situation is for Mrs Fontana,' he said at last.

'Who?'

'Sofia's mother. I think she stands to gain an inheritance.'

'And?' Panebianco was being awkward. He could follow the logic if he wanted.

'And seeing as she has no children any more, who will she pass it on to, do you think?'

'Her niece, Olivia?' Panebianco scratched below his lip as he considered this. 'That works, just. Assassination now for an inheritance much later when suspicions will not arise. That would take a cold bitch. Is this your idea?'

'It's a hypothesis. I'd prefer no one knew about it yet. I am particularly minded not to tell the Carabinieri,' said Blume.

Panebianco looked at Blume and nodded slowly in acknowledgement of the trust Blume was placing in him. 'I need a magistrate if I am going to look in any detail.'

'Start working on it. Pretend I am not suspended. And prep the magistrate. It'll make you look good.'

'As if this were my idea?'

'You can have it if you want. It might not be right.'

Panebianco shook his head. 'She was the shooter? Or . . .'

'Her boyfriend, Marco. He seems weak. He seems like the type who would do anything for her. Now, seeing as I was followed by a man in a Skoda, and Marco's brother drives a Skoda, and may be inclined to look after his baby brother, or may even stand to gain some inheritance, I'd like you to look into it.'

Panebianco was already tapping at his keyboard. 'Meanwhile the Carabinieri and the investigating magistrate are following the political angle.'

'Yes. With reason,' said Blume. 'After all, Manfellotto was almost certainly killed by some rogue elements of the service or on the orders of someone with things to hide. What they don't realize, is that she was killed much as a nomad tribe might first try to help, but then finally kill an injured companion.'

'Nomads do that?'

'I don't know,' said Blume. 'It's just a metaphor. Elephants, then. I'm sure some animals do that.'

'Not elephants, I think . . .' A photograph of a young man in a Carabiniere uniform appeared on Panebianco's screen. 'Not the world's handsomest, is he?' remarked Panebianco.

'That's Paolo Aquilone?'

'Yes.'

'Wow,' said Blume. 'His younger brother got all the looks. Check him out, Rosario. Marco Aquilone.'

'Why would I want to "check him out"?'

'The sheer contrast.' Blume was peering hard at the screen and ignoring Panebianco's touchiness. 'Hey, do you think he has curly hair underneath that cap?'

Panebianco glanced at the screen. 'It's under a cap. You can't tell.'

'Pity,' said Blume. 'But the way the cap sits sort of high on his head, isn't that the sign of curly hair?'

'Just accept that you can't tell from this picture. There will be others. I'll get them for you.'

'Thanks, Rosario.'

'Don't mention it. By the way, Principe has been replaced. Alice Saraceno has taken over.'

This was not news to Blume, but he did not appreciate being one of the last to know officially. The least Principe could have done was a courtesy phone call.

He resolved to pay Principe a visit later that day.

Twenty minutes later, with printouts, his notebook, razor, phone charger, and another shirt in his bag, Blume headed towards the exit.

'Wait!' Panebianco called him over, and pointed to a picture of a young man with curly black hair in civvies. 'Paolo Aquilone as he presents himself on Facebook. You were right about his hair.'

It was him. The person who had followed him the other day. Blume gave Panebianco a slap on the back.

'I get the feeling you're making progress,' said Panebianco.

'With the case yes; with my life, not so much. The thing now is to get the case to work in my favour so I can get back in here to boss you around.'

'I look forward to it. How's Caterina?'

'She's fine. Better. Better off without me.'

'You've split up?'

'I've said too much.'

'Well, if there is anything I can do.'

'As a matter of fact,' said Blume, 'I no longer have access to my service car.'

I was hoping you wouldn't take me literally.'

'Too late,' said Blume, giving him a second slap on the back.

40

BLUME WENT thundering up the Via Nazionale bus lane in Panebianco's Volkswagen Polo on his way to see, and hopefully surprise, his estate agent.

When he walked in and demanded to see the 'manager', since he still could not remember Valentino's real name, a young woman, whose fine features were ruined by pockmarked skin that she had tried to cover with too much makeup, told him that it was unreasonable for him to demand to see the manager if he did not remember his name. And anyhow, he was not a manager. He was an area director, if – she underscored the 'if', even making a little mark in the air with her finger – *if* they were talking about the same person.

'You people post more flyers than takeaway pizzerias,' said Blume. 'I thought the idea was you smiled and played nice with any walk-in.'

'We are a serious operation.'

'And I am a serious customer. He's in there, isn't he?'

'You still have not made it clear who you mean by "he",' she pointed out.

'Smells of aftershave,' said Blume. 'Wears a Valentino suit two sizes too small, with wide lapels.'

Her scornful demeanour vanished and was replaced by a smile that revealed a crooked eyetooth. She waved him closer as she lowered her voice, 'I once asked him what make of aftershave he used, but he didn't get the hint.'

'I can tell him if you want.'

She pulled back. 'Oh no. Don't say I said anything. His name is Mario Melandri.'

'Thanks. Don't worry. I won't say you said anything.' Blume made to go through the door.

'Let me warn him.'

'Nah, I prefer it this way.' He made a point of barging through the door and Mario Melandri leapt up like a teenager caught masturbating. A glossy magazine fell from his lap, landing open on the floor and revealing a two-page spread of men in hard hats pointing at a high-rise building surrounded by yellow cranes. He smiled and wiped his palms on the front of his trousers. 'I wasn't expecting anyone.'

Blume opened his bag, took out his charger, went over to a wall socket, and plugged in his phone, then turned his attention to the agent who was slowly sitting down again, his hand warily suspended above the phone on the desk. Blume unlatched and opened a window, and said, 'First of all, where's my stuff?'

'Mr . . . Blume?'

'Commissioner Blume.'

'In storage, Commissioner Blume.' He seemed more pleased with himself for getting the name right than awed by the official title. 'Do you need to see the receipts? Or do you need the address?'

'You didn't warn me beforehand. You just sent in your men, removed my stuff. In a single day. You had that room cleaned out within hours.'

The agent beamed proudly.

'The only people I know who are that efficient at emptying a flat are thieves,' said Blume. 'How much were you thinking of charging me for the privilege?'

Melandri began searching though the papers on his desk that had started flapping in the wind from the window, but Blume could see they were just brochures and publicity. 'It will be written down somewhere. I'll have it brought in.'

'You were going to deduct it directly from the rent you passed on to me, right?'

'You agreed to removal charges when you signed.'

'Fine. So, whatever you were going to charge me for the removal and the warehousing, you are now going to charge me half that amount. So, what is half the amount?'

'I can't do that.'

'I know you can.'

'Are you threatening me?'

'Not yet. But you were trying to pull a fast one on me, because you detected a certain distraction in me. That's fine. But I am focused now.'

'I wasn't.'

'And now the good news is that when you finally get round to telling me that you have found a particularly good deal for me, and can cover the removal costs yourself, when you have done that,' Blume raised his voice over the beginning of a protest, 'I am going to turn right round and give you the money back again.'

This gave Valentino pause, as he knew it would. 'I don't understand.'

'Trust me. It's all going to work out for you. We have agreed you are not charging me for the removal, just as I am not going to charge you for the damage to the goods that I and my police colleagues are sure to find, and now you are about to tell me the excellent warehousing deal.'

'Three hundred euros a month.'

'So that makes €150. That seems fair.'

'No, that was already half price.'

'The hell it was. €150. Even that strikes me as a bit steep.'

'It's air conditioned and damp proof. Speaking of which . . .' he motioned at the window.

'No,' said Blume. 'Keep it open. You smell far too strongly of after-shave. I bet it's green. It smells green. Is it?'

'I don't know what you mean,' he said stiffly. 'I do sometimes dab a little cologne on a handkerchief I keep in my pocket. I use it to freshen up if I am meeting clients. 4711.'

'4711?'

'That's what the cologne is called: 4711.'

'Well, as a client, I say lose the aftershave. Now, back to the storage issue, am I going to have to add the cost of mould to the damage already done?'

'That's not fair. There is no mould.'

'I am sure I and an officer from the *Vigili Urbani* can find some. That stuff you removed from my parents' study was pretty old.'

'€250 a month.'

'Not so much old as antique, and precious. Irreplaceable and invaluable in some cases.'

'€200 a month for storage. Any lower, and I am running at a loss.'

'Deal,' said Blume. He stuck out his hand, forcing Valentino to take it. 'That argument is completely closed now.'

Finally, he sat down, leaned forward, and folded his arms on Valentino's desk. 'Now, a promise is a promise. I said you would be getting the money back, and seeing as I now know I am dealing with an honest man, I would like to rehire you to find me somewhere to live. Oh, ho! I see your face has brightened already. That's great. Thing is, I don't have much time to waste searching. Now I am already paying you €200 a month for storage, a vast sum that reduces the amount I can pay by a corresponding amount, but I have the rent from my place, which is €1,800. I need a decent apartment for a single person. It does not have to be central. If you put me in a trendy district full of students, I'll break your legs. The place I want does not have to be large, it does not have to have a lift, but it must not be on the ground floor or basement. It must cost no more than €1,000 a month and it must be ready by tonight.'

Valentino had taken a piece of headed notepaper and was writing down the demands like a hostage ordered to write the ransom note.

'Tonight?'

'Yes, and I am staying in this office until you find one.'

'For that price, you'll have to share.'

'I am not sharing. That is a lot of money.'

The insult to his professional knowledge gave Valentino courage. 'If you want to be anywhere within the ring road, you need to share at that price. There is no room for dispute. I don't know when the last time you rented was, but the market has changed. Unless you are prepared to make a long commute every morning.'

Blume shrugged. 'I can commute. You can get a lot of thinking done in a car.'

'It would be easier if you were prepared to share.'

'You expect me to spend years in miserable confinement with some poor bastard just to make this day a little easier for you?'

'Look, can I close that window?'

Blume relented. It was clear that if he wanted a flat immediately, he was going to have to make some compromises. His compromise did not, however, include allowing Valentino his freedom back until some sort of a solution had been found.

There was a moment of rebellion from his hostage, which Blume defused easily enough with a ready lie.

'I've checked up on you.' He paused. It really would be more useful if he could remember the man's name. 'Your record isn't perfectly clean, is it?'

'That charge was dropped.'

He had guessed right. Estate agents bullied old people and browbeat the young. Valentino was bound to have forced some ghastly remainderman deals on old women. As his old friend Paoloni used to say, everyone's a creep.

'I need to make phone calls. A lot of phone calls.'

'Make them.'

'I can't. Not with you sitting there.'

'Why not?' asked Blume.

'It's like some people can't piss when there are others around? I can't make phone calls.'

'Do your lies humiliate you? I'll sit outside the door. I have an appointment, but it's quite late in the evening. So you have all day.'

He returned to reception, pulled out his book, and started to read.

He read a chapter on the amazing plasticity of children's brains, which he found depressing. As far as he could make out, his brain and life had probably started their downward spiral from his eighth birthday. By lunchtime, he had learned a sort of nursery rhyme, thanks to which he now knew all the kings and queens of England from William the Conqueror to Elizabeth II, though to what end he was hard pushed to say. He phoned Principe, and got no reply. He went over the ten presidents. Yes, they were still pointlessly there. He felt restless. Now it was a real book he was dealing with, he was able to hop to the appendix, where he finally learned the Memory Key.

He decided to go out for a late lunch, by now trusting Valentino and the girl to work hard on his behalf even without his glowering presence. When he returned, he called Principe in vain, tried to flirt a bit with the receptionist, who subsequently vanished for an hour. He spent another while in the company of Fisher who had a 'sure-fire' trick for remembering the periodic table. Fisher's method relied on imagining a table, colours, images, and faces based on a peg-system story that read like a bad trip on magic mushrooms. Besides, he already knew all the elements, though not in the right order, thanks to the Tom Lehrer song that his father not only used to sing in the shower, but also frequently played on the record player.

There's antimony, arsenic, aluminum, selenium,
And hydrogen and oxygen and nitrogen and rhenium . . .

The hardest bit was at the end.

> *And argon, krypton, neon, radon, xenon, zinc, and rhodium*
> *And chlorine, carbon, cobalt, copper, tungsten, tin, and sodium . . .*

He could hear Lehrer's voice, but when he tried it, his tongue always tripped between 'neon' and 'radon'.

Valentino opened his office door. 'Are you singing?'

'Yes,' said Blume. 'And waiting.'

'Well, you may end your song, Commissioner.' Ceremoniously, he ushered Blume in, went round, and sat behind his desk, and carefully brought his hands together as if he were protecting a small delicate object.

'We have found you a place.'

'Great.'

'€900 per month, which is an incredible bargain. Especially since it's in the Borgo. Via dei Tre Pupazzi.'

Blume sat back and waited for the 'but'.

'But I just couldn't get you one that was immediately available.'

Blume knew he has been asking too much for a flat in one day, but he wasn't keen on going back to the lonely hotel on Via Aurelia. 'How long?'

'Eight days.' He flinched slightly, though Blume had not stirred. 'It's the best I could do. The best I can do.'

'You find anything else?'

A shake of the head, a setting of the mouth in a frown of defiance. He had pushed Valentino far enough.

'OK,' said Blume. 'I'll think about it. Let me use your computer a moment.' He found the number of the hotel and phoned them to book another week. They quoted a price per room that was €10 lower than he had been paying. One night free. Wonderful. He needed a toothbrush, underwear and, come what may of it, he needed to get his clothes out of Caterina's flat. And he also needed to find out why Principe was not answering his damned phone.

41

THE SUN had come out. The white chapel in the corner of the piazzetta was almost blinding. The gleaming cobbles shone like obsidian, and the potted plants around Principe's building seemed to have been reinvigorated. The rain had rinsed the scooters and cars bright and new.

The building itself had benefited less from the general cleansing. The upper floors were still the colour of dried blood, the lower floors a sickly yellow and grey. The rain, delayed and partially absorbed by the weeds growing on the roof, was still seeping over the edge, sloppy and muddy. The wind caused the windowpanes to flex just enough to shift the light and give the illusion of a figure moving about behind them.

He took out his mobile and called Principe for the umpteenth time. It went straight to voicemail, as he now knew it would. He called the number of the apartment he was looking up at, and let it ring. Finally, he went to the front door and pressed the column of intercom buttons starting at the top and working his way down. Two or three voices, querulous, suspicious, indifferent, responded, and he simply said police, open, and they did. He walked up to the top floor. He went over and started hammering on Principe's door, ringing the bell and cursing him. Eventually the neighbour opposite poked out his head.

'Is there a problem?'

Blume took his finger off the bell, and turned round. 'That depends how you want to look at it. But I'd say no, there's no problem. Except maybe for you.'

'Me? What have I done?'

'Nothing. In fact, it might be to your advantage if you play your cards right. When's your next rent due?'

The man looked at Blume, then quickly shut the door.

'Don't bother calling the police!' Blume shouted after him. 'We're here already!'

He stopped thumping, and stood quietly in front of the closed door, then took a few steps back, and sat down, his knees seeming to give way at the last moment. He pulled out his phone and called Panebianco.

'Rosario, I'm just round the corner. I need you to come with a few people, fire brigade, and an ambulance, though what we probably need here is a mortuary van.'

'You are at a fucking crime scene?' Panebianco was not usually an easy man to fluster.

'Natural death or suicide,' said Blume. 'I can't tell yet. In fact, I haven't even seen the body yet.'

'Who is it?'

'Filippo,' Blume murmured.

'What?'

Blume cleared his voice. 'Magistrate Filippo Principe.' He raised his knees and pressed his back against the wall. 'You know, Rosario, it's so close you would make it here faster on foot.'

'We need the cars. Equipment bags, markers, seal off the area.'

'I wasn't thinking.'

'Just to be sure, you haven't seen a body?'

'I don't need to.'

'Are you in the apartment?'

'No.'

'Well, that's something.'

'You know it really is quicker to walk here.'

'We won't be long.'

Blume hooked his arms around the outside of his knees, bent his head, and waited for reinforcements.

Forty-five minutes later, Rosario walked out of the apartment glancing briefly at the distorted lips of metal where the edge of the door had been forced by five strikes of a fire axe, and said to Blume, 'Do you want to come in?'

'No,' said Blume. 'That might complicate matters.'

'Good,' said Rosario with evident relief. 'That solves a lot of potential problems, what with your personal friendship with the deceased and the fact you are suspended.' He looked at Blume's face and added, 'The death is not suspicious. The ME is tending towards accidental overdose. The only thing that is a little out of place is that you called it in. Now, as it happens, we have since found out that he missed two medical appointments, one meeting with Captain Zezza of the Carabinieri, and a meeting with Magistrate Saraceno to whom he was surrendering the Fontana and Manfellotto investigations. She's on her way over.'

'Saraceno's coming here? Will she be investigating this case, too?'

Panebianco was still finishing his earlier line of reasoning. 'The way I see it, you had solid grounds for a search of his apartment. He was not responding.'

'What are you on about?'

'I need to know what made you suspect he might be dead.'

'I just felt it. It was in the air. They are going to find lots of painkillers and alcohol in him.'

'I would love to be clear here, Commissioner. In what role did you come here?'

'As a friend, Rosario. I came here because I am his friend, or was his friend.'

Panebianco puffed out his cheeks and blew on his fingernails, and looked miserable. 'You kept phoning him, he did not answer, so you came here, is that it?'

'Right.'

'Do you always phone him that often? You see what I am getting at here?'

'I do, and you're right: months could go by without my calling him or seeing him.'

'So all these calls were connected with the murder case at the university. In other words, you were calling him in your role as an investigator. Even though you are not really supposed to be investigating. That's what I mean by role. You can't just explain this away as a question of friendship without it touching on disciplinary matters. That's going to be a problem for you.'

Blume sat still, thinking how much he was going to miss having someone to talk to, anger beginning to well up in him at the way Principe had just left him like that. He had walked casually and sadly out of life, and left it to Blume to get on with it all, until it would be his turn.

'I get it, Rosario.'

'Very messy. And of course Saraceno, who called me while I was in there, says she is very anxious to talk to you.'

'Fine. I'm here, aren't I?'

At that moment, the lift doors opened and out stepped a woman who, now that he saw her, Blume recognized from the Tribunal. She was wearing wooden beads and a colourful wide patchwork silk shirt. Her hair, perfect silver, was long but firmly tied back. She was wearing Converse trainers, skinny jeans, and small round steel-framed glasses.

He stood up and tried to make his expression as pleasant as possible as he shook hands with the magistrate, but the culture of the 1960s was one of his least favourite things. Apart from fucking up western education systems, popularizing massive drug abuse, and securing pensions and healthcare for themselves, while leaving a devastated economy and environment for the generations that came after them, a sizeable section of them insisted on wearing their hair long into their old age, as if framing their furrowed faces and wrinkly little mouths with long strands of grey hair preserved their youth. He immediately judged Alice Saraceno as guilty of not accepting the passing of the years. He also firmly believed in the principle that all public prosecutors should be bourgeois conservatives. It went with the job description. Trying to look leftist or, worse, trying to *act* leftist while prosecuting people for upsetting the status quo was hypocritical. The woman had no business jailing people while looking like some ditzy failed artist who believed in bare feet and candles.

'We have a lot to talk about, Commissioner. I believe you are the person who called this in?'

Blume nodded. She had a Tuscan accent, which softened him a little. He was a sucker for a woman with a Tuscan accent, all those aspirated words. *Hommissario*, she had called him.

'I am very sorry about Filippo. I knew him for a long time. He mentioned you a few times, often in glowing terms. I would like to go in there and take a look around. Will you be here for me afterwards?'

An order framed as a polite question. That was nice.

'Of course, Magistrate,' said Blume.

'We shall not talk about the Sofia Fontana case. That can wait for another time.'

She went in, and Blume remained standing, pacing the small corridor, suddenly more nervous than before.

Ten minutes later, she was back, her feet now hidden in blue plastic bags, blue latex gloves on her hands.

'You really were close to the magistrate, weren't you?'

Blume stopped pacing and looked at her carefully. She had found something.

She caught the look of comprehension in his eye, and shook her head firmly. 'Chill. I want to keep this as relaxed and informal as possible. Call me Alice.'

She made a subtle signal with her hand, and Panebianco, looking suitably contrite, appeared at the doorway.

'Aha, a witness to the interview,' said Blume, 'so it is a formal questioning.'

'This is completely informal, Commissioner.'

'What have you found?'

'In a moment. Just let me ask you, have you ever been in the apartment?'

'Yes, *Giudice*.'

'Alice, please. Recently?'

'Yes.'

'So the forensic team are going to find your fingerprints and DNA if they look around.'

'Forensic team?'

'They're below. Actually, maybe we could go downstairs, get out of their way?'

Blume started down the stairs, ignoring the magistrate's surprise that he was foregoing the lift. He walked out of the building, greeted the head of the forensic team on his way in.

'What have you got for us, Alec?'

He stood back, put up his hands. 'No. This is not my case. Nothing to do with me.'

He watched as the magistrate spoke to the team leader, who was now stealing a few glances in his direction. The sky had darkened again. Eventually, Alice Saraceno detached herself from the group and came up to him.

'You look like a man who could do with a drink. You work round the corner, where's a good place?'

Blume took her to the meanest, most miserable bar he knew, where they served nothing hip or healthy. He expected her to order a mineral water and to get served a dead Ferrarelle in a warm plastic bottle, but she surveyed the place quickly, and then him, and ordered two beers.

'I think that's the safest option here,' she said, settling down next to him, allowing her knee to knock against his. She poured her beer and drank.

'Principe was a magistrate, investigating a case in which a woman in care was apparently killed. That's the only reason a scientific team is in there now. But his death was accidental, or perhaps he wanted it?'

Blume gulped back half his glass, and relaxed a little. This Alice was not so bad.

'I think he wanted it.'

'Do you know the family. *Is* there family?'

He explained about the estranged daughter and Alice shook her head sorrowfully. 'You work with someone, you never imagine the things they are going through.'

She pulled out an iPhone whose case was decorated with coloured butterflies, and Blume felt a resurgence of hostility. She turned the phone round, and there was a picture of a desk, with a drawer open on it. The next picture showed a blue-gloved hand holding an envelope, and the third showed a letter.

'Suicide note?' asked Blume.

'No. Well . . . It foresees his death. It says that in the event of his death, he wanted it to be known that Alec Blume had absolutely no idea of the existence of any will or legacy, and was not to be inconvenienced by "misguided and busybody public prosecutors". He may have meant me, but I can think of others.'

Blume knew she was watching him closely as she spoke. He did not have to feign surprise at what he was hearing.

'The note also says that you will be inheriting a substantial amount and may want to reconsider your career.'

'It says that?'

'Yes.'

'Does he use the third person, or is it addressed to me?'

'Good question. It is in the third person. It seems written for investigators,' she finished her beer. 'I had better get back now.'

Blume waited. She was going to add a lot more before she really did leave. The casual aside technique. Even if you knew it was coming, it was still somehow effective.

'Another thing . . .'

Here we go.

'His note says that you are welcome to speak to his daughter and explain why he left half his fortune to you and the other half to his grandson. He also apologizes in advance for any legal hassles this may cause you, and mentions that his daughter will have a strong case if she contests the will. He then gives the address of his lawyer. You knew nothing of this?'

'No.'

'Good job it is a natural death or, at worst, death by misadventure. Otherwise, it would be a real hassle for you.'

'Well, aren't I just so lucky,' said Blume.

'Well, you're rich. Or very well off. Principe had powerful connections in his day, I remember. He used them against me a few times. He has a nice apartment, too.'

'The entire top floor is his,' said Blume.

Alice whistled.

'I'll get this,' said Blume, pointing to the beers. 'After all, I can afford it.'

'Let's hope that daughter is a reasonable woman. All right, Alec. Bye for now. We also need to talk about the murder of Sofia, but *con tutta serenità*. That can wait until . . . tomorrow? Say 10 a.m. at my office? Oh, and maybe if you wrote down your actions from when you last saw Filippo Principe until you made that call to Panebianco, including the people you were with, at what time that sort of thing.'

'OK.'

'You saw the note. It won't be a problem, Alec. I know you better than you think. Principe would talk about you sometimes.'

'Really?'

'Yes. There is a coda to the note. A postscript. It is intended for you, and it's pretty personal. I think you should read it without anyone here, especially not an investigating magistrate.'

'When it's released from the custody chain, I'll read it.'

'We don't have to wait that long, Alec. I photographed it with my iPhone, and sent it to your email address. As a favour. Can you pick up your email on your phone?'

'Apparently it can be done.'

'But not by you? Well, read it the first chance you get.' She gathered her Tolfa bag and swung it over her shoulder and left the bar.

Blume walked the few hundred metres back to the station. The staff room was empty, save for Rospo, whom he ignored. He went into his office, shut the door, fired up the computer, and pulled down the email with the attached JPEG file. The words were clear and easy to read on the computer screen, and the scrawled message was short.

Dear Alec,

Stop mistaking solitude for peace. If you find people who love you, hold them close, even if they are noisy and full of faults. If people you love die, try to find new people. You might not succeed, but do not invite loneliness into your life. Once it's there, it pretends to be its exact opposite, a companion that you are reluctant to leave.

Loneliness is not your friend. Keep an eye open for when it approaches, disguised as privacy, peace, independence, or freedom. I know you. I knew you.

Filippo.

42

S HE HAD answered the door thinking it was Elia, back from football.
'I need my clothes.'

She didn't like the way he said it. He was full of the sort of aggression he usually reserved for work. His eyes were moving all over her, appraising, judgmental, and analytical, perhaps even lustful – anything but loving. His eyes, which changed colour according to what he wore, sometimes green flecked with shards of blue, sometimes blue flecked with green, were flat grey. She looked down to avoid them, and saw his big scuffed shoes, which caused an unexpected ripple of affection in her chest until he killed it completely by saying, 'As you can see, I have not put a toe over the threshold.'

She did not want him in, nor did she want to shut the door in his face, so she simply turned and walked into the living room without saying a word.

'I'm coming in then, all right. Tell me to stop if you want me to stop.'

She was too tired to say anything and remained in silence on the sofa.

His footsteps had a familiar rhythm. He brought with him his familiar smell, too, but it was tinged with something else, as if he had washed his hands or his clothes in a volatile liquid. Alcohol. That was it: a faint taint of alcohol and something else. Something truly unpleasant.

'I am going into the bedroom, and I am going to fill a case, OK? It will take me no more than two minutes. All my stuff is in two drawers.' He was speaking to her as if she were immensely stupid, which is how she felt. She had to put his words together one by one and then nod to indicate that she understood what he was saying. But even if she understood the words, she did not quite recognize the person who was speaking them. He disappeared into the bedroom, and true to his word, was back within a matter of minutes, holding a bulging suitcase and, once again, scanning her body rather than looking at her. She took a cushion off the sofa and covered her belly and groin with it.

'You're looking well, considering,' he said.

'Considering.'

'The bruise on your face looks like a tan. It almost suits you.'

'That's a scary sort of thing to say, Alec.'

'What is?'

'That my beat-up face suits me.'

'But it does, sort of. You look . . .'

Again, he gave her a long appraising look. When he was suspicious, he was capable of looking into her with his gaze, when he was in his ordinary self-obsessed mode, she was invisible. Penetrated or invisible, depending on his mood: the definition of an abusive relationship.

'Anyhow, I've found a place. Well, I think I have.'

She didn't understand.

'I mentioned it? I rented out my old place, like you asked. So I can't go back there.'

'No, that is one of the forty-three thousand things you have forgotten to mention.'

Blume nodded his head slightly and glanced sideways, which he seemed to think was a more subtle way of expressing exasperation at her distraction than plain eye-rolling. Clearly, she had no right to forget salient events in his life.

'An African woman,' he said. 'I am sure I told you this. Maybe the bang on your head made you forget? Fine woman. Pale little English husband. Like a white grub. You'd wonder what makes two such mismatched people come together.'

'Utter mystery. So where are you staying?'

'In a hotel for a while. Nice place. Run by invisible priests.'

The irony in his tone was a relief because it marked a momentary passing of the barely repressed rage that he had brought in with him. She felt the muscles in her arms and neck relax a little, as his voice returned to its normal timbre.

'You are a fucking bully,' she told him, stealing some of his rage. 'You were frightening me. You still are.'

'Sorry. I don't mean to.'

'Men, they do that. They do it all the time. I thought you might be different.'

'Can I sit?' asked Blume.

She nodded.

'I don't suppose anyone has phoned you, to tell you about Principe.'

'No, what about him?'

He told her. When he heard her gasp in sympathy, he went on, and in the end, he had told her just about everything that had happened since they last met.

'I am going to make some tea,' she said after a while. 'Do you want some?'

'Tea?' Blume had never seen the point in the beverage. 'Wait!' He was overcome with a generous impulse. 'I'll make it.'

He boiled some water and made a passable attempt at keeping the contempt from his voice, as he kept returning to the living room to read out the names of her teas. 'Lady Grey, Melissa, Mountain Flower, Darjeeling, English Breakfast, Irish Breakfast . . .'

He did not even harrumph when she asked for honey instead of sugar.

'Look, I am sorry about Principe,' she said, taking the cup from him.

'So am I.'

'You're angry, too.'

'He did it on purpose, basically, but without quite doing it on purpose. I bet when they do the autopsy, they'll find that his overdose was minimal.'

'And so now you are rich,' said Caterina.

'I would prefer not to talk about it.'

'You could quit.'

'So could you. You have money coming your way from that woman, Emma.'

'We are both suddenly well off,' she said.

'Wait till the taxman has a look, and the lawyers, and the Finance Police in the case of Principe's properties.'

'You get money, but still no optimism.'

'It comes from the death of a friend, and it has not arrived, and I am not sure I want it anyway.'

'Being wealthy is not going to change you in the slightest,' said Caterina with a laugh. It was the first time she had laughed in days.

She pushed the cushion away. If he had walked over, and lain down beside her and put his head on her stomach, then perhaps everything could be resolved, but she could already feel the return of subdued hostility, basically his default mode. She knew he was angry at being abandoned.

It was what made him tick, and Principe had just overwound his mainspring. 'It's OK to be angry,' she said.

'Don't give me that psychobabble. I don't need someone to tell me it's OK to be angry, any more than I need someone to tell me it's OK to be hungry, or OK to take a shit.'

'Forget I spoke.'

'That wasn't aimed at you.'

'Sure it was.'

'No,' said Blume. 'It wasn't.'

'Well, then don't lob fragmentation grenades into conversations and not expect unintended victims.'

'You're right.' He fell silent for a moment, then aimed an idle kick at his suitcase on the floor, and opened his hands. 'Also, I'm really sorry about what happened . . . I mean the loss, the miscarriage.'

He paused and looked at her, and she covered herself with the cushion again. 'I should have been there for that,' he said, though without much conviction in his tone. 'I should have been there for you, but I especially should have been there for that. But I wasn't, just as I wasn't here for Elia, and so I think it's for the best. I am obviously not cut out to be a good father to anyone.'

Her thoughts exactly, but now that he had voiced them, she was not so sure. If he was capable of acknowledging the problem, maybe he could fix it. She resolved to tell him the truth. She opened her mouth to tell him, and out came different, slyer words. 'You should have visited, true, but the accident was hardly your fault, was it?'

This was his chance. If she could not depend on his intellectual honesty, then at least she could hope in his investigative intelligence, which surely told him that she would have found out by now. All he had to do was launch into an explanation as to why he went to subvert her witness. She would allow him to be as self-absolving as he wanted. She wouldn't agree with his motivations, and she did not even expect his defence to be anything but self-serving, but she would be happy to hear him tell her the truth at least about his actions. They could maybe build on that.

If he told her the truth, then she might return the favour. The abruption was under control, they said. There had been no miscarriage. She would almost certainly be able to bring the pregnancy to its full nine-month term.

That was half the truth.

The other half was that she had scheduled a termination of the pregnancy for the following morning.

She could not find the courage to say, 'I am going to abort your child because I don't trust you', but she did have the courage to look straight at him. She was shouting so hard inside her head at him that she felt sure the thought waves had to cross the room and make him see what was at stake. She prayed for him to make the right decision, to look her in the eye and begin his next sentence apologetically, as he shamefully disclosed his pig-headed betrayal that had put her in hospital: 'As a matter of fact', or 'Look, there is something I need to tell you', or 'Listen, about that barber . . .'

For God's sake, Alec, she thought. You think the hospital discharged a woman who had just miscarried after an accident? Look at me sitting here, flushed, plump, my skin shining like butter beneath the bruising, my legs already swollen, my hair lank, my breasts larger. You have been looking at me suspiciously since you came in. You know, even if you don't know you know.

'Actually,' began Blume. 'There is something – excuse me.' He pulled his telephone out of his pocket.

'Don't answer,' she said.

'I have to, it's Questore De Rossi.'

The conversation was one-sided with Blume replying only in monosyllables. But as she watched the colour draining from his face and his knuckles whitening as they clutched the phone, she realized it could not be good news. Then he started pacing, which meant he was nervous but thinking.

The questore said something else, and any traces of deference in his voice vanished. 'Do as you fucking see fit, sir', were his final words.

He shook his head in a gesture of disbelief. 'Hippy bitch.'

'And who might this latest object of your hatred be?'

'Magistrate Alice Saraceno. She ordered a search of Pitagora's villa this morning. She must have given the order while she was on her way over to Principe's. Apparently, she thinks she can play me like that.'

'Why now?'

'She got a tip-off. Someone phoned up the news desk of *Il Paese Sera* and asked to speak to the crime reporter, and told him to pass on a message to the investigating magistrate in the Manfellotto–Fontana cases. The caller did not specify which magistrate, which may have been a tactic . . .'

He was beginning to speak to himself rather than her.

'What was the message, Alec?'

'Oh, right. That the murder weapon was at Pitagora's.'

'And was it?'

'Apparently. Hidden in the garden. Captain Zezza conducted the search in person. They found it cleaned, stripped down, and wiped. But of course that midget De Rossi is furious, because he took a political punt on Pitagora's innocence, and me. As if I am the one who betrayed him.'

'So you were wrong?'

Blume crossed his arms and scowled at the floor. 'It has to be a set-up.'

'Not wrong, then?'

'I can't say for sure,' said Blume.

'If De Rossi gambled on you, he should be prepared to take the consequences when he loses,' said Caterina. 'I did.'

43

THE MAN had a head like a round-nose bullet, and it was as deeply tanned as his arms, face and, Blume imagined, his whole body. This was not the sort of man to have a bikini line, or whatever the male equivalent was. He had even gone to the trouble of oiling and shining his head to give it a coppery sheen. It looked hard and impermeable, as if it had never had a hair follicle. The skin over the skull was taut and youthful, the hand he offered Blume powdery dry, the handshake firm, hard, and decisive. He was wearing cargo pants and a white polo shirt that set off the darkness of his arms.

'Mr Aquilone? I was looking for your son, Marco,' said Blume.

By way of reply, the man stepped back and ushered him inside the small apartment, and led him straight into the compact kitchen, whose surfaces gleamed and where not so much as a teaspoon had been left in sight. They sat at a steel-topped table that would not have looked out of place in a morgue, in the middle of which was a white bowl full of green apples.

'Coffee?' Mr Aquilone slid open a narrow drawer and extracted a capsule, which he slotted into an espresso machine. He fetched a square white cup. The machine hummed electronically and the coffee trickled down.

'Long or short?'

'Ordinary – short. Whatever.'

He handed Blume the cup. 'No sugar, I'm afraid. No milk either. Lactose intolerance. Anyhow, it spoils the taste. That's Illy coffee. The guy's a Communist, but he makes good coffee. So, what rank are you?'

'Commissioner.'

'Excellent. What has Marco done?'

Blume sipped his oily coffee. 'You have another son, I believe?'

'Paolo. Yes. But you are not here for him, are you?'

Blume ignored the question. 'What makes you think Marco is in trouble?'

The man folded his arms, and Blume noticed a white line snaking across his forearm. He caught Blume's gaze and flexed his triceps causing the scar to whiten still further. 'An accident with phosphorous. Night training with idiots.'

It was hard to make out the man's age. 'Are you still in the Carabinieri?'

'No. Retired. Two former colleagues and I run a gym now.'

'That going well?'

'What the fuck do you care, Commissioner? You're here to question or arrest Marco, but I have not seen him in several days. If I did, I'd hand him in, no problem.'

'If I were here to arrest him, I wouldn't have come on my own.'

'Maybe you have backup around the corner. I don't know how these things work. I was never on civilian duty.'

'First Tuscania parachute regiment, you left in 2002.'

Curt nod.

'But you must know something about civilian policing from your other son.'

'You mean my first son, Paolo.'

'Yes, him. He's a *vice brigadiere*.'

'In Naples. A hard posting. Still, not quite as hard as Iraq.'

'He was back in Rome recently?'

'He visits me regularly. Never stays more than one night when he comes, so he is not a burden. He's a good son.'

'Is Marco a good son?'

'If you've finished with that cup, give it to me, so I can wash it.'

He picked up Blume's coffee cup and carried it over to the sink, where he held it under a jet of hot water until not a germ could be left on it. He wiped away the drops with kitchen towels and dropped them into one of four differentiated bins that slid neatly from under the sink.

'Do you mind my saying that you don't seem surprised or upset that Marco's in trouble? You seem remarkably uninterested in what it may be about?'

'I wish he had got into trouble earlier.' The words were directed at the sink. 'It might have done him some good. As for what it's about, I am assuming something squalid that a father would not want to hear about.'

'What sort of thing?'

'Drugs, blackmail, corruption of some sort. Maybe he was selling exam papers. Maybe he's been caught in bad company.'

'He mentioned nothing of a murdered girl?'

'No, he did not.' Marco's father finally turned around. 'Are we talking about a murder case?'

'Yes,' said Blume. 'Let me ask you, Mr Aquilone, do you know Olivia, Marco's girlfriend?'

He nodded. 'Yes, I've met her.'

'She had a cousin called Sofia.'

Marco's father shook his head. 'I'm not saying she didn't, but I know nothing about her.'

'Really? Not even the name?'

'No. I mean he might have said something once, but I doubt it. He and I don't talk much, you see. He's more of a mama's boy.'

'I thought she was dead,' said Blume.

'She's not dead! Or she wasn't last time I heard, which was a while ago, I admit. She left us when Marco was 7. So now you know what sort of woman she was.'

'Not really. What sort of woman was she?'

'The sort who could walk out on her children, leave her husband, a soldier, with a mother's work. It's odd you should come here so ill-informed of the facts.'

'It's odd your son never mentioned the death of his girlfriend's cousin. Do you have a weapons collection, Mr Aquilone?'

'No, I do not. Weapons are tools for killing. When you have no more need to kill, you have no more need for weapons.'

'Did you kill anyone in Iraq?'

'Not in Iraq. I shot at a UCK militiaman in Macedonia in 1998. He went down, but the kill was never confirmed by anyone. That's it.'

'No more shooting after that?'

'I like to keep my hand in, but I do not keep weapons. I visit a range, and the weapons are stored there.'

'So you never even heard of Sofia?'

'Like I said, we don't talk much.'

'How about Olivia?'

'As I said, I met her, all right.'

'You don't like her?'

'She is too much woman for someone like my son.'

'Your son is a good-looking kid.'

'He should be. He spends all day grooming himself.'

Blume glanced at the muscle-toned sunlamped man in front of him and said nothing, but he felt his eye flicker in contempt, and it was picked up immediately.

'I look after my body. My son grooms himself like a girl. As for the rest of it, I have no idea what goes on in his head. Now you come here talking about dead cousins and asking me if I have any weapons, which, I repeat, I do not. Whatever he has done, you can be dammed sure I am not complicit in it. We are strangers to one another.'

'Yet he lives here.'

'When it suits him.'

'Did you ever take him to that firing range?'

'When he was a kid, we used to go out to my father's place near Todi. There was a field there, and my father had some old weapons. He was a damned good shot.'

'Who, your father or Marco?'

'Marco. My father was a lousy shot for an *Alpino*. A lousy father, too, come to that.'

'So your father was also in the military.'

'Killed Greeks and Albanians in the Second World War, or at least shot more or less in their direction. He was a good engineer, so he says, but never learned to shoot straight. But I am not one to speak ill of the dead. Marco was a better shot than his brother, Paolo, though you would hardly believe it.'

'Why would I not believe it?'

'Paolo chose a police career. Marco chose to become what he has become.'

'You don't like him any more?' asked Blume.

Aquilone folded his hands over his forearms.

'But you did like him in the past, when you went out shooting in the Umbrian countryside, didn't you? Do you miss your son, then, Mr Aquilone?'

'I think you had better leave now.'

'Where is he? Where is Marco?'

'I have no idea. Like I said. I would hand him over at once if I thought he had done something wrong.'

'What about Paolo?'

'Paolo would not do something wrong, so I would never have to make that painful decision.'

'You misunderstand,' said Blume. 'Would Paolo hand over his younger brother?'

'I think you have asked enough questions, Commissioner.'

'Just one more request.'

'What?'

'Call Paolo.'

'Now?' He slipped a phone out of his cargo pants.

'No, not like that,' said Blume. 'Like this: "Paolo! Come in here. We're in the kitchen!" Like that.'

'I think you are completely . . .'

A well-built young man with irregular features and curly hair, stepped over the threshold.

'It's OK, Papà. I'll take it from here.'

'Paolo,' said Blume. The man in front of him had all the same handsome features of his younger brother, except they looked like they had been thrown on to his face haphazardly. The fleshy lips were close to the nose, and the eyes were large, but close together. Marco's high cheekbones were there, too, but looked like injuries. One of his ears was cauliflowered. His hands were large and powerful.

'Papà, really, it's all right.'

Blume turned round to see the father slowly drying a large bread-knife, his eyes fixed on Blume. Slowly he put the knife down, laying it on the counter and covering it with a cloth with the care of a priest cleaning and putting away the communion chalice. Then he left the room, making no noise with his footsteps.

'The car you followed me in is parked outside,' said Blume. 'No work for the Carabinieri in Naples?'

'I am off duty. Back on this evening. I am leaving soon.'

'I won't be stopping you, I hope,' said Blume. 'Tell me about Marco.'

'My brother has some issues with his sexuality.' Paolo glanced nervously behind him, then went over, and closed the kitchen door. 'He is not ready to come to terms with it. This makes him behave oddly.'

'What sort of issues?'

'I don't know what's wrong with him. Issues. I look after him, but he's secretive. Yes, I followed you because I was worried he had done something – he wouldn't talk about it.'

'Do you think he is capable of killing?'

'No.'

'Of course you would say that,' said Blume. 'They seem to have found a rifle in Pitagora's garden. *The* rifle, probably. Anyone could have put it there.'

'Exactly, anyone at all.'

'Your brother is one of Pitagora's students.'

'I don't believe he has ever been to Pitagora's private residence.'

'No? Any idea where he is right now, by the way. I was hoping to catch him here.'

'I'm afraid not.'

'A lot of Carabinieri have passed through Pitagora's place in recent times. One more in uniform might not have been noticed. You could have dropped a rifle into the grass, no problem.'

'My uniform is in a locker in Naples. I brought no rifle into any garden.'

'Relax. I want to teach you a trick for remembering numbers. Are you listening?'

Paolo's screwed his ugly face into a pained expression. 'I don't have much time.'

'Sit down, listen, and don't answer me back.'

Paolo scowled, but he sat down at the kitchen table. Blume removed the knife from the counter and placed it between them.

'What's that for?'

'It made me nervous, behind my back. Do you know what a vowel is?'

'Do you think I'm an idiot?'

'You're a Carabiniere,' said Blume spreading his hands. 'You must know the jokes. Anyhow, the vowels don't count. You can use them however you please.'

'What vowels don't count?'

'All of them. OK, so a zero is a S or a Z. Got that?'

'I don't know what you are talking about.'

'When you see a zero, think of an S or a Z instead. Then you can add some vowels. So you see a zero, you think Z and then maybe the vowel O – twice if you want. What word do you have?'

'Zoo.'

'Good. So instead of a zero, you picture a Zoo.'

'When do I do this?'

'When you are trying to remember a long number. I am not responsible for this. It is an ancient system.' Blume pulled out his notebook and pointed to a page where he had copied out the numbers 0 to 9 and the letters to which they corresponded. 'The number 1 is a D or a T. Make a word. You can put the vowels before or after or both.'

'Eto'o. The footballer.'

'Excellent. I never thought of using names,' said Blume. 'So next time you see a 1 that you need to remember, convert it into a picture of him. This will help you in cards, too, by the way. Now a 2 is the letter N. Add a vowel.'

'No.'

'What – oh, I get it. Very funny. But your word has to be something you can see, that you can turn into a picture. You can't picture a "no" so easily.'

'Anna. No, that's got two n's.'

'No problem. As long as there is nothing between them. See how it works? But Anna is no good unless you have an image of a particular Anna.'

'There is one in my office. She's pretty hard to forget. Most beautiful woman alive as it happens.'

'OK. From now on, think of your beautiful Anna instead of number 2. The number 3 is represented by the letter M.'

'Amo, Ama, Oma Mao . . .'

'All right, when you find a word with an image, choose it. The number 4 is an R. Five is an L, 6 is a SH, a J, or a soft G, 7 is a K or a hard C, 8 is a V or an F, and 9 is a B or a P.'

'OK.'

Blume spun his notebook round. 'So, say you want to remember the number 27, what would you do?'

Paolo looked blank.

'You would find a word that has the letter N, for the 2 and then a C or K for the 7. Throw in some vowels between them. Come on, think of a word.'

'NOCS. The Carabinieri special forces.'

'I know what it is, but that would be 270 N-C-S. The S is a zero. But you have the hang of it. See how it works? You need to remember 270, you see Carabinieri in balaclavas. Apparently it can be very useful when gambling.'

Paolo was frowning at the page, evidently interested, but Blume turned over the leaf and tapped an email address written in the middle. 'See that? That is Marco's email address. Marco_08@hotmail.com OK? Name, and what you imagine is the year he signed up.'

'Yeah. He uses this address.'

'Convert 08 back into letters.' Blume flicked the page back.

'Zero is S or Z and the 8 is F or V,' said Paolo eventually.

'Let's use S and F,' said Blume. 'Throw in some vowels – any name suggest itself to you?'

Paolo looked blank again, then it dawned on him. 'Sofia. I get it. But that's just sheer coincidence.'

Blume leaned over and flicked his notebook forward a few pages. 'I would tend to agree with you, except, look, there. That's Sofia's address: Sofia_347@hotmail.com. Now reverse those numbers back into letters – the system was designed to go the other way, but . . . go on, humour me. The 3 is an M.'

'M,' said Paolo. '. . . R . . . C or K.'

'MRC,' said Blume. 'Put in two vowels and you get Marco. That is no longer a coincidence. Your brother called himself Marco-Sofia, and she called herself Sofia-Marco. A little lover's game, see? And now Sofia is dead.'

Paolo suddenly slapped the table causing the knife to jump. Blume leaned back, slowly.

'Little shit,' said Paolo. 'Two-timing . . . *stronzetto*.'

'You didn't know?'

'No.'

'Marco, meanwhile, seems angry with you, even if you are driving round, following policemen who might suspect him. Why would that be?'

'Because I give Olivia what he can't. That's why!' Paolo stood up. 'And instead of . . . he sneaks off . . .' He spun round and looked fiercely at Blume. 'Did that little fucker kill Sofia?'

'I don't know,' said Blume sadly. 'I was hoping you might tell me.'

'Little bastard's a good shot. Better than me.'

'If Olivia found out Marco was cheating with Sofia?'

'She'd murder them both,' said Paolo immediately.

264

'Or maybe get Marco to kill Sofia?'

Paolo looked shocked. 'No. I was kidding. He's a good shot, but he's no killer.'

'Thing is, Marco is hard to find these days. If you come across him, Paolo, perhaps you'd bring him to me?' asked Blume. 'And maybe you don't mention any of this to Olivia?'

Paolo nodded.

'Good man,' said Blume. 'This will do your career no end of good as well, if it all works out.'

'No, it won't. Betray my brother – and to the *Polizia*?'

'I am not asking for a betrayal. Maybe he has nothing to do with it.'

A sparkle of hope lit Paolo's eyes. 'Have you other hypotheses?'

'Just one,' said Blume. 'It's a good one. I just need to follow the advice of a woman.'

44

A s he crouched over his notebook, which was almost as wide as the rickety hotel table, writing down the facts of the case, he had the sensation that the ceiling was sinking downwards.

He wrote down the names Marco, Sofia, and Olivia and drew lines upwards from each. Marco's line split in two, one ending with his father, one with his brother, Paolo, a new entry in his notes. He circled Olivia, then circled her again.

He leaned back in his chair, closed his eyes, counted to twenty, and opened them. The ceiling had moved up again, but not by enough to make him feel comfortable. He could do with some air. He examined the window. To open it would require some force to break through the layers of pigeon shit and grime that had glued it closed on the outside. Then all the flakes along with the pieces of grey feather and the strings of soot hanging from above would float into the room, and he would be breathing them all night. He turned on the TV, a massive CRT device that threatened to topple off the dresser and crush his feet.

He got off his bed, a movement that meant he was already standing by the door and, seeing as he had not felt happy about taking off his shoes and allowing the carpet in his room to fork its filthy pile between his toes, he was fully dressed and ready to leave his room. He grabbed his Fisher book on his way out.

He descended a flight of stairs at the end of the corridor and discovered an entire wing with a vast ballroom stretching into a veranda and on into the deserted garden beyond, dimly illuminated by a tottering row of white solar lamps that seemed to have been stuck into the grass by a drunk who did not quite make it to the end of the lawn. His footsteps over the wooden dance floor were very loud, so he tried to tread a little more lightly, and turned his steps into a shuffle, a waltz and a little step to the side and a bow to the hundreds of empty seats. He checked the doorway to make sure no one other than the insects and rodents was watching him dance. A majestic staircase with wistful banisters painted gold circled downwards into the bowels of the hotel, and the smell that came up was of rotting vegetables. A few metres away, an identical staircase went upwards. He followed this and found himself back in the hotel lobby, which was empty. No one was at the reception desk. He walked down a dirty plush corridor full of closed doors with half an idea of finding the restaurant, though if he found one he'd try to order only food that came from a tin. Instead, he found himself in a dimly lit bar, with little coloured lamps that reminded him of a place he had been in once in New York, or perhaps reminded him of how he imagined New York bars to be. In any case, it was a place that held out some sort of promise of intimacy and companionship, or at least dignified loneliness on a barstool, such as a handsome movie star might suffer. A few people were muttering, some young people in a corner were laughing, and a television was on and tuned to Discovery Channel, on which a man in a hat was racing through vast tracts of arctic wilderness.

Still in a New York frame of mind, he ordered a whiskey sour, just to see. The barman, who was below the legal driving age, nodded confidently, and came back with a glass brimming with ice and pale whiskey. Blume sipped it out of interest.

'This is neat bourbon,' said Blume. 'Not a whiskey sour.'

The barman wagged a finger in vigorous disagreement, then went away, and came back with a bottle of Jack Daniels. 'There,' he said, pointing at the label.

'Exactly,' said Blume. 'It says bourbon. Actually, it doesn't say bourbon. But that's what it is.'

'There,' insisted the barman. 'It says sour.'

Quality Tennessee Sour Mash Whiskey, read Blume, noticing for the first time it scanned and rhymed like a country song. He gulped back his drink. 'Just so you know,' he said, 'that is not a whisky sour.'

'You drank it,' accused the barman.

Blume took the bottle and poured himself another. 'Put it on the tab. Room 666.'

'We don't have a room 666.'

Blume fished out his enormous clunky brass key. 'Room 17, then. Do you have any cigarettes?'

'Brand?'

'Rothmans.'

'No.'

'Gauloises Blue?'

'No.'

'OK, you tell me the brands you do have.'

'Marlboro, Camel, MS, Merit, or Lucky Strike.'

'Lucky Strike it is,' said Blume.

'We don't sell cigarettes here.'

'Are you trying to be funny?'

The barman looked offended. 'There's an automatic dispenser in the lobby.'

'You're sure?'

'Sure, I'm sure. You need your medical or tax card for the machine. It checks your age.'

'OK, have a beer waiting for me when I get back.'

Getting cigarettes out of the machine turned out to be hard work. Eventually it accepted his medical card and his money, but instead of change, made up the difference by adding a giant pack of brown rolling papers and three lighters to his Lucky Strikes.

Back in the bar, he settled in a corner and watched men in orange battle their way through a blizzard on TV, and sipped his drink. The bar was not such a bad place, and the idea of sitting here all evening, maybe eating nuts or something that came out of a packet not previously opened in the hotel, seemed enticing enough. Outside it had started to rain again, but it was warm in the bar. He opened his cigarette packet and smelled the tobacco. Lovely. He tilted the pack and tapped a cigarette on to the table, before remembering smoking indoors was no longer permitted. He would have to go out in the rain, or huddle in the doorway. He could compromise and light up and walk around the large empty concourses and ballrooms, where no one would be bothered. Besides, most of the hotel staff he had seen seemed to be aged 16, and the few older ones were dark-skinned and probably didn't have their papers in order.

He opened his book.

Try to recall the first ten presidents that we learned in Chapter 7. The trick is not to try too hard. In fact, don't try hard at all. Just think of Günther's journey from his bed to the swimming pool and the bar at the end. Literally, enjoy the trip, and salute the presidents as you see them, for you will see them.

For the next ten, use your own house. Start at the front door. If a room is large enough to hold a double bed and a wardrobe, you may place three presidents in there. Do not place any behind the door where you can't see them! Reduce to two presidents (or whatever you are choosing to remember) for smaller rooms. Perhaps just one for a utility cupboard, toilet, hallway, or narrow bathroom.

And before you set about it, remember what the medieval monks have taught us about effective mnemonics. You want your characters to be in movement, colourful, and you want to exaggerate. Exaggeration – think dirty. Not disgusting, because then your mind blocks it. Dirty, titillating, like the medieval sculptures and drawings. If you can't think of anything, or don't want to for moral reasons, try comedy (if you are not so moral as to lack a sense of humour). You can do this by substitution or inversion. For example, substitute a cat for a towel and imagine drying yourself after your shower.

If you have not been following these instructions, if you have refused to follow the room methods or learn the Memory Key, and are reading this book just to see what it is all about, fine. I have no problem with that. But consider how important room and space are to memory.

In many languages, when we are marshalling arguments, we put them in locations. In the first place, in the second place. And it's not just in English. The Germans say _an erster Stelle_, the Italians say _in primo luogo_, the Spanish say _en primer lugar_, the Portuguese say _em primerio lugar_. In French _aux abords de_ means the area around, and _d'abord_ means first of all. It has all to do with place.

We Americans have taken this idea of place very much to heart. We say, 'Don't even go there', meaning do not bring the discussion to that theme, and 'I'm in a really good place right now'. When things go badly, we want to 'move on' and put things 'behind us'. Again, it is all to do with placing intangible things in virtual spaces.

Or talk to a stage actor. These are people who learn off hundreds of lines. They use all sorts of methods of course, and I hope some of them will be reading this book. But what always works, the moment when they really begin to get their lines, is when they are rehearsing on the stage in the positions where they will be reciting them.

So, if possible: practise in the same place you will have to perform.

If you want to pass exams, try this: study different subjects in different rooms. It sounds crazy, but it works. Try to review in the same context you learned.

I might even add, though I shouldn't, that if you learned something while smoking or drinking, you'll remember it better doing the same.

Blume fingered the packet on the table. It seemed like a lot of effort to resume a vice that he had had under control for so long. With difficulty, he pushed the cigarette back into the pack. It was something to look forward to.

He pulled out his phone, and checked the time. Ten in the evening. The hotel was surrounded by stone pines and thickets of glossy buckthorn. He called Panebianco.

'Hey, Rosario. You called. Are you at home yet?'

'Just in.' There was a curtness to the reply.

Only now did he remember. 'I forgot to give you back your car.'

'I noticed.'

'But you didn't phone. Avoiding me is more important than getting a car back?'

Panebianco waited a few beats before answering, 'I was busy.'

'I'll get you your car back tomorrow. Or the day after, if that's all right with you. I still have a few things to do.'

'No problem,' said Panebianco in a voice that strongly suggested the opposite.

Blume hung up, ordered an Old Fashioned, and explained all about David Augustus Embury to the young barman.

'Just remember,' said Blume as he swirled the ice with his finger, 'once you learn six basic cocktails, you have effectively learned how to make a thousand. A good barman in America can earn $250,000 a year.'

The barman hadn't known that.

'OK, so I am going to ask for a Sidecar. Remember the proportions for this, as for so many cocktails, are 8–2–1. Just think of the region of Veneto, or something.'

'Why Veneto?'

'V-N-T,' Blume started to explain. 'Actually, you're right. You may as well just remember 821.'

Blume offered some more on-the-job training to the barman as he mixed a Daiquiri (same as the whiskey sour except with rum, yes, brown would do).

After a while, he wandered out of the bar, reassured by the barman, now his friend, that it did not close until two. He lit up outside. The nicotine rush was exhilarating. Cones of pressure pushed at his eyeballs from inside, his head felt light, and the taste in his mouth was disgusting. A sort of alarm bell had gone off in his head, warning and celebrating at the same time. He enjoyed the first cigarette in ten years, but not as much as he had been expecting. He inhaled the second cigarette deeper, and held it in his lungs longer, then spat into the rain and coughed a bit. Better.

He had moved from bourbon to gin and tonics, which were his natural drink, now that he remembered. The mixture of fizz, steel, and juniper berry seemed to freshen the mouth and mind at once. After a while, he moved closer to a pair of women talking in whispers, but they continued whispering for ten more minutes, then vanished. He did not even see them go. He went sadly to the toilet but returned giggling at a joke that had re-entered his head from years ago about a guy who punished his foul-mouthed parrot by locking it in the fridge for half an hour, and now the bar was empty, apart from him and the barman, bar boy, really, he was educating. But the night was over already. Disappointed, he saluted the barman and returned to his room and fell on to the horrible bed. 'Pharmaceutical coma,' he said to himself, and sank into a catatonic sleep.

Kissing you is like licking an ashtray, a girlfriend had told him once, possibly quoting from some anti-smoking advertisement. In any event, he had not been very sympathetic to her complaint but now, as he awoke, and tasted his own stale mouth and ran the tip of his tongue against the back of his teeth, he realized she might have had a point. There was definitely something ashy as well as cloying about the taste in his mouth.

His head felt remarkably clear, though his hands had been infused with a strange reluctance to do what he wanted, as if the commands from his brain were moving slowly. He ordered his hand to stretch down and pick up the sock from the end of his bed, which it did, eventually. His foot, leg, and fingers cooperated reasonably well in getting the sock on, but when the idea arrived that he might need to take them off again if he was going to have a shower, his limbs gave up in exhaustion, and he lay down again and stared at the warped ceiling. His hair itched. It was five in the morning. *Freezing, agreed the contrite parrot. Terrible experience. But what the fuck did that chicken do?*

He slipped back into sleep but a strange vibrating sensation in his chest woke him. It turned out not to be cardiac arrhythmia but his telephone alarm, which he now remembered setting for half past five.

He showered.

Caterina would neither like his appearance nor the fact of his appearing, but it could not be helped.

45

She left the building at 6 in the morning, just as the traffic lights stopped flashing yellow and cars started coming in twos and threes rather than singly. It was bitterly cold and damp, which afforded her grim satisfaction. That is how it should be. She had borrowed her mother's shapeless coat for the occasion, ostensibly to protect against the cold, but mainly as a form of disguise. And it had worked, she hardly knew herself.

The morning sickness had left her a few days ago, but as she woke up at 5 this morning, she had been unable to eat for the nerves. The combination of the cold, the early morning air, the empty stomach, and the sense of dread reminded her inappropriately of going on a foreign holiday. She even felt a perverted version of the excitement that she remembered from those holidays, taken on her own, later with her husband, but never with Alec. The cold was like that she had felt in London all those years ago. She remembered her dear husband's heartfelt envy at the ability of the English to park their cars in front of their house. How would he have aged?

But in the Bible of Blume, having to remember where you parked your car every morning was good mental exercise: the equivalent of a five-minute run for the brain cells, he had told her. The bullshit he came out with.

Her car was parked at the end of the street, next to a bar frequented by *Vigili Urbani* and shift workers. Someone was leaning against its side, and she pushed her head down and advanced, hoping the person would understand her intention and remove himself without her having to speak. It was a miserable enough morning.

But the figure stayed there, leaning in a posture that was far too casual for the cold, too slouching for that hour of the morning. People up and about at 6 do not slouch. She kept her head down, and looked at the familiar scuffed brown shoes.

'I'd like to accompany you, if I may,' said Blume. 'And apologize while we are on our way.'

She had not mentioned anything to anyone. Nobody knew of her appointment.

'Do you want me to drive?' he asked. He had that smell about him again. Soap and alcohol oozing from his pores. It reminded her of formaldehyde, but she was not prepared to deal with it now.

'The hell I want you to drive. Do you know where I am going?'

'Yes. That's why I am here. Accompanying you is the least I can do.'

'You stupid bastard.'

He nodded, accepting, but there was something in the way he did it, like an old master nodding wisely as his protégé finally formulated and delivered an insight, that made her even angrier.

'Did you hack into a computer, no, you can't even turn on a mobile phone. Did you spy on me?'

'I know you, Caterina. I know that if you make a decision, you take the earliest possible opportunity to put it into effect. I was not sure it was going to be today, and I don't know if I was going to hang around all day, but I guessed right. The first available day at the earliest possible hour. That's you. No room for doubt on some things.'

Another insult. Was it deliberate? But he had guessed right.

'How did you find out I was still pregnant?'

'I replayed the scene of our last meeting in my head, over and over. And I kept seeing the cushion in front of you, and the way you held it, and the look on your face. What I don't understand is how I failed to understand it at the time. I could see you were pregnant yesterday as we sat there talking. But you told me the child was lost, and you don't lie, not really, not like I do. That meant you had decided you were going to end your pregnancy. This became clear to me last night as I was going over stuff in my head. Ruling out your mother, I guessed you would go by yourself.'

'I could have called a friend to drive me, and what then?'

'You don't have any friends, not like that. But I did think you might get a taxi. So I kept my eyes open for that, since you can't drive home by yourself after an operation like that.'

'Are you here to hand out medical advice?'

'Let me drive. I have something to confess, and I want to have an excuse to be looking forward, away from your face as I say it.'

She handed him the key, and sat in the passenger seat.

'You know the accident you had. You went to talk to the barber who had withdrawn his statement?'

At last. It was as if she had grown used to a small sharp something, like a jagged sliver of ice, being lodged somewhere around her ribcage. She turned on the CD player. Einaudi's repetitive melodic music filled the car and Blume, typically, incorrigibly, even as he was confessing and apologizing, lifted his hand and turned the volume almost all the way down.

She turned the volume up again, but not as loud as before. 'That music makes me feel more relaxed. It's therapeutic.'

'It always makes you cry,' corrected Blume.

'Sometimes the key changes can make me cry.'

'Good job he doesn't seem to know how to do them, then,' said Blume.

He finished telling her what he had done, and how sorry he was, and how miserable, too, and the last track, 'Bella Notte', came on.

'I don't expect you to think much of me for confessing to this only now,' he said, 'also because I know you knew I knew you knew.'

'It's too early for me to follow you. Yes, I knew.'

'I know. I figured it out. The barber has been questioned three times now by Panebianco. He'll have found out about my visit. It was Panebianco who told you, right? I am glad he did.'

'You figured it all out using memory and logic. You replayed the scene of me on the sofa, you worked out the probable dynamics of the visits to and conversations with the witness, you worked out what I would do, when I would do it, and waited for me, then appeared in a triumph of rightness, and you expect me to accept it as some sort of apology? Do you even get where we are going, what you are making me do to myself, to you . . . and to . . .'

Einaudi chose that moment to change key.

She did not manage to say anything more until they had reached the hospital. He parked the car in the lot, already half full, and gave her the key.

'I don't want you coming in with me,' she told him, 'and I don't want you here waiting for me, and I don't think I want to hear from you afterwards either.'

He nodded. 'I know why you are doing this.'

'Really, why?'

'You want to hurt me. You want to repay me some of the damage I have done. I accept your choice, but I wish you would not make it.'

She swallowed her tears and found her throat suddenly hoarse and dry with anger.

'Repay you? You think this is about revenge?'

'Partly. And partly, I'll grant you, my incapacity to behave like a responsible adult.'

'You cannot be allowed to think that your behaviour, your flaws are so important that they determine what I do with my body. Because you'll never grow up I must submit my body to this violence?'

'Then I don't know what to think,' said Blume.

'Good. Because if you are left in a state of total loss as to why all this is happening, then you'll at least have some idea of how I feel.'

She climbed out of the car and wrapped herself up against the cold wind. He got out, too, but kept the car between them. Typically, he was not dressed warmly enough, and she could see him wince as the cold wind bore into his chest and his eyes, and he brought his hand up to protect them.

He waited until she was almost out of earshot, then used the wind and distance as an excuse to scream her name at the top of his lungs.

She turned round. He had his arms out, like a character in an *opera buffa*. 'Everything is unravelling.'

She willed herself forward, but her feet refused to comply; she was not moving back, and he showed no sign of moving forward. They stood still 50 metres apart, the wind howling between them.

46

'WE HAVE had an interesting development, Commissioner, and I feel you really should be part of this,' said Captain Zezza.

Blume, sheltering from the rain beneath the awning of a bar on the Circonvallazione Gianicolense in front of the clinic, took a deep drag on his cigarette and pressed his phone to his ear.

'I heard.'

'The murder weapon has been found at Pitagora's villa. It was confirmed this morning. It is the weapon that fired both shots. It has been stripped down and cleaned. The lab hopes some DNA traces can be found, but it would be useful to know if the person who cleaned the weapon is also the person who fired it.'

'That would be the logical thought.' Blume flicked his cigarette against a billboard sign advertising one of the many funeral parlours that fronted the hospital complex. *Why cry twice? Funerals from as little as €100!*

'Pitagora was charged, and is currently at liberty on his own recognizance. Circumstantial evidence, circumspect magistrate, that Alice Saraceno. She does not want to make any mistakes.'

'And neither do you,' said Blume. 'But you know you already have, which is why you are calling me. Remind me who filed a complaint that got me suspended? Who wanted me out of his investigation?'

'Where are you?' asked Zezza.

'What do you care?'

'Let me hazard a guess that you are not at the Courthouse, for a meeting with Saraceno that begins – right now, as a matter of fact.'

'It must have slipped my mind,' said Blume. 'So you know I was supposed to have a meeting with her. Oh, OK, I get it, she told you to phone me.'

'She is minded to close the Principe case immediately, and is looking forward to resolving the Manfellotto–Fontana cases in which she will commend you and me for our excellent work.'

'I don't know about you guys, but magistrates don't have that much clout in the police. She can praise me all she wants, but who the hell is going to spend their free time reading a case report except for other magistrates and lawyers? Superiors on my force only look up past cases when they are trying to screw you.'

'Well, the Principe affair, your inheritance. It would be nice for that not to be investigated too closely.'

'Tell her, nice try.'

'You are not going to help? You'll allow Pitagora to go through all this?'

'I don't see why not. A Fascist agitator getting his comeuppance from a leftist magistrate?' Blume lit another cigarette. Like cherries, you could never have just one. 'Tell you what, I'll meet you at Pitagora's place. You show me where the weapon was found, I'll have a chat with the professor himself. I have one or two things to ask him anyhow.'

'I am very grateful,' said Zezza.

'Don't be. If I can screw you in any way, I will. Also, I need a lift. Send a car round.'

While waiting Blume made a call to the Courthouse and was put through to Magistrate Saraceno.

'I forgot,' he said as soon as she answered. 'I am sorry.' He almost felt like telling her all about Caterina.

'Aren't you already in enough trouble, or do you no longer care because money is coming your way?'

'I don't follow.'

'You can leave the police.'

'To do what?' asked Blume.

'You wouldn't have to respond to commands. I think you'd enjoy that freedom, Commissioner.'

'Were you going to ask me about Pitagora this morning?'

'That and other things,' said Saraceno. 'We can reschedule.'

'Have you opened any other lines of inquiry?'

'Such as?' He voice was wary.

'Sofia's co-workers,' said Blume. 'Interview them.'

'You suspect one of them?'

'I think you need to talk to them,' said Blume. 'Interview them, not as suspects. Get the pulse of the place where they work. Another thing I suggest you do . . .'

'Go on.'

'Can you look up Sofia's predecessors? Permanent senior research and lab assistants. Just tell me how many there have been over, say, the past five or six years.'

'What's this about?'

'A permanent research job in an Italian educational establishment? That's golden, and it's for life. And yet I get the distinct impression that Sofia had several recent predecessors. Why would that be?'

'What made them quit, you mean?'

'Exactly. Or who. Why did they quit?'

'No one looked into this before?' asked Saraceno.

'No,' said Blume. 'Too many men running the show. No one ever thought to ask Sofia about what was happening in her life. No one thought she was important enough.'

'That's very sensitive of you.'

'The fuck it is. Just run a quick check on Sofia's predecessors, will you? Names, how long they were there. Phone me when you do that.'

'Do you feel you have the prerogative to give me orders, Commissioner? Do you feel threatened as a man that I give the orders and you follow them?'

'I thought I was Alec and you were Alice. Back to Commissioner again? Just check. Then call me back. As a favour. Oh, one more thing, take all the names of Sofia's bosses and colleagues and cross reference them with gun club memberships in Latium and Rome.'

Ten minutes later, he was climbing into the backseat of a Carabinieri squad car. They used the siren and show-off driving to get him to Pitagora's villa in less than 15 minutes.

When they arrived, the gates were wide open, as were the doors of the house. Parked haphazardly on the gravel and the crabgrass were two Carabinieri cars, lights flashing. Nearer the door was an Isuzu D-Max SUV belonging to RaCIS, the scientific unit. The Carabiniere driver and partner saluted him with deference, using the *Voi* form of address, turned their car around, and left.

There was none of the tension and excitement, the coming and going, the crackling of radios and efficiency of movement that were so much a part of a moving investigation. There were no ambulances or mortuary vans, no sealing off of the area, no white-faced recruits and grim-faced unit commanders.

He walked through the 'weeds of forgetting', as Pitagora had called them, towards the house, so rustic and remote despite being surrounded by the city.

'Blume!' Captain Zezza came up and slapped him on the shoulder. He looked at him closely. 'You do not seem well. Have you been eating badly?'

Blume ignored the question and nodded at the RaCIS vehicle. 'Still looking for stuff, are they?'

'Just a few more checks.'

'Where's Pitagora?'

Zezza pointed to a door at the end of the hallway. 'In there. He's in what he calls his memory theatre. It's a room in the centre of the house. There are two Carabinieri with him. Not that he will flee. A man his age, with his connections, has nothing to fear from the courts. He'll get house arrest, and then that will be extended to allow him to continue working in the university and it will be as if none of this ever happened – though maybe it didn't?'

'Still fishing for help, Zezza? Where was the weapon found?'

'In the overgrown weeds outside.'

'No one thought to look until now?'

Zezza looked uncomfortable. 'As a matter of fact, we did.'

'But you didn't see the rifle?'

'Look, can we talk frankly to each other, now?'

'Sure. We're friends and allies now: you, me, the hippy magistrate.'

'The rifle wasn't there,' said Zezza.

'No,' said Blume. 'That figures. But it can be made to look like your mistake.'

'I personally logged them in the company of an *appuntato*. We drew up a report but forgot to present it to Principe.'

'Because you were holding back on him.'

'Also because there was nothing to report. The rifle wasn't there.'

'This corridor has weapons in it,' said Blume, pointing to the paltry collection of rusting old weapons hanging haphazardly here and there on the walls, just above head height.

'They are decorative. Anyone can see that. We took down the weapons from the wall, and examined them. They were all decommissioned collector's pieces. Old weapons. The ones you see there now. The only nearly modern weapon was an Enfield .22, but its barrel was filled with lead. That ancient-looking revolver is a replica. Those swords are irrelevant. It may as well be a butterfly collection.'

'The suspect had a weapons collection, the murder weapon was found in his garden, but you missed all this. It's going to look like you are an incompetent, Zezza. I'll be doing my best to reinforce the idea, by the way.'

'That rifle was put there by someone.'

'Why did you conduct another search? It was an anonymous tip-off, wasn't it?'

'Yes. Do you have any idea who might have put it there?'

'Someone making a desperate attempt to distract us,' said Blume.

'You're going to make me wait.'

'Yes,' said Blume, with a large smile. 'I am. A career-damaging long wait for you, Captain.'

They walked in silence to the end of the corridor. Zezza opened the door and held it open with ironic courtesy as Blume passed through. The space they entered was almost large enough to be a gym. The walls were lined with tall bookcases and at the far end was an arched fireplace, over which hung a collection, slightly more impressive this time, of swords, spears, and other white weapons. But the central feature was a large, brightly painted scale model of an ancient Greek theatre, as large as a baby's playpen, set on top of a purpose-built dais raised about half a metre from the floor. Two Carabinieri were standing next to it, pulling out sections of the theatre. One had hunkered down and was peering from behind the stage, like a giant behind the scenes. The other had discovered to his delight that the semicircle of stepped seats surrounding the stage was made up of seven separate wedges that could be lifted out.

'No little men inside there?' asked Blume as he reached them.

The Carabiniere who had been peering through the back of the model stood to attention, and Blume turned round to see Zezza had been silently tracking his footsteps.

'At ease,' said Zezza.

'The professor was just explaining this Colosseum to us . . .'

'It's so obviously not the Colosseum,' said his partner. 'He explained that.'

'Whatever. It should have little people in it, and maybe some animals, too.'

'And lighting,' suggested his partner. He looked at Blume and Zezza, as if for permission. 'These segments come out. The central one is largest, then three on either side. You peer through the seven arches like my colleague was doing and imagine the rising tiers, the seats in front of you, peopled with things you need to remember. The professor gave us a list of Roman emperors to picture sitting in the first few rows.'

'Yeah, but first he taught us a great trick for remembering anything just using the Roma football team. What you do is you take the last match and beside each player you associate an emperor . . .'

'. . . or a number or anything,' added his colleague.

'And if you know the numbers the players wear, or remember the scores of the matches, then you can use that.'

'Where is the professor, *appuntato*?' demanded Zezza.

The young man straightened up. 'There he is.' He pointed to an empty chair. 'He was looking up a book, he must have . . .'

Blume went over to the bookshelves. A sliding wooden ladder was attached to a brass rail running along the ceiling, but the shelves did not go that high. He climbed up and found there was a narrow walkway, a ledge running along a gable from when the villa was extended. It ran behind the last two rows of bookshelves and was invisible from below. At the end was a narrow door. He walked to it, glancing down to see the two Carabinieri staring up at him as he floated majestically above the leather volumes, while Zezza stared daggers at then. The door opened to a short flight of stone steps that led into an internal courtyard, which, unlike the front garden, was carefully tended. A white pebble path marked out a square of very green lawn, in the middle of which was a small fountain. He crossed the path, went through an arched doorway and down a few more steps, and found himself at the rear of the villa. He walked round again just in time to meet Zezza, whose jaw was clenched so tight he was unable to open it wide enough to respond to Blume's cheerful greeting.

47

Z EZZA WAS off checking whether Pitagora had taken his car, when Blume's phone rang. He answered without looking, expecting Magistrate Saraceno to be calling back.

'I was wondering if you'd like to chat?' said Pitagora's voice.

'Are you hiding in a bush or something, or are you on the run?'

'Of course not. I simply became bored, and I don't like being kept at another's convenience. I shall present myself before the Communist magistrate later today, with my solicitors.'

'Where do you want to meet? I could ask why, but I suppose you'll tell me when I arrive.'

'I'd prefer not to say where, in case someone is listening to your line. Someone following the orders of Magistrate Alice Saraceno,' he said placing exaggerated emphasis on the name.

'I can assure you, even if this conversation is being recorded, it'll take weeks before she hears it.'

'Unless she's standing there, listening. Are you there, Magistrate Saraceno?'

'Don't be so melodramatic, Professor. Just tell me where you are.'

'No.'

'Well, that's going to make it kind of hard for us to meet, isn't it?'

'Have you seen my memory theatre?'

'Nice, but I thought you would have gone full scale, a whole room, perhaps.'

'I am in another memory theatre. Across the field of forgetting. Figure it out, Blume.' He hung up.

Blume thought about it for a few moments, and then walked through the crabgrass and weeds, unnoticed. It was easy to move around the villa undetected. He reached the gate, and slipped out in what he guessed was simply the inverse of the movements of the man who had come to plant the murder weapon.

He stepped gingerly across the slippery wet cobbles of the Appia Antica, checking carefully for speeding drivers, entered a gateway in a wall opposite, and made his way down a footpath towards the San Callisto Catacombs. He drew in deep breaths, filling his mouth with wet air and the faint camphor of the cypresses that lined the walk. He spat on to the cindery path to clear out some nicotine, then filled his mouth with saliva and his throat with mucus, and spat again. Better, but he could still feel the yellow tar sticking to the back of his throat, dangling on his tonsils, disgusting now but threatening to become enticing later. At the end of the lane stood a priest watching.

'Afternoon, Father.'

The priest closed one eye and peered at him. 'Are you all right?'

'I have taken up smoking again after 10 years,' confessed Blume.

'Ah, now that's a pity. Make the next one your last for another 10.'

'I will. Is the back gate open?'

'To get to Via delle Sette Chiese? Yes.' The priest pointed towards the church. 'Just go straight on, past the church, unless you want to go inside, of course.'

'No thanks, I've seen the catacombs.'

'I am sure it was a very long time ago, probably on a school trip.'

'Yeah, well they won't have changed much, will they? I mean that's basically the big thing about the catacombs. They don't change.'

'My, my. Not the catacombs, I meant the church. Visit the church just for a moment.'

'Another time, perhaps.'

Blume hurried away, walking at a brisk pace towards and past the church on a dead straight avenue towards another gate set into a wall, this time skirting Via delle Sette Chiese. He made his way across the road on to Via Ardeatine and headed towards the entrance to the Cave Ardeatine memorial.

Yellow signs warned that the area was under video surveillance and a guard was present at the entrance, but otherwise it was deserted. He walked in and headed towards the innermost area, where he found the professor standing head bowed.

'I didn't know if you would understand my message or if you would come,' said Pitagora. 'Did you walk?'

'Yes.'

'I have been sitting in hallowed ground calling solicitors and some other contacts. It seems blasphemous. I was right to have faith in you. Few others would have immediately understood what I meant about the other memory theatre.'

'The largest memorial in the country to Nazi atrocity, visited year in and year out by politicians chasing votes? It's not so hard to figure out.'

'Not for you, Blume. For others, I am afraid it is. That leftist magistrate will never work it out. All she thinks about is Palestinians.'

Blume sighed. 'Professor, I am not political.'

'Everyone's political.'

'Not at your level of intensity. I will say, it is hard to figure out how you can reconcile being here with your Fascist beliefs.'

'Fascist, not Nazi. Italian, not German. I wish people would remember the difference. And old as I am, I was only a child when they did this.' He waved his hand at the memorial all around them. 'My father worked for the authorities that collaborated with the Nazis. I remember this slaughter.'

'You just said you were a child,' said Blume.

'Children remember. I was born in 1938. I was 6 when they killed these people. But you know how I found out?'

Blume shook his head.

'The smell. The villa I still live in was the family home, built by my grandfather. The wind carried the smell from here to there. There is nothing like it: 335 dead bodies less than a kilometre away, across open fields. It is hard to forget. I don't mean I found out when I was 6. But I remember the smell all over the garden, coming in the windows, sitting in the air at night, getting sweeter and thicker and more nauseating day after day until my parents finally gave up and we left the house for weeks. I found out later what it was.'

Pitagora picked up a pebble. 'Jews put a small stone with their left hand on the headstone of a tomb as a mark of respect, did you know that?'

Blume shook his head.

'It shows that someone visited the grave. Jewish graves used to be just a mounds of stones to show the place of burial. Once the stones were scattered, no memory of the grave or the person remained. By adding a stone, you helped mark the spot and keep the memory.'

Pitagora pointed to the long list of names inscribed on the wall. 'The most remarkable thing about that list is the sheer variety of trades.

Professor of literature, tailor, mechanic, fruit stall holder, shopkeeper, lawyer, policeman, general, cook, driver, tax lawyer, insurance salesman, shoemaker, waiter.'

He turned round so his back was to the wall, and then slowly slid down till he was seated. 'Ask me a number.'

'I'm not in the mood for games.'

'This is no game. This list of the murdered was the first I ever committed to memory.'

'Victim 99.'

'Angelo Di Porto. He worked in a shop. One of the 75 Jews in here. A Jew, like you.'

'I'm getting fed up with your saying that,' said Blume.

'See, everyone is touched with some anti-Semitism. Check your background. Look at your name. Be proud of your heritage. Of course, there was a much more famous Di Porto. Celeste di Porto. Ever hear of her?'

'No.'

'A famously beautiful, nowadays we would say sexy, Jewess. She was known as the "Star of Piazza Giudia" where she worked as a waitress. She became a Nazi collaborator. She would walk up and down Via Arenula, along the Tiber there, fantastically dressed, a real head-turner. She would graciously greet old friends from the neighbourhood, and those friends would then be grabbed by the police and disappeared. Eventually her name changed from "Star" to "Panther". She sent hundreds of her companions to their death. After the war, she became a seamstress and a Catholic and lived happily ever after, dying peacefully in 1981. She didn't cut her own throat, and, here's the thing, neither did any surviving Jew do it for her. Why is that?'

Blume shrugged, then sat down on the ground opposite Pitagora, ignoring the dampness, and tucked his knees up. Caterina would have killed the foetus by now. Was that the wrong way of looking at it? He wouldn't say kill, and he wouldn't attribute the killing to her. He wished his thoughts started off as careful and forgiving as that. His thoughts as they came out in their raw state were so ugly. He refined them as they slipped to the front of his mind, and polished them some more before he spoke them, and still people said he was blunt.

'That's right, sit down. They should have killed her. Violence is justified in some cases. You need to clear away the evil, weed it out.'

'You said you had something to tell me.'

'I didn't kill anyone. I have never killed anyone.'

'Fine,' said Blume.

'You believe me?'

'Up to a point. You knew what Manfellotto was going to do in 1980 and you did not act to stop it.'

Pitagora kept his head bent and addressed the words to the ground.

'There were coup-plotters and generals and prelates and bombers and CIA and Greek colonels, Mafia, Ndrangheta, and the Banda della Magliana, but once an operation is completed, successful or not, it's over. All the real effort, more complicated than any operation, comes afterwards and it is dedicated to hiding evidence of who knew what. That's all it is, really. The network consists of people who knew, keeping an eye on each other and making sure no one spoke out of turn. The only reason we do this is for shame. This Manfellotto business caused panic. No one suspected for a moment that she was going to break silence.'

'Maybe she wasn't.'

'Then why did someone try to kill her? And eventually succeed.'

'I'll tell you who it was if you tell me who you think it was,' said Blume.

'Swiss Catholics. The bankers. The same people who organized the kidnappings and murders of the 1980s. They funded the people who did the deeds. They were the people around Calvi, and they faded back into the shadows when he lost power and then his life. Wojtyła restored some of them to obscure positions of power, but Ratzinger has made the mistake of promoting some of them back into visibility. Those are my referents.'

'The hippy magistrate is going to be delighted when you tell her all this,' said Blume.

'No she won't, because I am not going to tell anyone but you.'

'I am flattered. These people sent someone to kill her in the hospital, then.'

'Why ask? You told me you know who it is, Commissioner.'

'The hospital murder – I have no idea,' said Blume. 'That's your territory. The original shooting – that was simply a mistake. The real target was Sofia Fontana.'

'The witness who got shot outside the university?'

'She was not a witness: she was the target. Both times. Everyone has assumed it was Manfellotto, including you and all her ex-*camerati*, and you are now ready to tear yourselves apart over it. But it was Manfellotto who strayed into the path of a bullet meant for Fontana, not the other way round. It was an accidental shooting.'

'Stefania was an innocent bystander, in some miserable settling of accounts between non-entities?'

'As innocent as if she were just some woman standing in a train station, planning her day and her life.'

'Are you sure?'

'Yes.'

Pitagora laughed, and then put his head in his hands.

'You're responsible for Stefania's death, too, Blume.'

'How do you figure that?'

'We had a meeting. It is pointless asking me who was there. At the meeting, I happened to mention that Stefania seemed to have changed personality and had, maybe, just maybe started remembering, even though the doctors said that was impossible. I had no idea they would be so swift and brutal.'

'But you had an idea that they would act?'

'I thought they were going to anyhow. I was just trying to make myself seem useful, show I was on the right side. You will not credit this, but I also loved her. I hated her actions, loved her person. We Catholics can do that.'

'Good for you Catholics. But how am I to blame?'

'You mentioned that Stefania remembered me as Pasquale Pinto. That made people worry.'

'But you already knew her earlier memories were intact. Clearer than ever because they were the only ones left,' said Blume.

'You forget the psychological power of specificity,' said Pitagora. 'That detail, my old name, brought it home to some people how vulnerable we all were. And that's all because you thought you were clever spotting that Pinto was a Jewish name.'

Blume slumped back against the inscribed wall. 'Is it?'

'It is one of those names that can be Gentile or Jewish,' said Pitagora. 'If you are interested, delve into my background, but I suggest you look at your own first.'

They sat in silence. Blume pulled up his knees to hide his phone from Pitagora who was not looking in his direction in any case.

'Tell me, Professor, your former pupil, Ideo, the animal behaviourist, you mentioned him the other day; he wanted you to endorse his book.'

'Review it. Yes. He turned up in person two days ago to give me a signed copy. He included me in the dedications and cites my work over and over again. He showed me the index.'

'Two days ago?'

'Yes,' said Pitagora. 'He made an appointment first. Why . . . Ideo?'

Blume allowed Pitagora to think it through for himself. '*He* put the weapon in my garden? Are you telling me Ideo is a killer? Ideo? He writes about voles, and the magic of dogs and the breeding habits of amphibians. He literally would not harm a fly.'

'Not a fly perhaps. A woman, yes,' said Blume.

Pitagora shook his head. 'I think you are barking up the wrong tree there, Commissioner. You found out he visited, and you are clutching at straws. No, the people who put the rifle there are the same people who killed Stefania. And before you ask, no, Ideo has nothing to do with any of those groups.'

Blume nodded, as if accepting the professor's words. The chill of the ground was seeping up his spine. He should get up, but still he sat there. It was peaceful. A place of horror, now a place of peace.

Pitagora swept his hand around the cavernous space. 'Do you know why the Germans shot dead 335 people?'

'Because of the attack on Via Rastella,' said Blume. 'Ten prisoners for every German soldier killed.' He slipped his phone out and started tapping on the keys.

'Except there were only 32 killed in the attack on the day. So they chose 320 prisoners to be shot, but then another German soldier died, so they had to find another ten victims. In the meantime, Stella the Panther intervened to have some names changed around. Then some Italian officials, my father among them, intervened in an effort to save a few more names. But all this did was confuse the situation and in the end, they found they had 335 people. It was a rounding error, and this really bothered the Germans, who hate numerical imprecision. So the Germans decided the 5 extra hostages had to go back, but others, more sensible and less fanatical about balancing the books, argued that if they released the extra 5, they would to go back and report what had been done to the other 330. So they killed them, too.'

'When the Germans killed them all, they dynamited this area, which did not stop the stench from reaching my house, but did hide the visibility of the fact. Just as they continued to hide the extermination camps by locating them in other countries, and then hide the exterminations in the camps from the inmates. But it doesn't make sense if you think about it. They killed all these people to make a very bold statement. Ten of you for every one of us, and it worked. But then they buried the bodies secretly in this quarry, and then killed the unlucky extra 5 for fear of them telling of the shameful act. It would have made more sense to drop the corpses into centre of the city as a warning, except that as soon as they had killed people, they became ashamed, hid their faces, and never again told the truth.'

'I can't tell if you're repentant or not, Professor.'

'I am a complicated man. So was your friend Principe, the magistrate. He was one of them.'

'One of who?'

'The people who have suppressed the truth and memory for all these years of the Republic. He struck deals with killers, turned them into free-lancers for the deviant sections of the secret state. In his long career, he probably met whoever killed Manfellotto, came to an arrangement with them. Not in this case, but some time in the past. That's how it works. Everyone does a little bit; everyone has a little bit of guilt.'

Blume stood up. 'I need to get out of this place. It's getting a bit heavy, talking between these mounds full of martyrs. Literally walking through the valley of death. I want to go outside and look at some ordinary people driving ordinary cars.'

'I was hoping . . .' Pitagora could not manage to speak as he tried to keep up with Blume's fast pace towards the exit. 'Can you slow down?'

Blume seemed to speed up if anything.

'Did you hear me?' He was wheezing and Blume had already vanished behind the wooden lattice entrance. Blume stepped back through the gap. Pitagora caught his breath and collected his thoughts.

Blume allowed Pitagora to pass through the gap first. As he did so, someone grabbed him without violence but in a firm grip. Captain Zezza was standing there with four other Carabinieri. Two squad cars were parked right up against the memorial plaque.

'Thanks for the text, Commissioner,' said Zezza. 'You saved me some embarrassment. The magistrate has given me a detention warrant for

Pitagora. Conspiracy to commit murder is the charge, but she's rather depending on you to help her with the details.'

Pitagora stared at Blume.

'You need to talk about that meeting with your Swiss banker friends,' said Blume. 'Feeling bad is not enough. You were instrumental in her death. And as far as I can see, your main motivation was fear, which is to say cowardice.'

'Double-dealing Yankee Jew. You think I am going to help you after this?' He tried to shake off the grip of the Carabinieri pushing him towards the squad car. 'I'll be out in hours.' Pitagora turned and shouted at Zezza. 'I'll fuck you all up, including you, Captain. Blume's just having fun at your expense and mine.' An *appuntato* solicitously placed his hand on Pitagora's silver head to stop him banging it on the car roof. Pitagora swung round in the seat to stop the door from being closed and shouted back at Blume, 'Check your blood lines. I told you I knew you better than you do yourself.'

'He'll be pleading insanity in court,' Blume said to Zezza, who looked worried.

'You have to tell them why they killed Manfellotto,' shouted Pitagora. 'It is in your stars that you must behave this way. Accept your part in this, Blume. You are Mercury. I am Pitagora, I am the Sun, and I am also Pasquale Pinto.'

'See what I mean?' he said.

48

'I AM sorry it took me so long to get back to you, Alec. You were right. Five assistants in four years. Sofia was the sixth. Do you want their names?'

'I don't think I need them. You'll be talking to them, won't you?'

'I have already talked to three of them on the phone. One, the penultimate, filed a harassment complaint. Another is suing the Institute for wrongful dismissal. That's what really hurts. These women had filed complaints with us, and no one thought to talk to them. Even a basic cross-referencing would have brought this out. Professor Ideo's name is on record. Seven complaints from women. I don't see how he can still be working there.'

'And yet he is,' said Blume.

'And I simply cannot believe that no one thought to check up on the boss of the victim. That was very remiss. I realize Principe was your friend . . . but even so.'

'*De mortuis nil nisi bonum*,' said Blume.

'It's not his fault, or not as much,' said Saraceno graciously. 'The whole Manfellotto connection led the inquiries in the wrong direction.'

'Would you have checked if I had not mentioned it?' asked Blume.

'Of course I would have!' She sounded outraged.

'I need to go now. What's the next step?'

'I am issuing a warrant for his arrest, and it will be executed immediately. I have two substitute magistrates who are dragging up all the details of his life, and the women he bullied and molested will be giving statements. Ideo is a member of the Porta Neolo shooting club. A little detail that was also overlooked. He has a hunter's licence. We may even have a trace on the rifle. His grandfather fought in Libya, and there are records of several gun licences in his name. Ideo lives in the same house his grandfather once owned. With his mother, by the way. The man is 49 and he lives with his mother.'

'I knew that. So how long?'

'Till we pick him up? Now, basically.'

'Good. Maybe half an hour?'

'What?'

'You know. In half an hour's time, as opposed to immediately?'

'Wait, Blume, where the hell are you now?'

He hung up, without answering, pocketed the phone, and peered into a cage containing a fat rat.

'Who was that?' asked Ideo, dropping three more food pellets into the food dispenser in the next cage.

'Work,' said Blume. 'It's non-stop. You're better off here with your cages. I wouldn't want to be in one of them though.'

Ideo straightened up and set the tray of pellet food on a table beside him.

'Were you talking about Sofia's case?'

'As a matter of fact, I was,' said Blume.

Ideo pulled on a pair of latex gloves. 'Any progress?'

'Oh, yes. Lots,' said Blume.

Ideo opened the cage and took out a fat rat, and started to stroke it. 'Glossy, isn't he?'

'I'm not so keen on rats, really,' said Blume. 'I suppose he is glossy, if that's a good thing. I am already a little uneasy about not wearing the protective clothing.'

'Don't be. It's safe in here. It's been a while since we tested anything really deadly in this lab.'

'That is a comfort,' said Blume.

'So any arrests, or are you not allowed to tell me?'

'Imminent arrests,' said Blume. 'You'll be reading about it soon enough, but, no, I can't say much more.'

Ideo nodded. He brought the rat up to his chin and nuzzled it a bit. Blume almost expected the creature to purr. Then he put it back in its cage, and turned to face Blume. 'You know I miss her enormously.'

'Sofia? Of course you do. So does her mother. And there is a kid called Marco, who was secretly in love with her while going out with her cousin. He'll miss her, too.'

Ideo's face darkened. 'Marco? She never mentioned him.'

'Young, very handsome. We still need to talk to him, to rule him out of our inquiries.'

'He's gone missing?'

'Yes. Suspicious behaviour, isn't it?'

'Very,' agreed Ideo.

'So I suppose you'll be getting a new researcher to replace her?'

'No one can replace Sofia. She was a wonderful, wonderful girl. Especially with dogs.'

Blume looked around the laboratory, causing Ideo to laugh. 'None in here. That's in a different facility. Experiments with dogs are not popular even if they don't suffer.'

'Apart from the lack of freedom.'

'They are adaptable animals,' said Ideo. 'Shall we go to my office?'

'Any chairs in it yet?'

Ideo laughed. 'No!'

'Then we may as well stay here,' said Blume. 'Tell me about your former assistants.'

'I'd rather not. I did not get on well with them.'

'And with Sofia?'

'She was wonderful. She didn't want me, of course. Couldn't get beyond my body and its imperfections. That was perhaps the most superficial thing about her. Women are like that. They obsess about appearance. Their own and others'.'

'So your belly and bald head were off-putting to her?'

Ideo clasped his hands around his stomach, like a defensive pregnant woman. 'She was beginning to see my mind. She was beginning to understand that that's all that counts.'

'And then she got killed before she could understand fully.'

'Yes.'

'And now no one can have her.'

'You speak as if she simply ceased to exist.'

'She's dead,' said Blume. 'That's not existing.'

'Not at all,' said Ideo. 'It's just matter rearranging itself. All of us, even you, Commissioner, are made of the elements that came into existence after the Big Bang. We literally have infinity inside us.'

'I may be made of stardust,' said Blume, 'but I still see being dead as dead.'

'When a person dies,' said Ideo, 'do you think their personality simply evaporates?'

'Yes. Actually, I can think of several colleagues ostensibly alive whose personalities seem to have evaporated already.'

Ideo wasn't listening. He wasn't even looking at Blume now. He had tilted his head back, like a lecturer in a large hall or a preacher in a church, the better to project his voice. 'That's not how it is. Matter has memory. If a good person existed, she will serve as a template for another good person, perhaps a better one. In the future, there will be a better version of Sofia and a better version of me. There will be worse versions, too. But her spirit, if you like to call it that . . .' Ideo paused at a sudden sound of voices and feet. 'What's that?'

'Sounds like a group of men outside,' said Blume. 'Tell me this, Professor, you'd like to be a sort of guru, wouldn't you. Like Pitagora managed. With admirers.'

'Pitagora is an old fraud.'

'Why didn't you just let her go? Like the others. Their complaints don't seem to have cost you your job. Why did you have to kill her? We know about the gun club. The rifle still has DNA on it. You must know how hard it is to get rid of that.'

Ideo nodded. 'Persistence is such a feature of nature. That's why Sofia won't disappear as a pattern, you see. She was different. Let's hope the resonance of her former being resonates into a new vibration. I am sure it will.'

Blume had never seen a smoother transition. One second the concerned work colleague and boss, the next an admitted murderer, with no change of register.

'Did you make a phone call?'

Ideo looked momentarily confused, then his face cleared. 'Oh, you mean claiming responsibility, in the name of the Justice and Freedom Party? That was good, wasn't it?'

'Justice and Order Party.'

'Even more inspired on my part. Pitagora left his office door open. There was a phone sitting on the desk as I came down. I just grabbed it. I hoped I could use it to confuse things. I wasn't even sure it was Pitagora's phone until I saw the phone book was empty.'

'I don't understand.'

'Pitagora used to boast about never having to write down any phone number. A phone without contacts had to be his. Then I heard I had hit not just the wrong person, but that monster Manfellotto – well, it was too good. "Justice and Order". Talk about thinking on your feet.' He shook his head in slow self-admiration.

'No one saw you in the CNR building?'

'White coat,' said Ideo with a smile, flapping at the one he was wearing. I look like I belong there, and I know the layout, too. Just as I knew the layout of the university. I was seen by about 15 students, but not one of them actually saw me. I am invisible to the young. All they see is professor, old man, bald, fat.'

'Did her rejection of your advances hurt you more than the others'?'

Ideo nodded his head, but did not bow it. 'You think you understand, but you don't.'

'No. Quite the contrary,' said Blume. 'I don't understand. I don't even begin to understand, and God help me the day I do.'

He walked out the twin sets of double doors, leaving Ideo in the middle of the room with his cages and pellets. A group of six Carabinieri, two in uniform, were in the corridor. Two of them had their weapons drawn and pointed downwards.

They all stared at him as he emerged.

'He's in there.'

Still they did not move.

'Unarmed.'

The plain-clothes commander nodded at the biohazard notice.

'It's OK,' said Blume. 'Just a whole load of trapped animals.'

49

V ALENTINO WAS in a terrible state of excitement.

'Do you like panoramas, Commissioner? You know, beautiful vistas of nature and the countryside, the mountains of . . . whatever. The ones to the east of the city.'

Blume demurred.

'OK, forget the panorama, how about no traffic and your own underground parking?'

Blume was more enthusiastic at this prospect. Valentino piled on the glories. Loads of space to walk your dog, definite possibility of a metro line sometime in the next decade. The whole area run by a consortium and not the City of Rome, so the neighbourhood was actually clean. All Blume needed was an €80,000 deposit, which would give him 30 per cent ownership and he would pay rent on the remaining 70 per cent to the construction company, with the option to buy the property in increments of 10 per cent. Once he got to 50 per cent, he could sublet if he wanted.

'Every time you buy more of the property, the rent goes down!'

'Unless they put it up,' said Blume. 'Where is this paradise whereof you speak?'

'Borgata Fidene. It's so new it's not even on Google. Well, it is on Google but don't look it up, because it might put you off. They photographed it in the past when it was a big excavation hole. The reality is much better. When I heard of this place, I thought immediately of you, because you are a modern man who doesn't mind a commute. This is a modern place, you understand? Open spaces, IKEA, a cinema with 20 theatres, one of the city's biggest shopping centres on your doorstep, perfect tranquillity. Fastweb is your phone supplier. Fifth floor. Unbeatable. Green fields. You don't have to be in Rome to be in Rome. Even before the metro gets there, there is already a train that goes straight to the centre of town.'

'No trains run to the centre of Rome,' said Blume. 'One of those little quirky oversights that make us all love the place so.'

'Trastevere, then. That's close. So, do you have €80,000? Or maybe €160,000, that way you can sublet immediately? If not, I can help you arrange a loan.'

'You never said what size it was.'

The voice became sly and confiding. He had evidently been saving this pearl for last. 'You'll never guess.'

'250 square metres?'

'What?' The disappointment in his voice was comical. 'That's the size of an entire floor. Oh, you were joking, weren't you?'

'So how big?'

'80 square metres. Net floor area. Actual walkable area. In Rome but out of the chaos.'

'No, not interested,' said Blume, cutting him off.

He walked outside the hotel and was surprised to find that the clouds had, at last, moved higher into the sky and turned white. The reflection of the sun on the wet leaves of the bushes made him put on his sunglasses. He lit a smoke, and wondered about the greenfield site in Borgata Fidene. Out of Rome, away from the chaos every day. Until the city caught up with him, of course. If they developed there, they would develop around it and eventually he'd be back in the city, but that could take years, and he would be dead by then.

He didn't remember cigarettes being so thin and burning away so quickly in his hand. Had they always been like that? He lit another.

Panebianco phoned him to ask for his car back.

'I left it at Caterina's. Sorry about that. I'll get it later on.'

'Is everything OK?'

'It was badly dented already, you know.'

'I meant Caterina.'

'Her too,' said Blume.

His spirits were lifting with the air pressure. Everything would be finished by the end of the day. He took a taxi from the hotel to the Trullo district.

Olivia's mother was not pleased to see him again, but her mild hostility was nothing to the glare of sheer hatred he received when he walked into the living room and found Olivia seated there.

'I was really hoping to catch you,' he said.

Olivia, who was wearing a short purple cotton skirt that may have been some form of night-time wear, slowly uncrossed her legs, flicked her hair back from her forehead, reclosed her legs while sitting up straighter in her chair.

'Commissioner, why don't you sit there opposite me?'

Blume shook his head. 'I'll remain standing, I think.'

'You don't trust yourself not to look up my skirt, is that it?'

There was not too much looking up to be done since the skirt did not travel any distance down.

'You're not irresistible, you know,' said Blume. 'Some men might not even find you attractive.'

'Then they are not real men. I'm sorry, Commissioner, but there's no point in either of us pretending otherwise. Every day, hundreds and hundreds of men of all ages turn as I pass.'

Olivia's mother had been following the to-and-fro and now thought it time to intervene. As she drew her breath to say something, Blume said, 'I don't suppose I could trouble you to make me a coffee, Mrs Visco?'

'You just want rid of me.'

'Exactly. So if you can think of something that takes longer to make than a coffee, I would appreciate that even more.'

'How dare you!'

'Mother!'

She left.

'Can Marco resist you?'

'No.'

'What is he to you?'

Olivia looked at the back of her hands and found the answer there. 'You know the way some unmarried women wear a wedding ring, to keep old creeps like you from propositioning them?'

'I do indeed,' said Blume good-naturedly.

'Marco's my wedding ring.'

'Where is he now?'

She smiled with exaggerated sweetness at the imbecility of his question.

'You know he almost got arrested for you?'

'No, I didn't know that.' She grabbed long strands of hair in her fists and with a deft movement he had seen Caterina do, only more slowly, she formed a sort of old-fashioned bun at the back of her head and pushed in a hair slide that she conjured out of thin air. The effect was to outline the angles and shadows around her sharp cheekbones, and expose her pixie ears.

From the kitchen to his left came the sound of her mother reminding everyone that she was there.

'Is that it?' said Olivia. 'You came all the way here just to tell me that Marco has fucked up his life again?'

'When's the last time you heard from Marco?'

She slowly shrugged a bare shoulder out of her T-shirt, then covered it up again. 'A few days.'

'You know he was seeing Sofia?'

'I know now. Paolo told me.'

'And what about you and Paolo. Does Marco know about that?'

'Who cares – well, you do, apparently. Why?'

'Because men who get hurt can become evil.'

'Only if they are evil to begin with.'

'No one is evil to begin with,' said Blume. 'Just release him, Let him find his level, whatever it is. Maybe he just needs a woman who is a bit dumber than him.'

'Brain damaged, then. I'll tell him you suggested that might make him happy.'

Blume fingered his eyebrow trying to remember his reason for coming.

'Are you running out of things to ask me?'

'No. You know arrests have been made and the investigative phase is over?'

'Sure.'

'So you're safe.'

'Because I didn't *do* anything, Inspector.'

'Exactly. So you can tell me. Were you thinking about it? Did you ever discuss it with Marco?'

'What are you talking about?'

'Getting rid of Sofia.'

She smiled at him. 'You are so offensive, Inspector. And your mind is full of violence. You hate me, but I think you hate women in general. That's what this is all about. Now leave.'

'Tell your mother I'm sorry I couldn't stay.'

'I bet you are sorry. You're like a dog in search of a home, Inspector.'

'Commissioner.'

'You think I or anyone else gives a fuck?'

Olivia stood up and came up close to him, and for a panicky moment he thought she was about to stand on tiptoe and kiss him on the lips, until he realized she was showing him the door. She opened it for him. The sharp light of the winter morning was unforgiving on the grubby little place but illuminated her beautiful features.

50

T HE RED bedcover and the yellow bulb in the ceiling filled his tiny bedroom with a bloody hue, and he was finding it difficult to read the small print in Pitagora's book. But Blume could not make head or tail of it:

We might imagine humankind to be formed of a forest of inverted trees that change position, for what is our head but the roots of our being, and what do we do but move?

Humans, walking, trees. Upside-down trees. OK, he could remember that. Blume stuck his finger into the middle of the book and opened another random page.

Though our materialist world is inimical to virtues and misunderstands the Greek concept of goodness, for whereas <u>agape</u> is to <u>amor</u> as <u>agathos</u> is to . . .

Nope. He turned over another wad of pages.

For the same twelve keys to a good memory are the same twenty-four keys to happiness. And if it is happiness you seek, the thirty-six rules of the golden . . .

Blume thought about this. All in all, he felt it was pretty safe to say he wasn't after happiness. The idea seemed as uninviting as heaven threatened to be eternally dull. Misery endured became, after some practice, misery enjoyed. Still, on the off-chance he was missing out on something, he read on:

Then these are the twelve steps you must take: Study, contemplate, debate, discuss, converse, change, seek novelty, hate your rivals, fear criticism, seek praise, strive after excellence . . .

Now there was something. Hate as a path to happiness. He flicked forward.

Once upon a time . . .

Good, he liked anything that started this way.

. . . there was a nameless place. Then people came to live there and they needed something to remember it by. So they gave it a name that was a function or a description. Florence is where all the flowers grow, Rome was named after Romulus. The Jews always named a place after the deed that had been done there. When God called on Abraham to kill his son, Abraham called the place Jehovah-jireh, which means the Lord will provide. When the Romans saw tall trees, they called them Abies, which means high-rising. Poplars are poplars because they populate everywhere. The American Indians remembered every-thing by storing their memories in the vast landscape, on mountaintops, beside rivers, in forests, at the roots of ancient trees, at water springs, and on the shape of the horizon. Their environment was their memory store, and it was so exten-sive and filled with landmarks they had no need of writing. When they were forced to move, they lost contact with their memory store and began to forget everything about their culture. The only things they are allowed to remember now are the battles they lost . . .

Blume pulled out his phone and glanced at the time. Time to go. He was looking forward to this.

He had the taxi drop him off at the end of Caterina's street, where he knew there was an all-night florist manned by a deeply depressed Pakistani who, Blume knew (because he had asked), earned €4 an hour. But the flowers looked as miserable as their seller, and he remembered her saying something about not liking red flowers, or yellow, or red and yellow together. He bought a small cactus with a ribbon round it.

On the way up the road, he popped into the video store and asked for the newest video game they had. He was staggered by the price, but felt sure Elia would appreciate the latest Battlefield, even if Caterina did not fully approve.

He licked his finger and removed a stain of some sort from the lapel of his jacket. He had sprayed on some herbal essence that Caterina had bought him for his birthday. It smelled like fermenting fruit and made him sneeze, but presumably she liked it.

The table was set, red tablecloth and all, the one without the stains, and Elia sat there, looking solemn and bored and angry.

'Did she keep you waiting for me?' said Blume, sitting down beside him.

'Yeah, she did. I'm starving now.'

'Sorry. I think she wants to be formal. Here, I got you a present.' He handed over the plastic bag. Elia pulled out the DVD glanced at it, then tossed it straight back in.

'*Cazzo*,' said Blume, 'you have it already.'

'I wish,' said Elia.

'Ah, she won't let you play it because it's rated for over-18s.'

'My machine won't let me play it. That's a PlayStation disc. I have an Xbox.'

Caterina came in, cactus still in hand. 'Where were you thinking I should put this? On top of the piano?'

'What piano?'

'No, just testing you for Alzheimer's.' The giggle that followed sounded very tense. Her skin was taut and shiny.

'How is your father?' asked Blume.

Caterina put the cactus on the floor beside the sofa, then, with her foot, pushed it out of sight.

'A good dose of lung cancer or something is what he needs. God forgive me. Elia, ignore what I just said. And never smoke.'

She left the room slowly, like she was nursing a sprain, saying, without turning round, 'By the way, Alec, you reek of alcohol and cigarettes. What's that about?'

'Alcohol? As for the smoke, well, you know, people in the hotel.'

'Your hotel is extraterritorial? Not subject to the laws of the state in which smoking is banned in public places?'

'Yeah, well, it is sort of out of this world. Owned by the Vatican, I think. And they're foreign – obviously because they are in a hotel.'

'Liar.' She spoke the word from the kitchen and it sounded casual, almost friendly, and she hadn't returned to the smell of alcohol, though how she could possibly have picked that up was a mystery. It was hours since his last drink.

She had made them lasagna, Blume's and Elia's favourite dish, and one at which she excelled. With a stately and cautious gait, she brought it to the living room table, refusing his offers of help. The last time they had eaten at this table had been when they had a dinner party with school friends of hers, a squad of bores none of whose memories coincided with anything to do with his life. They had just made him feel old and lost.

The lasagna was not her best effort. What wasn't hard was chewy; the meat was dry, crumbly, and tasteless. They ate in almost complete silence, save for the crunch of the overcooked pieces of pasta. At one point, Blume exaggerated the crunching sounds, and Elia had a fit of the giggles, but his mother didn't notice.

Elia was dismissed, and went without complaint. Caterina sat down on the sofa, but instead of pulling her legs up under her, sat with her hands on her lap, and asked him about the case. Adopting the slightly formal tone that she seemed to be insisting on, he ran through the whole case from beginning to end, clarifying some ideas in his own mind as he spoke them aloud, which, he discovered, was quite therapeutic. By the time he had finished, he felt quite good about how it had gone and optimistic about the next few days.

'Will he get away with it, do you think?'

'Professor Ideo?' Blume considered. 'Maybe. You never can tell.'

'That doesn't bother you too much, does it?'

'It's how things work, or don't work. We have the lousiest court system in the western world. Or the most inconclusive, which may be the same thing.'

'Are you interested in that case you sabotaged?'

'I had almost forgotten about it.'

'The preliminary judge released the daughter and criticized the preventative arrest. Adelgardo Lambertini has been put under house arrest and ordered to sign in once a week. Medical certificates helped there. Are you pleased?'

'Yes,' said Blume.

'Well, I am glad to get such a direct response from you for once. But you don't have to look quite so pleased.'

'That's not it,' said Blume. 'I am smiling for a different reason. But I am waiting for you to tell me what it is.'

She glanced at the door, the way she did in the bedroom when she was nervously checking again that Elia was not home. Then she turned her face towards him, and he was unsure what to make of her expression, at once so bright and so sad.

'What do you think you know, Alec?'

'I think you are still pregnant. You did not have an abortion.'

He felt a lurch as her eyes filled with tears. Surely, he had not got that wrong.

She smiled at the teardrops that landed on her blouse.

'You're right.'

Quite of its own accord, Blume's hand made a fist and thumped the armrest.

'So you take this as a victory?'

'Victory, triumph, fantastic news, call it what you will. We are going to have a son.' He laughed.

She laughed, too, but with considerably less joy. '*I* am going to have a *child*.'

'Fine. A girl's fine. Girls are great. Probably better if it's a girl. Is it?'

'It's too early to tell. And I probably won't get amniocentesis. It's less used now than – you don't even know what that is, do you?'

'Is it that thing where they give you a . . . they take a . . . they put you into a . . . no, I don't know what it is.'

'No, you wouldn't. In most of the ways that count, you're still basically an adolescent. The reason I called you here tonight is to tell you I do not want you to be the father.'

Blume felt the same wave of nausea and light-headedness the cigarettes had induced in him a few nights before, and he found his hand reaching for his pocket in search of them. Had he known she was going to say this? His muscles seemed to have seized up as in a dream. He was not sure if they would respond to his commands, so he simply sat there, immobile, considering the idea that he could be asleep and dreaming this moment.

Caterina had tilted her head and was looking at him the way she did sometimes, with curiosity as well as pity.

'Poor Alec. I am sorry. What were you expecting, though? You abandoned me again in the car park this morning, then you phone me up to ask to come round for dinner. I don't know where to begin. And you have started drinking and, I think, smoking, but that's minor. You can give them up. You can't give up being you.'

His tongue was stuck to the roof of his mouth, and he did not seem to be able to produce saliva. He swallowed dry air, and tried to speak. 'I think, legally speaking, I am allowed . . . Can I recognize her?'

Caterina stepped across the space between them and sat on the armrest and stroked the side of his face with the back of her hand. 'Yes, of course you may.'

'Great.' The voice that came out of his throat was an alien croak.

'You can contribute, you can visit, and you can watch her grow up. But you can't bring her – or him – up. You can't live with me any more.'

'Ah, you say that now.'

She ignored his effort to assume a bantering tone. 'Yes, I say it now. I could have said it when I was angrier with you, and it would have been easier. I could have not said it to you, and left you adrift. But I chose this way because it is the hardest way, and the hardest way is always the right one.'

'Well, if that were true, football would be quite a different–'

'Alec!'

'What?'

She put her finger to her lips. 'It's all right. Stop trying to talk your way out of your pain. I know you're hurt.' She took her finger off her lips, and touched his forehead.

'Won't Elia miss me? A bit?'

'Yes, he will. Much more than a bit.'

'I suppose he's almost grown up now, and I came late on the scene.'

'He'll survive. He'll miss you, but he'll survive.'

'And you?'

'I'll miss you too. I am transferring out of the department. It will effectively mean a demotion. I am going back to immigration affairs. At least I'll know what I am doing.'

'I can put in a good word for you.'

'You! A good word.' She bent down her head and made a sound like a long eeeee, then threw her head back and abandoned herself to laughter. He hadn't seen her laugh so hard since they had watched a Peter Sellers movie. And it was infectious.

Elia appeared in the doorway in his pyjamas, a big expectant grin on his face, and demanded to know what was so funny, and his mother tried to explain, contextualize, and yet mitigate the implied insult to Blume. Elia tried to join in the laughter, but it was no longer all that funny.

Blume ran his hand through the child's hair. 'Your mother seems to think that having me on her side won't necessarily advance her career. You had to be there,' he added.

Elia wanted to hang around in case there were more sudden outbursts of merriment, but after a while his mother sent him to bed.

' 'Night, Alec.'

' 'Night, Elia.'

Half an hour later, just as Elia was falling asleep, Blume slipped quietly out the door.

51

A house of contemplation should be built in open space where the air is pure. It should be as far as possible from the haunts of women, the noise of the market, the rumble of horses, the sight and sound of ships, the baying of dogs, all noises that are offensive to the ear, the groaning of stinking carts. In length and width, it should be of equal measure, and the windows shall be disposed so that neither more nor less light enters than nature herself requires. The roof should not be too low, nor slope too steeply, for that way it will close off your mind and memory. It should be free of dust and blemishes, nor should it contain images or paintings. The walls should be white, there should be but one single entrance and the stairs leading to it should not be tiring. It should afford a view of outdoor areas, trees, gardens, and whatnot, because through the sight of delightful things is our memory strengthened.

(Boncompagno da Signa, 1215)

'Isn't that a magnificent view?'

'The IKEA that is set on the hill cannot be hidden.'

'From up here, you can choose what to look at. You don't have to look at the IKEA.'

'And yet somehow I do,' said Blume. 'But eventually they'll build another high-rise tower in front of me and then I'll have to look at that instead.'

'The consortium went bankrupt. The building work is finished.'

'Unlike the roads,' said Blume.

'The City of Rome is legally obliged to pay for them. I am telling you, this is a once-in-a-lifetime opportunity. Top floor, too. That view of the hills . . .'

'And of the IKEA.'

'From this side you can look back to the city. In a few years this place could be worth two million.'

'Once Italy returns to the lira,' said Blume.

'I'll leave you to look around on your own, shall I?'

Blume walked around the empty apartment. The windows on one side looked out towards the natural park of Veio, home of the Etruscans. The windows on the other looked out at a building development that had taken a huge bite of a hillside. In the distance, the rising heat from Rome made the cold air shimmer. The neighbourhood looked and felt like an airport without any planes, and he was in a watchtower looking out. They had cemented over the past and left it without soul or without memory. No one walked on the half-finished streets below. No one else lived in the high-rise apartment block, no one else had turned up for the showing.

He walked out of the apartment. Then back in.

The estate agent, who was looking with admiration at his own reflection in the gleam of the brand-new metal lift doors, caught the movement, and rolled his eyes. For the past half hour, he had had to scrape and bow and smile as the tall, sarcastic bastard in the suit who had arrived an hour late with the improbable excuse that he had been at a friend's funeral, walked around the apartment, a look of loathing on his face, criticizing every aspect of it and the landscape below.

He had not had a commission in 40 weeks. The estate agency paid him a paltry €550 a month, yet were still considering letting him go. No one was buying in this climate, and the criminals who had built this block were asking a stupid amount for such a lonely godforsaken place. His boss said he might as well learn the trade, practise his spiel, and test his patience on awkward customers like this. Nothing to lose. Except an evening he would prefer to be spending warm in the company of his girl, even just sitting together on a sofa, snuggling, and watching something stupid on TV.

'Excuse me?'

He set his face to smile and turned round.

'I'll take it,' said Blume.

Appendix

Memory Key 1 – The Major/Phonetic System (from *The Memory Key: Expand your mental capacity by* 2^7, Profile Books, Los Angeles, 2009)

1	2	3	4	5	6	7	8	9	0
t	n	m	r	l	sh	g (hard as *good*)	f	b	s
d					j	k	v	p	z
					ch	c (hard as in *cup*)			c (soft as in *city*)
					g (soft as in *general*)	qu			

William James (*The Principles of Psychology*, vol. I, p. 668) calls it a 'figure-alphabet' and one of the 'ingenious' methods of 'technical memory'. As he explains, 'whatever is to be remembered is deliberately associated by some fanciful analogy … Each numerical digit is represented by one or more letters. The number is then translated into such letters as will best make a word.'

Other writers have used many other names for this memory key which, remember, is for learning off numbers, playing cards and dates, but not facts or poetry or faces (see Appendices B and C for these).

Key words can be constructed by placing vowels before or after the consonants listed above. Thus, to remember the digit 1, you might think of a tie, tea, oat or tee and so on. It must contain only the consonant t or d (die, aid, doe – or 'dough' since the gh is silent). Remember also that 'h', 'w' and 'y' may also be treated as vowels. So the number 7 might be coo, key, cow, quay, wake, yak or ache.

Here is a list of key words for the numbers 0–20.

0	1	2	3	4	5	6	7	8	9	10
zoo,	tie,	Noah,	ma,	ray,	eel,	ash,	key,	Eve,	pie,	daze,
ace,	tea,	knee	me	ear	loo	jay,	oak,	hive,	ape,	toes
ass	day					hash	yak	fee	bee	

11	12	13	14	15	16	17	18	19	20
tit,	tin,	time,	door,	tool,	dish,	tack,	toffee,	tub,	nose,
tide,	dune	tomb	tire	dial	tissue	dick	dive	dop	noise
diode									

I trust to your inventiveness to continue up to 100 (which might be daisies, thesis, disease) and then to 999. When you get there (it will take about three months of studying), my advice is to re-use the same images but recontextualise them with a strong enveloping theme. For 1,000–2,000, encase the same images in ice, for 2,000–3,000, surround them with fire, and so on until 10,000. So that if 14 is a door, 1,014 is a door in a block of ice, 2,014 is a door on fire. Choose your own. Personally, I use ice, fire, amber, hair, grass and flowers, honey, plastic bubble-wrap, dirt, tar and molasses, coloured glass and blood.

I explain this and the room-method in more detail on my website, which I urge you to visit.

ALSO AVAILABLE BY CONOR FITZGERALD

THE NAMESAKE

When it comes to murder it's all in a name.

When Magistrate Matteo Arconti's namesake, an insurance man from Milan, is found dead outside the court buildings in Piazzale Clodio, it's a coded warning to the authorities – a clear message of defiance and intimidation.

Commissioner Alec Blume, all too familiar with Rome's criminal underclass, knows little of the Calabrian mafia currently under investigation by the magistrate. Handing control of the investigation to now live-in and not-so-secret partner Caterina Mattiola, Blume takes a back seat. But while Caterina questions the Milanese widow, Blume has an underhand idea of his own to lure the arrogant mafioso out of his hiding place . . .

'Exquisitely written in a quietly elegant style, and dotted with nuggets of coal black humour'
IRISH TIMES

THE FATAL TOUCH

In the early hours of a Saturday morning, a body is discovered in Piazza de' Renzi. If it was just a simple fall that killed him, why is a senior Carabiniere officer so interested?

Commissioner Alec Blume is immediately curious and the discovery of the dead man's notebooks reveals that there is a great deal more at stake than the unfortunate death of a down-and-out . . . What secrets did he know that might have made him a target? What is the significance of the Galleria Orpiment? And why are the authorities so intent on blocking Blume's investigations?

'Alec Blume is an inspired creation . . . Highly recommended'
GUARDIAN

'Set in Rome in the murky world of art forgery, it's beautifully written and has a deliciously laconic sense of humour'
IRISH TIMES

BITTER REMEDY

There's no cure for murder . . .

Commissario Alec Blume, on health leave and fleeing his partner Caterina, has retreated from Rome to central Italy. At the Villa Romanelli he enrols on a natural remedies course conducted by a young woman named Silvana.

But far from recuperating or resolving his differences with Caterina, a feverish Blume becomes isolated and sluggish with sickness. Increasingly ill-at-ease in the stifling environment, the dark history of the crumbling villa and its once-magnificent gardens draws him in. And when a Romanian girl who works for Silvana's ambiguous fiancé Niki asks for his help, Blume finds himself dragged into the shadowy case of a missing girl, and the secret horrors of the garden's malign beauty.

'Fitzgerald's terse but lyrical style is perfectly suited to evoking the poisonously claustrophobic atmosphere in which Blume operates, and contributes handsomely to an excellent police procedural'
IRISH TIMES

'Blume is an engaging hero'
SUNDAY TIMES

ORDER BY PHONE: +44 (0)1256 302 699; BY EMAIL: DIRECT@MACMILLAN.CO.UK

DELIVERY IS USUALLY 3–5 WORKING DAYS. FREE POSTAGE AND PACKAGING FOR ORDERS OVER £20.

ONLINE: WWW.BLOOMSBURY.COM/BOOKSHOP

PRICES AND AVAILABILITY SUBJECT TO CHANGE WITHOUT NOTICE.

WWW.BLOOMSBURY.COM/CONORFITZGERALD

B L O O M S B U R Y